Stephanie LAURENS

'When it comes to dishing up lusciously sensual, relentlessly readable historical romances, Laurens is unrivalled.'
—*Booklist*

'Laurens's writing shines.'
—*Publishers Weekly*

'One of the most talented authors on the scene today… Laurens has a real talent for writing sensuous and compelling love scenes.'
—*Romance Reviews*

'Stephanie Laurens never fails to entertain and charm her readers with vibrant plots, snappy dialogue and unforgettable characters.'
—*Historical Romance Reviews*

'Stephanie Laurens plays into readers' fantasies like a master and claims their hearts time and again.'
—*RT Book Reviews*

No.1 *New York Times* bestselling author **Stephanie Laurens** began writing as an escape from the dry world of professional science, a hobby that quickly became a career. Her novels set in Regency England have captivated readers around the globe, making her one of the romance world's most beloved and popular authors. *The Tempting of Thomas Carrick* is her fifty-ninth published work. All her works remain in print and are readily available. If Stephanie isn't writing, she's reading and, if she's not reading, she's tending her garden.

Visit Stephanie's website at www.stephanielaurens.com.

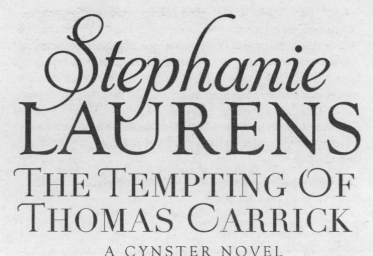

Stephanie
LAURENS

THE TEMPTING OF
THOMAS CARRICK

A CYNSTER NOVEL

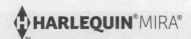

HARLEQUIN®MIRA®

Harlequin MIRA is a registered trademark of Harlequin Enterprises Limited, used under licence.

Published in Great Britain 2015.
Harlequin MIRA, an imprint of Harlequin (UK) Limited,
Eton House, 18-24 Paradise Road,
Richmond, Surrey, TW9 1SR

© 2015 Savdek Management Proprietary Limited

ISBN 978-1-848-45365-4

60-0215

Harlequin (UK) Limited's policy is to use papers that are natural, renewable and recyclable products and made from wood grown in sustainable forests. The logging and manufacturing processes conform to the legal environmental regulations of the country of origin.

Printed and bound by
CPI Group (UK) Ltd, Croydon, CR0 4YY

Other titles from **Stephanie Laurens**

CAST OF CHARACTERS

In Glasgow:

Carrick, Thomas	hero, nephew of Manachan Carrick
Hemmings, Quentin	Thomas's maternal uncle
Hemmings, Winifred	Quentin's wife, Thomas's aunt-by-marriage
Hemmings, Humphrey	Quentin's son, Thomas's cousin
Andrea	Humphrey's intended
Anglesey, Lady	a grande dame of Glaswegian society
Crawley, Lady Janet	a young lady of Glaswegian society
Vilbray, Miss	a young lady of Glaswegian society
Mack, Miss	a young lady of Glaswegian society
Manning, Mrs.	receptionist of Carrick Enterprises
Dobson	clerk of Carrick Enterprises

At Carrick Manor:

Carrick, Manachan, Laird Carrick, The Carrick	the head of the Carrick Clan
Carrick, Niall (deceased)	Manachan's brother, Thomas's father
Carrick, Katherine (deceased)	Niall's wife, Thomas's mother
Carrick, Nigel	Manachan's eldest son, laird-elect of the clan
Carrick, Nolan	Manachan's second son
Carrick, Niniver	Manachan's third child and only daughter
Carrick, Norris	Manachan's fourth child and youngest son
Ferguson	butler
Kennedy, Mrs.	housekeeper
Edgar	Manachan's manservant
Gwen	cook
Burns, Joy	clan healer
Burns, Faith	senior maid
Sean	head stableman
Mitch	stableman
Fred	stableman
Watts, Alice	healer's apprentice
Edge, Mrs.	previous clan healer

On the Carrick Estate:

Bradshaw	crop farmer
Bradshaw, Mrs.	Bradshaw's wife
Forrester	crop and timber farmer, kin to Bradshaw
Forrester, Mrs.	Forrester's wife
Egan	retired farmer living on the estate
Watts, the (family)	clan family, including midwife

At Casphairn Manor:

Cynster, Lord Richard	Lucilla's father
Cynster, Catriona, Lady Cynster, The Lady of the Vale	Lucilla's mother
Cynster, Lucilla	heroine, twin to Marcus
Cynster, Marcus	Lucilla's twin brother
Cynster, Annabelle	Lucilla's younger sister
Cynster, Calvin	Lucilla's younger brother
Cynster, Carter	Lucilla's youngest brother
Algaria (deceased)	Catriona's and Lucilla's mentor, kin to Manachan
Polby	butler
Broome, Mrs.	housekeeper
Agnes	Lucilla's apprentice
Matilda	Lucilla's apprentice
Jenks	head stableman
Gatehouse, Mr.	sheep farmer

Visitors at the wedding include:

Cynster, Helena, Dowager Duchess of St. Ives	Lucilla's paternal grandmother
Cynster, Lord Sebastian, Marquess of Earith	Lucilla's cousin★
Cynster, Lord Michael	Lucilla's cousin★
Cynster, Christopher	Lucilla's cousin★
Cynster, Prudence	Lucilla's cousin★
Rawlings, Antonia	Lucilla's longtime friend
Cynster, Persephone	Lucilla's cousin★
plus numerous other Cynsters	

*cousin★ = term used loosely;
their fathers are first cousins*

One

"Good morning, Mr. Carrick."

Thomas looked up from furling his umbrella and smiled at Mrs. Manning, the middle-aged receptionist seated behind her desk to one side of the foyer of the Carrick Enterprises office.

Mrs. Manning held out a commanding hand. "Let me take that for you, sir."

As the door to the stairwell swung closed behind him, Thomas strolled across and dutifully handed over the umbrella.

Mrs. Manning's thin lips curved approvingly as she took it; despite her habitually stern demeanor, she had a soft spot for Thomas. The company offices occupied the front half of the first floor of a building on Trongate, close to the bustling heart of the city, and the widowed matron ruled over her empire with a firm but benign hand.

"You have no meetings scheduled this morning, Mr. Carrick—just the discussion with the Colliers late this afternoon." Mrs. Manning glanced across the room. "And nothing's come in this morning that falls to you."

Opposite the reception desk, a long polished counter ran along the wall, and there were numerous pigeonholes set in the wall above. Before the counter, Dobson, the general clerk, was quietly sorting letters and deliveries; an ex-soldier and man of few words, he nodded in acknowledgment when Thomas glanced his way.

Turning back to Mrs. Manning, Thomas murmured, "In that case, I'll take the opportunity to go over last month's accounts."

"You'll find them on the bureau behind your desk, sir."

The foyer was paneled with fine-grained oak. The half-glassed door through which Thomas had come bore the company name and logo—the outline of a steamship superimposed on a square crate—in exquisitely wrought gilt signage. Round marbled-glass bowls suspended by heavy chains from the stamped-metal ceiling shed the steady glow of gaslight upon the scene. The ambiance was all restrained prosperity—the sort that was so assured no one thought to make anything of it.

Yet it wasn't old money behind Carrick Enterprises. Thomas's late father, Niall, had started the import-export business thirty-five years ago; as a second son with no inheritance, Niall had had to make his own way in the world.

In that, Niall had been joined by his brother-in-law, Quentin Hemmings. Although Thomas's father had died long ago, Quentin was still very much a part of the day-to-day running of Carrick Enterprises.

As Thomas headed for the open door leading to the inner offices, Quentin appeared, filling the doorway, his gaze on a sheaf of papers in his hands.

Almost as tall as Thomas, Quentin exuded the air of a gentleman of ample means quietly yet definitely satisfied with his lot—and, indeed, marriage, family, and business had all treated Quentin well. His brown hair might have been thinning somewhat, yet his face and figure remained that of a vigorous man still engaged with all aspects of life.

Sensing an obstacle in his path, Quentin glanced up. His face lit as his gaze landed on Thomas. "Thomas, my boy. Good morning." Quentin brandished the papers he held. "The contracts with Bermuda Sugar Corporation." Quentin's hazel gaze sharpened. "There's just one thing…"

Fifteen minutes later, after having agreed that Quentin should seek further assurances as to delivery dates from Bermuda Sugar, Thomas finally stepped through the doorway and strode down a narrow corridor. Lined with offices on the side overlooking the street and with storerooms on the other, the corridor ended at an imposing door that led into a large corner office—Thomas's. Quentin's office lay at the other end of the corridor, filling the other front corner of the building.

Thomas was five paces from his door when another tall gentleman stepped out of the adjacent office, papers in hand—Thomas's cousin Humphrey, Quentin's only son; he glanced up, saw Thomas, and halted, grinning.

When Thomas paused alongside him and arched a laconic brow, Humphrey's grin turned puckish. "You are going to have to choose which of Glasgow's finest you favor, and soon, or the situation will descend into feminine war. And when it comes to hostilities, ladies are more inventive than Napoleon ever was. There will be blood on the ballroom floors—metaphorically speaking, at least. Mark my words, young man!"

Thomas chuckled. "Where did you hear that? Or should I say from whom?"

"Old Lady Anglesey. She collared me and bent my ear over you and your peripatetic interest. Luckily," Humphrey went on, "I was clinging to Andrea's arm and she acted as my shield, but I was nevertheless conscripted as a messenger." Andrea was Humphrey's intended, although they were not yet formally engaged.

Along with Humphrey, Thomas had accompanied Quentin and his wife, Winifred, to a society soirée the previous evening. Considered one of the most eligible bachelors in Glasgow, Thomas was a target for the matchmakers, and even more for enterprising young ladies attracted by his appearance and persona as much as by his wealth.

Thomas heaved a sigh. "I suppose I'll have to choose sometime, but I keep hoping I'll find someone like Andrea." Someone who fixed his interest and held his attention. Someone with whom he felt a real connection.

"Ah, well." Still grinning, Humphrey clapped Thomas on the shoulder. "We can't all have the luck of the gods."

Thomas laughed. He glanced at the papers in Humphrey's hands.

Humphrey promptly waved them. "Rosewood headed for Bristol." Excitement tinged his tone. "I think I can persuade the company that Glasgow would be a better destination."

"That would make a nice addition to the mahogany we've coming in." Thomas nodded. "Let me know if you pull it off."

"Oh, you'll hear—you'll definitely hear." With another wave of the papers, Humphrey took off down the corridor, no doubt to consult with one of their brokers about how best to wrest—not to say steal—the deal away from the Bristol merchants.

Thomas stepped into his office. He shrugged out of his greatcoat and hung it on the stand behind the door, then closed the door and walked to his desk. He didn't immediately round it and sit in the chair, but instead he paused before it. His fingertips lightly brushing the desk's smooth surface, he gazed out of the corner window. The bustling thoroughfare of Trongate stretched before him, thronged with carriages and pedestrians going about their business; the calls of drivers and the cracks of their whips came faintly through the glass. From the left, through a gap between two buildings, the glint of fleeting sunshine reflecting off the pewter waters of the Clyde drew his eye.

This office, this place—Thomas had elected to make this the center of his life. He intended to craft an engaging life around his position as half owner of Carrick Enterprises, and the next step along the path to his goal was to select a suitable wife. The right sort of wife for a gentleman of the type he intended to become—a pillar of the wealthy business community with a supportive wife on his arm, with children attending the right schools, and a house in the best quarter. Perhaps a hunting box in the Highlands. He had it all reasonably clear in his mind.

Except for one thing. The first thing.

No matter how many young ladies of good family, passable or better beauty, and impeccable social credentials his aunt steered his way, he simply didn't—couldn't—see any of them as his.

Not while Lucilla Cynster still stood so vibrant and real in his mind.

By deliberate design, he hadn't set eyes on her for more than two years; he'd hoped the inexplicable grip she seemed to have on his psyche would fade if it wasn't fed—if his eyes didn't see her, if he didn't hear her voice, if his awareness wasn't teased, abraded, and impinged on by her nearness. Yet it hadn't.

He didn't even have to close his eyes to conjure her in his mind, with her emerald-green eyes slightly tip-tilted in a finely featured face haloed by fire-red hair; the colors of her eyes, soft pale pink lips, and that flaming hair were rendered even more vibrant by the unblemished ivory of her alabaster complexion.

Every other young lady he saw paled in comparison. They were insipid. Colorless.

And not just in appearance; Lucilla's vibrancy extended to her soul and was something that marked her, in Thomas's experience, as unique.

Wonderful. Alluring.

She attracted him, captured his senses, and commanded his awareness at some level beyond understanding. His understanding, at least.

She was considered a witch of sorts; it wasn't hard to see why.

For instance, there he was, standing and thinking of her when it was quite definitely the last thing he wanted, much less needed, to do.

Brusquely shaking his head, shaking all thoughts and visions of Lucilla from the forefront of his brain, he rounded the desk and sat in the comfortable leather chair behind it. If trying to focus on which young lady might be suitable as his wife was hopeless, at least he could deal with business—one aspect of his life in which thoughts of Lucilla rarely intruded.

He spent the next hours reviewing the company's past month's trading. All was going excellently well; along with the port, trade of all sorts was booming, and the company was well placed to reap the harvest his late father and Quentin had long ago sown. Although Quentin was still fully active in the firm, Thomas and Humphrey saw themselves as the ones to grow the company into the future, something Quentin openly encouraged.

Business was good. It was absorbing, too.

A tap on his door had him glancing up. "Come."

The door opened, and Dobson entered, a small sheaf of letters in his hand. "Mail, sir. Just got in."

"Thank you, Dobson." Thomas set down his pen, leaned back, and stretched his arms over his head.

Dobson set the letters on the tray on the corner of Thomas's desk and, with a taciturn nod, retreated, closing the door behind him.

Thomas lowered his arms, relaxed for a moment, then sat up and reached for the letters. There were five. Sorting through them, he found three notifications from the company's bank, detailing payments made. One thick envelope was from a shipping captain Thomas knew, who occasionally reported on prospects he came across in far-flung ports that he thought Carrick Enterprises might be interested in pursuing. That missive in his hand, Thomas was reaching for his letter knife when his gaze fell on the last letter in the pile.

The plain envelope was addressed to Mr. Thomas Carrick, with the "Carrick" heavily underlined. Across the corner opposite the post-office stamp was scrawled: Bradshaw, Carrick.

Setting aside the captain's letter, Thomas picked up the one from Bradshaw and squinted at the stamp.

Carsphairn.

Frowning, Thomas lifted the letter knife and slit open the envelope. There were two sheets inside. Sliding them out, he smoothed the pages, then leaned back in his chair and read.

And grew increasingly puzzled.

The missive was, indeed, from Bradshaw, a farmer on the Carrick estate. Thomas's paternal uncle was Manachan Carrick—*The* Carrick, laird of the clan. Thomas had been born at Carrick Manor, on the estate, although that had been an accident of sorts, a twist of fate. He'd spent several summers there with his parents while they'd been alive; after their deaths when Thomas was ten, he'd spent a full year at the manor, embraced, nurtured, and supported by the clan. He owed Manachan and the clan a great deal for that year, but as time had passed and he'd healed and returned to normal boyhood life, Manachan and Quentin, his co-guardians, had decided that Thomas would be best served by going to school in Glasgow and living with Quentin and Winifred and their children. And so he had.

Thomas had still visited the Carricks every summer, spending anything from a few weeks to a few months with Manachan's four children and other children of the clan, but even more with Manachan himself.

Thomas had been—and still remained—closer to Manachan than even to Quentin, whom he saw every day. Even when much younger, Thomas had intuitively realized that Manachan and Niall had been close, and with Niall's death, Manachan had transferred that degree of closeness, of connection, to Thomas, Niall's only child.

Quentin, Winifred, and Humphrey were Thomas's Glasgow family, yet Manachan was the family closest to his heart. Thomas understood Manachan and Manachan understood him, and that understanding sprang from something deep in their bones.

It was precisely that understanding that made Bradshaw's letter so difficult to comprehend.

Not the details—they were plain enough. Bradshaw—

Thomas could easily picture the burly man; he'd met him on and off over the years—wrote that, despite the season, by which he meant the planting season, being so advanced, no seed stock had as yet been supplied to any of the estate's farmers.

Frown deepening, Thomas looked unseeing across the room while shifting his mind from shipping times and the effect of the seasons on transport, and delved into his memories to recall the impact of the march of the seasons on the land. The Carrick estate lay in the western lowlands, in Galloway and Dumfries. It was already late to be sowing, surely?

Refocusing on the letter, Thomas read again Bradshaw's plea that he—Thomas—should intercede with Manachan over the matter of the seed supply.

"Why can't Bradshaw speak with Manachan himself?"

That was what Thomas couldn't understand. If there was a problem on the estate, then as laird of the clan, Manachan was the person to take that problem to. He always had been, and Thomas had never known any of the clan to feel the least reluctance over approaching his uncle. For all his fearsome reputation outside the clan, within it, Manachan was held in high esteem and, indeed, affection. He might be a cantankerous old bastard on occasion, but he was theirs, and to Thomas's certain knowledge, Manachan had served the clan faithfully and had never, ever, let them down.

Manachan would fight to his last breath for the clan.

That was the role of the laird, one Manachan had been born to; it was the principle on which he'd lived his entire life.

Admittedly, Manachan was now ailing somewhat and, over the past year, had allowed his eldest son, Nigel, to assume some of the day-to-day running of the estate. But Thomas couldn't imagine Manachan *not* keeping his hand on the tiller, much less *not* keeping abreast with all that was going on in the clan.

Thomas had learned of the change in estate management via letters, several from Manachan—although, now Thomas thought of it, none in recent months. A brief missive had come from the estate's solicitor, and one from Nigel himself. Also a note from Nolan, Manachan's second son, and one from Niniver, Manachan's only daughter, inquiring when Thomas next planned to visit. None of those communications had spelled out the change, but rather had alluded to it.

Thomas hadn't visited Carrick Manor for the last two years—the years during which he'd been trying, and failing, to steer his life forward—for the simple reason that Lucilla Cynster lived at Casphairn Manor, in the Vale of Casphairn, which abutted the southern border of the Carrick estate.

Ever since his fifteenth birthday, whenever he'd visited, he had—one way or another—run across Lucilla. Sometimes just to see, on other occasions to interact with. He would never forget the Christmas Eve they had shared, trapped by a blizzard in a tiny crofter cottage.

The last time he'd been at Carrick Manor, they'd met at the local Hunt Ball and had chatted and waltzed—and it seemed he would never forget that experience, either.

In order to forge ahead along his defined life path, he'd sought to expunge his memories of Lucilla by avoiding her—which had meant avoiding the Carrick estate.

Bradshaw's letter suggested that something on the estate wasn't quite as Thomas had thought. But was that fact, or was it Bradshaw's interpretation? Or was it Thomas's interpretation of Bradshaw's interpretation?

Thomas pulled a face. He scanned the letter one last time, then tossed the sheets onto his blotter. He stared at them, aware of the thick letter from the shipping captain waiting for him to open it and learn what exciting possibilities the New World might have to offer Carrick Enterprises...

Abruptly, he pushed back from the desk and stood.

When push came to shove, clan came before company.

He shrugged on his greatcoat, then glanced out of the window. The wind had increased; he picked up the hat he'd left on the stand the week before and strode out of the office.

In the foyer, Mrs. Manning wasn't at her desk; she was doubtless taking dictation for Quentin or Humphrey. Dobson was beside his counter. When he looked up, Thomas met his gaze.

"I'm going for a walk." The handsome clock on the wall above the pigeonholes showed the time as just before noon. "I'll probably find lunch while I'm out. Please tell Mrs. Manning I'll be back in plenty of time for the meeting with the Colliers."

Dobson nodded. "Aye, sir."

Thomas pushed through the outer door and went quickly down the stairs, then stepped out into the bustle of Trongate. He let his feet take him where they would—he knew the town so well he didn't need to think of where to go, but simply what he needed.

Right now, he needed space, and air, and reasonable quiet in which to consider the likely possibilities and weigh his options. Down by the river, on Low Green above the banks of the Clyde, seemed appropriate to that part of his brain that directed his feet. He strode down Trongate, turned right into Saltmarket, and followed the pavement south toward the steel ribbon of the river.

His mind already juggling the possible implications of Bradshaw's assertions—assertions that hadn't exactly been spelt out—he was only dimly aware of those around him as he paced down the street.

But one voice reached through his abstraction and jerked him to awareness.

"I don't know. It's brown, after all. Why are they all brown this year?"

Thomas halted so precipitously the messenger following at his heels ran into him.

The boy bounced off, ducked, and muttered an apology, before scurrying around Thomas and continuing on.

Thomas barely noticed, his gaze riveted by the two men standing before the wide window of a gentleman's outfitter; they were discussing the hats arrayed behind the glass.

Thomas blinked, then smiled. "Nigel. Nolan."

The pair turned, surprise on their faces.

Thomas crossed the pavement and offered his hand. "Well met, both of you. What brings you to Glasgow?"

Not that he cared; whatever had brought them there, the pair were the answer to his not-quite-formulated prayer. Through them he could learn what was behind Bradshaw's letter without journeying to Carrick Manor.

Nigel—the elder, fractionally taller than Nolan although several inches shorter than Thomas—looked blank for half a second, then he smiled. "Thomas!" He gripped Thomas's proffered hand. "It's good to see you!"

"Indeed." Nolan—blond where Nigel was brown-haired, with blue eyes instead of Nigel's brown—shook

Thomas's hand once Nigel released it. "We didn't want to disturb you at work, and there's so much to do here." Nolan gestured about them. "Always something to fill the time."

"How long have you been here?" Thomas asked.

"Just a day or so," Nolan replied.

Thomas wanted to discuss Bradshaw's letter, but the open street wasn't the place. Sinking his hands into his greatcoat pockets, he asked, "Have you dined yet?"

Nigel shook his head. "We hadn't got that far."

Nolan pulled out a fob watch—a handsome piece Thomas hadn't previously seen. Nolan glanced at the face. "Twelve already—I hadn't realized."

"If you haven't any plans," Thomas said, "let me take you to lunch at my club." He tipped his head back the way he'd come. "The Prescott in Princes Street—it's not far."

The brothers exchanged a glance, then both turned similar smiles on Thomas. "Excellent notion," Nigel said.

Nolan nodded. "It'll give us a chance to catch up with how things are going with you—Papa always asks, and he'd love to know."

* * *

It'll give us a chance to catch up with how things are going with you.

The Prescott Club was the premier gentleman's club in Glasgow, refined and restrainedly elegant. Over the following two hours spent within its hallowed precincts, in the grandly appointed dining room and later in a corner of the smoking room, Thomas discovered that Nolan's words had been more polite response than actual intention.

When it came down to it, the pair were interested in little beyond themselves, and that little largely revolved about what entertainments were on offer that might appeal to their hedonistic souls.

Thomas had forgotten why it was that of Manachan's four children, the company of these two—of his own sex and nearest to him in age—so grated on his nerves.

Nigel and Nolan were quick to remind him.

Although only thirteen months lay between Thomas and Nigel, with another thirteen months between Nigel and Nolan, the pair always made Thomas feel more like, if not their father, then at least an uncle. They always seemed a good decade his junior; their current focus on horses, all manner of horse racing, and lightskirts seemed more appropriate to young men of twenty or thereabouts rather than the pursuits of well-bred gentlemen in their late twenties.

The distinction, Thomas had to admit, was one of degree. Most of his friends appreciated fine horses, but the subject didn't dominate their conversation. Most gentlemen of their age had a social interest in the sport of kings, but few were devotees of the track, much less the more questionable dives catering to the industry with which Nigel and Nolan seemed to be well acquainted. As for women, the difference between Thomas's socially acceptable encounters with society's bored matrons and Nigel and Nolan's exploits in the local brothels could not have been more marked.

Glad that, it being lunchtime on a weekday, the club was only thinly patronized, Thomas waited out his cousins' rambling, rather boastful discourse, and finally found the right moment to say, "From your letters, I gathered that you"—Thomas looked at Nigel—"have taken up the reins of the estate to some extent."

Nigel responded to the question in the words and nodded. "The old man's grown weak—too weak to ride about."

"No real illness," Nolan put in. Popping another candied walnut into his mouth, he shrugged. "Just old age."

"Exactly." Nigel glanced down at the table between them. "It was getting too much for him, so he asked me to help out—to take over the organizational side of things. Seeing to the farmers, that sort of thing. So I have been."

In between gadding about, it seemed. Thomas swallowed the words and mildly said, "I'd heard that there was some problem with the seed supply this year—that the planting's not yet done."

Nigel made a scoffing sound and waved the comment aside. "All in hand. Going with a different system. It'll work out better in the end for the clan. They just don't realize that yet."

Thomas wondered how not getting seed into the ground could possibly result in a better crop.

Before he could pursue the point, Nolan stirred. "Why do you ask?" When Thomas met Nolan's blue eyes, Nolan arched his pale brows. "I didn't realize you were keeping such close tabs on the estate, cuz."

Thomas swiftly weighed his options, but could see no reason to prevaricate, and perhaps it was best that Nigel learned there was unease among the estate's farmers, all of whom were clan. Thomas dipped his head to Nolan, acknowledging the point. "I'm not." He looked at Nigel. "One of the farmers wrote to me and mentioned the matter as a problem." Thomas could see no reason to mention Bradshaw's name nor that the man had requested that Thomas speak directly to Manachan.

Now that he'd learned of his cousins' recent exploits and taken the measure of their current interest in the estate, Thomas had to wonder if Nigel really was performing as well as he would no doubt like to think. Manachan's shoes were large—very large.

Nigel fell ruminatively silent at Thomas's words, as if digesting unwelcome news, but, eventually, he slowly nodded. "I didn't realize they were put out by it. You can leave the issue with me—I'll deal with it."

Thomas hesitated, then offered, "It might well be that all that's required is an explanation of your new strategy." Whatever that might be.

"Indeed." Nigel nodded more definitely. "I'll take care of it."

"We're going back tonight." Nolan drained his glass, set it down, and eased forward in his chair. Across the low table, he caught Nigel's gaze. "We'd better get on." Nolan glanced at Thomas and smiled. "And leave you to get back to your desk, cuz."

Nigel humphed and finished his drink. Thomas did the same and rose as his cousins got to their feet.

Together, the three made their way out of the club. They paused on the steps to shake hands and, with faintly awkward expressions of familial bonhomie, to bid each other adieu.

Then Nigel and Nolan strode off to the stable where they'd left their curricle, and Thomas headed back to the bustle of Trongate.

* * *

Thomas sank into the chair behind his desk. The two pages of Bradshaw's letter still lay on his blotter. He regarded them for a moment, then picked up the sheets, folded them, and set them in the bottom drawer to the left, where he kept all correspondence relating to the estate.

As he pushed the drawer closed, the question of what his cousins had been doing in Glasgow resurfaced in his mind. He'd asked, but they hadn't actually replied, not specifically. They'd told him at length of all their carousing, real and quite possibly imagined, but they hadn't touched on what had brought them there. Thomas knew the clan coffers would never stretch to cover the profligate lifestyle his cousins had described; he'd taken their descriptions with a very large grain of salt. They'd either exaggerated or fabricated. Possibly both.

Yet something—some reason—must have brought them to Glasgow. Why else had they come?

After a moment, he shrugged. "Presumably they came on estate business." And, in reality, the estate and its business were no business of his. "And, thank God, I am not their keepers."

With that heartfelt statement, he lifted the top file from the pile on his desk; opening it, he settled to review the company's dealings with Colliers, a shipping line operating out of Manchester who were looking to expand their business in Glasgow, and who were hoping that Carrick Enterprises, with whom they had several lucrative agreements, would help ease their way.

Twenty minutes later, a tap on the door heralded Quentin. His uncle stood in the doorway regarding Thomas, then with a smile, Quentin nodded at the file in Thomas's hands. "The Colliers?"

Thomas laid the file down. "They'll be here at four."

"Well, when you're finished with them, don't forget you're expected for dinner in Stirling Street tonight." When Thomas wrinkled his nose, Quentin grinned. "Your aunt sent a message, just in case you were in any danger of forgetting."

Thomas sighed and tipped his head back against the chair's raised back. "More young ladies."

"Undoubtedly." Quentin's expression was amused. "As neither she nor you are going to give up, you'll just have to weather the course."

If only Thomas could be sure there would be a prize worth winning at the end. He raised his head and nodded. "I'll be there."

His grim tone had Quentin chuckling as he retreated down the corridor.

The interruption had broken Thomas's concentration; his thoughts, freed, tugged him back to the question of what had brought his cousins to Glasgow...

He shook aside the distraction and refocused on the Colliers file. "Regardless of what brought them here, because they were here, I don't need to go down to the estate—and for that, I should give thanks."

And because he didn't need to journey to the lowlands, he could concentrate on taking the next vital step in forging the life he wanted.

All he needed to do was find some young lady strong enough, vital and vibrant and enthralling enough, to oust Lucilla Cynster from his mind.

* * *

Two mornings later, Thomas walked into the Carrick Enterprises office to find Dobson standing before Mrs. Manning's desk. Mrs. Manning was seated behind the desk as usual. Both she and Dobson were staring at a letter set prominently across the top of the blotter. There was a certain expectant tension in the air.

Dobson and Mrs. Manning glanced at Thomas, then Dobson reached for the letter, but Mrs. Manning snatched it up and held it out. "Good morning, Mr. Carrick. This just arrived by courier."

"I see." Strolling forward, Thomas took the packet. "Thank you."

Dobson snorted. "Surprised the boy didn't bowl you over."

Thomas had seen a courier dart out of the building just before he'd reached it, but couriers were commonplace in that part of the city. He was wondering why this particular delivery had excited such concern when Mrs. Manning obligingly added, "It's from Carsphairn, sir."

Shock lanced through Thomas. "Ah." Manachan? Or something else? He studied the envelope, but it wasn't franked by his uncle's hand... Was that good news or bad? "I'll be in my office."

Without haste, without again looking at the packet, he made his way down the corridor, into his office, and to his desk. Standing before it, he picked up the letter knife, slit the packet, and withdrew a single sheet of paper, folded twice. His face like stone, his emotions under tight control, he unfolded the sheet and read...

That the Bradshaws, the entire family of seven—Mr., Mrs., two sons, and three daughters—had been taken violently ill the day before. The family of the same Bradshaw who had previously written to Thomas.

The letter he held had been penned by a neighbor, Forrester. Forrester confirmed that, as Bradshaw had told Thomas, the seed stock for the farmers had not been delivered, and as far as anyone knew had not even been ordered, and no one knew want to do. Forrester explained that he and his family had called on the Bradshaws, who were kin, and discovered the entire family gravely ill and wracked with pain. Forrester stated that they'd sent for the clan healer, who lived at the manor. And that Bradshaw had begged Forrester to write to Thomas and let him know immediately—because they believed that someone hadn't liked Bradshaw informing Thomas about the problem with the seed supply.

Lowering the letter, Thomas stared unseeing at the view down Trongate. "Good God." Logically, there was no reason to link the Bradshaws' sudden illness with Bradshaw writing to him about the seed supply. However, in the circumstances, he couldn't swear that there was no connection. He had told Nigel and Nolan, and while he couldn't imagine his cousins doing anything so nefarious—something idiotic, perhaps, but cold-bloodedly poisoning an entire family was something else again—he had no way of knowing who else they had told.

No way of knowing what was going on on the Carrick estate.

No way of guessing if someone else might have an interest in their farmers not being supplied with seed.

Families fell ill for all sorts of reasons. The healer had been sent for, thank heaven, and if the family were still alive… "Pray God she can pull them through."

Thomas knew the healer, one Joy Burns, a woman devoted to her calling. She would do her best; that wasn't in question.

Despite the unstated insinuation contained in the letter, at first glance, there seemed no reason to assume cause and effect. However, although Thomas hadn't mentioned Bradshaw's name, for anyone familiar with the people on the estate, it wouldn't have been all that hard to guess that the outspoken and frequently belligerent Bradshaw had been the source of the complaint. And then the Bradshaw family had fallen ill—on the day after Nigel and Nolan had returned to Carrick Manor.

It wasn't, Thomas realized, simply a case of three potentially connected facts—Bradshaw writing to Thomas, Thomas mentioning the matter to his cousins, and the Bradshaws falling ill—but also the timing. More than all the rest, it was the timing that made his hackles rise.

He'd been making his way in the business world for nearly a decade. If he'd stumbled across a situation like this in a business context, he wouldn't be even entertaining the notion of coincidence.

He stood in his office, staring out of the window, while he struggled to make more from the scant facts he had.

When all was said and done, *something* was going on on the Carrick estate—and he had no idea what.

After several long moments evaluating his options, he swiveled on his heel, walked out into the corridor, and strode for Quentin's office at the other end.

When push came to shove, clan trumped damn near all else.

It absolutely trumped personal considerations.

He couldn't not go down to the estate and find out what was going on. He owed the clan, the Bradshaws and the Forresters, and even more, Manachan, that much, at least.

His interference might be unwanted, even unnecessary; he hoped the latter would prove to be the case, but regardless, he couldn't ignore the renewed plea in Forrester's letter.

He had to go back and do whatever he could. That was all there was to it.

Two

It was midafternoon when Thomas rode into the stable yard behind Carrick Manor. The *clang* of his gray gelding's hooves on the cobbles brought first one, then two, then three clansmen from the stable.

Sean reached Thomas first. The burly stableman caught Phantom's bridle; as the big gray quieted, Sean looked up at Thomas, relief in his face. "You surely are a sight for sore eyes, laddie."

Mitch and Fred came striding up, smiles on their faces, warmth in their eyes. "Welcome back, Mr. Thomas," Fred called.

"Aye." Mitch tipped his head back to meet Thomas's eyes. "Good thing, too."

Thomas returned their smiles. "It's good to be back." The response came by rote, yet, as he swung down from the saddle, he realized it was true. A sense of simple happiness, the expectation of meeting old friends and family he held dear, had slid through him in the instant he'd turned off the highway and started down the long drive.

Handing the reins to Mitch, he said, as much to himself as to the three men, "I shouldn't have stayed away so long."

Sobering, he glanced at Sean, the eldest of the three

and officially the head stableman. "Forrester sent word about the Bradshaws."

Whatever was going on, it wouldn't involve these three. Thomas knew where their loyalties lay—with Manachan and the clan—and no power on earth could have changed that. Aside from all else, the three were, like Thomas, clan orphans, orphans Manachan had taken in and watched over.

"Aye." The smile had fallen from Sean's face, too. "Bad tidings."

"Bad doings, you ask me," Mitch growled.

Sean glanced at his subordinate—but, Thomas noted, Sean didn't dismiss Mitch's suggestion of foul play.

Thomas shifted. "I'll see what the laird has to say."

"Aye." Fred nodded. "You do that. Be good that he knows."

About to turn for the house, Thomas paused, his gaze on Fred's bland countenance. Then he looked at Mitch and finally at Sean; the three didn't meet his eyes but were glancing at each other. "Manachan has been told about the Bradshaws, hasn't he?"

The three exchanged another glance, then Sean—still not meeting Thomas's gaze, which Thomas found very odd—shrugged. "Can't rightly say, can we? What we do know is that all in the house have been ordered not to tell hisself anything that might bother him."

"Ordered on pain of being sent away," Mitch added in another low growl.

Things were definitely not as they used to be—not as he'd assumed they were. Thomas gave a brief nod. "I'll go and speak with him."

As he turned away, Sean asked, "You staying?"

Striding for the house, Thomas glanced back. "I'll

probably ride out to the Bradshaws'." He nodded at Phantom. "Walk him for now."

Sean tipped a finger in salute.

Facing forward, his hands in his greatcoat pockets, Thomas continued to the house, climbed the front steps, and crossed the porch to the front door. Unsurprised to find it unlocked—this was the country, and one of the more isolated pockets, at that—he opened the door and walked into the front hall.

Into a scene of domestic confusion.

Four figures stood in the middle of the hall, talking in quiet but urgent tones, and all showing signs of consternation. Ferguson, the butler, was frowning and looked worried, while the housekeeper, Mrs. Kennedy, was as distracted as Thomas had ever seen her. The two footmen, waiting nearby, were openly anxious.

All four glanced at Thomas as he paused just inside the open door. For one second, all looked blank; Thomas realized that with the light behind him, they couldn't immediately see who he was. He reached back and pushed the door shut, then stepped forward; they recognized him, and relief washed over their features.

Thomas's chest tightened. "I heard about the Bradshaws. I've come to see the laird."

Beneath his breath, Ferguson muttered, "Thank God for that." More loudly, he said, "Welcome back, Mr. Thomas."

Mrs. Kennedy bobbed a curtsy and echoed the sentiment. The footmen, both of whom Thomas recognized from years past, nodded in greeting.

All were transparently glad to see him, which was nice in a way…and worrying in another.

Ferguson glanced at one of the footmen. "Grant can show you—"

Frowning, Thomas cut in, "Where is the laird?"

Ferguson and Mrs. Kennedy exchanged a glance, then Mrs. Kennedy carefully said, "In his room, sir. He rarely comes down, these days."

Thomas managed not to swear. The last time he'd been there, Manachan had been striding around the place, hale and hearty. "I know the way—I'll see myself up. But what's your current problem?"

Another glance was exchanged, but this time it was—again—one of relief; all were glad he'd asked.

"It's Faith Burns, sir." Mrs. Kennedy gripped her hands tightly before her. "She's the senior maid."

Thomas nodded. "I remember her."

"Yes, well." Ferguson ran a hand through his hair, something Thomas had never seen the normally unflappable man do. "Faith's gone missing. She was here last night. All was normal and as it should be. But she didn't come down this morning—or, leastways, none of us have seen her."

"Her bed's made," Mrs. Kennedy said. "But we can't tell whether she slept in it or not."

"And her sister—our healer, Joy—left last night to go out to the Bradshaws," Ferguson explained, "so we can't ask her if she knows where Faith's got to."

Mrs. Kennedy folded her arms and clasped her elbows. "It not like Faith to just up and go."

"What about other family?" Thomas asked.

Ferguson shook his head. "They're the last of the Burnses, and neither of them married."

Thomas thought, then grimaced. "I can't see anything else you can do except keep searching. Get Sean and the others to ask around in case Faith had to leave for some reason last night."

Ferguson nodded. "I'll get Sean onto that."

Mrs. Kennedy pulled a face. "I just can't see Faith leaving without a word to us, but the Wattses are second cousins. Sean might try them."

Thomas suddenly realized what—or, rather, who—was missing. "Where's Nigel?"

Ferguson didn't actually sniff, but the impression was there. "Off to Ayr with Master Nolan. Left yesterday morning, bright and early."

They'd ridden back from Glasgow only to leave the next day? Thomas struggled to keep his reaction from his face; what were the pair playing at? If Manachan was too ill to lead the clan, it was Nigel's place to step up.

Thomas looked from Mrs. Kennedy to Ferguson. "Is Edgar with the laird?" Edgar was Manachan's manservant, a silent and staunchly loyal man.

Ferguson nodded. "Edgar stays with the laird as much as he can. If he's not fetching something, then he's within call."

Thomas fought to keep the frown from his face. They were speaking of Manachan as if he was an invalid... He shrugged out of his greatcoat and handed it to Ferguson. "I'll go up. I'll be with the laird if you need me."

Stepping past the group, Thomas strode down the hall and beneath the archway into the adjoining hall that lay at the bottom of the main stairs. He took them two at a time.

The gallery was exactly as he remembered it; overall, very little seemed to have changed.

Except that Manachan was keeping to his room.

Thomas knew which room that was, but he had only

rarely been inside. His uncle wasn't young, but throughout Thomas's life, Manachan had been hale and hearty, brazenly and boldly so.

Fronting the dark-stained oak door of the master suite, Thomas paused to steel himself against what he might find within. He'd known Manachan was "ailing," but to his mind, an ailing Manachan had not equated to a man keeping to his room. "Ailing" certainly hadn't suggested, at least to him, that Manachan would retreat from his people and essentially abdicate his role as laird.

That wasn't the Manachan he knew.

He raised a fist and rapped lightly on the door, then waited.

He half expected to hear his uncle's voice bellowing an irascible "Come." Instead, soft footsteps approached the door, and it cracked open.

Edgar looked out; behind him the narrow foyer that linked Manachan's bedchamber on one side and his sitting room on the other lay in semi-darkness. Tall and lean, his face all long planes and pallid skin, his dark hair falling across a wide brow, Edgar blinked at Thomas— then the relief that was making Thomas increasingly concerned flooded Edgar's features.

"Mr. Thomas, sir! How very good it is to see you."

There was not a shred of doubt in Thomas's mind that Edgar's heartfelt tone was an accurate reflection of the man's feelings. Damn! What was going on?

Before he could ask to see Manachan, Edgar turned. Leaving the door open, an unspoken invitation, Edgar moved to Thomas's left, into the bedroom. "Sir—look who's come!"

Thomas stepped into the foyer. He paused for a second for his eyes to adjust to the dimness, then he closed the door and walked into the bedroom.

Manachan lay upon the bed, atop the covers and propped in a semi-reclining position on a mound of pillows. A shawl covered his legs, but he was dressed in shirt, cravat, and trousers, with a long velvet smoking jacket over all.

Although his skin was pasty, and he'd lost significant weight since Thomas had last seen him, Manachan was still a very large man. Although he no longer appeared robust in the sense of being vigorous, there remained a great deal of muscle and bone in his solid frame.

Yet just the act of turning his head toward the door spoke of weakness. Lassitude. The enormous, weighty lethargy of the chronically ill. The eyes that rose to Thomas's face were the same soft blue he remembered, yet the sharpness and shrewdness that had been a hallmark of his uncle's attention were...not missing, but faded and fuzzy.

Almost as if Manachan now viewed the world from a distance, through a screening veil.

Manachan's gaze traveled over Thomas's features, then his face softened and his lips curved in a smile. Weakly, he raised a hand. "Thomas, m'boy. Good of you to visit."

He went forward and took Manachan's hand in one of his; with his other hand, he lifted a straight-backed chair, positioned it beside the bed, and sat. Still gripping Manachan's hand, he studied his uncle's face and tried to mask his shock.

Manachan might have grown weak, yet his faculties seemed intact. His expression turned wry. "No, I'm not dying. Just brought low. But I'm not getting any worse, although I'm not sure if that's a blessing or a curse."

Edgar made a distressed *shush*-ing sound.

Thomas caught Manachan's gaze. "How long? How long have you been like this—confined to your room?"

Manachan arched his brows as if trying to remember, then glanced at Edgar.

"He was first struck down last August," Edgar quietly supplied. "He's been up and down since then, but never back to his old self."

Manachan snorted. "Sadly, not even close to my old self. It seems that old self of mine has slid away, and this is the best that's left." Manachan's gaze grew sharper. "Not much use to anyone anymore, but luckily Nigel is here to take over."

"You're still the laird." Edgar said it before Thomas could, and there was a wealth of defensive stubbornness in the words.

Manachan snorted dismissively. "Not much of a laird, given I can't get out and about to see what's what."

When Manachan glanced his way, Thomas met his gaze. "Speaking of what's what, why didn't you write and tell me?"

Manachan lifted his heavy shoulders in a slight shrug. "What's to tell? I'm old, boy. My past misdemeanors are catching up with me, and I just have to bear it. Old age comes to us all."

Thomas cast a reproachful glance at Edgar.

The thin man responded, "We were instructed that you were not to be bothered with…the master's failing."

Thomas looked back at Manachan.

Manachan squeezed his hand. "Allow me my dignity, boy. No one but those who have to need to see how low I've sunk."

It wasn't easy, but Thomas forced himself to swallow that—along with the acid guilt that he hadn't come back to the estate before now, that he'd stayed away for the past two years purely in pursuit of his own agenda and a cowardly wish to avoid Lucilla Cynster.

He drew a deep breath, and let it out with "Very well—I'll allow, but that doesn't mean I agree."

There was so much he didn't agree with about Manachan's current situation that he wasn't sure where to start, but today, there were more urgent matters on his plate.

Refocusing on the problems immediately before him—those facing the clan and the lairdship—he recaptured Manachan's gaze. "I received a letter from Bradshaw, and also one from Forrester, saying there were problems with the supply of seed stock for the season's plantings. They wanted me to intercede with you about the matter."

Manachan frowned, the expression starting in his eyes and slowly transforming his face. "Seed supply? But…" His gaze grew puzzled, then Manachan glanced at Edgar. "What's the date?"

The request was rapped out—still weak, but the tone more like that of the Manachan Thomas knew. Clearly, that man lay inside somewhere.

"April twentieth," Edgar promptly supplied.

Manachan's gaze swung back to Thomas. "The crops should already have been planted, shouldn't they? Or at least be about to go in?"

Thomas nodded. "But there's been no seed supplied,

at least not to the farmers on the northern farms—and, I suspect, not to any in the clan."

Still puzzled, Manachan's gaze turned inward. "There must be some delay…or something." Refocusing on Thomas, he said, "Ask Nigel—he'll know."

"Nigel and Nolan are in Ayr, and have been for the last few days. They were in Glasgow before that—I don't know for how long."

That that was news to Manachan was clear. His frown returned, darker and more definite.

"And now," Thomas said, freeing his hand from Manachan's and rising, "the Bradshaws have fallen ill. Seriously ill. The whole family."

"What?" Manachan stared at Thomas, then glanced questioningly—almost accusingly—at Edgar.

Edgar folded his hands and piously intoned, "We were ordered not to bother you with any disturbing news."

"The devil you were." Manachan's tone boded ill for whoever had given that order. He didn't say anything for several moments, then he looked at Thomas. "Where are you going?"

"To the Bradshaws' farm."

"Good. Go and find out what the deuce is going on. Take Joy, our healer, with you."

"She's already there—the Forresters sent for her and she went last night."

"At least someone's thinking," Manachan muttered. After a moment, he looked up at Thomas from under his shaggy brows. "Go and be my eyes and ears, boy. See what you can learn—not just about what's stricken the Bradshaws, but about this business of the seed supply. As Nigel's not here to ask, he can't be surprised if we ask others for information."

Thomas nodded, but the comment disturbed him, suggesting as it did that, even in Manachan's mind, all responsibility for the estate now rested with Nigel. It was one thing for Nigel to be acting in Manachan's stead, but Thomas hadn't imagined that Manachan had abdicated his role so completely, to the extent of thinking to be careful about stepping on Nigel's toes.

Then again, Thomas hadn't known how weak Manachan had grown. Perhaps the change had been necessary.

Regardless... He stepped back from the bed. "I'll come and report when I get back."

He waited for Manachan's nod, then turned and strode for the door. Closing it quietly behind him, he paused, puzzled by the changes and wondering again just what was going on, then he shook aside the distraction and went down the stairs.

After collecting his greatcoat from Ferguson, who confirmed that they still hadn't located Faith Burns, Thomas strode out of the house and back into the stable yard.

Mitch had Phantom waiting in the aisle of the stable. "Thought he may as well stand in the warm."

Thomas smiled his thanks.

As he mounted, Mitch added, "Sean's off to the Wattses' to see if they know anything of Faith. Odd, that—she's no giddy girl to go waltzing off anywhere, and, really, whereabouts around here is there anywhere to go?"

Thomas grimaced and nodded; it was a pertinent point. But how did a maid simply disappear? "If anyone needs to know, I'm off to the Bradshaws'—with the laird's blessing."

Mitch nodded. "Good thing, too. Hope Joy's got them well again. We'll be waiting to hear."

Thomas walked Phantom out into the yard. The sun had dipped behind the Rhinns of Kells, and the light was already waning. "I doubt I'll be back before full dark."

"Aye, but we'll keep an eye out, any case."

Thomas tipped his head, then tapped his heels to Phantom's sleek sides. The big gray shifted smoothly into a trot, then into a canter. Once out of the stable yard, Thomas turned the gelding to the north and eased the reins.

* * *

The Bradshaws' farmhouse lay along the northern boundaries of the Carrick estate, where the country was less hilly and the fields more open. As he rode in that direction, Thomas noted that many fields lay fallow; some were partially tilled, but none bore the neater regimentation of planted rows. The estate primarily ran sheep, with a small herd of cattle and two small goat herds; only a handful of farmers had fields useful for grain, most of which went to supplying the clan's needs through the rest of the year.

With the fields not yet planted, the concern of the farmers over not having a sufficient crop—of having only a single crop that year instead of their usual two—appeared, to Thomas, to be justified; as far as he recalled, year to year, the clan used most of the grain produced on the estate.

The shadows were lengthening when he rode up the slight rise to the front of the Bradshaws' long stone farmhouse. As the temperature had also started to fall, he was surprised to see the front door left ajar.

A glance confirmed that no hint of smoke was wafting from the chimneys—which seemed decidedly odd. It was late April, and while winter had lost its grip, warmer days, let alone evenings, were some way off.

He dismounted and tied Phantom's reins to one of the rings set in a post to one side of the door, then walked to the doorway and looked in. The light from the open door reached only so far, and the windows were fully curtained and no lamp had been lit; he couldn't see deeper into the shadows wreathing the long room, but regardless, he saw no one, and no one stirred. He couldn't hear anyone, either; silence, undisturbed, enveloped the house.

He raised a hand and rapped on the wooden door frame. "Hello? Bradshaw?"

The eerie silence stretched, but then a creak followed by a weak shout came from deeper in the house.

Thomas stepped across the threshold. Leaving the door open, he strode through the main room, beneath an archway, and into a long corridor; the shout had come from that direction.

The first door he came to stood ajar. He pushed it open and found himself looking into the Bradshaws' bedroom. Mrs. Bradshaw lay curled and slumped in an armchair by the cold fireplace. She looked dreadful, her face a ghastly hue, her graying hair bedraggled and coming loose. She was fully dressed but didn't stir at Thomas's arrival; she was breathing through her mouth, and her breath came in shallow, barely there pants. A pool of half-dried vomit lay beside the armchair.

Thomas's gaze shifted to the bed. Bradshaw had fallen across it. He was also fully dressed but, like his wife, had curled up and looked haggard and drained. He, too, had emptied his stomach, apparently violently, beside the bed, and his skin was the same ghastly shade as his wife's.

Unlike her, Bradshaw was awake, but only just; as Thomas looked his way, Bradshaw tried to raise a hand in greeting—in supplication—but couldn't.

The action—and the helpless plea in the man's wretched gaze—sank talons into Thomas's soul. "Wait." Rapidly defining what he most needed to know, he asked, "Where's the healer? Did she reach here?"

Bradshaw managed a fractional nod.

Thomas frowned and glanced down the corridor. About to search further, he glanced back to see Bradshaw moisten his cracked lips.

"She came…last night." The words were a bare thread of sound. "Forresters were here…got her here."

Abandoning the doorway, Thomas strode to the bed. He swiftly surveyed the nightstand, the dresser, but there was no water he could offer Bradshaw. Leaning closer, ignoring the stench, he concentrated on Bradshaw's lips.

Bradshaw seemed relieved he was nearer. He summoned the effort and croaked, "Joy came and saw us, then she looked in on the bairns. She put her head in to say…that she was going to make us something… heard her go to the kitchen…talk to Forrester." Bradshaw closed his eyes. His lips, his features tightened. A soft moan escaped him as pain seemed to wrack his entire body.

Helpless, Thomas watched.

As the spasm eased, Bradshaw drew in a shuddering breath and whispered, "Joy never came back."

Thomas was no healer; he had only instinct to guide him. Placing a hand on Bradshaw's meaty shoulder,

Thomas gripped. "Rest. I'll get help." As he straightened, he murmured, "Hold on."

"The bairns…" Bradshaw moaned.

"I'll check on them." Thomas turned and went to do so, not knowing what he might find.

To his relief, while all five children were in similar straits to their parents, they were all alive.

All showed signs of having been subject to violent, stomach-cramping pain; all five children lay listless, close to comatose, in their beds. Like their parents, all were dressed.

The Forresters had found the family ill and had sent for the healer. Thomas couldn't imagine the Forresters leaving their kin—not unless the healer had arrived and reassured them. Joy Burns must have believed she was capable of caring for the Bradshaws and making them well again. So she had arrived late last night, checked over the Bradshaws, understood what ailed them, and sent the Forresters home. All that had to have happened during the night.

And Bradshaw hadn't seen or heard from Joy since.

It was now late the following day—nearly night again.

So where was Joy?

Leaving the room that was occupied by Bradshaw's two sons, Thomas paused in the doorway to Bradshaw's room to say, "I'm going to find Joy and sort out what's going on. I'll bring help as soon as I can."

Bradshaw managed an infinitesimal nod and closed his eyes again.

Thomas went back into the farmhouse's large main room—sitting room, dining room, and kitchen all in one, although the kitchen was partially walled off from the dining room. Through an archway, the huge fireplace used for cooking that filled the center of the far wall of the kitchen was visible, but there was no sign of any fire in that hearth, or in the nearer fireplace in the sitting area. There had been a fire burning there, but it had burned to cold ashes.

A glance out of the open door confirmed dusk was steadily falling. No point opening the curtains. His eyes now adjusted to the dimness within, Thomas looked around and spotted a lamp sitting on the dining table. Skirting the sofa and armchairs, he walked to the table, picked up the lamp—and realized it was empty. By the look of the wick, the lamp had burned until it ran out of fuel.

Setting the lamp back down, Thomas walked into the kitchen. There had to be matches and surely another lamp.

Joy Burns lay curled on the stone floor.

She looked even worse than her patients.

Thomas swore. For a moment, he simply couldn't think, then his brain started working again. Stepping around Joy, he crouched by her side. "Joy?"

He lifted one of her hands. It was limp, without life.

He touched her face; her skin was deathly cold. He patted her cheek lightly, then more firmly, but her lashes didn't flicker. Her features didn't shift.

She was breathing, but so shallowly he could barely detect it. He couldn't see any signs that she'd emptied her stomach, but the way she lay—arms and legs curled tight, her skirts tangled beneath her—suggested she'd been in extreme pain. He searched for a pulse at her throat; all he found was a thready tremor.

The Bradshaws might be sleeping the sleep of the exhausted, but he'd known none of them, even the children, had been unconscious.

Joy—the healer—was.

The situation was bizarre.

Also beyond serious. Eight lives—seven Bradshaws plus Joy—hung in the balance, and of them all, Joy seemed to have the most tenuous hold on life.

Thomas had no ability to help any of them—not directly.

Cursing softly, he levered his hands under Joy, praying that, unconscious as she was, he wasn't causing her more pain. Straightening, he lifted her. She was a tallish, well-built woman, now a dead weight, but he managed to angle her through the kitchen archway and around the dining table.

Gently, he laid her on the worn sofa before the cold hearth.

Stepping back, he glanced at the grate, debated whether spending the time to get a fire going would be well spent—decided against it.

His clansmen desperately needed help, and given their healer was among those struck down, he knew of only one place he could get that vital help from.

* * *

He rode hell for leather for the Vale, striking east to join the road near the village of Carsphairn, then thundering south before veering down the long drive that led to Casphairn Manor.

It had been over ten years since he'd last ridden that way. Then, he'd trotted slowly, balancing two squirming deerhound puppies across his saddle. He'd given the pups—Artemis and Apollo—to Lucilla and her twin brother, Marcus. As the manor rose before him, he wondered if the dogs still lived.

Pulling up immediately before the front steps, he swung out of the saddle. He released Phantom's reins, knowing the horse wouldn't stray, then climbed the steps and grasped the iron chain that connected with a bell somewhere inside; he tugged the chain and heard a distant *clang*.

In less than a minute, footsteps approached, a measured tread, then the door opened, revealing the butler—the same one Thomas remembered from his last visit.

The butler looked at Thomas and, somewhat to his surprise, smiled in recognition. "Mr. Carrick, isn't it?"

Unable to keep the grimness from his features, Thomas nodded. "I—my clan—need help. I've just come from the Bradshaws' farmhouse to the north. The entire family—Bradshaw, his wife, and their five children—are all gravely ill and in pain." Thomas had to pause to haul in a breath against the constriction banding his chest. "And our healer is there, too, but I think she's dying. She's unconscious, and I couldn't revive her."

"Good gracious!" The butler was as shocked and as concerned as Thomas could have wished. "You'll need Miss Lucilla, then."

Thomas managed not to frown. "I was hoping Algaria might come—or, if not her, then Lady Cynster."

The butler's expression grew commiserating. "I'm afraid, sir, that Algaria passed on several years ago, and Lady Cynster is holidaying with Lord Richard on the Continent. It's Miss Lucilla who is—so to speak—holding the fort, healer-wise. But I'm sure she'll aid you—of course, she will."

Thomas knew she would, but... Jaw setting, he forced

himself to nod. Clan trumped personal considerations. "Very well. If I could speak with her?"

"Ah." The butler grimaced. "She's at the grove at the moment, but she should return very soon."

Having swallowed the necessity of having to appeal to Lucilla herself—of having to meet with her, look into her eyes, and hear her voice again—Thomas wasn't inclined to further delay. "The grove?"

"The sacred grove." The butler waved to the north. "Where she prays to the Lady. Mr. Marcus is with her."

Looking in the direction the butler had indicated— on the way back to Carrick lands as the crows flew— Thomas narrowed his eyes. "Where exactly is this grove?"

Three

L ucilla had finished her devotions.

The ancient trees of the grove—a dense mix of beech, spruce, fir, and birch—ringed the small clearing, enclosing her in a living shell of shifting green. Branches extended overhead, tips entwining to create an arched ceiling, cocooning all within from the wind—in effect, from the world.

Opening her eyes, she softly exhaled. Part prayer, part meditation, part simply communing with the land around her—and with the deity that claimed it as Her own—the quiet moments, as always, left her feeling anchored, more assured. More connected with the flow of life and with her own destiny, her own thread among the myriad strands.

Moving slowly, ceremonially, she rocked back from the rectangular stone of the rustic altar before which she'd been kneeling; originally rough-hewn, but now worn smooth by the centuries, the unadorned rock was more symbol and practical support than anything else.

She rose, feeling the skirts of her riding habit shift about her legs, and paused. Fingertips lightly brushing the smooth stone, for just one moment more she resisted the tug of the world beyond the grove; she knew what frustration awaited her there, yet it wasn't something she could avoid.

Avoiding life wasn't in her lexicon, much less in her stars.

Surrendering to the inevitable, she relaxed the meditative leash she'd imposed on her mind and allowed it to return—not to her duties in the Vale, to the role she filled, the tasks she confidently and capably performed, but to its abiding obsession. To brooding over her preordained fate, and when said fate would come to claim her.

She'd been waiting for the past ten years.

Along with her cousin Prudence and their best friend, Antonia Rawlings, she'd been presented to the ton nine years ago. As she'd fully expected, not one gentleman, eligible or otherwise, had caught her eye. But then she'd already known that her future did not lie south of the border but here, on the Lady's lands.

The man she was fated to marry was here, too—occasionally. She'd assumed that, over time, he would find his way to her side. Over the past decade, they'd met several times, and every time the connection—real, intense, and undeniable—had flared, growing stronger, more compelling, with each repeated exposure. And he knew it; he was as susceptible to that irresistible force, as governed by it, as she.

She'd schooled herself to patience, even though patience was not one of her primary virtues.

And waited.

Impatience was dangerous; it fed a reckless, willful part of her she had long ago learned to keep restrained.

She'd continued to wait.

Recently, she'd started wondering if waiting was her correct path—or whether, perhaps, she was supposed to act, to do something to initiate their inevitable union. While acting would certainly suit her temperament significantly more than passively waiting, every time she asked the question of the universe—of the Lady—the answer came back a resounding "no."

Wait. She was supposed to wait for him to come to her.

If he didn't hurry up, she would be in no good mood when he eventually got around to approaching her.

They'd last met at the Hunt Ball two years ago. They had chatted and shared a waltz—and her heart had soared. That waltz. Those ineluctable moments and their implication had been impossible to mistake, to misconstrue. To ignore.

After that night, she'd expected him to call any day. For the next month, she'd lived in a state of giddy anticipation.

But he hadn't come.

More, he hadn't set foot on the Lady's lands since.

A sound reached her—the shifting of a stone on the path leading into the grove.

Her senses immediately focused. Even while her mind was telling her it was doubtless some animal or bird, her senses reached, found—and knew.

Slowly, she turned.

As if her thoughts had finally conjured him, he was standing ten feet away, where the crooked path leading to the grove opened into the clearing. Tradition held that only the Lady's representatives and their consorts could enter Her grove—yet, as he was to be her consort...

He looked...even more elementally hers than she recalled. An even more perfect construct of her desire. Dark hair, a brown so dark it appeared black in most lights, fell in fashionably cut waves about his well-shaped head. Arched dark brows framed eyes of a curious and compelling shade of golden amber, a complex, mesmerizing blend of pale hazel and gold. Sharp cheekbones rode above aesthetically austere cheeks, complementing a squared chin and finely drawn, mobile lips.

She hadn't forgotten his height—significantly greater than her own—or his physique, a riveting combination of muscles stretched over long, heavy bones; she had no difficulty imagining that his physical form had been created by the hand of some god in that god's own image.

He was a strikingly handsome man, but what most commanded the attention of any female was the ineffable aura of power that clung to him. That pervaded the very atmosphere around him.

She was no less susceptible than any other woman—but she had power of her own.

Noting that he was, somewhat curiously, dressed in clothes more appropriate for town, with a greatcoat thrown over all, she clasped her hands, drew in a breath, raised her chin high, and looked him in the eye. "Thomas Carrick."

She said nothing more. What more was there to say? She wasn't about to fall into the same trap she had two years ago and assume his presence meant anything at all.

Thomas held Lucilla's emerald gaze. *This* was why he'd been avoiding her—that look, that unvoiced challenge.

It was as if she, the female she was, had some direct link to all that was male in him—she only had to meet his eyes, and he felt as if she'd sunk talons into his psyche and tugged.

She possessed—no, she embodied—a certain haughtiness, a highhandedness, an imperious feminine confidence that fascinated and drew him.

It wasn't anything so mundane as attraction. This struck much deeper, more forcefully, more enthrallingly.

And that was on top of all the rest—all that made up her undeniable allure.

Her head didn't even reach his shoulder; she was petite, delicate, yet well rounded and womanly. Richly red, her fabulous hair was today caught in a knot at the back of her head, leaving soft, puffed waves framing her heart-shaped face. A redhead's alabaster complexion was the perfect canvas for her startling eyes—brighter, more intense, than the green of the forests—and her lush rose-tinted lips, crafted by some angel's hand.

For a long moment, he simply looked at her—met that green gaze, felt the connection, visceral and so real—then he forced air into his lungs and tipped his head. "Miss Cynster."

At the formality, one of her brown brows arched.

He seized the moment. "I arrived at Carrick Manor in response to a summons, and subsequently rode out to the Bradshaws' farm—it's on the northern edge of the estate."

Faint puzzlement blooming in her eyes, she nodded. "I know it, but not well. I've met the Bradshaws."

That made things easier. "They're ill—very ill. Whatever struck them down happened, I think, the night before last. Others found them yesterday and sent for the clan's healer. As far as I can make out, the healer arrived late last night, and the others left the Bradshaws in her care." He paused, then simply said, "I arrived at the farmhouse less than an hour ago. I think the healer—Joy Burns—must have had some sort of seizure. I think she's dying—she's certainly very low. I don't think she had time to treat the Bradshaws at all—they're still very ill."

Lucilla blinked. "But they're alive?"

Lips tightening, he nodded. "For the moment."

"I'll come." The words were past Lucilla's lips before she'd thought—not that she had to think, not in this. A summons such as Thomas had brought was her reason for being—at least for being the Lady's representative in those lands.

He eased out a breath. "Thank you. The clan doesn't have another healer, at least not that I know of."

She shook her head. "No." She looked around for her gloves, spotted them on a mossy rock by the altar. Bending, she picked them up. "Joy was training a younger woman, but I spoke with Joy a few months ago, and she said...Alice, I think the name was, wasn't yet up to taking on the role in any independent way."

Pulling on her gloves, she walked toward Thomas, but her mind was already ranging ahead. "Joy would have taken all she needed, and I carry the essentials wherever I go, so there's no reason I need to go back to the manor and fetch anything..." She halted beside Thomas and, surprised, reached with her senses...

Abruptly, she looked at him. "What did you do to Marcus?"

Thomas grimaced and gripped her elbow.

She struggled to suppress her reaction to his touch. Even muted by the velvet of her riding jacket, it scorched.

But her twin...was where she'd left him at the entrance to the path, but he wasn't...aware. He wasn't thinking.

Thomas turned as if to follow the path out of the grove, but she stood her ground. And waited.

She'd grown very good at waiting, thanks to him.

His lips tightened, but—wisely—he didn't attempt to physically urge her on. "My clansmen need your help urgently. Cynster—your brother—would have argued. Persuading him to let you ride north with me, even if he came, too, would have taken time." He met her eyes. "Time Joy Burns and the Bradshaws may well not have."

She held his gaze. "So...?"

"I tapped him on the head. Not too hard, but he's unconscious."

She drew in a long breath, searched his eyes, then shook her head, twisted her elbow free of his hold, and started walking. "You do realize he's never going to forgive you for that?" And as Marcus would be his brother-in-law eventually, "never" was going to be a very long time.

Falling in beside her, Thomas shrugged. "If it means I get you to the Bradshaws in time to save them, I'll live with his animosity."

The images—of Joy Burns lying on the kitchen floor, as still and as cold as death, and even more those of the Bradshaw children, wracked and weak in their beds—had filled his mind as he'd ridden away from Casphairn Manor. Realizing that Marcus, being with his sister, would almost certainly be standing guard—almost certainly looking out over the Vale—Thomas had foreseen the inevitable argument and delay, and had acted to avoid both.

He'd circled and reached the grove from higher ground. He'd left Phantom a short distance from where he'd spotted Marcus's and Lucilla's mounts, then quickly, but with a woodman's caution, he'd made his way to where he'd guessed the grove had to be.

Not far from the entrance to the path into the grove, Marcus had been sitting on a rock, looking out over the Vale; he'd been so deep in his own thoughts that Thomas had had no difficulty coming up behind him without Marcus realizing.

One swift blow was all it had taken. He'd caught Marcus before he'd toppled and laid him carefully on the ground.

Marcus was still there, exactly as Thomas had left him, when, beside Lucilla, Thomas stepped clear of the enclosed path.

Lucilla halted and looked down at her twin, then she crouched and touched his cheek, his neck. Apparently satisfied, she reached into Marcus's jacket pocket, rummaged, and drew out a small notebook and pencil. She opened the notebook, flicked to a blank page, and started writing.

Thomas shifted, impatient to get on. The sense of urgency that had sent him racing to the Vale was escalating with every passing minute.

"Trust me." Lucilla's words were clipped. "Neither you nor I want to leave him without an explanation."

Recalling the level—warning—look he'd received from Marcus the last time their paths had crossed—at the Hunt Ball—Thomas had to accept that she knew of what she spoke. Cynsters were not known for being understanding over territorial incursions, and knocking Marcus out and whisking his twin sister away was not going to endear him to Marcus.

Thomas frowned. "Your parents are away, so he's running the Vale."

Lucilla nodded. She glanced at the sky, which remained clear, then tucked the open notebook into her twin's hand. Then she rose. "As long as he knows—from me—where I've gone, he won't come after me. Not unless I send for him."

Thomas inwardly admitted that Marcus turning up unannounced was one encounter he was happy to know he wouldn't have to face. He reached for Lucilla's arm. "We need to get going."

Lucilla allowed him to keep a light grip on her arm as they made their way over the rough terrain to where she'd left her horse. A flighty but very fast black, the mare pricked up her ears as they approached. Lucilla untied her reins. "What's the fastest route from here?"

She asked the question to distract him—and herself—as she drew the mare around. She would have to allow him to lift her to her side-saddle; there was no other option.

Steeling herself against his touch, she stood beside the mare and waited.

Somewhat to her surprise, Thomas's lips set, and he looked almost grim—almost as steeled against the moment as she. "North," he replied, then he closed his hands about her waist and hoisted her up.

He released her the instant she was stable, but the few seconds of contact, the sensation of being entirely within his control, had been every bit as riveting, as senses-stealing, as she'd expected.

As exhilarating, as transfixing.

Ostensibly busying herself settling her boots in her stirrups, from beneath lowered lashes, she watched him stride to a big gray that had been cropping the sparse grass a short distance away. She watched him grab the gray's reins, then swing effortlessly up to the saddle, the movement drenched with male power and grace, and a certain sense of reined aggression.

Realizing that she'd stopped breathing—that the moment had only set an edge to the need that, with him close once again, was rising within her—she drew in a tight breath, raised her head, lifted her reins, tapped her heel to the mare's side, and trotted forward to join him.

This might not be anything like the reunion she'd hoped for, but in the circumstances, she would take whatever situation the Lady handed her. And once she'd done her duty for those the Lady held within her care, she would turn the opportunity to her own purpose—to fulfilling her own very real need.

Thomas was waiting, every bit as impatient as she. Without further words, they set out, riding as fast as safety allowed for the Bradshaws' farm.

* * *

They rode up to the Bradshaws' farmhouse as the last glimmer of daylight was fading from the western sky.

Lucilla reined in before the farmhouse door, kicked free of her stirrups, and slid to the ground; she didn't need the distraction of feeling Thomas's hands close about her waist at that moment. Untying her saddlebag, she glanced at him.

Already dismounted, he reached for the mare's reins. "I'll stable the horses. Joy's on the sofa in the main room."

Lucilla nodded. Her saddlebag in one hand, she headed for the front door. Opening it, she paused, waited a moment for her eyes to adjust to the dimness, then walked in.

The Carrick healer was still lying on the sofa. There was no fire, no light, no warmth in the house. After setting her saddlebag on the table, Lucilla went into the kitchen, but the lamp she found was empty. The stove was cold, the fire in the kitchen hearth long gone to ashes. No candles lay in sight. Walking back into the main room, she scanned the furniture, the mantel—and saw a candle in a holder sitting beside a tinderbox.

She made quick work of lighting the candle, then carried it to the sofa.

Two minutes were enough for her to confirm that Joy Burns had passed beyond her ability to help. The healer was still alive, but barely, and she wasn't long for the world.

Lucilla straightened; she looked up as Thomas came inside and shut the door.

"How is she?" He crossed to stand behind the sofa and looked down at Joy. His face hardened. "She hasn't moved since I laid her there."

Lucilla hated to say the words, but she'd had to often enough to know the importance of simply saying them. "You thought she was dying, and you were right. There's nothing I can do to help her. I'm sorry." After a moment, she added, "As she hasn't moved, I don't think you could have done anything for her, even when you first found her."

His face had set, the lines harsh and unyielding; for a moment he said nothing, then he glanced up and met her eyes. Briefly, grimly, he nodded. "The Bradshaws?"

"Pray they're in better straits." She lifted the candleholder from the small table beside the sofa and turned to the archway she assumed led to the bedrooms. "I'll check on the youngest first—the little girl, isn't it? Which room is she in?"

He came around the sofa and pointed to an open door

to the right of the corridor. "The three girls share that room. The two boys are in the end room, and Bradshaw and Mrs. Bradshaw are in the room to the left."

"I'll examine them all—children, then the parents." She walked into the corridor.

Behind her, he said, "The lamps had burned down. I'll see if I can find more lamp oil."

Without looking back, she nodded. "And if not that, see if you can find more candles. I—we—will need better light."

Pushing open the door to the girls' room, she went inside.

To her relief, the youngest girl, about seven years old, seemed to be recovering; she roused from what appeared to have been normal sleep when Lucilla laid a hand on her brow.

Quickly reassuring the child, Lucilla checked on the older girls, about thirteen and fourteen. Both also roused, but were weaker, groggier, than their younger sister.

But all would live; Lucilla was certain of that.

It seemed odd that the youngest, and most lightweight, should be recovering fastest, but assuming the same would hold true for the others afflicted, Lucilla returned to the youngest girl and encouraged her to describe what had happened, what she'd felt and when. The child's report was clear enough; all the family had started to feel ill from about noon the day before. One by one, they'd started vomiting, then had taken to their beds, but the cramps hadn't stopped. The girl complained that her stomach—by which Lucilla confirmed she meant her abdominal muscles—still hurt dreadfully.

By the time the Forresters had arrived late in the afternoon, the entire family had been laid low. The Forresters had said they would send for the healer, but the girl knew no more; she'd fallen asleep.

She'd woken again that morning, but she hadn't felt well enough to do anything at all, and had continued to lie in her bed, drifting in and out of sleep.

The girl's eyes looked sunken. Lucilla had noticed that the child had been moistening her lips in between speaking; she had glanced around, but the water jug on the dresser was empty, as were the glasses each girl had on her nightstand.

Then the girl blinked up at her and in a thready voice asked for water.

Lucilla patted her hand and rose. "I'll bring some. Just close your eyes and rest, and I'll bring you some water and perhaps something else to drink soon. But first I want to check on your brothers and parents."

Her eyes already closing, the girl nodded.

In the boys' room, Lucilla found much the same situation—the ten-year-old was recovering more quickly than the sixteen-year-old. As in the girls' room, each boy had been provided with a bucket, and although the smell was dreadful, the evidence led Lucilla to conclude that whatever they'd eaten since breakfast the day before hadn't stayed down, which explained the prevailing weakness.

She reassured both boys and moved on to their parents' room.

There, she found further confirmation that what was principally ailing the Bradshaws now was lack of nourishment, lack of water, and overall exhaustion brought about through the pain of their earlier violent spasms.

But the spasms themselves seemed to have passed.

Mrs. Bradshaw seemed the most dragged down; Lucilla theorized that as a working farmer's wife with a large family, of said family, Mrs. Bradshaw very likely had the lowest reserves.

Lucilla had to climb up on the bed to examine Bradshaw himself. A bear of a man, he roused as she was leaning over him. His eyes opened, then flared wide.

Having been told that she resembled some people's idea of an angel, she was quick to reassure him. "Mr. Thomas brought me to help." Bradshaw knew her by sight, and the mention of Thomas's name helped recognition flow.

Bradshaw tensed to sit up, but she pressed him back. "No. Just rest. You're too weak to help yet, and you need to get better if you're to help your family—all of whom are recovering, too." Shifting back off the bed, she looked around the room, confirming that here, too, there was no water. "Just wait and I'll bring you something to drink. Your wife is still sleeping deeply, and there's no need to disturb her. At this point, it's best she sleeps."

She left the bedroom and walked back into the main room. A quick glance at the sofa showed that Joy hadn't stirred. Lucilla checked the healer's pulse; it was barely there, and slowing, fading. The glow of lamplight spilled out from the kitchen. Carrying her single candle, she headed that way.

Thomas was working at the kitchen table, filling a second lamp. He looked up as she appeared.

She answered the question in his eyes. "The Bradshaws are already recovering. Whatever it was, they vomited it up, and now that's done, they'll recover well enough."

"So it was something they ate?"

"That's what it looks like. Something that caused a violent stomach reaction. Something like a poison, but one that doesn't stay down, and once it's out, it no longer affects them. They're still in some pain, but it's from muscles strained through prolonged retching, not from any continuing ailment. I'll make a tisane that will ease that, but first they need some water." She'd been looking around for whatever the Bradshaws used to fetch water, but hadn't spotted anything useful.

Thomas pointed, and she turned to see a large metal ewer sitting in the shadows close by the back door. "It had rolled and spilled. I tipped what little was left into that glass on the sideboard. Joy must have had the ewer in her hand when she had her seizure."

Lucilla paused, then, without looking again at Thomas, walked over and picked up the ewer.

"What?"

The demand—more like a poorly worded command— had her glancing his way. She hesitated, but he was probably the right person to tell. "You asked about poison. I don't know what it was the Bradshaws ate, although I suspect they ate it at breakfast yesterday. But Joy was poisoned, and by something quite different. Something she most likely ate either while here, or when she was close to here." She paused, calculating, then shook her head. "I don't think she could have eaten it before she left the manor. She wouldn't have made it this far, let alone been in any state to reassure the Forresters enough for them to leave the Bradshaws in her care."

Thomas's hands had stilled, the lamp half filled. He searched her face, then said, "Our healer was poisoned?"

She grimaced. "I know it sounds unlikely, but I'm prepared to swear that Joy is dying of poison, one of the more potent ones. But how she came to take it in"—she raised her free hand, palm up—"that's impossible to say.

She could have eaten a mushroom she thought was safe, but that was actually another species. Although it sounds far-fetched, it happens often enough, even to people who think they know what they're doing."

He held her gaze, then quietly said, "So the Bradshaws are severely ill because of one sort of poison, and our healer sent to aid them is dying of another sort of poison."

She sighed. "Yes, I know. What are the odds? But I can only report what I know, and I know Joy is dying of poison. No seizure, or heart failure, or any other cause of death looks quite the same." She raised the ewer. "I'm going to fill this."

She turned and opened the door.

"The well is to the right, toward the barn."

She went out, drawing the door closed behind her. The twilight was deepening and the air had grown chill, but she wasn't planning on being outside for long. The rear yard was paved, and the well stood in pride of place in the center of the expanse; there was light enough to see her way.

The stone well was open, but shaded by a small pitched roof. The bucket had been left down and was already full; she bent to the task of hauling it back up. Swinging the sloshing bucket to the side of the well, she unhooked the handle. Steadying the ewer between her feet, she was about to lift the bucket from the well wall and pour the water into the ewer when three cats and five kittens came running from the barn, mewing plaintively.

The cats made straight for a gray enamel bowl on the ground beside the well. The bowl was empty.

The cats twined about the bowl and Lucilla's skirts.

"You poor things." She bent and picked up the bowl,

tipped the bucket enough to splash water into it, then carefully set it down beside the well.

The cats had backed off. She stepped away and watched as the three older cats crept forward. Noses extended, whiskers twitching, they approached the water.

They got to within a few inches, then pulled up and, lips curling, backed away.

Two of the kittens made a dash for the bowl. One of the larger cats hissed and batted them away.

Casting what she could only describe as dark looks at the gray bowl of water—and, incidentally, at her—the cats grumbled and slunk away, back toward the barn.

Lucilla looked at the bucket of water, and a chill slid down her spine.

A second's thought was enough to transform suspicion into certainty.

Jaw setting, she gripped the bucket and tipped the water back into the well. She left the empty bucket by the side of the well, tipped the water out of the gray bowl, swiped up the empty ewer—and remembered the glass of water on the sideboard and someone who might well be thirsty.

She burst into the kitchen just as Thomas lifted the glass from the sideboard. "No!" She flung out her free hand. "Don't drink that."

Thomas looked from her to the glass, then looked back at her, at the ewer dangling, obviously empty, from her other hand. "The *water*?"

His tone was both horrified and incredulous.

She slumped back against the door and nodded. "It's tainted. Even though they're desperate, the barn cats won't touch it."

Catching her breath, she pushed away from the door,

walked to the table, and set the empty ewer down. She studied it for a moment, then quietly said, "Something—somehow—got into the well water two nights ago. The Bradshaws drew water in the morning and drank it with their breakfast."

"And fell ill."

She nodded. "But, of course, when people are ill like that, the first thing anyone does is give them water. More water."

"So the illness—the retching and pain—continued."

Raising her gaze, she met Thomas's eyes. "Whoever did this—and I can't think of any alternative but that someone put something in that well—it was a dastardly thing to do. The children—" She broke off; fighting to quell a shiver, she wrapped her arms around herself. "If it had continued, they would all eventually have died. There would have been no end to the pain."

Thomas swore beneath his breath. He looked at the glass in his hand, then stalked to the door, opened it, and flung the contents outside.

Lucilla continued to stare at the ewer on the table. Eventually, she said, "What a twist of fate. The Bradshaws are recovering because they haven't had any water for the last day. If Joy hadn't fallen ill herself—"

"She would have continued to give the Bradshaws water, not realizing she was poisoning them with it." Thomas's jaw felt like stone; inside, he was raging. But there was no one on whom he could vent his anger, no one on whom he could avenge his clansmen. Not yet.

He forced himself to draw in a huge breath and refocus on what was important here and now. "The Bradshaws. They need water—water they can safely drink."

Lucilla shook herself, as if shaking free of similarly

vengeful thoughts. "Yes. And they need it urgently. I can't give them any tisanes to ease them, not without water to brew those tisanes." She looked at him. "Which farm is closest?"

"The Forresters'. I'll ride there—they'll help."

She nodded. "If I boil the water, I can use it to wash and clean. The youngest two—I can make them more comfortable, at least."

He hesitated. "I'll need to borrow the Forresters' dray to bring back any decent amount of water. I'll be an hour, possibly two. Will you be all right here on your own?"

She looked at him as if he was speaking in tongues, then she waved him away. "Go. I'll be perfectly all right."

He went.

Lucilla finished reassembling the second lamp. She lit the wick, turned it low, then left the lamp on the table beside the sofa. After checking Joy Burns and finding little change, she took the other lamp and explored the various small rooms off the kitchen and the wash house. After deciding what she could use for each task, she set to work hauling in water from the well, filling the copper, then building the fire beneath it. Once the water had boiled for ten full minutes, she doused the fire, ladled water into a pail, then set the lid back on the copper and got to work.

She scrubbed floors and replaced the used buckets. Despite the chill in the night air, she cracked open several windows, encouraging the cool drafts to clear the stench of sickness from the house.

That done, she fetched more of the boiled water, still warm, and used damp cloths to wash her patients' hands and faces, all the while being especially careful not to allow any of the water, boiled or not, to touch anyone's lips.

The youngest girl and younger boy awoke and remained awake, but all the others were still drifting in and out of sleep. Remembering the small canteen attached to her saddle, Lucilla wrapped a knitted shawl she found in the Bradshaws' room about her head and shoulders, and went out to the barn to find it.

She was pleased to discover the canteen was full of pure, fresh water from Casphairn Manor's well. She took a small sip, then returned to the house and poured small amounts of water into two glasses she took from the very back of a shelf. Those she gave to the girl and boy, then she found another glass, one she deemed safe enough, and took some water to Bradshaw.

He roused enough to drink it down, but immediately fell back, exhausted just by doing that much. Lucilla watched sleep reclaim him. She checked on his wife, then left them both sleeping.

Returning to the main room, she pulled a chair up to the sofa, sat, and, taking Joy Burns's hand in hers, kept vigil.

She'd done this before, with Algaria, with others, and knew she would do so many more times in her life— holding the hand of the dying as they approached the veil.

The moments ticked past, then she bent her head and prayed.

The small clock on the mantelpiece chimed twelve times before she heard the distant rumble of an approaching dray.

She walked out to discover that Thomas had brought two full barrels of water.

He drew the rear of the dray as close as he could to the kitchen door. Stepping down, he nodded at the barrels. "The Forresters will be here as early as they can. Until then, we'll have to work with the barrels where they are—I can't lift them by myself."

"No matter," she said. "It's untainted water, and that's what counts."

The next hours were busy. Thomas unhitched the Forresters' horse and led it to the stable, while she set two different tisanes brewing. While they steeped, then cooled, she rinsed and dried glasses and bowls, using the precious untainted water sparingly. She didn't know what had been put into the Bradshaws' well, but boiling alone might not negate its effect; she wasn't taking any chances.

Thomas had come back inside, looked in on the Bradshaws, and was sitting silently beside Joy when Lucilla carried a tray laden with doses of her tisane into the main room.

He rose and went to take the tray. Together, they went into each room and woke each Bradshaw. He helped them to sit while Lucilla helped them drink. Thomas was relieved by the improvement in the youngest children; color had started to return to their cheeks and they moved, albeit carefully, on their own.

"They should all be like that by morning," Lucilla told him.

All the Bradshaws roused enough to recognize both him and her, which was also reassuring. When Mrs. Bradshaw, the weakest and still most affected, struggled to thank them, he hushed her. "Just rest and get better—that's the best reward you can give us."

Lucilla's lips gently curved. She gave him an approving nod, then she lifted the tray with the empty glasses and led the way out of the room.

He picked up the lamp and followed. Pausing in the

doorway, he glanced back, took in the clean floor, the clean, unused buckets left in case of need, and the other signs of order restored and neatness reimposed.

After closing the door, he followed Lucilla along the corridor. He hadn't expected her—the granddaughter of a duchess—to scrub soiled floors in a farmhouse, yet the floors had been washed and scrubbed, and she had been the only able body there. Then again, he'd seen how she had worked when they'd been stranded in a crofter's cottage ten years before, and she'd helped deliver the crofter's babe. Granddaughter of a duchess she might be, but she'd never shied from doing whatever was required to aid those who needed and asked for her help.

Ducking under the low lintel of the archway, he stepped into the dimness of the main room. In the glow cast by the lamp set beside the sofa, he saw her, still carrying the tray, peering at the face of the small clock on the mantelpiece.

"We'll need to dose them again at about four o'clock."

He hesitated, then asked, "What is it you're giving them?"

She glanced at him as if surprised by his interest, but answered, "What we've just given them is a blend of herbs that will ease the pain and settle their stomachs. At four o'clock, we'll give them a half dose of the same thing, along with a half dose of a strengthening tonic. Later, when they're ready to get on their feet, they should have more of the latter." She started toward the kitchen. "They can sip that throughout the day as needed. I'll make up a bigger batch to leave with them. By evening, I'll be surprised if they aren't all feeling a great deal better, although full recovery will take another day or so." Pausing in the kitchen doorway, she glanced back. "The most important thing is to ensure they have no more of that tainted water."

He nodded; when she continued into the kitchen, he ambled after her and set the lamp on the table. "The Forresters are near enough to supply them. Forrester's already offered. I'll arrange for the well to be tested, but that will take months."

"The effect might pass. They can use the cats to check if the water's still bad." She paused, then said, "That reminds me."

Leaving the tray on the table, she picked up the lamp, walked to the kitchen door, opened it, and went out. Curious, Thomas followed as far as the door. He propped one shoulder against the frame and watched as she went to the well, bent and picked up a bowl, then returned to the water barrels and filled the bowl from one.

She glanced at him. "As the barn cats were so instrumental in sounding the alarm, so to speak, the least we can do is see to them, too."

He didn't argue, just watched as she returned to the well, set down the bowl, then straightened and called, "Kit, kit, kit."

One after another, the cats came out to investigate. Soon, the bowl was surrounded by furry heads, all lapping furiously.

When the cats were replete and sat back to groom their whiskers, Lucilla brought the bowl back to refill it. Still lounging, he asked, "Artemis and Apollo—are they still about?" By which he meant still alive; the pair would be just over ten years old, which was a very good age for a deerhound.

She nodded. "For years, they went everywhere with us, Marcus and me—at least, wherever we allowed.

They used to come to the grove with us without fail, but now their legs aren't up to the journey." Her lips gently curved. "They usually laze about the manor in the best spot of sunshine they can find. Or if not that, they stretch before the fireplace that has the best fire—they move from hearthrug to hearthrug, depending on the state of the blazes."

He humphed. He watched her take the refilled bowl back to the well. He remained where he was as she returned. When she halted before the door and arched an imperious brow at him, he met her gaze and simply said, "Thank you for coming and helping the Bradshaws."

She shrugged lightly and waved him back.

Slowly straightening, he stepped back, and she stepped past—almost touching yet not, a teasing of his senses, one he hadn't anticipated and therefore hadn't guarded against. He clamped down on his instinctive reaction.

Apparently oblivious, she continued into the kitchen. "It's my duty to help." She glanced back at him. "As I did with the crofters—the Fieldses—all those years ago."

Closing the door, he frowned. "I thought your duties, as such, were limited to the Vale."

"The Lady considers these lands—the Carrick estate, all of it, it seems—to be part of her domain, too. Hence all the people on the estate are in her care, so if they need the sort of help I can give"—she spread her hands—"I'm here."

Halting at the end of the kitchen table, he watched her sort through the various herbs she'd pulled from her saddlebag. After several moments, he shifted. "I'll go and check on the Bradshaws."

She nodded without looking up.

After confirming that all was quiet in the bedrooms,

he sank into the chair beside the sofa. Resting his elbows on his thighs, linking his hands and propping his chin upon them, he watched Joy Burns. He wished she could rouse enough to tell him what had happened, whether her taking poison had been a terrible accident, or...

His mind balked at supplying the rest of that thought. Who would knowingly harm a healer, and why?

Yet coincidence, coincidence. One too many coincidences had brought him there, and now here was another.

Time passed, and Lucilla joined him. She'd turned the lamp in the kitchen low; the light was muted, shades of shadows and night, when she bent over Joy, felt for her pulse, then quietly murmured, "She's sinking. It won't be long now."

He rose and drew up the other armchair. Lucilla sank into it, and he returned to the other.

Together, they sat and watched Joy Burns die.

Later, he carried Joy's body to the wash house. Lucilla spread a sheet on the bench, and he laid Joy down. Lucilla straightened Joy's limbs, her clothes, then drew another sheet over Joy's empty shell.

They stood side by side for a moment, then turned and left, closing the door and returning to the house to continue caring for the living.

At four o'clock, they did their rounds, waking the sleeping Bradshaws and administering doses of Lucilla's combined remedies.

By the time they'd tidied things away, set all ready for making breakfast, and Lucilla had put up her prepared tonic for later, the sun was lightening the eastern sky.

He found a cache of tea. Lucilla made a pot for the two of them. Taking his mug, he walked through the main room to the front door. He opened it and looked out, then he stepped out, tugged the door almost closed, and sat on the stone stoop. Cradling the mug between his hands, he sipped the strong tea and gazed out over Carrick lands, to where the sun was painting the skies with pale gray, blush pink, and soft orange.

Some time later, the door opened, and Lucilla stepped out. Like him, she'd brought her mug. She sat next to him; the stone step was only so wide—less than an inch separated their hips and shoulders.

Without a word, she, too, sipped her tea and looked out at the dawn as the sun rose over a landscape that was familiar to them both.

Minutes passed, then without looking away from nature's splendor, he asked, "The poison in the well—do you have any idea what it might be?"

She looked down; she frowned at the mug in her hands. "No, not really. It could be something organic, like a fungus or mold, or mineral-based." She paused, then added, "If I had to wager, I'd put my money on the latter."

He sipped, lowered his mug. "Why?"

From the corner of his eye, he saw her raise her head.

"Because a fungus or mold would have taken time— weeks or months—to grow to the point of poisoning the well. Any illness would have come on gradually, over a long period, not as it appears to have done, all in one morning." Her gaze on the horizon, she sipped, then said, "Salts of some sort. That would be my guess."

He let that settle between them, then asked, "I take it we're in agreement that, although Joy could have, for some reason, eaten a mushroom or some other poisonous plant while on her way here, it's very strange that a healer of her experience, one who was born and lived all her life in these parts, should have made such a mistake?"

He made the statement a definite question.

Lucilla frowned. "Yes. Beyond strange, heading toward incomprehensible." She waited, sipping her tea. When Thomas said nothing more but simply stared broodingly out at the fields, she decided it was her turn to ask questions. "What brought you back to the estate?"

He shifted on the stone beside her, then settled again. "I got a letter—two letters. The first from Bradshaw, telling me there was a problem with the seed supply for the season's planting. I happened to run into Nigel and Nolan in town, and they assured me it was...some change in procedure. Something like that. Yesterday, Forrester sent a courier with a note to tell me that he and his wife had found the Bradshaws very ill. Forrester confirmed the difficulties with the seed supply." He paused, hands clasped about his mug, then said, "I decided I needed to come down and see what was happening for myself."

She'd harbored a tiny kernel of hope that she might have contributed to his reasons for returning, but...whatever the reason, he was at last there. She sipped, turning over his words. Puzzled, she said, "Our farmers have already planted or are in the process of doing so." She glanced at him. "I haven't heard of any new procedure, or any seed shortage, but if there has been any disruption to the supply, Marcus would know."

He met her gaze briefly. "I'm sure the situation will sort itself out." He looked forward again.

She did the same, the warmth from the tea slowly seeping through her.

Silence descended, wrapping about them, but it was comfortable, unstrained—comforting.

Then he murmured, "Your butler told me Algaria had passed on—I hadn't known. He also said your parents were traveling in Europe—I thought that, as Lady of the Vale, your mother never left the area."

Thomas raised his mug and drained it while inwardly cursing his own curiosity; he knew very well why some errant part of him wanted to know if a Lady of the Vale could live elsewhere.

"Mama could have left at any time—we're not tied to the Vale in any tangible way. But our duties…" Lucilla paused, then went on, "It's by our own choice that our duties bind us. Mama has never traveled out of the country before, but she's gone down to London, or to Edinburgh and elsewhere, often enough. But she never left the Vale except when Algaria was there to stand in her place. Now that I can do the same, Papa persuaded her to go and experience all the sights she's always longed to see."

She paused, sipped, then went on, "Neither Mama nor I would ever leave the Vale untended—without one of the Lady's chosen to care for her people."

He'd assumed as much, which was why he'd long ago decided that she would never be—could never be—the lady for him.

She continued, "It's not just our role as healers, but as…foci, or figureheads. Just being there gives the people a central figure, one that draws them together, that gives them hope and bolsters them in times of trouble, and keeps the community united."

He knew that was so, understood that well enough to entertain no ambition to steal her away. She was the embodiment of the future for the people in the Vale, and they were good people. She was theirs.

And that being so, she could never be his.

That errant part of him that, despite all, wanted her, didn't like that truth, but he couldn't argue it, couldn't fight it.

His empty mug dangling from his fingers, he stared out at the fields as the rising sun bathed them in golden glory. Both he and she were tired, but not exhausted. They had worked all night, yet a sense of quiet euphoria filled them. The Bradshaws were much better, and all were sleeping normally—even he could see that.

Suddenly, she leaned against him, her shoulder against his upper arm, her tipped head resting on his shoulder. Lids low, she sighed, then murmured, "You don't mind, do you?"

He looked down at her, at her flaming red hair; wisps had come loose and curled, lit to brilliance as the sun touched them. "No." He was passably good at lying. Having done so, he decided he might as well be hung for a wolf as a lamb. He raised his arm, letting her settle more comfortably against his side, then draped that arm about her shoulders. She might be delicately built, but she was very real. And wholly feminine.

Feeling the subtle warmth of her stealing into his muscles, he drew a careful breath. He forced himself to look out over the fields and state what he knew had to be. "Once we're sure the Bradshaws are on the mend and the Forresters arrive to relieve us, I'll escort you home."

Best to underline the limit of their association—for himself even more than for her.

Four

The Forresters arrived in a pony trap at ten o'clock that morning.

By then, Lucilla had made breakfast for the Bradshaws, as well as for Thomas and herself. After dispatching Thomas to milk the by-then-distressed cow, she had rummaged and found oats, and some barley, too. She had made a large pot of thick porridge, adding fresh milk to make it creamy. The two youngest Bradshaws came to the table, but the others ate propped up in their beds. The rapidity with which the steaming bowls, liberally laced with honey, had emptied had reassured her.

The Bradshaws were firmly on the road to recovery.

When Mr. and Mrs. Forrester walked into the house, she had a large batch of the strengthening tonic prepared and put by, enough to see the whole family back to robust health.

After going around the bedrooms with both Forresters and explaining the improvements she expected to occur over the next few days, she led Mrs. Forrester into the kitchen, leaving Mr. Forrester conversing with Thomas in the main room.

Both Forresters had been shocked to hear of Joy Burns's death but, rustically stoic, had accepted the

mystery of it as "just one of those things." Neither she
nor Thomas had alluded to any deeper suspicions; no
sense in starting rumors over something they could never
prove.

After instructing Mrs. Forrester on the correct dos-
age of the strengthening tonic to administer to each of
the Bradshaws—and reassuring her that there was no
danger if any of them took too much—Lucilla helped
unpack the baskets of food and supplies the Forresters
had helpfully brought.

With everything for the Bradshaws' further care organized, she turned her mind to the most pressing item
on her personal agenda: How to keep Thomas with her—
or, alternatively, how to remain by his side.

Regardless of the reason for his return, he was there.
In his continued absence, she'd wondered if she should
act and bring him to her, but she had always sensed she
wasn't supposed to; the current situation was, presumably, the reason for that. He'd been summoned by others
and he'd come, but now he was there, acting to keep him
there long enough for them—her and him—to take the
next step along their preordained path, namely to marry,
was patently something she should do.

That it fell to her to do.

How to do so, however...

He had said that he would escort her back to the Vale,
but when they reached there, how was she to get him
to stay?

The Forresters had brought more water. Thomas and
Mr. Forrester came into the kitchen, crossed to the rear
door, propped it open, and went out. They returned a minute later, carrying one of the water barrels between them.

Lucilla rushed to clear a space on the counter along

the rear wall. The men set the barrel down, made sure it was steady, then went out to fetch the next.

Shifting various pans from the counter to create more space, Lucilla heard Thomas, outside by the dray, say, "So neither you nor any of the farmers have been given any explanation for the delay in the seed stock?"

"No," Forrester replied. "When we asked, we were told that we'd get the seed when it came in, and that was all there was to it. Any of us questioned—as Bradshaw did—why the seed was late, we were told it wasn't our concern." Forrester's ire was plain. "Can you imagine? Telling us—who grow the crops, who get the seed into the ground—that it's no concern of ours when we get the seed? Preposterous!"

Lucilla stepped back as the men brought in the next barrel, the second of three.

When they went back to the dray, she made a show of rearranging some pans so she could remain close enough to the door to overhear their exchanges.

"I take it," Thomas said, "that none of you spoke directly to the laird."

"No—although we would've if we could've. We were told it was Mr. Nigel we had to deal with. Not that that would've stopped us, but none of us has seen the laird these past months. Seems he's been poorly and keeping to his room."

"So I'd gathered," Thomas said in reply.

Manachan was ill? That was the first Lucilla had heard of it, but, although the Vale and the Carrick estate were geographically connected, the people on the two properties shared few familial ties, and so the usual conduits of gossip—sister to sister-in-law, cousin to cousin—weren't there.

Frowning to herself, she left the pans and moved further into the kitchen. To keep her hands busy, she started repacking her saddlebag while rapidly reviewing all she knew.

Something, quite obviously, was going on on the Carrick estate. The peculiarities of Manachan being ill and no seed being provided for planting were the least of it. The Bradshaws' sudden illness and Joy Burns's death added darker layers to the situation.

Thomas had been summoned and had been left no option but to come down to the estate and involve himself in sorting things out; that, too, was plain enough.

And, wisely, he'd asked for her help.

So she was now involved, and as the people on the Carrick estate were under the Lady's protection, too, to her mind that was entirely appropriate.

By extension, she needed to remain involved until she and Thomas got to the bottom of whatever was going on, and sorted matters out in whatever way said matters needed sorting.

She glanced up as Thomas and Forrester carried in the last barrel and settled it alongside the others.

Yes, she had a vested personal interest in remaining by Thomas's side, but solving problems for the Lady's people was what she was supposed to do. It was part of her role, a part of the code by which she lived.

The clop of hooves and the ponderous crunching of wheels on the gravel outside had all of them in the kitchen looking toward the front of the farmhouse.

Thomas frowned and led the way to the front door. Forrester followed. Lucilla set down her herb packets and hurried in the men's wake. Wiping her hands on her apron, Mrs. Forrester brought up the rear.

Thomas opened the front door, looked outside—and inwardly swore. Leaving the door open, he walked out and down the step to the heavy, old-fashioned curricle that had come to a halt, rocking on its springs, before the farmhouse.

The reins in his hands, Sean met Thomas's eyes, a warning in his.

Beside Sean, swathed in a blanket over a thick overcoat, sat Manachan. Large though he was, in contrast to Sean's hale and hearty form, Manachan looked frail. His pallor was more pronounced in the clear morning light, and his crippling lack of energy showed in the effort he had to expend to simply raise a hand in greeting.

Thomas rounded the horse and went to Manachan's side. He gripped the hand Manachan had raised. "Sir—we didn't expect you."

Manachan nodded weakly, yet nevertheless managed to infuse the action with his customary dismissive irascibility. "The Bradshaws," he all but wheezed. "How are they?" Using Thomas's grip for leverage, Manachan started the process of getting himself out of the carriage.

For a moment, Thomas was fully absorbed with balancing his uncle's weight; the last thing he wanted was for his laird to fall on his face.

Lucilla had taken in Manachan's state in one swift glance; she didn't need to see more to know the old man was seriously ill. What the devil had happened to him? But he was still The Carrick, the laird, and despite the inadvisability of him having come out all this way, he was behaving appropriately—as a laird should.

Glancing at Forrester, she saw that he was as shocked by Manachan's state as she was, but he wasn't hiding it as well. Moving past him, she stepped off the stoop and circled the horse to where Thomas was endeavoring to keep Manachan upright. "The Bradshaws arc much improved," she stated.

Manachan had been looking down at his own feet; he hadn't seen her approach. At her words, he glanced up at her from under beetling brows—but he recognized her instantly, which gave her hope for his condition.

"You, heh, miss? I heard your mother was from home."

"She is." Stepping to Manachan's other side, Lucilla calmly twined her arm in his. "Thomas fetched me, and I've treated the Bradshaws—all of them." She glanced at the couple on the stoop. "And now the Forresters have come and will keep watch over the family. They should be entirely recovered in a few days."

Between them, she and Thomas managed to guide, steer, and support Manachan into the house. They eased him down onto the sofa before the fire; he sat half slumped, laboring to catch his breath. Forrester had busied himself stoking the fading fire in the hearth, coaxing it into a blaze. At Lucilla's suggestion, Mrs. Forrester had rushed off to make a pot of tea.

Leaving Thomas and Forrester to explain what they would to Manachan, Lucilla followed Mrs. Forrester into the kitchen and set about searching for biscuits.

She found a crock filled with a mixture of biscuits of various types. She started hunting through it, pulling out the shortbread, softer and more suitable for a man in Manachan's state.

Mrs. Forrester glanced through the open archway at the men, then brought an empty plate to Lucilla. Standing beside her as she arranged the shortbread on the plate, Mrs. Forrester whispered, "I had no *idea* the poor laird was so low. I'm sure Forrester didn't have any clue, either."

"Nor did I." Lucilla glanced at Mrs. Forrester. "No one in the Vale has heard anything about Manachan being ill."

Mrs. Forrester lifted a shoulder. "We knew he was ailing—but there's ailing and *ailing*, as you would know." She shook her head. "He was always such a... well, *vigorous* man. It's sad to see him so...pulled down."

"Indeed." Lucilla was already considering what to do about that. Now she'd seen how unwell Manachan was, there was no question as to where her duty lay. Manachan was The Carrick, the laird, and he lived under the Lady's protection, regardless of whether he accepted that or not.

She picked up the plate she'd piled with shortbread and walked back into the main room in time to see Thomas, seated in one armchair, lean closer to Manachan and quietly ask, "Are you all right?"

The concern in his tone, the anxiety in his face, spoke clearly of the depth of his worry for his uncle. She moved closer and offered Manachan the plate. "We'll have the tea ready in a moment."

Manachan nodded and lifted one of the shortbreads from the plate. He moved slowly, with will and thought required to perform even that simple act.

Lucilla glanced at Thomas, but his gaze was on Manachan. Looking back at Manachan, she asked, "Has Thomas told you about Joy Burns?"

Thomas murmured, "I did."

"Bad business," Manachan muttered around his first bite of shortbread. His gaze was fixed on the flames in the hearth. After a moment, he swallowed, then said, his words not quite distinct, "She was clan—she'd been with us all her life."

Lucilla turned as Mrs. Forrester bustled up with the tea tray. When the farmwife glanced inquiringly at her, Lucilla nodded for her to pour. They handed around the cups, and Lucilla sat in the other armchair. The Forresters retreated to the kitchen, uncomfortable in the company of those they regarded as their betters, at least when it came to taking tea.

Thomas's attention was on Manachan, on the struggle to get the teacup from saucer to lip. Lucilla waited until Manachan had taken a long swallow, then quietly said, "I know Joy had an apprentice. Do you know if she's ready to step into Joy's shoes?"

Manachan didn't move his head, but cast her another of his assessing glances. A minute ticked by; she waited patiently, her gaze locked with his.

Then he humphed. "As you say, Joy's been training another—Alice Watts."

Lucilla knew the family. "The midwife's daughter."

"Aye." He nodded, moving his head only fractionally. "That's her. Slip of a thing, and quiet, too, but according to Joy, Alice is clever enough and willing to do the work and learn..." He paused, then sighed gustily. "But I don't know that Alice can step up to the healer's role—I doubt she's come that far."

Manachan glanced sidelong at Lucilla; for all his frailness, his gaze was still shrewd, the mind sunk in his worn frame still acute. "I don't like to ask..." He let the sentence trail away.

"You don't have to ask." Calmly, she set her cup on its saucer, balancing both in her hands. Avoiding Thomas's gaze, she looked solely at Manachan. "I'm obliged by my station to aid your people as well as those in the Vale. I should check on Alice and see how far along in her training she is, and ensure that she possesses the requisite knowledge to properly care for your clan and that she has any and all support she might need."

Manachan blinked; for a moment, he looked nonplussed. "Your...remit, as it were, extends to the Carricks?"

She inclined her head. "It does." Over the years, she'd confirmed that what she thought of as the Lady's mantle extended far enough north to encompass all the Carrick lands. Even there, at the northern boundary farthest from the Vale, she could still reach for the Lady and feel Her presence.

Her revelation had given Manachan pause; from the expression in his blue eyes, he was wondering whether the Lady's dominion posed any challenge to him. Regardless, she wasn't about to return to the Vale and meekly wait for him to summon her. If Joy Burns hadn't known how to effectively treat him, then it was unlikely her half-trained apprentice would.

Manachan studied her, unblinking, for several moments, then his features softened, and with a touch of graciousness, he inclined his head. "If you have the time to visit Carrick Manor, I and my clan would welcome your advice." Manachan's gaze slid to Thomas. "Our first thought must be for the clan, to ensure the people and the bairns are as safe as they can be, and that means having an effective healer."

Thomas read the message in Manachan's eyes. His uncle thought he'd been clever to encourage Lucilla to aid them; for Thomas's money, the instant Lucilla had laid eyes on Manachan, she'd decided she would be going to Carrick Manor. He might not know her all that well, but he knew how she responded to what she perceived as need; if people needed her help, they got it.

He strongly suspected Manachan would have her help whether Manachan wished it or not.

Which left him—Thomas—in a difficult position.

He wanted Lucilla to help Manachan—to treat him, if she could persuade the old man to it. If anyone could help his uncle regain at least some of his previously rude health, he firmly believed she was that person. In addition, ensuring that the clan had an effective healer was another vital issue she and only she could properly address.

On the other hand, he didn't want to spend any more time in her vicinity. Being within her orbit helped him not at all; the effect she had always had on him had, it seemed, only intensified over the last two years. She was worse than a distraction; she was a compelling being who drew him, his attention, his focus, like a lodestone.

He forced himself to take a sip of tea while the internal tug-of-war between what he wanted for Manachan and the clan, and what he wanted for himself, raged within.

Lucilla urged Manachan to take another shortbread, which he did.

The small moment of domesticity seemed strange, yet comforting.

After a moment, Manachan asked about the Bradshaws; Thomas listened with half an ear as Lucilla described their symptoms and the suspected cause.

Manachan's gaze shifted to him. "The well's tainted?"

Thomas met Lucilla's gaze, then said, "I'll have samples sent to Glasgow." He looked at Manachan. "It'll take a while, but we'll find out what's behind it. Meanwhile, the Forresters will supply the Bradshaws from their well."

"Forrester's agreed?"

"He has."

Manachan brooded for several minutes, then he held out his empty cup on its saucer. Lucilla took it from him; she rose and carried her cup and Manachan's to the kitchen.

Manachan waited until she was out of earshot to lean closer to Thomas. "The Bradshaws. Should I go in and see them, do you think?"

Thomas considered, then shook his head. "Bradshaw and his wife were the worst affected. They're sleeping now. If you go in, they'll be flustered and embarrassed that they can't greet you properly."

Manachan grimaced; he didn't argue, yet it was clear from his expression that he wanted the Bradshaws to know of his coming, of his support.

"Perhaps," Thomas suggested, "we could have the youngest two come out and speak with you. They're recovered enough to greet you, and they'll tell their parents that you were here."

Manachan brightened. "Good enough."

Lucilla returned. Thomas explained his plan; somewhat to his surprise, after one searching glance at Manachan, she agreed without comment. The youngest two Bradshaws were duly prepared; as the pair had come out for breakfast, they were already washed and dressed. A quick brushing of hair and tugging down of clothes, and they were ready to greet their laird.

Thomas stood to one side of the hearth and watched

Manachan talk with the pair. Lucilla came to stand alongside him. After a moment, he murmured, "I'd forgotten how good he is with children." His uncle was frequently testy, sometimes belligerent, always calculating, but when it came to children, he seemed instinctively to know what to say and how to say it.

Lucilla regarded the group on the sofa. Her lips curved in subtle appreciation. "Your uncle is a cunning old soul with a big heart."

The Forresters were in the kitchen, preparing a sustaining luncheon for the Bradshaws. Manachan and the children were absorbed with their conversation.

Thomas seized the moment and quietly said, "About you coming to Carrick Manor—we can't ask you to leave those in the Vale without your...services, not with your mother absent, too. I was thinking I should escort you back there, and perhaps tomorrow you could ride over." *And bring Marcus with you.* Thomas was fairly certain her twin would act as an effective barrier to any contact between them. Especially as Marcus would be nursing a sore head, most likely in more ways than one.

Lucilla shifted her gaze from Manachan and the children to him. She met his gaze; her emerald eyes narrowed fractionally, then her chin firmed. "That won't be necessary. Casphairn Manor is only an hour from Carrick Manor. If, as seems likely, I need to stay for a few nights, I'll send a note to Marcus. If anyone in the Vale needs me, he'll send for me, but we have no sickness there at present." She glanced at Manachan, then met Thomas's eyes again. "As I told your uncle, I have a duty toward those on the Carrick estate, too, so at this time, my path is clear, and it leads to Carrick Manor."

There was nothing he could say to refute that, and

given her focus on Manachan—despite the raging awareness she ignited in his blood, simply by standing close,
by *being* there—he wanted her to help his uncle.

Clan trumped personal considerations.

He repeated that like a mantra as, Manachan's visit
with the children concluded, he and Lucilla, with Sean's
help, got Manachan back into the curricle. Forrester and
Sean had shrouded Joy Burns's body in a canvas sheet,
and strapped the wrapped body to the curricle's boot.

Thomas saddled and fetched his, Joy's, and Lucilla's
horses. With Joy's and her saddlebags in her arms, Lucilla was waiting by the curricle when he led the horses
around to the front of the farmhouse. Approaching, he
steeled his senses against the contact necessary to lift
her to her saddle—saw her gaze grow distant and realized she was doing the same thing.

Which made his life not one whit easier.

He released Phantom's reins and tied Joy's horse to
the rear of the curricle. Accepting Joy's saddlebag from
Lucilla, he secured it to the saddle while she did the
same with her own saddlebag, setting her horse prancing. He turned and steadied the black mare, then stepped
to where Lucilla now waited—holding her breath.

He gripped her waist and lifted her. Felt again the
suppleness of her slender form between his hands. He
deposited her in her side-saddle, then had to force his
fingers to ease, to let her go.

Inwardly cursing, he swung on his heel, grabbed
Phantom's reins, and swiftly mounted.

Sean was already turning the curricle. Nudging Phantom in the curricle's wake, Thomas settled to ride alongside Lucilla.

All the way back to Carrick Manor.

Some part of him—the rational, logical part that knew spending time with her was inimical to the future he wanted—wondered how it had come, so inexorably, to this.

Another part of him, a part he normally kept well suppressed, didn't care. Not in the least.

* * *

By the time their small cavalcade clopped into the manor's stable yard, Thomas had managed to refocus his wayward brain. Nevertheless, he was relieved when Lucilla dismounted without assistance; she was an excellent horsewoman and rode with an easy grace that his senses had registered even though he'd striven to keep his eyes from her svelte form.

He had questions to which he needed answers; keeping the list firmly in the forefront of his brain, he handed Phantom's reins to Mitch and went to help Sean assist Manachan from the curricle.

Meanwhile, Lucilla spoke quietly to Fred, directing his attention to the canvas-wrapped body at the rear of the curricle. The shock in Fred's face was mirrored in Mitch's as, with the horses tethered, Mitch returned to help with the unloading and realized just what the bundle was.

Sean remained stoic, but once Manachan was steady on the cobbles and Lucilla came to join them, Sean saluted and stepped back. "I'll give the others a hand."

Manachan briefly met Sean's eyes, then nodded. One hand gripping Thomas's arm, Manachan reached for Lucilla's; she deftly caught his hand and wound his arm in hers, stepping closer to help steady him.

As they made their slow way to the house's side door, Thomas reflected that, while Manachan was far larger and heavier than Lucilla, with her spine of steel, she seemed to have no difficulty steering him, and that in more ways than one.

They entered the house and slowly continued along the dimly lit corridor toward the front hall.

Sean, Mitch, and Fred had elected to bring Joy's body in by the front door; Thomas, Manachan, and Lucilla reached the front hall in time to witness the shock and consternation that ensued when Ferguson, Mrs. Kennedy, and several footmen and maids—all of whom, for some reason, had already gathered in the front hall— learned of Joy Burns's death.

"No!" Mrs. Kennedy, a stout matron who had faced any number of emergencies while barely batting an eye, looked as though she would faint.

The youngest maid smothered a small scream, then burst into tears. The two older maids patted her shoulders, but they, too, looked stricken and stunned.

The footmen were white-faced. Even Ferguson looked thoroughly shaken.

Everyone was staring, increasingly ashen and wide-eyed, at the bundle of Joy Burns's body. No one had yet noticed Thomas, Manachan, and Lucilla emerging from the side corridor.

Thomas frowned. Before he could ask, Manachan raised his head and rumbled, "What's going on?"

All the staff whirled.

All blinked, then all the others looked at Ferguson.

The butler cleared his throat but was plainly still rattled. "Laird Carrick, sir...I—we..." Ferguson briefly closed his eyes and drew breath, then he opened his eyes and said, "It's *Faith* Burns, sir. We found her not five minutes ago. She'd fallen down the stairs in the old wing. She's dead, sir." Ferguson glanced at the bundle Sean, Mitch, and Fred were balancing across their arms. "And now Joy's dead, too." Ferguson looked at Manachan, then lifted his gaze to Thomas's face. "Whatever's going on, sir?"

Thomas wished he knew.

Manachan grunted and waved to a chair against the wall. Thomas and Lucilla helped him to it. Once he'd sat, with Thomas on one side and Lucilla on the other, Manachan demanded to be told everything.

With the rest of the staff at their backs, Ferguson and Mrs. Kennedy stood before Manachan and between them related how they'd searched the rambling old house, high and low, and sent Sean and others to the nearby farms. Only after they'd eliminated every other possible place had one of the footmen thought of going into the disused wing.

That particular wing was called that for a reason; Thomas couldn't recall the last time any of the rooms within it had been opened, much less used.

"Lying there, she was," Ferguson said. "Sprawled at the bottom of the stairs with her neck broken. Seems she'd been dead from the night we'd last seen her." Ferguson paused, thinking. "Two nights ago, that would be."

Mrs. Kennedy, still pale, but with her composure returning, nodded. "Poor Faith. She must have tripped…" Breaking off, Mrs. Kennedy frowned. "We thought it an accident." Her tone suggested she was no longer so sure.

Manachan shifted, then in a more vigorous tone barked, "Where's Nigel?"

Ferguson exchanged a glance with Mrs. Kennedy. "The young master's still in Ayr, sir. He and Mr. Nolan left three mornings ago, and we haven't seen them since."

Footsteps from the rear of the hall had everyone glancing that way. Lucilla watched a slight young lady and a tall, gangly young gentleman walk out from under an archway at the rear corner of the hall.

Both halted, clearly surprised to have come upon such a gathering.

Lucilla recognized Niniver Carrick, Manachan's third child and only daughter; slender, with pale blond hair, she blinked at the assembled company. The dark-haired young man, barely more than a youth, who halted beside Niniver, Lucilla assumed to be Norris, Manachan's youngest son; the resemblance was faint, but there. Norris and Niniver were dressed in day clothes suitable for a morning about the house.

Niniver recovered first. She focused on her father. "Papa—it's…good to see you down. We came to ask what was happening about luncheon. The gong hasn't rung."

Manachan humphed. He looked at Mrs. Kennedy and Ferguson. "Luncheon has been put back by an hour or so."

Norris frowned. "Why?" Then his gaze fixed on the wrapped body now resting on the tiles, and his features went blank. "What's going on?"

"Never mind that." Manachan waved his hand testily. "What do you know about anyone going into the old wing?"

Norris's frown didn't ease. "The disused wing?" When Manachan nodded, Norris replied, "As far as I know, no one's been in there for years."

Niniver nodded, then it was her turn to ask, "Why?"

Manachan sighed, and in a few terse words, told them. Their shocked surprise was transparently genuine;

Lucilla doubted the pair knew anything about either death. But what increasingly concerned her was Manachan's flagging strength; she could hear the effort each breath cost him. He'd called on reserves to go out to the Bradshaws' and was now fading fast.

She caught Thomas's eye; she let her gaze flick to Manachan and *thought* at Thomas—and was relieved when, lips tightening, he nodded.

The instant there was a suitable break in the comments, Thomas said, "Sir—I suggest we leave Ferguson and Mrs. Kennedy to deal with the situation and get luncheon under way. Meanwhile, we should get you upstairs."

Manachan glanced at Thomas, then softly grunted and tensed to rise. From the way Thomas's lips thinned, and the faintly pained demeanor of the staff as they watched him, assisted by Lucilla, haul Manachan to his feet, Lucilla surmised that Manachan's ready capitulation was seen by all as an indication of just how weak he truly was.

Once he was on his feet, she beckoned one of the burlier footmen to take her place; she wasn't confident of supporting Manachan up the stairs. Freed from her position by his side, she circled to come up beside Thomas. Her voice low, she spoke to him and Manachan. "I'll see to the bodies, both of them."

Manachan met her eyes, then dipped his head. "Thank you, my dear."

Stepping back, Lucilla watched the trio pass beneath the archway through which Niniver and Norris had come; beyond lay a small hall into which the main stairs debouched. The trio awkwardly wheeled to the right and started up.

Lucilla turned and regarded the staff. She glanced at Joy Burns's body, and Sean, Mitch, and Fred bent to lift it again. She looked at Ferguson and Mrs. Kennedy. "Faith Burns—I take it she and Joy were related?"

Mrs. Kennedy nodded. "Sisters. Last of the Burns family hereabouts."

"I see." That certainly accounted for the earlier consternation. Lucilla tucked the information aside for later examination. "What have you done with Faith's body?"

* * *

If Thomas had been disturbed by Joy Burns's death, he was deeply troubled now.

So was Manachan. Once Thomas had, with Edgar's help, settled Manachan on his bed, Manachan grasped Thomas's sleeve. "Something's going on. I need to know what."

Unable to keep the grimness from his expression, Thomas nodded. "We'll get to the bottom of it." Whatever "it" was.

Manachan's eyes searched his; his grip on Thomas's sleeve tightened. "Will you stay until this is sorted out?"

Thomas couldn't recall Manachan ever asking him for help; a laird did not ask for help—a laird gave it. "Yes, of course." He closed his hand over Manachan's and briefly squeezed.

"Good. Excellent." Relaxing against the pillows, Manachan released him. "Come and tell me what you learn."

An order. "I will." Raising his gaze from Manachan's increasingly pallid face, Thomas exchanged a meaningful glance with Edgar. "Meanwhile, just rest."

After quitting Manachan's room, Thomas paused in the gallery, then went in search of Lucilla.

He eventually tracked her to the library. She was seated behind Manachan's huge desk, writing a letter.

Thomas inwardly sighed. He closed the door; she glanced up at the snick of the latch but immediately returned to her task.

He started down the long room. "It was one thing for you to stay in this house when the only dead body we had on our hands died in a farmhouse miles away."

She didn't even glance up. "I'm not leaving. Your uncle needs help, and so does your clan."

"Your family will come down on Manachan's head like avenging angels if anything happens to you while you are, however nominally, in our care." His words were clipped. He halted before the desk. "That concerns Manachan and the clan, too."

She waved at the letter. "I'm explaining the situation to Marcus. He'll appreciate the need for me to remain here." She wrote another line. "I'm asking him to send some clothes for a few days' stay."

Thomas leaned his fists on the edge of the desk.

She glanced briefly up at him but continued calmly writing. "I can assure you Marcus won't create a fuss."

Thomas had no doubt that her twin had been conditioned from an early age to stay out of his sister's way. "Lucilla." His gaze on her face, he waited until she looked up at him. "It's too dangerous for you to stay."

She had, he realized, already signed her letter. She held his gaze and, without looking away, set the pen aside and picked up the blotter. Emerald eyes, intensely green, the vibrant hue highlighted by tiny flecks of gold, never wavered. "Thomas," she said, "I'm staying."

And you have neither the right nor the power to gainsay me.

Lucilla held back those words, but she was prepared to utter them if he drove her to it. His amber eyes narrowed; they searched her eyes almost as if he could read that unuttered sentence inscribed therein.

His lips tightened even more; at the edge of her vision, she saw the ripple of his sleeves as muscles bunched beneath.

Eye to eye, metaphorical toe to toe, she waited.

She wondered how long she could manage without breathing.

Just when she was starting to feel a touch light-headed, the tension holding him eased. His muscles unknotted, then he straightened. "Very well."

His tone was beyond clipped. She might have won that round, but he was not happy with the outcome and had in no way conceded the game.

His gaze lowered to her letter. He nodded curtly at it. "Let me have that, and I'll get Fred to ride over and deliver it."

Blotter in hand, she glanced down at her missive. There was nothing more she needed to tell her twin; Marcus was exceptionally talented at reading between her lines. Then she remembered; she looked at Thomas and arched a brow. "Would you like me to ask Marcus about the seed supply?"

He considered it; she could see him silently evaluating the pros and cons. But at last, he shook his head. "No." He met her gaze. "Nigel is supposedly managing the estate. I should ask him first." His brows rose cynically. "Again."

She was growing used to reading between his lines, too. "So you don't step on his toes?"

His lips thinned, but he nodded. "Precisely."

When he said nothing more, she blotted the letter, folded it, and inscribed Marcus's name on the front. There was no reason she could see to seal it. Rising, she held out the folded sheet.

Thomas closed his fingers on the paper just as the deep *bong* of the luncheon gong reverberated through the house.

For a second, he held Lucilla's green gaze, then she released the letter. Sliding it into his pocket, he waved her to the door. "As you're determined to stay, I'll show you the way to the dining room. I'll get this sent off before I join you."

Smiling with a satisfaction that carried a definite hint of approval, she started up the room.

Patently thrilled at getting her own way.

Inwardly shaking his head—at her, at himself, at his unexpected predicament—he followed her to the door.

* * *

Luncheon was served in the formal dining room, although they were using only one end of the long table. The room was lined with wood paneling to head height; the higher reaches of the walls were plastered and painted, and played host to ornately framed landscapes interspersed with mounted stag and boar heads. The windows were lead paned and relatively small; even though the dark brown curtains were open, the illumination in the room was softly dim, as if shadows hovered about its edges.

Four places had been set, two on either side of the table, at the end closer to the door. Norris and Niniver were already seated opposite each other; Lucilla went to the place beside Norris, who stood and drew the chair out for her.

As she sat and settled the heavy skirts of her riding habit, she glanced across the table and saw Niniver watching her. The younger girl had caught her lower lip between her teeth. The expression in her cornflower-blue eyes was uncertain.

Norris resumed his seat.

Sensing his impatience, Lucilla said, "Thomas will be here shortly."

Norris met her gaze, studied her for an instant, then nodded.

A moment later, Thomas appeared. Ferguson followed at his heels, bearing a soup tureen.

Once Thomas had taken the chair opposite Lucilla and they'd all been served and had started to eat, Norris glanced at Thomas. "I didn't know you were coming down."

Answering Norris's unvoiced question, Thomas explained about the letter from Bradshaw, his meeting with Nigel and Nolan, and the subsequent letter from Forrester, which had brought him back to the estate.

Lucilla quietly ate her soup and listened as Thomas described what he had discovered at the Bradshaws' and his ride to the Vale to ask for her aid. She detected no animosity between Thomas, Niniver, and Norris; if anything, both Niniver and Norris appeared to view Thomas's arrival with a species of wary relief. Lucilla could sense the link between Niniver and Norris, the two youngest children, but their emotional ties to Thomas were significantly less, no doubt due to his recent absences compounded by the difference in age.

"Are the Bradshaws all right?"

Lucilla looked up at Niniver's question and realized it was directed at her. "Yes. We discovered their well was tainted. Thomas fetched fresh water from the For-resters, and once we had that, I treated the Bradshaws. By the time we left, they were on the road to complete recovery."

"The Forresters are there, looking after them." Thomas set down his soup spoon.

A footman removed their soup plates while Ferguson laid platters containing a simple cold collation before them. They served themselves. As they settled to eat, Norris said, "So now we have both the Burns sisters unexpectedly dead, and if I have it correctly, both died on the same night."

Thomas studied Norris. "Do you know anything pertinent about either death?"

Norris shook his head. "No—nothing. It wasn't as if I knew them that well. Not as people."

Lucilla placed Norris as being somewhere around twenty years old. He reminded her of several of her younger male cousins; he had the same unfortunate way with words. Despite how his last statement had sounded, she was certain he'd intended it merely as a statement of fact, rather than any reflection on the relative standing of young master of the house and the staff.

Bearing out her reading of Norris, Thomas accepted Norris's comment with a noncommittal grunt.

A moment later, Norris ventured, "The one thing I don't understand is why Faith went into the disused wing. No one's been in there for years."

Lucilla glanced at Thomas, then Niniver, but it seemed Norris's puzzlement was shared by all.

When no one said anything further, she returned her gaze to Niniver. "How long was Joy Burns the clan's healer?" She arched her brows. "Do you know?"

Niniver grimaced. "I can remember the healer before her, old Mrs. Edge." Niniver glanced at Thomas. "You must remember her, too." Looking back at Lucilla, Niniver went on, "Mrs. Edge retired and Joy took over as our main healer about fifteen years ago."

"Was Joy Mrs. Edge's apprentice?" Lucilla asked.

Niniver shrugged lightly. "She might have been, but Joy wasn't an apprentice—not for as far back as I can recall."

Chewing, Thomas nodded. He swallowed, then said, "Joy was a recognized healer from long before Mrs. Edge left." He frowned as if trying to bring something into focus, but then shook his head. "When Norris was born and things didn't go well with my aunt, I remember Joy being called in to spell Mrs. Edge, so she's been—she was—a recognized healer at least from that time."

So for twenty years at least. "And she was from a local family?" Lucilla asked.

Niniver answered. "The Burnses have been on the estate, a part of the clan, for generations, but only the two of them—Faith and Joy—were left." Niniver's expression sobered. "And now they're all gone."

Lucilla focused on Thomas. Accepting his implied assessment that neither Niniver nor Norris was involved in any way with whatever was going on, she stated, "The one thing I cannot readily accept is that Joy Burns was a competent and experienced healer, one who grew up and lived all her life on the estate, yet our only explanation for her death—at least to this point—is that she mistook some fungus or herb and ate something that killed her."

Thomas grimaced. "I agree that's not a very likely thesis." He met Lucilla's emerald eyes. "But until we uncover a more plausible option, that's the only possibility we have."

Which proves we need to investigate further.

He could all but hear the words, even though neither he nor Lucilla gave voice to them. Her determination to get to the bottom of who had killed Joy Burns, how, and why was all but palpable. She wasn't going to let the matter rest; aside from all else, Joy Burns had been a peer of sorts.

The plundered platters were replaced with a bowl of trifle.

While they consumed servings of the sweet treat, Thomas examined his motives and Lucilla's. Despite not wanting her to involve herself in learning what was behind the recent deaths, he felt forced to acknowledge that, were he in her shoes, he would do...exactly what he knew she intended to.

He also could not argue that, when it came to investigating the mysterious death by poison of a healer, she was better qualified than he.

By the end of the meal, when they rose from the table, he'd achieved a degree of acceptance. Following her out of the dining room, he asked, "What are you planning on doing next?"

She glanced at him, briefly searched his eyes as if registering his resignation. "I'm going to speak with the housekeeper and the cook." They'd reached the front hall; she halted and looked around.

"I'll take you and introduce you." Niniver had followed them from the dining room. "If you'd like."

Seeing the shy diffidence in his cousin's fair features, Thomas—reluctantly—kept his lips shut.

"Thank you." Lucilla smiled at Niniver.

Norris, who had trailed them from the dining room, stepped past them, strode for the main stairs, and went quickly up.

Lucilla pointed in the same direction. "That way?"

Niniver nodded, and the two women walked toward the stair hall and the corridor to the kitchens that ran off that.

"Do you know Alice Watts, Joy's apprentice?" Lucilla asked.

"Not really," Niniver returned. "We…have never been encouraged to associate with the staff." She hesitated, then added, "Or, in my case at least, with the wider clan."

Thomas stood looking after the pair as their voices faded. Niniver's words rang in his mind, sparking memories. Reminding him of why Norris in particular showed no interest whatsoever in the clan, in the people or the estate. Returning to the household after a full two years' absence, he was seeing it anew, through clearer eyes.

Faintly frowning, he considered, then trailed after the two ladies as far as the bottom of the stairs. There, he paused. Lucilla would be safe with the housekeeper and cook in the kitchen, which left him free to pursue his own line of investigation.

As she and Niniver passed out of his sight, he turned and climbed the stairs.

Five

Lucilla sat at the well-scrubbed deal table in the servants' hall, a mug of tea cradled between her hands. As she had assumed, the lull after luncheon was the perfect time to interview Mrs. Kennedy and the cook, a surprisingly thin woman named Gwen. Although several maids were clattering and chatting in the scullery, washing and drying the luncheon dishes, all the rest of the staff were out and about their duties elsewhere; the servants' hall, off the kitchen, was warm, comfortable, and relatively private—the right sort of place to encourage confidences.

Niniver had introduced Lucilla to the two women and had added a request that they freely answer whatever questions Lucilla posed. For a moment, Niniver had hesitated, dithering, but then had retreated. For which Lucilla was grateful; both Mrs. Kennedy and Gwen had relaxed and had proved amenable to sitting with her and telling her all they knew of the Burns family, and of Faith and Joy.

Both women knew who Lucilla was; they saw nothing odd in her sitting with them and sharing a pot of tea. They sat opposite her, mugs in their hands, their thoughts revolving about the dead women.

"I still can't believe it." Mrs. Kennedy's eyes were red-rimmed. "Both gone—just like that. On the same night. And them the last two of the Burnses."

Gwen snorted softly. "Can't believe it is right." She looked at Lucilla. "Well, you're a powerful healer, too, so you'd know. However could Joy have picked the wrong sort of thing and eaten something that poisoned her?"

"Exactly." Mrs. Kennedy's lips pinched. "As for Faith going into the disused wing and falling headfirst down the stairs—why would she have done any such thing? She'd worked in this house since she was a girl—she knew the place, even what's now the disused wing, like the back of her hand. She could have walked the whole place blindfolded. Falling down the stairs?" Mrs. Kennedy made a disgustedly dismissive sound. "Nonsense!"

"Aye—and they were both hale and hearty when they sat down to dinner with us all that last night," Gwen offered.

"Indeed they were," Mrs. Kennedy said. "And then... they were dead."

Both women looked confounded, as if they were still having difficulty believing that was truly the case.

Lucilla let a moment pass, then asked, "I take it you know of no one who wished the sisters, or the family, ill?"

Both women regarded her, then, slowly, they shook their heads.

"Well liked, they were—the pair of them," Gwen said.

Reviewing all she knew, and all that she didn't, Lucilla asked, "That last night they were here. What do you think they—each of them—did after you all parted for the night?"

"Well, Faith remained up for a time." Gwen pointed to

an old tapestry bag set on the top of a big dresser. "She used to knit every night while she waited for the bell to make the laird's nightcap and take it up to him."

"Nowadays, that's often very late," Mrs. Kennedy said. "Because he sleeps such odd hours, I suppose."

Gwen nodded. "It was sometimes midnight or later before Edgar—he's the master's manservant—would ring."

"So did Faith take the laird's nightcap up to him that night?" Lucilla asked.

Mrs. Kennedy exchanged a look with Gwen. "Aye. She must have."

"Else we'd've heard about it, no question," Gwen said. "And, now I think of it, Edgar brought down the empty pot and cup the next morning on the tray, just like he always does. He didn't know Faith was missing—we'd only just realized that ourselves."

"So," Lucilla said, "Faith made up a pot of tea and took a tray up to the laird's room—I assume that's on the first floor?"

"Aye," Mrs. Kennedy replied. "It is. Not far from the head of the main stairs."

"Which stairs would Faith have used?" Lucilla asked.

"The staff stairs that go up close by the main stairs," Mrs. Kennedy replied.

Lucilla nodded. "All right. So we know that Faith made the tea and took the tray up, presumably by her usual route." She paused, then asked, "What would she normally have done next? Come back here?"

Both women shook their heads.

"She would have come straight up to bed," Mrs. Kennedy said. "All of us have rooms in the attics on the third floor. She would have taken the same stairs to come up."

"That's why Edgar always kept the tray and brought it down the next morning," Gwen said. "So Faith could go straight up and not have to wait and take the tray down again."

Lucilla decided she would need to look at exactly where Faith's body had been found. "All right—that accounts for Faith. She behaved normally until after she parted from Edgar at the laird's door. She should have gone up to her room, but, for some reason, she went into the disused wing and ended up falling down the stairs. Let's turn to Joy. She lived here, in the manor, didn't she?"

Both women nodded.

"Her room was next to Faith's," Gwen offered.

"Very well. So tell me what you know of what Joy did that night. When did the summons to aid the Bradshaws arrive?"

"We were all already in bed." Mrs. Kennedy shot an affectionate glance at Gwen. "Some of us, the kitchen staff at least, would probably have been well and truly asleep."

Gwen grimaced, but nodded. "Aye—I don't remember much. Just hearing the back bell ring like the dickens and Ferguson go down."

Mrs. Kennedy leaned her elbows on the table, her mug held in her hands. "Ferguson came up a minute later and knocked on Joy's door. I'd got up to see what was happening. Ferguson told Joy about the Bradshaws needing her help right away, and Joy nodded and said she'd go. She said there was moonlight enough for her to find her way." Mrs. Kennedy met Lucilla's eyes. "Like Faith, Joy was born on the estate—she knew the land that well she never had a qualm about going out in the dead of night."

Lucilla nodded. Piecing the events together in her mind, she asked, "About what time did Joy go downstairs?"

"Would have been about half past ten—maybe a little later." Mrs. Kennedy paused, then went on without prompting, "Joy would have come straight down to this hall. I've seen her get ready to go out before, and she always did things in the same order."

Lucilla wasn't surprised; she did the same.

"She would have got down her saddlebag," Mrs. Kennedy continued. Both she and Gwen raised their gazes, looking beyond Lucilla. Mrs. Kennedy nodded, indicating the spot. "She kept it up top of that same dresser next to where Faith kept her knitting."

"Aye," Gwen softly said. "But it's not there now, so she must have taken it."

"She would have filled her canteen and collected any food she thought she might need, although I doubt she took anything from the larder that night. No need, and she was in a hurry. She would have left the saddlebag and her canteen sitting on the table right here." Mrs. Kennedy tapped the table in front of her. "Then she would have gone to the still room and fetched her packets of herbs and such. She would have come back, put everything on the table, then packed it all into her saddlebag." Mrs. Kennedy paused, then raised her eyes to Lucilla's. "I've seen Joy do that so many times, I can almost see her doing it right now."

Lucilla nodded; a strong, almost certainly exact memory then, one burned into Mrs. Kennedy's mind. And Joy's movements made excellent sense to Lucilla; when called to tend someone, she did much the same. "So Joy finished packing her saddlebag, picked it up, and walked out of the house."

Gwen nodded. "Sean had her horse already saddled and waiting—he'd heard the young Forrester lad come riding in, so he knew Joy had been summoned. Sean said as Joy was her usual self when she fetched her horse. Said she mounted up and rode off, just like usual." Gwen paused, then drained her mug.

Lucilla placed each fact she'd gleaned into the proper order, then took a mental step back and surveyed what she'd learned. "From all you've told me, when Joy came down here to gather her things and pack her saddlebag to go out to the Bradshaws', Faith was here, sitting and knitting."

Both women blinked, then Gwen nodded. "Aye— that'd be right. The pair of them would have spoken."

"Did they get on?" Lucilla asked.

"Oh, aye—they were two peas in a pod in some ways," Gwen said. "Not to say they always agreed, but there was no bad blood between them. Close, they were."

"So we can assume they would have chatted—about what, we don't know." Which, Lucilla felt, was a potentially pertinent point. Eyes narrowing, she let the vision in her mind play out. "So Joy laid out her bag and her canteen, then she went to the still room to fetch her herbs, leaving Faith here..."

Lucilla was accustomed to getting flashes of insight, but this one left her chilled. Carefully, she asked, "Do we know what time Edgar rang for the laird's nightcap?"

Gwen shook her head. Mrs. Kennedy started to do the same, but then her expression cleared. "As it happens, I can guess. It was a little while after Joy went down. I heard her door close, then her footsteps headed off toward the stairs. It was perhaps…ten minutes later? I was falling asleep again when I heard the bell ring in Ferguson's room." Mrs. Kennedy nodded at the panel of bells above the door of the servants' hall. "Same bells as those are on the wall between Ferguson's room and mine. Normally, I don't register them, not if I'm asleep, but that night I wasn't yet, what with having got up."

Gwen was studying Lucilla's face. "If it's important, you could check with Edgar—he tends to keep track of how much sleep the laird gets."

Lucilla nodded, but she could now see how someone might have poisoned Joy Burns. She could even guess how. But where had they been while Joy and Faith had been talking?

The kitchen was separated from the servants' hall by one long wall; two wide archways, one at either end of the wall, connected the rooms. The scullery and other preparation rooms lay beyond the kitchen. The door that led into the servants' hall was directly behind Lucilla; turning to scan that wall, she saw two narrow doors set into the walls on either side of the main door. She pointed to one. "Is that a larder?"

"Aye," Gwen replied. "We have two. One for dry goods and the other for cooked meats and such. Nice and large, they are."

Lucilla rose and stepped over the bench seat on which she'd been sitting. She crossed to one larder door, opened it, and looked in. Shelves ran along three sides, packed with bags and packets of flour, dried beans, sugar, and other comestibles; there was plenty of room for a person to stand in the space between. "Do you have any trouble with mice?" she asked. "I know Cook grumbles at home."

"Used to," Gwen replied. "But there's some new bait stuff Ferguson got that works a treat. There's a packet of it in there. Look under the bottom shelf to the left of the door."

Lucilla did, and saw the blue, red, and white packet of rat poison. The packet was open. She didn't reach for it; she didn't need to. The chill that slid through her was sharp and acute.

She straightened, shut the larder door, and turned to face the room. Thinking, juggling. One thing still didn't quite fit. Focusing on Mrs. Kennedy and Gwen, she asked, "Where did Faith sit while she was knitting? Do you know?"

Mrs. Kennedy tipped her head back, toward the kitchen. "She used to sit before the fire in there. It's the only one we make sure to keep going, and she needed it well up to make the laird's tea quick smart. He's particular about it being made properly, with the water freshly boiled."

Lucilla had it all now; she even knew where to look for the proof of how Joy Burns had been poisoned. Not that it would do much good. She nodded to Mrs. Kennedy and Gwen. "Thank you."

She should find Thomas and tell him what she'd learned, what she now thought, but there were several other things she still needed to know. She returned to the bench and slipped back into her previous place. "I understand that Joy had an apprentice who will be taking over as healer. Alice Watts. Can you tell me how far along in her training she is?"

Mrs. Kennedy exchanged a glance with Gwen. "From what Joy said, Alice was on the last leg of the training."

Gwen nodded. "Almost, but not quite done."

"She's been sent for to come and fill Joy's shoes." Mrs. Kennedy grimaced. "She's another would have taken Joy's death hard, but the Wattses sent word she'll be along as soon as she's packed her things."

"She knows she has to come and live here," Gwen added. "She should be here tomorrow."

Lucilla reviewed the list of questions she'd wanted to ask, then nodded. "I think that's it for the moment. If you could show me where the still room is, I won't take up more of your time."

Both women shifted, but neither moved. They exchanged another glance, then Gwen made a get-on-with-it gesture at Mrs. Kennedy. The housekeeper primmed her lips, then she drew breath and looked at Lucilla. "We don't know if this is the right thing to ask, miss—my lady—but we, all the staff, we were wondering if you might be able to convince the laird to take something. So dragged down he is, yet beneath it all, he's a strong man."

"I can build a body up with food," Gwen said, "but with him it doesn't seem to stick, not anymore. Joy was certain she could give him something that would help, but she didn't think it her place to push, especially not with him being her laird, if you know what I mean."

Lucilla did. She seriously doubted many people had the backbone to inveigle Manachan to do anything, much less on an issue that might well have touched his pride.

Mrs. Kennedy leaned forward. "If you could see your way to saying something, Lady, it would mean a lot to us."

Lucilla held up a hand to stay further pleas. "I've already decided the laird needs my help—the sort of help such as I can give. That's partly why I'm here." She paused, then added, "No one in the Vale had any idea he was so poorly, or I, or my mother, would have been here earlier."

The relief that shone in both women's faces was clear. "So you'll speak with him?" Mrs. Kennedy asked.

Lucilla couldn't lie. "I'll help him. Quite how I'll go about it, I can't yet say. He isn't the easiest person to persuade to do something he'd rather not do."

"Howsoever you manage it," Mrs. Kennedy said, "you'll have the gratitude of the entire clan."

Rising, Lucilla smiled and let that comment pass, but she doubted it was accurate. Something very serious was going on at Carrick Manor and on the estate, and whoever was behind it was, almost certainly, a member of the Carrick clan.

She stepped over the bench seat. "If you could show me the still room?"

"Of course." Mrs. Kennedy rose and waved to the door. "I'll take you—it's back along the corridor and off to the left down some steps."

* * *

Lucilla didn't spend much time in the still room. As Joy Burns had left the room prior to meeting her end, Lucilla hadn't expected to find any clues. After a few minutes circling the room, noting and approving all Joy had done and finding everything she expected neatly labeled and stored, she stepped out, pulled the door shut behind her, and headed back into the maze of corridors. Following the directions Mrs. Kennedy had given her, she made her way into the disused wing.

The spot at the bottom of the wing's main stairs where Faith Burns's body had lain was easy to identify; even in the dim light that seeped past the drawn curtains and drifted down the stairwell from uncurtained windows on the first floor, Lucilla could see that the dark floor-boards were covered in an inch of dust except for the area at the bottom of the stairs, which had been scrubbed.

She'd seen Faith Burns's body when she'd directed the staff in properly laying out the sisters in the ice-house; Faith had been taller and bigger boned than Joy. Faith had fallen with such momentum she'd fetched up against the wall on the other side of the corridor, her neck broken.

Given what she suspected about Joy Burns's death, and what she could now imagine of Faith's, and how both might tie together, Lucilla stood in the corridor, staring unseeing at the lower treads of the stairs while she wondered whether she should press for the magistrate to be summoned.

But she couldn't prove anything. Most importantly, she had no idea what it was that either Joy or Faith had suspected and spoken to the other about while they'd been in the servants' hall and kitchen; she felt sure such a conversation had occurred, and that it had led to the deaths of both sisters. That was her theory, but that was all it was—a theory, a conjecture, a set of connecting suspicions.

Conversely, although it stretched credulity in some ways, it could easily be argued that Joy had died by eating something poisonous by accident on the same night that her sister had died by accidentally falling down the stairs.

"Preposterous," Lucilla muttered. But how to prove it?

A footstep, soft, muted by a rug, had her glancing up—all the way up to the top of the rather steep stairs.

Thomas looked down at Lucilla standing at the base of the stairs, her upturned face lit by the soft daylight washing through the windows beside him.

He saw her fine brown brows slowly rise. The look she directed at him was plainly interrogatory.

He mentally sighed. "I was trying to work out why Faith might have come this way. It's not a faster way back to the kitchens."

Lucilla reached for the banister and started up the stairs. "According to Gwen, the cook, and Mrs. Kennedy, Faith wouldn't have been returning to the kitchens. She had no reason to."

He frowned, conscious of his attention bifurcating—his mind following their discussion, his senses locking on her. "What about the tray she took to Manachan's room?"

"She left it with Edgar, as she usually did."

He forced himself to move back, further from her as she reached the top of the stairs.

She stepped into the upper corridor, halted, and met his gaze. "If Faith had followed her usual habit, she would have taken the staff stairs up to the attics and her room."

She leaned sideways to look past him, along the first-floor corridor. "What's along there, and does it connect to the area where Faith should have been?"

He stifled another sigh; she'd already learned more than he had. Maintaining a decent distance between them, he turned and waved down the corridor. "There's a door a little way along that opens into the gallery. In the gallery, it's just past the entrance to the staff stairs for the main wing—the ones Faith would have used to come up from the kitchens, and presumably, later, to continue up to the attics." He met Lucilla's gaze as she looked at him. "So why did Faith come this way?"

"Because she heard something?" Lucilla glanced at

the windows; three sets along the corridor had their curtains open. She nodded at the curtains. "Were those left open?"

"No. I opened them so I could see to search." He glanced down. "But there's only one scuff." He pointed to a fresh mark in the layers of old beeswax at the top of the stairs, just to one side of the threadbare runner. "The sort you might expect if she'd tripped, skidded, and then fallen. Other than that…the runner in this area was flat and all looked normal."

Lucilla glanced around at the floor just back from the stairs. "But what did she trip over?"

Her own feet? He didn't say the words, but that was the only explanation he'd come up with. He wasn't sure he liked or approved of Lucilla's involvement, but as had happened in the crofter's cottage ten years before, he felt a sense of connection with her, an affinity that had nothing to do with any physical phenomenon but was rather an instinctive ability to interact and work with her, fueled by a recognition that, together, they were more effective than either working alone.

She was the only person he'd ever felt such a connection with, which was another aspect of her he didn't want to dwell on.

Still glancing around, she frowned. "Where did Faith's candle go?"

He blinked. "I don't know. But if she tripped and fell, it should have fallen with her."

They peered down the stairs, but the runner and the dark-stained wood of the stairs showed no evidence of any spilled wax.

"Hmm. The staff would have picked it up." Lucilla stared at the stairs. "They must have straightened the runner, too. It would have been pushed around, wouldn't it? As Faith tumbled and fell?"

They both considered the runner, which lay smooth and taut beneath its wooden restraints.

Focusing on the clear patch in the dust coating the floor below, he grimaced. "She must have pitched forward quite dramatically to have landed all the way over there, up against the wall."

Lucilla made a *hmm* sound, then turned away from the stairs. "Did Edgar and Manachan know anything?"

"No. Assuming this happened shortly after Faith had delivered Manachan's nightcap, both he and Edgar were awake, but they heard nothing." He caught her eye. "What else did you learn from the staff?"

She readily gave him what he suspected was an edited, but essentially accurate, accounting of all she'd learned. At the end of her recitation, she paused, then said, "I know that the deaths of both sisters *could* be ascribed to accident, but it's the timing I find most troubling." She drew breath, then looked along the corridor. "I'm having difficulty accepting that Joy and Faith spoke in the kitchen—with Faith in the kitchen itself and Joy in the servants' hall, so they would have spoken loudly— and then Joy dies of poisoning and Faith falls down the stairs." She looked back and met his eyes. "Especially as I can now see how someone who was in the house at the time, who was close enough to the servants' hall to hear Joy and Faith's conversation, could have poisoned Joy, and then later pushed Faith down the stairs."

He held her gaze for several long seconds, then demanded, "How?"

She told him. She concluded with "So I think we

should find Joy's canteen and see what the contents can tell us."

"It was attached to her saddle. I'll get Sean to find it."

"Warn him not to drink from it." She paused, then said, "I'm not sure I'll be able to smell anything, not now. But we can test for such things, can't we?"

Feeling grimmer by the minute, he nodded. "I'll send samples with those from the Bradshaws' well." After a moment, he added, "But the results will take...probably weeks to come through."

She shrugged lightly. "Both women are already dead... Oh, I see." She met his gaze. "What it was they discussed and our hypothetical murderer heard and killed to conceal. There might still be a threat."

"Indeed." Jaw setting, he reached for her elbow. Ignoring the effect simply touching her had on him, he gripped and turned her along the corridor. "Let me show you which door leads into the main wing, so when in the gallery, you'll know it's the door you don't need to go through." The thought that someone in the house— or with access to it—was harboring some mysterious and murderous intent was unsettling enough; that she was there, under the same roof, made matters immeasurably worse.

Made an emotion he didn't recognize rise up and grip him. Coerce and compel him.

Somewhat to his surprise, she made no demur at his taking control; instead, she walked beside him, courtesy of the narrowness of the corridor rather close, her velvet riding skirt brushing the material of his trousers. Once he was sure she was, indeed, consenting to leave the scene, he eased his grip, then released her altogether.

He would have increased the distance between them, but there was no space.

Lucilla found herself dealing with a rather odd fracturing of her awareness. On one level, she was increasingly exercised over the matter of the Burns sisters' deaths, and very conscious of the tug of duty on that score, yet simultaneously her sensual awareness was reveling in Thomas's nearness. In his touch, however brief.

The toe of her riding boot hit something, and she stumbled. "Oh!" She pitched forward—

Thomas caught her and hauled her upright. Hauled her to him.

She ended in his arms. Locked against him, her palms flat against his chest.

The first thing she registered was the heat of him, the warmth that seeped through the layers of fabric and sank into her.

Into her flesh, feeding her senses.

They came alive on a giddy rush of anticipation.

She raised her gaze to his eyes. In the same instant registered the sudden tension that had gripped him, that had turned taut, resilient muscle into granite and steel. The arms that held her so securely felt less malleable than iron.

But it was his eyes that most gave him away; the gold-flecked amber burned.

She didn't stop to think. To question.

To give him time to snap his shields back into place.

The Lady might help and create the chance, but it was up to her to seize it.

Stretching up on her toes, she barely paused to whisper "Thank you" before she pressed her lips to his.

For one instant, her confidence wavered. What if he didn't respond?

Then she sensed it—a sharp hitch in his breathing, a leaping, uncontrollable, barely reined impulse to seize.

She'd felt that reaction in herself—she recognized it in him.

All doubt evaporated. All caution fell.

She pressed her kiss on him, sure, certain.

Stepping boldly into him, she slid her hands up his chest and over his shoulders, savoring the heat and the strength beneath her palms, then she reached further, to his nape, and slid her fingers into the thick, heavy locks of his hair.

The feathery touch caught her, steadied her.

All her senses alive, she turned her mind from conquest to persuasion.

Drawing one hand from the silk of his hair, she placed her palm against one lean cheek and gave herself over to the communion of the kiss.

Thomas was lost, his anchor gone, swept away by a tide of ferocious yearning. His, but equally hers. Her longing had poured into him, inciting a response he had no hope of reining back. Of taming. Of restraining.

He wanted her; he always had.

But the part of him that wanted her—still, regardless—was the part of him he normally kept leashed, controlled. Hidden.

It hadn't been her kiss, the sharp and shocking pressure of her lips against his, that had shattered the chains, that had broken the lock and flung wide the doors of his inner prison.

It hadn't been the searing heat of her touch as she'd slid her hands up his chest and over his shoulders, an evocative, provocative come-hither act that yet had felt curiously innocent.

Even her fingers tangling in his hair—he was more than experienced enough to set all such temptations aside.

But the feel of her palm, her fingers, lightly riding against his cheek…

It was as if by that touch she'd tamed him. Slayed all resistance and claimed the man he truly was.

He'd always known she was dangerous. That she and she alone could rule him.

He hadn't wanted that. He still didn't want that. Yet…

Her lips tasted of a heady blend of rose and nectar. He couldn't resist the temptation to sip.

Just a little. A bit.

Slowly, inexorably, the muscles in his arms tightened and he gathered her to him. His head bent—whether to his will or hers he didn't know—but with irresistible expertise, he seized control of the kiss, until then a mere shadow of what, between them, a kiss could be.

He showed her that reality. With brutal candor, he laid the possibilities bare; as she had started this, he was only too willing to finish it—to tease her as much as her not-so-innocent kiss was teasing him. Parting her lips, he claimed them, then angling his head, he claimed every inch of her mouth, of her tongue, with his. Claimed all the luscious softness and tasted her burgeoning passion.

Instead of drawing back, as he'd assumed she would, from the deliberate and blatant claiming—from an exchange that, between one heartbeat and the next, had stepped over all acceptable lines straight into ravenous, rapacious need, into barely contained greed—instead of being shocked and pulling back, she pressed closer yet, her breasts flattening against his chest, her nipples hard pearls he felt even through his clothes.

The heavy ache in his groin intensified.

The compulsive need he'd always felt for her welled, washed through him, and rode him even harder.

Slender and supple she might be, all delicate bones and silken limbs, but the *fire* in her—a nascent blaze as yet, but one formed from elemental passion and desire— was, to him, to the real man within, temptation incarnate.

Giddy, reckless, consuming, and entirely out of control, the kiss raged, waged—not a war but a clash of desires. Of needs, of wants.

Not opposing, but melding. Flowing together, twining, and growing.

Hers intentional, he harbored not a doubt; his undeniable—unable to be denied no matter his wishes.

He knew they had to stop, to cease and desist before he lost all hope of ever stepping back from her. Of ever letting her go.

But her hand remained on his cheek, her touch scalding in a way that had nothing to do with heat, effortlessly holding him captive. Holding his senses, snaring them in a net of want from which he couldn't break free.

His senses and his mind were literally reeling.

She seemed to know, to realize.

But instead of comprehending the danger, pulling back, and letting him go, she reached—with her lips, with her body, with the gentle pressure of her hand on his cheek.

A sudden clattering *clang* of hooves on cobbles snapped them both free; on a mutual gasp, both pulled back from the kiss.

The sharp clatter was followed by shouts and calls.

For one instant, they remained locked together, gazing into each other's eyes. Both of them were breathing rapidly. His pulse thudded in his ears.

Then the calls rising from below hauled them both fully back to the here and now.

They stepped apart. Side by side, they moved to the window.

That end of the disused wing overlooked the stable yard. On the cobbles below, they saw Nigel and Nolan, still mounted, their horses dancing, infected by the brothers' transparently ebullient spirits.

Nigel had called for the stablemen—that had been the summons Thomas and Lucilla had heard—but Sean, Mitch, and Fred were taking their time.

Thomas watched as the stablemen slowly ambled across the yard and—it seemed grudgingly—held Nigel's and Nolan's horses. Apparently oblivious to the almost sullen disapprobation radiating from their clansmen, the brothers continued exchanging comments with each other as they dismounted, then haphazardly flung their reins toward the stablemen and started toward the house.

There were no greetings exchanged between the stablemen and the young masters of the house. As far as Thomas could see, there hadn't even been any true acknowledgment of each other—a remarkable contrast to when he'd ridden in.

Frowning, he stepped back from the window. Less than a second's thought sufficed to suggest that making his presence known to Nigel sooner rather than later would serve everyone, Manachan especially, best.

He looked at Lucilla. She was still gazing down at the stable yard, at the stablemen leading the horses away. Even though he couldn't see her eyes, from her pensive, assess-

ing expression it was clear that she'd detected the strain between the two groups of men and, like him, found it curious.

"I should go and break the news to Nigel." He took
another step back. When she turned to look at him, he
pointed over his shoulder at the door just along the corridor. "That's the door to the gallery in the main wing."
Briefly, he met her gaze. "I'll see you later."

He didn't wait to see if she would reply; he turned on
his heel, strode to the door, and escaped.

Lucilla watched him go. He left the door ajar; whether
he'd meant to or not, it was a clear invitation to follow.
Which she fully intended to do.

The kiss…had been everything she'd wanted. Even
more than she'd dreamed of. But now Nigel and Nolan
had arrived, such personal matters had to be set aside—
for the moment. Until later.

With the prospects for later flitting through her mind,
she stepped out—and felt something catch beneath her
boot heel, nearly tripping her again.

She halted, stepped aside, and looked down. A ripple
in the runner along the edge closest to the window was
the obstacle. Frowning, she glanced back at the stairs.
"Could that be what Faith tripped over?" But the stairs
were too far away for even the most uncoordinated person to have tripped there, and then reeled far enough to
have fallen down the stairs.

Lucilla humphed. In the interests of safety, she attempted to use the toe of her boot to flatten the runner—
and realized there was something beneath it. Something
solid.

Crouching, she lifted the edge of the runner—and
uncovered a short length of candle.

"So that's where it went." Picking up the length—the

top broken from a longer candle—she smoothed back the runner. She was about to rise when the oddity of a piece of candle with no candleholder struck her. "And clearly the staff didn't come this far when they tidied up."

She glanced to left and right. Two low bureaus were set against the walls between the windows; their knob-like legs held them three inches off the floor.

She sighed, got down on her knees, then bent until her head was almost on the dusty floor, and looked beneath the bureaus.

The candleholder, a simple pewter one, was underneath the bureau to her left. Peeling back her jacket sleeve, she reached and hooked the holder out; it still contained the stub of the candle.

Getting back to her feet, the candleholder in one hand and the broken piece of candle in the other, she briefly studied both, then looked down the corridor. The head of the stairs was a good twenty feet away.

Puzzled, she set candleholder and candle on the top of the bureau. For a long moment, she stared at them. Then, beneath her breath, she murmured, "I can think of only one way that you ended up here, while Faith fell down the stairs all the way over there."

Her theory was increasingly looking like fact—far more like fact than she liked.

A distant rumble of voices reminded her that she had an imminent meeting she wanted to witness.

She turned and headed for the door to the gallery.

Six

The thick runner on the main stairs muted Lucilla's footsteps as she hurried down to the ground floor.

Thomas had already walked into the front hall. The rumble of male voices she'd heard had come from Nigel and Nolan when they'd opened the front door, but they'd paused on the porch, laughing at some joke; as she reached the bottom of the stairs, the pair pushed the front door wide and strolled in.

Intensely curious, she slipped unseen from the bottom of the stairs, keeping close to the newel post so that the side of the archway between the front hall and the stairway hall screened her from the three men.

Halting in the lee of the archway, she risked a quick peek. Thomas had halted just a few steps into the hall; he stood with his back to her, waiting for his cousins. She caught only a glimpse of Nigel and Nolan before they were blocked from her view by Thomas's shoulders, but they looked startled to discover Thomas there. Their laughter had cut off abruptly; the silence that followed lasted long enough to feel strained.

She'd seen Nigel and Nolan here and there over the years. Nigel was a few inches shorter than Thomas, but of more barrel-like build—a younger Manachan, in that respect. He had brown hair, a redder, lighter brown than Thomas's, and his complexion was ruddier, his features less refined. Some ladies might consider him ruggedly handsome, but in an aggressive, pugilistic fashion.

Nolan was of similar height, but slighter build, with fair hair loosely flopping over his brow. Finer boned, he seemed to exist in Nigel's shadow, a lesser man not just physically but also in personality; Nolan watched while Nigel acted.

Tilting her head, she waited to hear where the encounter would lead.

"Cuz," Nigel finally said. "What are you doing here?"

No hello, hail-fellow-well-met, or similar family greeting—in fact, no greeting at all. She tried to imagine any of her cousins greeting each other like that, and simply couldn't.

Thomas replied, his tone even, "I was summoned."

Even as the words left his lips, Thomas realized just what in the situation had been bothering him all along. Why the devil had Bradshaw, let alone Forrester, applied to *him*—far distant in Glasgow—and not to Nigel, the acting-laird? Regardless of whatever was going on, it was Nigel's responsibility to deal with it, a fact Manachan had confirmed. Which meant that the clansmen appealing to Thomas was a deliberate declaration of their lack of confidence in Nigel's leadership.

The scene in the stable yard seemed to bear out that conclusion; the clan didn't approve of Nigel.

From the way Nigel bristled, he already knew that. His "Oh?" was laden with rising aggression.

Thomas had no time for cousinly tantrums. "The Bradshaw family was taken violently ill—all of them, the children included. Why others insisted on sending for me, I have no clue, although I assume it's connected to the reason Bradshaw appealed to me about the situation with the seed supply." He paused, holding Nigel's gaze. "You recall I mentioned that when we met in Glasgow. As you've been in Ayr, am I to take it you've resolved the issue?"

Nigel looked uncomfortable but quickly sought refuge in a scowl. "I'm dealing with it, as I said I would."

Defensive dismissiveness laced his tone.

Thomas had no wish to engage in hostilities; despite being heir to the lairdship, Nigel had always resented the somewhat different relationship Thomas enjoyed with Manachan. Thomas had known that, on finding him at the manor, Nigel would see him as intruding on his turf. As for Nolan, who was standing to the side and watching the exchange unfold, Thomas had no doubt over where his loyalties lay; Nolan had always been fiercely supportive of Nigel and protective of Nigel's dignity.

"In that case," Thomas went on, "as you are now back and able to resume the duties of laird, you need to know…" Succinctly, he told them of Joy Burns's death, and of her sister's death on the very same night. He reported briefly on the recovery of the Bradshaws, courtesy of Lucilla's intervention, and concluded with Manachan's invitation to Lucilla to remain at Carrick Manor to oversee the transferring of the healer's duties to Joy's apprentice.

Nigel blinked. Nolan frowned. Both had shown surprise on hearing of Joy's and Faith's deaths, but Thomas detected no evidence of real concern, much less sorrow, even though, far more consistently than he, the pair had known the Burns sisters all their lives.

After a long moment, still frowning, Nolan glanced

at Nigel, then said, "I still don't understand, cuz, why you didn't simply send a message. Nigel would have seen the Bradshaws dealt with."

Thomas hung on to his temper. "As it happened, I had reason to speak with Manachan—and I'm shocked that he's been allowed to sink to his present state. But that aside, as to the Bradshaws, in case you've already forgotten, Nigel wasn't here. You were both in Ayr and not here to consult." He had to wonder what they'd been doing in the seaside town, but now was patently not the time to inquire.

Nolan shrugged negligently. "I don't know why you think you need to concern yourself with Papa—you don't. And the matter with the Bradshaws couldn't have been that urgent. They could have waited."

"As a matter of fact, they couldn't." Lucilla chose that moment to walk out from the stairway hall.

Thomas suspected she'd been lurking there for some time; since Nigel and Nolan had walked into the front hall, his nerves had been flickering in the way they did whenever she was near.

The effect of her appearance on his cousins was nothing short of shock—if she'd slapped them, she couldn't have stunned them more.

"Good afternoon, Nigel." Lucilla halted beside Thomas and inclined her head, first to Nigel, then Nolan. She saw no reason to offer them her hand; after hearing what they'd said, she didn't wish to encourage them even that far.

Both stared at her. Their expressions were not so much blank as suggestive of a medley of largely suppressed emotions.

She stared back at them, then, raising her chin slightly,

she allowed the hauteur she'd learned from her grand-mother to seep into her eyes.

Nigel belatedly remembered his manners. He bowed rather stiffly. "Miss Cynster."

Nolan inclined his head and echoed the words.

"Regarding the Bradshaws." She paused to confirm that she had the pair's full attention. "If your cousin had not gone to the farmhouse when he did, found Joy Burns dying and immediately fetched me as he did, if we hadn't discovered that the well was tainted and he hadn't fetched fresh water, the Bradshaws almost certainly would have died, and anyone who arrived to help them and who drank their water would have fallen severely ill, as well."

She'd caught and held Nigel's gaze. She continued to hold it mercilessly. "You were not here to act for your clansmen. Thomas was, and did. As acting-laird, you owe him thanks, although your father has already proffered his."

Shutting her lips, she waited, letting silence act for her and exact further penance from Nigel and his brother.

The pair had paled, but she doubted it was from shock, not now—more from suppressed anger. She was getting the impression that too few people in their isolated lives spoke to them so directly.

Certainly, she—and her plain speaking—appeared to be something to which neither had any idea how to respond.

"Ah." If Nigel had been holding a hat he would have been mangling it. "I—ah, take it you've been assisting the new healer. On behalf of the clan, you have our thanks."

Lucilla managed to keep her eyes from narrowing. "I

fear your gratitude is premature. I will be overseeing the settling in of Joy Burns's apprentice into the healer's role, but that will have to wait until she, the apprentice, arrives." She arched a brow in haughty question. "I gather she has to travel some distance to reach here."

While she didn't know how far away the Wattses' farm was, she did wonder if Nigel—the acting-laird—had any idea who the clan's healer's apprentice was.

"Ah…" Nigel glanced at Nolan but got no help there; Nolan looked equally blank. Looking back at Lucilla, Nigel essayed a smile. "I daresay she'll be here as quick as she can. But I fear I must leave you to Thomas to entertain." He waved at the dust coating his top boots. "I should change before dinner." Nigel glanced at Nolan, then looked back at Lucilla, and smiled again. "If you'll excuse us."

She didn't smile back, but inclined her head. "Of course."

Nigel's face hardened as he looked at Thomas. "Cuz—until later."

The pair moved past Thomas and Lucilla and headed for the stairs.

Thomas didn't turn to watch them go but, instead, met Lucilla's eyes as she looked up at him. She'd just defended him—unnecessarily, but still—and he wasn't sure how to react, or even if he should.

His cousins had paused at the bottom of the stairs. Both he and Lucilla heard a whispered question, the tone too low for them to make out the words.

They turned as Nigel reappeared under the archway. "Ah—we just wondered"—his gaze included them both—"if you were staying for dinner."

Thomas replied with a bald "Yes."

Beside him, Lucilla inclined her head regally. "I'll be staying until I'm satisfied that Alice Watts has settled in as the clan's new healer. That will likely be several days."

Nigel's smile was forced. "In that case," he said, "we'll see you later." With a vague salute, he turned back to the stairs.

Thomas stood beside Lucilla and listened to Nigel's and Nolan's boots thud up the stairs, and wondered, yet again, just what was going on.

* * *

Lucilla called blessings down on Marcus's head. Her twin had sent Fred back with all she'd requested— clothes, shoes, hairbrushes. Her maid, Jenna, had even thought to pack the jewelry Lucilla preferred to wear with each of the three simple country evening gowns she'd requested.

At the sound of the dinner gong, clad in green silk the color of spring leaves, with a necklace of peridots clasped about her throat and the matching bracelet dangling from her wrist, she left the room she'd been given in what was referred to as the visitors' wing and made her way downstairs. A glance into the drawing room confirmed that the family did not bother with any pre-gathering there; she continued to the dining room. Quick, light footsteps pattered down the corridor behind her. Lucilla paused before the dining room door and smiled as Niniver joined her.

Shyly returning her smile, Niniver murmured, "Good evening. I didn't know you would be staying." She waved for Lucilla to precede her.

"I suspect I'll remain for a few days. I've agreed to help Alice Watts take up the reins of clan healer." Walking into the room, Lucilla saw that Manachan was already there, seated at the head of the table. A tall, thin man with a somber demeanor stood behind his chair—presumably Edgar, Manachan's manservant.

Thomas was also there, seated on Manachan's right, two places down the table; he rose as she and Niniver entered.

Manachan glanced up at her from under his shaggy brows. "You'll excuse me from rising, Lucilla—if I may call you that?"

Smiling, she inclined her head. "You may."

Manachan waved to the place on his right, and Thomas drew out the chair. Lucilla moved to take it, noting that Niniver—after a brief nod to her father, who seemed to barely see her—moved to take the chair opposite Thomas, but one place further down.

A footman held Niniver's chair. She sat, then looked up the table. "It's good to see you here, Papa."

Manachan glanced at her; his expression suggested he was debating whether to be annoyed she'd mentioned it, or pleased. He settled for a noncommittal humph.

Lucilla kept her brows from rising. Coming from a large family, she was always curious about how other families behaved, especially among themselves.

Norris arrived. He blinked at Manachan, then curtly nodded. "Sir." Without waiting for any acknowledgment, he strode around the table and claimed the chair on Thomas's other side.

Then Nigel and Nolan strolled in. They saw Manachan and stopped dead. The looks on both their faces held more shock than surprise. Nigel recovered first. "Papa!" His gaze traveled to Lucilla, then returned to Manachan as Manachan looked at him. "Should you be down?"

Manachan wasn't pleased. He let silence stretch for

several heartbeats before saying, "I'm here, which is all that need concern you."

Nigel swallowed. "Yes—of course. We're…delighted you're able…"

"It was just a shock to see you." Nolan walked to the place opposite Thomas. He directed a severe look at his cousin. "We hadn't realized you'd recovered your strength to this extent."

"Well, I have." As Nolan sat and Nigel took the seat on Manachan's left, opposite Lucilla, Manachan waved at Ferguson, standing by the door, to start serving.

Given that beginning, Lucilla wasn't surprised that the conversation around the dinner table proved somewhat one-sided. Manachan asked about her parents' travels, and she duly described them. He then asked Thomas about a firm called Carrick Enterprises, of which, she learned, Thomas was part owner. She listened avidly as Thomas spoke of importing tobacco, sugar, and exotic timbers, and exporting fleeces, hides, and whisky. He mentioned several people—Quentin, Humphrey, and Winifred—who, from Manachan's wish to be remembered to them, she surmised were family of sorts.

The courses came and went, good hearty country fare more suited to masculine tastes, and well suited to this predominantly male family. The staff were silent and unobtrusive. Lucilla took only a small sip of the heavy red wine, and otherwise drank the clear mountain water. She ate, listened, and observed.

Manachan and Thomas spoke about the weather, and about fishing, shooting, and hunting in general, finally touching on county politics. Nigel and Nolan occasionally offered a comment, the tone of which only emphasized the difference between them and Thomas, which in turn underscored Manachan's attitudes toward the three. The old man treated Thomas like a youthful peer, someone whose opinions he valued and respected, while his sons he still saw as impertinent children, better seen than heard.

Lucilla reflected that, all in all, Manachan was an excellent judge of character.

Beyond Thomas, Norris ate with his eyes on his plate and his attention somewhere far away; Lucilla's brother Carter, an artist, often wore the same detached expression at meals. Norris barely registered the changing of the courses, much less the conversations, but unlike Carter's usually unintentional absorption, Lucilla sensed a deliberateness in Norris's behavior, as if his mental absence was his response to his family—his way of shutting them out.

She felt faintly shocked at that assessment, yet it rang very true.

In contrast, while Niniver also kept her eyes down and contributed nothing to the conversations, from time to time she would glance up, blue eyes locking on whoever was speaking, before looking down again. Niniver might be silent, but she was listening and observing as avidly as Lucilla; far from shutting out her family, she was engaged, watchful—and concerned.

It didn't take long for Lucilla to be certain of that last emotion.

As the main course was cleared, Manachan turned to Nigel and Nolan. "And what about you two, heh? What have you been up to?"

Lucilla focused her attention on the pair. Thus far she'd found them difficult to read. Cagey. Slippery.

But Nigel seemed to bloom under his father's gaze; he

relaxed and smiled. "We took a quick trip up to Glasgow, but there wasn't much of interest there." He tipped his head to Thomas. "Fell in with Thomas for lunch, then we headed back, and the next day we went to Ayr. We spent a few days there, doing the usual." Nigel shrugged nonchalantly. "The races were on. In between other things, we took a look at a few nags—that sort of thing. Just got back this afternoon."

A pause ensued while the dessert was served—Chantilly cream and a heavy charlotte.

After everyone had started eating and the footmen had departed, Manachan directed a lancet-sharp look at his heir. "I take it you've heard by now that the Bradshaws were taken ill, and that Joy Burns died while she was there helping them. As you weren't here to deal with the situation, I went out to the Bradshaws' to see what could be done."

Nigel's and Nolan's hands slowed. Their heads remained down, their gazes on their plates. Neither had known their father had left the house; Thomas hadn't mentioned that, and clearly, no one else had, either.

His deep voice giving no hint of his emotions, Manachan continued, "Quite aside from the Bradshaws' illness, I learned that no seed has yet been supplied to our farmers, those who grow our crops. Not to any of them. Yet unless matters have changed mightily, they're already late to be getting the first crop into the ground."

Nolan shifted slightly; Lucilla would have sworn he'd kicked Nigel beneath the table.

A second passed, then Nigel raised his head; his pale skin was flushed, although whether from embarrassment, frustration, or anger, Lucilla couldn't guess. "I've instituted a new system which, overall, will save the clan money. Funds it doesn't otherwise have. As I've been happy to explain to anyone who's asked, the new system works on a slightly different timetable. The seed is still coming and will be here when it needs to be, which is to say any day now. There's no need for the farmers to have it in their hands earlier—that was an inbuilt inefficiency of the old system."

Nigel had delivered his explanation with increasingly arrogant certainty.

Manachan frowned. After a moment, he asked, "So there isn't actually any problem with the seed supply?"

"No!" Nigel raised his hands in the air, and this time his frustration was transparently clear. "I have no idea why anyone would think there was—well, other than that they refuse to listen to a word I say."

Manachan stared down the table for a moment, then his gaze switched to Thomas.

Nigel's gaze followed his father's; his brown eyes grew agate hard. "And I cannot conceive," Nigel said, his voice low, dripping with rancor, "why anyone would think Thomas, who doesn't live here and hasn't been here for the past two years, would know more about how to run the estate than I do."

Thomas read the antagonism, the barely reined challenge, in Nigel's gaze, and tipped his head. "I, too, have to wonder why, given I'm no longer frequently here and you are acting-laird, anyone on the estate would appeal to me about such matters."

He wasn't entirely surprised when, after a moment of replaying his words, Nigel inclined his head and lowered his gaze, obviously mollified. Nigel had taken his comment as supporting Nigel's own position; he hadn't registered the critical question Thomas's comment had

underscored. Why *had* two senior clansmen gone to the
trouble of contacting Thomas and asking for his aid?

A glance at Manachan showed his uncle frowning.
Unlike Nigel, Manachan had caught the implication.

Thomas looked at Lucilla. Her green gaze was fixed
on Nigel. Her expression was neutral, but Thomas suspected that she, too, had heard the true question, the one
that yet remained to be answered.

In the circumstances, with Manachan, a well-beloved
father figure to the entire clan, having effectively handed
the lairdship to Nigel, the question of confidence in Nigel's
leadership was a sensitive one—for Nigel, for Manachan,
and even for Nolan, Niniver, and Norris. And Thomas,
too. While most often the title of laird was passed from
father to son—or, indeed, to daughter—the family that
held the lairdship was elected by the clan. A laird who
failed to hold the confidence of the clan could be replaced
by clan election, either with another of his own family, or
with someone of another clan family.

Thomas had assumed that, regardless of the reins
of the estate being passed into Nigel's hands, that
Manachan—being Manachan, the benign tyrant he'd
known all his life—would still have influenced decisions. Would still have been there, directing matters
from the wings.

Instead, Manachan had been laid too low to function
in any overseeing capacity.

Nigel had been running the estate entirely on his own.

Thomas gave his attention to his serving of charlotte.
The promise he'd made to Manachan, to stay until they'd
learned what was going on, resonated in his brain. Quite
how he, most likely without Manachan's direct help, was
going to learn what they needed to know, he wasn't yet

sure, but he now accepted that they did, indeed, need to get to the bottom of it. Thomas knew where his loyalties lay. With Manachan, yes, but as a Carrick, as his father's son, the clan, its people, were his ultimate concern.

Lucilla set down her spoon and looked at Manachan. "The Burns sisters. The staff have laid them out in your ice-house. Given they have no remaining family, a decision will need to be made as to their burial."

Manachan, Thomas, and Lucilla looked at Nigel, but he had his head down, eating dessert, and didn't notice their expectation.

Manachan grimaced. Looking at Lucilla, he said, "Our standard is burial four days after death."

She nodded. "So two days from today."

"Aye—in the morning, at the church in Carsphairn. There's a Burns family plot in the churchyard. Thomas"—Manachan glanced at Thomas—"will tell Ferguson. He'll know what arrangements need to be made." His gaze returned to Lucilla. Manachan paused, then said, "If you can, I think they—Joy and Faith—would have liked you to attend. To represent the other side, so to speak. Both were adherents of the old ways—they believed in the Lady."

She inclined her head. "I wasn't sure, but yes, I will be there."

Manachan's lips quirked. "One of your duties?"

"Yes."

When she said nothing more, Manachan grew pensive. "I realize it's an imposition, but as Alice Watts is not fully trained, I would appreciate your assessment of how the still room and all other matters pertaining to the healer's duties stand. How did Joy leave things—especially as she didn't expect to leave?"

"I've already taken a look at the still room. From all I can see, Joy had everything well in hand. She's got the basics well covered, and she had started preparing summer tonics." Lucilla seized the moment to ask, "One thing—what tonics did Joy prescribe for you? Alice will need to know to put more up."

Manachan waved dismissively. "Don't worry about me—I'm an old man. Look to the bairns first. Make sure Alice knows all she needs to cope with broken bones, burns, and cuts, and the usual childhood ailments."

If he hadn't been the laird, if he hadn't been sitting at his dining table surrounded by his children, Lucilla would have pushed, but there was something in Manachan's tone that warned her away from the subject of his medicines. So she inclined her head in polite acceptance.

For now.

The charlotte and all the sweet cream had disappeared. The footmen cleared the table.

Lucilla saw Ferguson enter bearing a tray with crystal glasses and three decanters. She glanced at Niniver, but the daughter of the house was sitting with her hands in her lap and her gaze on the table before her. Lucilla swiftly debated her options, then, looking at Niniver, shifted her chair back and rose. "Niniver—I believe it's time we retired to the drawing room."

The men hastily rose, all except Manachan. Niniver did, too, rather more slowly. She met Lucilla's gaze, then glanced at her father.

Manachan caught her gaze and nodded curtly.

Niniver recovered quickly. She looked at Lucilla. "Yes, of course." Laying her napkin beside her plate, Niniver waited for the footman to draw back her chair.

Thomas performed that office for Lucilla.

With a smile, she murmured her thanks, then, inwardly shaking her head over the lack of social eptitude displayed by the Carricks, followed Niniver into the corridor.

* * *

"I'm sorry." Niniver dropped into one corner of the sofa in the drawing room. "I should have remembered, but I'm so used to not having any other lady at our table."

Lucilla gathered her skirts and sat in an armchair facing the sofa. "I didn't think of it before, but are you living here without any female companion?"

Niniver grimaced lightly. "My old governess, Hattie, lives here, so technically I do have a chaperone. But Hattie doesn't approve of Papa or my brothers—she refuses to bear with what she calls 'their baseness.' She keeps to her suite of rooms upstairs, unless I need her to accompany me to some event. She never joins us at table."

"So." Lucilla settled more comfortably. "I recall seeing you at the Hunt Balls. I must admit that, other than those, I don't go into local society all that much."

"Nor do I." Niniver caught her lower lip between her teeth for an instant, then added, "And if it wasn't for Papa insisting, I wouldn't go to those, either." She wrinkled her nose. "I find all that—the balls, dinners, and parties—so...well, restricting. And unnecessary. The young gentlemen always complain about having to do the pretty, as they say, with us young ladies, yet it never seems to occur to them that some of us find being polite to them and pretending to be interested in them and their exploits equally excruciating."

Lucilla laughed. "I take it you harbor no fond dreams

of going into the ton, or even joining society in Edinburgh or Glasgow."

"Heaven forbid!" Niniver shook her head. After a moment, she looked across and met Lucilla's eyes.

Somewhat to her surprise, behind the pretty blue of Niniver's eyes, Lucilla saw a mind far more shrewd, quick, and calculating than she'd expected to see.

"You probably understand better than most," Niniver said, "being so centrally involved with your clan—even if you don't call it a clan, the people of the Vale are that, aren't they?" When Lucilla inclined her head, Niniver went on, "I was born here, in this house, on this land. I've lived here all my life, and although everyone assumes that, at some point, I'll marry and move away, I... don't think I want to. No—I already *know* I don't want to." Her blue gaze open and true, Niniver held Lucilla's eyes. "This is my home—I care about the place and I care about the people. My roots are here, and that's important to me."

Lucilla saw the strength in Niniver's delicate jaw, read the steadiness in her gaze—sensed the backbone her small frame and fairy-like features disguised. She nodded. "Yes. I understand."

She recognized devotion when she saw it.

Niniver's features eased. After a moment, she arched a brow. "Should I ring for tea?"

Lucilla waggled her head. "Not yet. Let's give them a few minutes more."

Niniver glanced at the pianoforte sitting in one corner. "I don't play—or at least, not well—so I can't entertain you with music."

Lucilla grinned. "I do play, but I don't feel so inclined." She hesitated, but finding Niniver to be something of a kindred soul was too good an opportunity to pass up. "You could entertain me by telling me about a topic I would like to know more about."

Niniver's blue gaze fixed on her. "Thomas?"

With Niniver's powers of observation confirmed, Lucilla nodded. "I've realized I know little about his background, and I'm curious." Mainly about his connection with the Lady, but she didn't want to reveal that much. "His relationship with Manachan and your brothers is... not quite as I expected, given Thomas and Nigel must be of similar age."

"Thomas is the elder by thirteen months." Niniver leaned back, getting more comfortable. "And there's another thirteen months between Nigel and Nolan."

"I've always assumed Thomas was born here."

Niniver nodded. "He was. However, he didn't grow up here. His parents—Uncle Niall and Aunt Katherine—lived in Glasgow. I've been told that they used to come here for all the holidays, so Thomas knew the clan and they knew him. I gather Uncle Niall—I can only just remember him—was well liked by everyone. He and Papa got along very well—I can still remember them laughing together, and coming in from hunting together. They were close, up until Uncle Niall and Aunt Katherine died in a carriage accident. I was only little at the time, and Norris was a baby. Our mama had died shortly after Norris's birth. And then Uncle Niall and Aunt Katherine died, too, and Thomas came to live here with us."

"How old was he then?"

Niniver screwed up her face in thought. "Ten—he must have been ten years old. He stayed for a year or so, and then he went to Glasgow, to go to school and live with Aunt Katherine's brother, Quentin Hemmings, and his wife, Winifred, and his son Humphrey, who is the same age as Thomas. From what I've gathered, Papa and Quentin, who were Thomas's co-guardians, thought that with Thomas inheriting half of Carrick Enterprises, he needed to learn about business and Glasgow." Niniver lifted a shoulder. "And with Nigel to take over after Papa, there wasn't any reason for Thomas to learn all that much about the estate."

Lucilla managed not to look puzzled; there had to be more. "How much time did Thomas spend here after he went to live in Glasgow?"

"Not that much. He came for the holidays, and sometimes stayed for a month or so in summer." Niniver shifted. "In those days, he was closer to Nigel and Nolan, but the older they grew, the more…different they became." She frowned. "Ever since they reached twenty or so, Thomas has seemed much older, much more mature and reliable than Nigel and Nolan." Niniver glanced across and met Lucilla's eyes. "Much more adult."

There was no arguing that, but what about Thomas's connection to the land? How had that evolved, and when? Although he'd been born with a link to the Lady, time was generally needed for such a bond to grow, strengthen, and mature.

Lucilla glanced at the clock on the mantelpiece. "We should probably ring for the tea trolley."

While Niniver rose and went to tug the bellpull, Lucilla inwardly frowned over what she'd thus far learned of Thomas's past.

She'd assumed he'd been born in the Lady's lands, under her mantle, and he had been.

He *was* Lady-touched; that was beyond question. Lucilla knew it, and Marcus did, too.

But given Thomas had spent so little time on the Lady's lands, either in childhood or as an adult, did *he* know he was Lady-touched? Did he understand what it meant?

Most important of all, did he know he was Lucilla's Lady-ordained consort?

He had to know, surely?

But if he didn't understand about the Lady...

When Thomas walked into the drawing room ahead of the tea trolley, Lucilla's gaze locked on him.

He saw and arched a brow. "The others have retired." He came forward and sat in the other armchair, shoulders square against the padded back, his long legs bent.

Despite the question humming in her brain, Lucilla drank in the inherent masculine strength on display; for a large man, he possessed a certain fluid grace, one that brought to mind the flexibility of steel rather than the rigidity of iron.

"Shall I pour?"

Niniver's question broke the spell. Lucilla glanced at her. Ferguson had positioned the tea trolley between the sofa and her armchair. Lucilla smiled. "Please."

Niniver did the honors, and Thomas passed Lucilla her cup, then accepted one himself. Lifting her own cup and saucer, Niniver sat back.

Lucilla sipped. She wanted to ask Thomas about his understanding of the Lady, but she couldn't think of any subtle way to introduce the topic.

She felt Niniver's gaze as she, too, sipped, then Niniver lowered her cup and looked at Thomas. "How are your uncle and aunt? And Humphrey?"

In other circumstances, Lucilla would have listened, eager to learn more about Thomas's life. Instead, she felt consumed by a welling urgency to confirm that he knew, that he understood—that he recognized what he was to her and, conversely, what she was to him.

She didn't know how long she sat there, her thoughts in a whirl, but her cup was empty when Niniver delicately smothered a yawn, then, somewhat unexpectedly, rose. "I'm for bed. I'll see you both at breakfast." Setting her cup and saucer on the trolley, Niniver walked out of the room.

Leaving Lucilla blinking after her. Then she glanced at Thomas and saw his understanding grin.

"Just as well we're not in London. Or even Glasgow." He set his cup and saucer on the trolley, then reached for hers.

Lucilla surrendered it. And mentally shook her wits into place. Niniver had handed her an opportunity—one she needed to use. "I…" She feigned a grimace. "I don't always sleep well when away from the Vale. I would like to stroll in the fresh air for a short while before I try to sleep, but I don't know where would be appropriate." She met Thomas's eyes and made sure her own gaze was limpid, devoid of intent. "Will you walk with me? I would prefer not to walk alone."

Thomas studied her green eyes. He could see no calculation therein, yet…he was fairly certain there was a subtle threat in her last sentence. She would walk alone if he didn't go with her—and he didn't want her walking alone, not with even the vaguest possibility that they might have a murderer lurking.

That said…while he would trust her with his life, he wasn't sure he could trust her in this. Could afford to trust her in this. He could remember all too well—indeed, with senses-stealing clarity—just what had happened the last time they'd strolled. Yes, she'd tripped. Yes, he'd caught her. But that kiss...she'd initiated that all on her own.

And she'd snared him. Hauled him out of his carefully controlled environment and shown him just what she represented.

Something elemental. Something so viscerally powerful and potent that if he surrendered to it, it would swallow him—all he was—whole.

He shouldn't walk with her.

Yet every instinct he possessed, every fiber of his being, wouldn't allow him to let her take even the small risk of walking outside alone at night.

He didn't let any of his thoughts reach his surface. Instead, he inclined his head. "Yes. Of course." Uncrossing his legs, he rose.

Seven

The side terrace ran along the length of the disused wing. That side of the house was clear of shrubbery; the terrace lay bathed in faint moonlight, devoid of shadows and with no bushes crowding the balustrade anywhere along its length.

It was the perfect place to stroll, knowing that no danger could approach unseen.

Of course, for him, the biggest danger walked by his side.

Lucilla was, indeed, plotting how to gain the insight she needed into his mind. Now that the question of what he understood about the Lady—about them—had risen, she couldn't concentrate on anything else. She doubted conversational inquiry would get her anywhere, or at least not get her the answers she wanted; she needed to shift their interaction to a different, more personal plane.

But how? He was ambling alongside her, slowing his pace to match hers, yet she sensed he was alert.

Given their shared kiss that afternoon—a highly satisfactory mutual endeavor—she wasn't sure what he might be anticipating. A repeat performance?

The notion held significant appeal.

While the far end of the terrace overlooked the drive

as it swept into the stable yard, the nearer reaches were abutted by empty stretches of lawn, and the rooms alongside and above were uninhabited; their privacy appeared assured. But how best to use it?

How best to use it to gain *all* she desired?

Abruptly, she halted; they hadn't been touching, so it took him an instant to realize she had.

She waited until he halted, too, and turned to face her.

Before his eyes could find her face, she stepped forward, hooked a palm about his nape, stretched up, and kissed him.

Again.

And, once again, she felt his instantaneous response.

Reassured, she stepped into him, into his arms as they rose and locked about her.

Into the kiss as it spun out, on, in a glorious upsurge of passion.

Angling her face the better to meld her lips with his, on her toes, she pressed closer yet. Glorying in the warm, solid wall of his chest, of his body so heated against hers, she twined her arms about his neck, clung, and gave herself up to delight.

And felt him grip her tight.

She'd parted her lips and welcomed him in; as he surged deep, claimed, and took possession, she rejoiced.

This was the reality she'd wanted to touch, the plane she'd wanted to reach.

The one based on, built on, that necessary understanding.

Plunged into a whirlpool of passion and desires, Thomas was lost, just as he had been that afternoon— just as, he realized, he always would be with her. Lucilla in his arms, her lips beneath his, her body pressed enticingly to his, was the definition of heaven to his senses.

A forbidden heaven filled with temptations too alluring to resist.

He couldn't prevent his arms from holding, from tightening about her as if to seize and keep her against him, his forever.

He couldn't stop his senses from rioting, from drinking in the treasure she offered; the sweetness of her mouth and tongue were an intoxicating nectar.

The pressure of her breasts against his chest, the long, slender lengths of her thighs trapped between his, the soft pressure of her belly against his erection—all sang a siren song to his whirling mind.

Addicting. She was that and more; her luscious lips, her supple body, and the vibrant, undeniable fire that burned within her made her the ultimate lure for him.

The sensation of falling—of simply going and not caring, of relinquishing control without further thought— jerked him back from the invisible brink. And let sanity return enough to recognize that the danger he'd intended to guard against had materialized and blindsided him.

Caught him. Trapped him.

He hauled back on his senses, pulled back from the kiss.

He couldn't afford to let her influence him, much less allow her to rewrite his path.

Determination coalesced, hardened.

But when he raised his head and looked into her eyes, the emerald so dark in the night, and saw the soft flush of pleasure tinting her alabaster cheeks and passion sparking in the depths of those mesmerizing eyes…the truth hit him like a blow.

She wanted him. Until that moment, he hadn't thought of her in this, but only of himself. He hadn't thought of what her actions in kissing him, in initiating such an engagement—not once, but twice—said of her, of her desires.

But he couldn't—simply couldn't—be the man he saw reflected in those eyes. The man she wanted him to be.

He cleared his throat. Eyes locked with hers, he softly said, "This…isn't wise."

Lucilla blinked, then studied him—searched his eyes, his face. He might have broken the kiss, but he hadn't—yet—set her from him. That he would at any second was obvious, but for that moment, she was close enough to read him in more ways than the obvious; she detected no hint of true rejection, of denial of what lay between them, in him.

She didn't understand why he'd uttered those words, but she had more important issues to address. "What do you know of the Lady?" More than anything else, she needed to know that.

Carefully, he set her from him—slowly, as if it took concentration to make his arms do as he wished.

She took heart from that. When she didn't step back, he did.

His frown showed more in his eyes than on his face. "The Lady?"

Thomas had no idea why she wanted to know that—what had so compelled her to ask that of all things, given the circumstances. He took an instant to consider, but the subject seemed safe enough—much safer than what had gone before. So he shrugged and answered honestly, "She's the local deity in these parts—in your Vale and for some here on the estate, too."

That his answer was, for some reason, important to her showed in her intentness, in the way she searched his face.

He narrowed his eyes. "Why do you ask?"

She blinked again. Several seconds passed before she replied, "Niniver happened to mention that you haven't, through your life, spent all that much time here. I... thought you had spent more." She shrugged. "So I asked."

To his surprise, she turned and started walking again, albeit more slowly. Her fingers lacing over her waist, her expression suggested she was both disturbed and thinking furiously.

He fell into step beside her.

She glanced at him. "But you were born here."

Her tone made the words something akin to an accusation, but he replied as if she'd posed a question. "Yes, but only by accident."

"Accident?"

Her tone now held a note of...latent panic? That couldn't be right. With a touch on her arm, he steered her through a side door and into the house—back into the safety of uncertain privacy. "My parents intended me to be born in Glasgow, but they came for a short stay, and I arrived weeks early."

"Ah."

Why those details should soothe her, he had no clue, but that single syllable had been infused with relief.

The shadows in the corridor made it impossible to read her eyes. He had no idea what was going on in her mind, but he knew without question that keeping distance between them was now imperative. She had to understand and accept that he was not for her, no matter what happened when they kissed.

They reached the stairway hall. He paused at the bottom of the stairs. "Do you know the way to your room?"

Lucilla nodded before she thought. *Damn!* She watched him step back.

"I need to speak with Ferguson. I'll see you tomorrow." He hesitated for a moment, his gaze on her, then he inclined his head. "Good night."

She seized one last moment to scrutinize his features, to try to fathom what he was thinking, but failed. Left with little option, she inclined her head in return. "Good night."

The last glimpse she had of his face as she turned and, raising her skirts, started up the stairs suggested concealed relief.

Why?

What on earth was going on between them? Instead of being the simple, straightforward, obvious path defined by the alignment of similar goals and desires that she'd always envisioned their way forward would be, their path to the altar was increasingly resembling a tangled maze—at least with respect to his intentions. His goals and desires.

Very rarely did she feel uncertain, but now she felt bemused, unsure—and on *this*, of all issues, the single issue most critical to determining her future. More, *both* their futures—his as well as hers.

She'd walked blindly up the stairs, through the gallery, and along the corridor. Sufficient light fell from the skylight over the stairwell for her to see her way, not that she'd been looking. Reaching the door of the room she'd been given, she opened it, walked through, and shut the door—all still in a daze.

While she undressed and donned her nightgown, she let her mind range as it would—over all the previous moments she'd shared with Thomas. Revisiting those moments, each separate interaction, critically reanalyzing every word, every look.

She had thought he'd known, that he'd understood, as she had, that he and she were fated to be consorts. Lovers. Spouses. Husband and wife. Ever since she'd truly *known* beyond question, during that Christmas Eve he and she and several of her relatives had spent in a crofter's cottage ten years ago, she'd interpreted his reactions toward her on the assumption that he knew and understood, too.

He was Lady-touched, as she was. He'd lived under the Lady's rule, or so she'd thought. She'd assumed he'd known...

But if he hadn't either known or understood, why had he behaved as he had?

She climbed into the large tester bed, lay back, and pulled the covers to her chin. Staring, unseeing, upward, she searched for an answer.

Her memory of each of their meetings was acute; reviewing all that had occurred, reliving each moment yet again...

No. She hadn't imagined anything. The intensity of the attraction that had flared every time they'd met, and that had escalated with the years, had been and still was impossible to mistake.

It had consistently been there, in his eyes, in the way his jaw set, in his touch.

Remembering the last time they'd waltzed, at the Hunt Ball two years ago, still made her tremble.

There was no possibility of denying such an attraction—and to give him his due, she didn't think he'd tried.

Instead, as he had that evening, he'd simply turned and walked away from it.

Walked away from her.

Which, she had to admit, confused her no end.

She knew intensely passionate men—every man in her family was built that way. She was far better acquainted with their foibles than she would ever have chosen to be.

But that meant that she should understand him. That his actions should make sense to her, in one way or another.

Yet at the moment, she didn't know what was going on—what issues, what considerations, were making him back away from an attraction that should have seen him fighting to keep her in his arms.

Instead, he'd let her go and walked off.

She didn't know whether she was insulted, or angry, or just plain confused.

With her thoughts gradually slowing, she closed her eyes and reached for the Lady—sensed her comforting presence, an elemental heartbeat softly rolling beneath the blanket of the night.

Gradually, the confused tangle of her thoughts sank deeper, leaving revealed the rocks to which she could—should—cling.

He wanted her—every bit as much as she now wanted him. Desire between them ran strongly, a rope connecting them no matter what either might wish or will. The

Lady had ordained that, and neither she nor he had the power to overcome, eradicate, or dismiss that.

The Lady had ordained that he and she would wed, that he—Lady-touched and therefore a guardian of his people, whether he understood that or not—would be her consort. Neither he nor she could step away from that destiny without suffering drastic consequences; their lives would never run smoothly or well, but would, instead, be shrouded in miseries.

But no matter what the Lady decreed, people, even those Lady-touched, still had free will.

If Thomas chose to walk away, he could.

Over the last year, she had wondered whether she was supposed to act in some way to bring about their Lady-ordained marriage. Acting—doing—would have been so much more in keeping with her character, her temperament, her usual way of facing and dealing with life's challenges. She'd questioned, but in the end, she'd accepted and waited...

Perhaps her time to act was finally here.

As she slipped over the threshold into sleep, it certainly seemed that convincing Thomas that he couldn't walk away from her and his Lady-ordained future was a task that fell to her.

* * *

Thomas woke restless and somehow dissatisfied. Unwilling to dwell on what his body seemed to think it lacked, he threw on his clothes and headed down to the stable to check on Phantom and Lucilla's mare.

Even though it was early, he avoided the breakfast parlor. He didn't need to learn if Lucilla was an early riser—she probably was.

He walked out of the front door and circled the house.

Alice Watts was due to arrive that morning. As soon as Lucilla had coached Alice in all she needed to do, he would escort Lucilla back to the Vale, to Marcus—who, no doubt, would be very ready to take back his sister and send Thomas on his way.

It said much of his mood that he was starting to feel glad that he'd been forced to knock Marcus Cynster unconscious.

On reaching the stable, he walked inside. A quick glance around found no Sean, Mitch, or Fred, which surprised him. He hadn't expected to see any of his cousins about at that hour, but the stablemen were usually at work by now.

Yesterday, he'd made time to speak with Sean about finding Joy Burns's canteen and getting some water from the Bradshaws' well, and sending samples from both sources off to Glasgow for analysis. As well as his other duties, Sean handled the various soil- and water-related tests the estate ran in the continuing effort to eke out the best from their lands. Thomas wanted to check that Sean had found Joy's canteen, and when he thought the results from the laboratory might come back.

But he would have to check later, because Sean was nowhere in sight.

Mentally shrugging, Thomas went down the aisle. He spent the next fifteen minutes grooming Phantom, then stepped into the next stall and started brushing the black mare's glossy hide. She shifted, not accustomed to him. Phantom hung his head over the wall between the stalls, as if intrigued by the mare's prancing. She quieted after that, allowing Thomas to groom her.

When both horses were gleaming, he relatched their stalls. He was replacing the brushes on the wall at the end of the stable when, in the distance, he heard a horse whicker.

The noise came from outside, from beyond the end of the stable. But he hadn't heard anyone ride up, and there weren't any horse paddocks in that direction.

Puzzled, he walked out of the stable. Another whicker carried on the breeze drew his gaze—to the old barn.

As far as he knew, it was used to store old carriages and carts no longer in use, old implements no one was ready to throw away just in case they were needed again. No horses of any kind had been stabled there for years.

He walked toward the barn. The closer he got, the more sounds he heard—the shifting stamp of horses' hooves on straw-strewn earth, the rattle of a stall wall as a horse bumped it.

And voices.

He walked through the open barn door and discovered that Sean, Mitch, and Fred were, indeed, at work. They were mucking out the stalls and feeding and grooming... Thomas counted along the line of stalls...eight horses.

Eight examples of prime horseflesh, with glossy coats and strong legs. Four had the deep chests of carriage horses, two the sleeker build of Thoroughbreds, while the last pair were hunters, heavy and powerful.

He stood staring for a full minute, then Sean, standing in a nearby stall, brush in hand, saluted him. "Morning."

Slowly walking forward, Thomas returned the greeting. Then he asked, "Where did these come from?" He faced Sean. "Who do they belong to?"

Sean looked him in the eye, then flicked a glance at Mitch and Fred before returning his gaze to Thomas's face. "Don't rightly know, do we? You'd do better asking Master Nigel."

Thomas studied Sean's eyes. "Nigel brought them here?"

"Him and Master Nolan." Mitch came to join them. "The pair o' them brought the beasts." With his chin, Mitch directed Thomas's gaze down the aisle to the barn's end. "And those, too."

Thomas peered into the shadows at the back of the barn and saw the outline of three carriages.

"Not as if we don't have enough work to do," Fred grumbled from a nearby stall.

"Aye." Sean got back to his brushing. "And the breeding season's already on us—not that that pair seem concerned about that."

Thomas heard the complaint for what it was; the clan had always saved money by breeding their own horses and donkeys to use on the estate's farms. In any decent season, there were usually a few extra to sell, helping the coffers just that bit more.

His earlier question of what was going on was translating into what the devil Nigel and Nolan were up to.

But as he walked deeper into the barn, Thomas acknowledged that although this problem-of-sorts, along with the matter of the seed supply, clearly lay at his cousins' doors, none of the more serious incidents could be attributed to them. They'd been away in Ayr when the Burns sisters had died and the Bradshaws had fallen ill.

He reached the end of the barn, where a large open area had previously played host to a jumble of old carts, drays, and carriages. All had been shifted and crammed somewhat haphazardly aside to accommodate three new carriages. Spanking new carriages, barely used. One was a sleek, elegant, high-perch phaeton, another a well-appointed racing curricle, while the third was a closed gentleman's carriage of distinctly modern design. Thomas opened a door and looked in. Fine leather, polished oak, and gilt trimmings met his eyes.

He closed the door and, for a moment, stood looking down at the barn floor.

He wasn't intimately acquainted with the clan's finances, with the profits and cash flows from the estate. He'd never sought such information; the clan had never been his inheritance—there had been no need for him to know such details.

That said, he was a businessman, one most others in Glasgow considered extremely shrewd. Even without knowing the details, he knew beyond question that the clan's wealth would not stretch to the acquisition of such carriages, let alone the horseflesh presently gracing the barn.

This, he suspected, was a part of the answer to their question of what was going on. He stirred and started back up the aisle. Drawing level with Sean, he met the head stableman's eyes and nodded. "I'll take your advice— I'll ask Nigel."

Jaw setting, Sean nodded back.

Thomas paused long enough to ask his questions about the samples to be sent for testing, and to hear Sean's reply as to how long it might be before the results came back: "A month or more, depending on how much work from others is already waiting to be done."

As he strode back to the house, Thomas recalled the scene he'd witnessed the afternoon before, when Nigel and Nolan had ridden into the stable yard.

He hadn't understood the sullen reception they'd received.

Regardless of all the other threads still flapping in the breeze, he was fairly certain he understood that now.

* * *

He was alone at the breakfast table when Lucilla walked in. She was wearing a day gown in a shade of bronzy-green that, combined with her fire-red hair, made him think of autumn.

The gown's fine material also revealed far more of her figure than either the velvet of her riding habit or the stiff silk of her evening gown had, which did nothing for his comfort.

Of course, after smiling in greeting, then filling her plate at the sideboard, she came to the place beside him. He rose and drew out the chair for her, held it while she sat and settled, then sank back into his own.

Clearly comfort wasn't something he was destined to experience any time soon.

Luckily, Norris, closely followed by Niniver, arrived. The pair served themselves and took the places opposite him and Lucilla. In between bites of toast and jam, Lucilla asked Niniver and Norris about Alice, and the conversation slid into safe arenas.

But just having Lucilla close played havoc with his concentration. As distractions went, she was as potent as they came, at least for him. If he'd been *restless* before, having her within his senses' reach only intensified the feeling.

He remained puzzled by her question about what he knew of the Lady. Why ask that? The implication and her reaction to his answer suggested she'd thought he would know more. But, again, why? What could she have expected him to know?

Despite the fact he had—he thought fairly definitely—

stepped back from her last night, and signaled his decision not to pursue the path she'd seemed hell-bent on
rushing down, her attitude to him this morning could
best be described as equable.

He had no idea why he could sense her mood so clearly,
yet he could. She was calm, serene—and focused.

He wasn't sure on what.

Before he could decide whether he needed to remain
on guard against her, Nigel and Nolan strolled in. The
pair greeted Lucilla, their siblings, and him with almost
identical, arrogantly insouciant airs. Unimpressed, he
waited until they'd served themselves and sat, Nigel at
the end of the table with Nolan to his left, next to Niniver. He waited while both started in on the ham and eggs
on their plates, until Nigel paused and reached for the
mug of coffee he'd poured himself.

"There are," Thomas said, his tone even and unin-
flected, as unaggressive as he could make it, "eight
excellent specimens of horseflesh, plus three new carriages, in the old barn."

Nigel froze, his mug halfway to his mouth. A heartbeat passed, then his gaze flicked up to Thomas's face.

Thomas arched his brows. "Who do they belong to?"

Nigel's gaze darted to Nolan. Impassive, Nolan looked
back at Nigel. Then Nigel turned to Thomas and smiled.
"Good cattle, aren't they? Very nice steppers."

"So they appeared." Thomas waited, his gaze on Nigel's face.

Nolan leaned forward, reaching for the jam pot. Picking it up, he grinned at Thomas. "There's no mystery,
cuz. We're looking after them for a friend. He's been
forced to sell up—trouble with his creditors, don't you
know? The horses and carriages in the old barn are the

ones he wants to keep, but he thought it wise to get them out of sight for the nonce."

Nigel was nodding. "He needed somewhere to keep them, and we had the room. No skin off our nose to house them."

Thomas thought of how much feed eight horses could go through, let alone the time taken for their care. In a level tone, he ventured, "The stablemen didn't seem quite so thrilled to have double the number of horses to tend."

Nigel humphed. "A surly lot they're turning out to be, even if they are distant cousins."

Seated closer to Nigel and Nolan than Thomas, Lucilla could feel the suppressed animosity both were directing his way—Nigel in particular. Given what she'd seen previously of Nigel's not-entirely-logical resentment of Thomas, she wasn't surprised when Thomas shrugged lightly and let the subject slide.

She'd also noticed Niniver watching the exchange—watching her brothers with a quietly suspicious air. If Thomas harbored doubts about the story of the horses—and she was well aware that he did—so, too, did Niniver.

But when Niniver noticed her regard, the younger girl smiled slightly and asked, "What are you planning on doing today?"

The question fixed the attention of everyone else at the table—all except Norris, who remained determinedly detached.

Lucilla saw no reason not to answer. "Once Alice arrives, which I gather should be soon, I'll go over the still room with her. We need to check on all the stores, and the decoctions Joy left steeping, and I need to make sure Alice is able to carry on by herself. I also want to walk through the herb garden with her and check that she has all the herbs she might need, so if there's anything missing, I can supply it from the Vale, rather than have her distracted by having to source obscure herbs while she's still settling in."

Nolan, forearms folded on the table, tipped his head. "So once you've done that, you'll be heading back to the Vale?"

The question was posed in a conversational tone, yet she sensed that both Nolan and Nigel—as well as Thomas—had a keen interest in her answer. Calmly, she replied, "That depends on what I find."

Nigel waved his fork. "How so?"

She studied him for a second, then said, "For instance, much depends on the stocks of specifics Joy has put by. Once I check what she's been making by way of tonics and medicines in general, and assess whether Alice knows how to replace them, I'll have a better idea of how long I'll need to stay. It may take a day or two to ensure that Alice has sufficient stocks put by to continue to supply all those Joy was treating."

Nigel frowned as if trying to remember. "I really don't think she—old Joy—was supplying anyone with anything vital."

Lucilla arched her brows. She knew the answer, yet still she said, "Surely she's been treating your father, if no one else."

Lips pursing, Nigel shook his head. "I would need to check with Edgar, but I'm fairly certain Joy wasn't making any potions for Papa."

"Whyever not?" Anything she could learn might be of use in convincing Manachan to accept the help she was determined to give him.

Nigel smiled, more than a touch patronizingly. "Nothing to be done, really." He shrugged. "The old man's just getting older. Unless you have some potion from the Fountain of Youth, there's not much anyone can do about that, is there?"

Refutation burned her tongue, but she kept her lips shut, unwilling to respond to that not-so-subtle goad. She could have informed Nigel that, in her experienced opinion, there was a great deal that might be done to restore his father's health, but rather than argue, she decided she would prefer a demonstration.

Coolly, she inclined her head, then pushed back from the table. She looked at Thomas. "Alice should be here soon. I'll wait for her in the still room."

Rising and pulling back her chair, Thomas merely nodded, then after she'd inclined her head to Niniver and her brothers, he followed her from the room.

* * *

Lucilla let the familiar ambiance of the still room close about her. Thomas had followed her down the steps and along the winding corridors to the room in the bowels of the main wing; he lounged in the doorway, one shoulder propped against the stone surround, his hands sunk in his breeches pockets, and watched her, while she ignored him.

She didn't want to ignore him, but she was finding that he and what to do about him were taking up too much space in her mind—space she needed to devote to Alice, once she arrived, and to determining what needed to be accomplished, and in what order.

She pottered about the room, circling the big table at its center, checking and noting the pots on the shelves running above the bench that lined the walls.

After several long minutes, Thomas stirred. Straightening in the doorway, he murmured, "Will you be staying here?"

Without looking his way, she nodded. "I don't plan on leaving until Alice gets here, and even then, I'll only be going to the herb garden with her."

It was interesting, she supposed, that she could accept his protectiveness—for that was what was behind his hovering presence—without any real irritation. Only from Marcus would she have accepted such a question with any similar degree of equanimity. Even had it been her cousin Sebastian, future head of their house, who had voiced it, she would have responded with a decided snap.

But there was someone lurking with murderous intent, possibly not in the house but at least on the estate. That was reason enough for protectiveness in any true man—and even more in he who was destined to be her consort.

He studied her for a moment more, as if debating, then sound drifted down from the ground floor; the corridor that led from the stable yard to the front hall was, more or less, directly above them. He drew his hands from his pockets. "That sounds as if Alice has arrived. I'll go and fetch her."

Lucilla didn't bother pointing out that Alice had to know the way to the still room—she'd been the healer's apprentice for at least two years.

Instead, she used the peace—both around her and in her mind—to formulate a program for the day.

When Thomas ushered Alice—a thin, pale woman in her early thirties with long fair hair and gentle blue eyes—through the door and Alice promptly bobbed a curtsy, Lucilla smiled and waved her up. "No need for that—we're both healers, and we need to work together. Curtsying, you'll discover, will only get in both our ways."

Alice's lips quirked; she fought to stifle a giggle and didn't entirely succeed.

Lucilla let her smile deepen. "Excellent. Now, sit down"—she pushed one of the two tall stools toward Alice and claimed the other for herself—"and tell me how far along in your studies you are."

Before Alice could speak, Thomas said, "I'll leave you two to it." When Lucilla looked at him, he met her gaze. "I'm going for a ride around the estate." He glanced at Alice. "To see what else has changed since last I visited."

To see if there are any other odd things going on.

Lucilla heard the words he didn't say. She nodded, then watched him turn and stride away.

Once he'd gone, she looked at Alice. "Did he ask you to stay with me at all times?"

Alice blinked, then regarded her as if she were clairvoyant. "Yes."

Lucilla smiled. "Don't worry. I happen to think that's a very good idea."

The Carricks had lost one healer; she saw no reason to risk another. While she might be safer with Alice, Alice would also be safer with her.

"Now," she prompted, "tell me how far Joy has taken you. Has she had you making any of the complex tonics?"

Eight

He'd agreed to be Manachan's eyes and ears, and the only way to get a decent view of the estate was from the back of a horse. Manachan had always ridden his acres, usually going out three or more times each week, regardless of the weather. He'd kept in close touch with all the clan families, had known how each of the farms was faring at any given time. Even when Thomas had last visited the manor some two years before, Manachan had still been riding out regularly. Thomas didn't like to think how deeply, if silently, his uncle would be fretting over his inability to get out and about.

A nagging sense of unease had driven him to ensure that Lucilla would always be with others, but now that was taken care of, clan duty called.

He'd sent word to Sean that he intended to ride; Phantom was saddled and waiting in the yard. Accepting the reins from Mitch, who had been waiting with the big gray, Thomas noticed a smaller horse—a neat bay gelding—also saddled and waiting. The saddle was a side-saddle.

He was about to mount when Niniver hurried out of the house.

In a black velvet riding dress, with a small cap set

atop her blond head, she came forward with a surprisingly determined stride. "Thomas—are you just going riding, or will you be calling at the farms?"

He paused, then admitted, "The latter."

Niniver halted a few paces away and met his gaze. "I often stop by the farms—do you mind if I ride with you?"

Did he? Of Manachan's four children, Thomas knew Niniver the least. Manachan overlooked her, too—but then he also largely ignored Norris, and even Nolan; when it came to his offspring, Manachan had a highly blinkered view, and that view was focused on Nigel. Then again, some would argue that, as laird, Manachan had always had so much to do with being father to the entire clan that he'd only had time left for one child and, naturally, that had to be his heir.

But if Niniver knew the farms and families... He inclined his head. "I would appreciate the company."

Niniver smiled, the gesture shy and fleeting, and turned to her horse. Mitch held the bay steady as she climbed the mounting block, then scrambled into her saddle.

Thomas mounted; settling Phantom, he waited. When Niniver trotted forward to join him, he swung Phantom's head down the drive. "Which way should we go?"

Niniver cast him a careful glance. "Do you want to do a circuit of all the farms?"

"That was my intention."

Looking ahead, she lifted her chin. "In that case, we'll do best to go east first, and then circle to the south. That way we'll end with the Forresters, and then the Bradshaws last of all."

Thomas vaguely recalled the eastern farms. He nodded. "You lead. I'll follow."

With a brisk nod, Niniver nudged her bay into a canter. Thomas kept pace and they rode out into the morning.

An hour later, as they headed toward the western farms, that "You lead; I'll follow" replayed in his head. Who would have guessed that Niniver was...as deft a manipulator as her father?

Thomas was fairly certain that was where she'd inherited the knack; if anything, he would have said that her subtle, quiet "steering" was even more effective than Manachan's often brash and blatant maneuverings. But as her direction aligned with Thomas's own interest, far from resenting her interference, he was glad of it. She showed him where to look and eased his way in learning all he'd ridden out to find.

At every farmhouse, she was welcomed with genuine smiles and warmth; even the workers they came upon in the fields were transparently glad to see her, and very ready to pause and chat and tell her—and Thomas, too—how their labors were progressing and how each saw their own corner of the estate.

Although they hadn't seen him for two years, the farmers still knew him and counted him as one of the laird's family. He'd come to ask their opinions, with Niniver beside him, and so they spoke without restraint. If there was a prickliness, it was directed at Nigel—the "young master" as they termed him—not at Thomas or anyone else. While no one mentioned Nigel's trips off the estate—that wasn't their way—all the comments were restricted to what was wrong here, in their world.

The further he and Niniver rode, the more farms

and holdings they stopped at, the more the problems mounted. None were major enough to be classed as emergencies; the lack of seed for planting was arguably the most worrying. Many of the gripes were merely minor irritations, but if left unaddressed, would fester and grow.

Most of the farms nearer the manor ran small herds of sheep, while the more southern and western holdings specialized in woodcutting and logging. Two farms ran cattle; three had goatherds. Again and again, Thomas heard the same comments, the same tune sung—that of a lack of interest and support from the manor. Bit by bit, a pattern emerged—one where Nigel was insisting that the farmers got their beasts or produce to market and secured the usual best price for the same, but without the help the manor had provided in the past, often acting as agent and helping to arrange transport.

As one farmer dourly stated, "Hisself wants us to do it all, but still pass the usual cut back to the manor. More, if our prices go down, he still wants the same amount. So now we do all the work, and he gets to sit in state on the manor's coffers."

Another explained, "We know as it's the clan's money and not just the laird's, but still…it's not fair."

Yet another stated, "This wasn't how it used to be in the old laird's time."

From that point on, Thomas looked even more carefully, and what he observed only increased his concern. Children wearing clothes they'd outgrown. Women in faded and patched gowns. Mothers who looked, to his eyes, too thin—certainly not as buxom as he recalled. Even some of the men showed signs of losing weight.

The Carrick estate had never been wealthy; its farms had never enjoyed the degree of prosperity of those to the south, in the Vale. But the Vale was managed on different principles, as a much tighter, more inclusive whole. That wouldn't have suited the Carrick clan, where the families were more fiercely and pridefully independent, but they'd always managed. Manachan had always ensured that they did.

But with Manachan ill and no longer able to manage the reins, it was clear things were falling apart.

Although Thomas didn't hear a single good word about Nigel, not even any neutral comments, the entire clan still held Manachan in high regard, and, to a large extent, that was protecting Nigel from concerted complaints and open opposition.

To the clan families, Manachan was still in ultimate charge with Nigel his temporary and less-able agent; although none precisely stated it, it was clear the families all believed that the current state would, with time, pass, and then Manachan would put right all the things that had gone wrong.

Together with Niniver, Thomas visited the Forresters, and then the Bradshaws. Forrester, who logged the northwestern forests and also cropped several large fields, confirmed all that Thomas had learned from others. The management of the estate was, if not yet in disarray, certainly unraveling.

The Bradshaws were considerably improved. Thomas sat at their dining table and let Bradshaw explain the full implications of the estate's crop farmers not yet having received any seed stock.

"We're too late, now, to get more than one crop this year, when usually we'd have two." Bradshaw paused, then more diffidently said, "And the way the manor's been talking, it sounds as if they're going to insist we pay the usual tithe, as if we'd had the two crops and not just one."

Thomas didn't need to ask what strain that would place on the farmers. Struggling to mask the degree of his disquiet, he nodded. "I'll make sure the laird knows." He couldn't promise that Manachan would put things right and adjust the levy on the farms, yet neither could he suggest that Manachan wouldn't. Or, as it might well be, couldn't.

For all his bluster and belligerence, Manachan had never allowed the clan to be harmed, and most especially not by any action of the manor. That wasn't how clan and lairdship worked.

After asking to see the Bradshaw children, on the pretext of having promised Lucilla he would bear tidings of them back to her, and confirming that all five were entirely recovered, he took his leave. Niniver said her goodbyes and followed him outside; from the smiles, even from the children, she was clearly a favorite visitor at the isolated farmhouse.

They mounted their horses and headed back to the manor.

Halfway back, there was a rocky shelf of land, a lookout of sorts. Niniver turned onto it and drew rein.

Following in her wake, Thomas pulled up alongside her.

They both sat and looked out over the fields. In the middle distance, the manor squatted like a dark deformed goblin amid its screening trees, its slate roofs looking rather like a hat. Remnants of morning mist still hung over the fields to the west, smudges of soft lavender against the dark green of the forests.

The sun was high overhead. Thomas's stomach suggested the time was somewhere about noon.

Niniver drew breath. "So." She glanced at Thomas, her blue gaze sober and direct. "Did you *see*?"

He thought better of her for having dropped all pretense that she hadn't been guiding him throughout the excursion. "Yes." He looked at the fields. He hadn't been trained to manage this sort of an estate, but if this had been his inheritance, he would have been seriously concerned.

He *was* seriously concerned, because these people were his clan.

"Papa needs to know."

He looked at Niniver. "You know. You've known all along. Why haven't you told him?"

Her lips twisted, and she faced forward. Her mount shifted, and she reined the gelding in. "Because I'm his daughter. I'm not his heir." That was stated without rancor. "And now Nigel is in charge."

A moment passed, then she met Thomas's eyes. "You're mine and everyone else's only hope of putting all the issues you've seen today before Papa. He'll understand. Nigel...doesn't want to see. He doesn't want to understand."

Thomas paused, then said, "I hadn't realized, not until this morning, just how completely Manachan has handed over control."

Her expression unreadable, Niniver swung her gelding around. "Papa has been too ill to do anything, not for nearly a year. But once he understands what's going on, he'll know what needs to be done."

She tapped her heel to the bay's side and set off for

the manor. Thomas swung Phantom around and followed her off the ledge and back onto the bridle path.

As they rode in single file between the fields, he weighed and considered, but all avenues led to the same unwelcome conclusion.

It appeared that neither Niniver nor the rest of the clan fully comprehended the change that had occurred. Thomas hadn't either, not until he'd arrived and realized just how ill Manachan was—and, apparently, had been for nearly a year. If Manachan hadn't been well enough to act for the clan for nearly a year, then Nigel truly was in charge of the estate. He wasn't acting as Manachan's agent, as his father's right hand, but entirely on his own authority.

Because of his illness, Manachan had been forced to cede complete control.

Theoretically, as laird, Manachan could take back what he'd given, but, realistically, could he?

Given Manachan remained so very weak, the answer to that was no.

Yes, Thomas would convey to Manachan all that he'd learned—all Niniver had ensured he saw and heard. Regardless of any inclination on his part not to unnecessarily trouble his uncle, Manachan would insist, and as laird, he had a right to know. But in the current situation, what could Manachan do? He could hint or suggest actions to Nigel, but Manachan couldn't—wasn't in any position to—ensure those actions were carried out.

Could he, Thomas, speak with Nigel? Given Nigel's antipathy toward him, the answer to that was an even more resounding no. Indeed, he had a shrewd suspicion that anything he suggested, Nigel would take pains *not* to do.

But even more disturbing, from all Thomas had seen and heard, it seemed that, in succeeding to the duties of laird, Nigel had decided to treat the rest of the clan as if they were his employees—as if they worked for him, rather than for the clan. Rather than in the way the Carrick clan had always operated, as a collective functioning under the overall leadership of the laird—subject to his rule, perhaps, but also entitled to his protection and active support.

That corruption of the system that had served the Carricks down the generations deeply troubled Thomas. As they neared the manor, he saw the conundrum before him clearly. His clan needed help, needed the relationship between laird and clan to change back to what it used to be. But with Manachan so ill and Nigel firmly in charge, what could he, a clan outsider, moreover one whom Nigel so resented, do to improve matters, to effect the changes that needed to be made?

The stable yard lay ahead when a point that had been nagging in the back of his brain leapt to the forefront. He called to Niniver, "Where are the hounds?" The Carricks had bred deerhounds for generations; there'd always been beasts in and around the manor, but since he'd ridden in, he hadn't seen one.

Niniver glanced at him, clearly assessing whether she should trust him or not. Eventually facing forward, she called back, her tone flat, "Nigel sold them."

"What?" Thomas was aghast. "All of them?"

"All that were in the breeding barn. He said they were an unnecessary drain on the estate."

Thomas studied Niniver's profile; as they slowed the horses to a walk, he prompted, "But…"

Manachan had loved his hounds. If Thomas remembered aright, so had Niniver.

"Sean, Mitch, Fred, and I moved some to old man Egan's farm. He had a barn he wasn't using."

So she and the others still had a hunting pack.

They turned the horses onto the drive. Thomas frowned. "I thought Nigel used to like to hunt with the dogs."

Niniver nodded. "He used to. But these days, he and Nolan go into the Highlands to hunt. Nigel said he didn't need the hounds anymore." She paused, then added, "Papa's last bitch passed last summer, about the time he fell ill. He hasn't asked after another and...I haven't told him about the others being gone." Reining in, she met Thomas's eyes. "I didn't want to disturb him then, and now he has more urgent matters on his plate."

Thomas wasn't about to argue. He met her gaze and nodded. "Indeed."

* * *

Thomas and Niniver walked into the front hall just as Ferguson, in the stairway hall, raised the padded mallet and struck the gong for luncheon.

The deep sound reverberated through the house.

Screams drowned the echoes.

The shrill sounds of terror sliced through the house, emanating from more than one throat.

They came from below, from beneath the main wing.

Thomas bolted for the steps leading down. Two flights; he leapt down the latter, landed in the lower corridor, then raced toward the still room.

The screams had stopped.

He rounded the last corner and saw Lucilla. And his heart started to beat again.

She and Alice were backed against the corridor wall, their gazes locked on the still room door—which was closed.

"Lucilla?" He forced himself to slow as he reached her—forced himself not to haul her into his arms, to lock her against him just to reassure himself that she truly was safe.

The face she turned to him was white—unnaturally so. Her eyes were huge pools of green.

He struggled to rein in his reaction; regardless, one hand rose to touch her upper arm. "What is it?"

Beyond Lucilla, Alice started gasping as if she couldn't catch her breath. Niniver pushed past Thomas and went to the healer. Murmuring soothingly, Niniver took Alice in her arms and rubbed her back.

Lucilla gulped; her gaze hadn't left his face. "Adder." She shuddered, then weakly raised a hand and pointed to the door. "It was just suddenly there, around our feet."

She took another, deeper, gulp of air. Then abruptly she clutched his jacket and turned into his arms. She pressed her forehead into his chest as his arms instinctively closed about her.

Adder? He fought to simply hold her and not crush her to him. In his mind, he heard Manachan's voice from long ago, warning him that adders were at their most deadly on emerging from hibernation—as they would be at that time of the year.

Lucilla's fingers fisted in his shirt. He dipped his head and heard her hoarsely whisper, "I *hate* snakes."

Most people did. Holding her against him—he wasn't sure he could force his arms to let her go—he glanced back at Ferguson, who had rushed down, too.

The butler had heard; he looked grim. "You and Miss Niniver get Miss Cynster and Alice upstairs." Ferguson reached past them for the doorknob and checked that the door was shut tight. He glanced down, and Thomas and Lucilla followed his gaze. There was a gap between the base of the door and the worn stone floor.

Two footmen arrived, clattering down the corridor.

"Just in time." Ferguson beckoned them forward. "There's an adder's got into the still room. I want you two to stand here and make sure the slithery thing doesn't come out."

Alice had finally caught her breath. "It's a big fat one," she said. "I don't think it could squeeze through."

Ferguson nodded. "We'll hope not, but meanwhile"— he looked at the footmen—"you two keep watch while I go and fetch Fred and his spade."

The footmen didn't look happy but nodded.

After one swift glance at Thomas, Ferguson turned and strode off.

"Come on." Keeping one arm about Lucilla, Thomas urged her in Ferguson's wake. "You might not have heard, but Ferguson rang the luncheon gong just before you and Alice screamed."

Walking slowly beside him, Lucilla managed a nod. "I heard."

After a moment, she drew in a breath and glanced back, confirming that Alice was following with Niniver, then looked forward and, her spine straightening, raised her head. "As it happens, I really could do with a cup of tea."

Her tone was a reasonable facsimile of her customary imperiousness.

Taking that as a sign that she was recovering from her shock, Thomas let his arm fall as they reached the top of the steps. A few paces more brought them into the corridor off the front hall. At the far end, Fergu-

son, aided by Mrs. Kennedy, was shepherding a flock
of maids and footmen, no doubt drawn by the screams,
back to the staff quarters.

Thomas and Lucilla turned in the opposite direction
and walked into the front hall; behind them, Niniver
called to Mrs. Kennedy and handed the still-shaken Alice
into the motherly housekeeper's care.

Nigel, Nolan, and Norris were standing in a loose
group in the hall.

Nigel frowned. "What was that all about?"

Thomas told them, adding that Ferguson and the staff
were dealing with the adder.

Nigel humphed and exchanged a glance with Nolan,
then the pair turned and headed for the dining room.

Norris, who hadn't frowned earlier, was frowning
now. "Why on earth would an adder go down there?
Where the stone is cold? They're only just out of hibernation—they should be heading to where it's warm."

And that, Thomas acknowledged, was a highly pertinent point. In that season, no self-respecting adder would
have gone slithering down into the cold stone bowels of
the manor. That was simply too hard to swallow, so...

Beside him, Lucilla shivered. "I don't care why it went
there, as long as it's gone by the end of luncheon. Alice
and I were in the middle of a making, and we need to
finish it today."

Despite her shiver, by the end of that declaration, her
tone had firmed to resolute.

Thomas waved her forward. "In that case, let's eat."

* * *

After luncheon, a rather short and subdued meal, Thomas
escorted Lucilla back to the still room. Alice was already
there, sorting various leaves on the central table. A foot-

man with a stout broom was perched on a stool in the far corner; he didn't look bored, but then he was watching Alice.

Pausing before the open door, Thomas quietly said, "I meant to ask before—were you and Alice in the still room all morning?"

Lucilla met his eyes, then shook her head. "We went out to the herb garden." She looked at Alice. "We gathered those leaves to prepare a decoction she'll need to know how to make."

"So the room was empty for a while."

She nodded.

He glanced at the door; it was fitted with a heavy lock. "I take it the room wasn't locked."

"No. Alice said Joy never locked it, so I didn't insist."

"Do you know where the key is?"

She moistened her lips with the tip of her tongue. He had to look away.

"There's a key hanging on a peg inside—I think that's it." Before he could say anything, she went on, "At Casphairn, we always keep the still room locked."

He nodded. "A sound practice. I think it best that we institute it here. I'll mention it to Manachan. Perhaps you could tell Alice that we're changing the rules."

Lucilla dipped her head. "Ferguson mentioned that he's already instructed one of the carpenters to fix a strip to the bottom of the door."

"Good." Thomas stepped back; he met Lucilla's eyes when she glanced his way. "I'll be with Manachan if you need me."

She held his gaze for a moment, then in her usual regal fashion, inclined her head. Then she raised it, walked forward, and gently shut the still room door.

Thomas turned and walked away. And started mentally organizing all the information he had to report to Manachan—who, when all was said and done, was still the laird.

* * *

He returned to the still room in the late afternoon. Lucilla and Alice were clearly tidying up. Pausing in the doorway, he caught Lucilla's eye. "If you're finished here, there are several matters I'd like to discuss with you."

She glanced at Alice.

Alice smiled. "I can finish the tidying."

Setting down the paper-wrapped packets she'd been gathering, Lucilla nodded. "Be sure to lock the door and take the key. Keep it with you—don't leave it anywhere."

Alice's expression sobered. "I won't."

Lucilla sent a smiling nod toward the corner where the footman was still sitting on his stool, then went to join Thomas. Stepping into the corridor, she studied his face. "Did you learn anything about what's going on when you went riding this morning?"

He glanced along the corridor, which remained empty, but rather than answering, said, "Let's go for a walk."

Outside, where they ran much less risk of being overheard. She nodded. "After spending all afternoon down here, some fresh air would be welcome."

He waved toward the stairs, then fell in beside her.

She sifted through the many questions crowding her brain. "Did you call on the Bradshaws?"

"Yes." He described how he'd found the family, confirming her assumption that the matters he didn't want to broach while within the hearing of others were of a different ilk.

His report continued as they climbed the stairs,

walked into and through the front hall and out of the front door. Closing it behind them, he waved her on; they circled the house via the narrow terrace that followed the walls and eventually connected with the wider formal terrace that ran along the disued wing.

The instant they were on that side of the house, he said, "I wanted to ask whether there was anything in the still room, perhaps some note from Joy, or something not as it should be, that might suggest a reason for someone to kill her."

She'd anticipated the question. "I looked, but there was nothing at all that even vaguely struck me as out of the ordinary."

"Did Joy keep a record of those she was treating? Could there be a clue there—someone she was treating for something they might not have wanted known? Had she ever treated Manachan?"

She held up a hand to stem his questions. "Like any good healer, Joy kept a ledger. She's been supplying tonics and tisanes for several people in the house, and also on the farms, but they are all for perfectly mundane ailments—no motive for murder there. Or, indeed, anywhere else, I'm afraid." She paused, then continued, "I'm concentrating on making sure Alice knows how to continue to supply all of the tonics Joy was making, and what to watch out for while doing it. There are a few of the stronger tonics I'll need to teach her more about before I leave." She drew breath. "However, to answer your last question, no. I looked back more than three years, and there's no record of Joy ever treating Manachan. No regular tonic—not even a pick-me-up."

Pausing, she met Thomas's eyes. "I truly believe Manachan could use the help a good healer can give.

I'd like to see if he'll accept something to help him regain his strength, but I know men of his age and temperament don't like admitting that their health is failing. I wasn't all that surprised to learn that Joy never had a chance to treat him."

Thomas paced alongside her for half a minute before saying, "My ride about the estate confirmed that there are…escalating problems. Difficulties that need to be addressed, but that Nigel prefers to ignore. That can't go on, but the clan farmers don't want to bother Manachan, deeming him to have enough troubles of his own. But they can't influence Nigel, either. And nor can I."

She nodded. "Because you aren't the heir, and you therefore can't step on his toes, and he already resents you because you are closer to Manachan, or at least closer in a different, more adult way than he is."

That she'd seen that so clearly—could state it so clearly— was a comfort in itself. He had never met any other lady who understood the complex relationships of a clan.

"It seems," she murmured, "as if all the issues impinging on the estate stem from Manachan's illness. Because he fell ill—and no, I don't know what he caught, but clearly he fell victim to something—his health crumbled and his strength fell away, and so he was forced to allow Nigel to take over the estate…" She paused, then, frowning, went on, "If Manachan was restored to something like his old self, could he retake control of the estate?"

"Almost certainly, although I doubt he would—at least not unless Nigel refused to properly deal with the issues arising in the clan."

"By properly, I take it you mean in accordance with Manachan's wishes."

He nodded. After a moment, he drew a deeper breath and asked, "Do you really think you can help him?"

"I can't be sure until I examine him, but…" Looking ahead, she seemed to choose her words. "He was always such a strong and robust man. His physical strength was a hallmark. From what I've observed, and from when we helped him back and forth from the curricle yesterday, it seems to me that while he's lost muscle tone—the strength in his muscles—he hasn't actually lost that much weight." She frowned. "His problem seems to be a lack of vigor—he seems far weaker than he should be, as if everything takes more effort than it ought, and he just doesn't have enough energy in him."

"Exactly." He couldn't keep the grimness from his tone. "I spent all afternoon with him, and even though I'd brought back information he needed and wanted to hear about the problems the farmers are facing, he was… so weak, it was distressing to watch him trying to focus enough to take it in." He paused, then confessed, "In the end, I couldn't bring myself to push him to act—by that time, it seemed that it was all he could do to simply keep breathing."

They walked on for several paces before he said, "The drive to and back from the Bradshaws drained him, and then he insisted on coming down to dinner because you were under his roof—a guest." He grimaced. "He's sleeping now, but only because Edgar told him you were staying, so he's determined to come down for dinner tonight, too."

"Hmm." They reached the end of the terrace and halted. Head up, she gazed across the last stretch of the drive and into the stable yard. Eventually, she said, "There's a limit to how much you can argue against the dictates of an old man's pride. However, perhaps we can use his coming down to dinner to our advantage."

He frowned. "How so?"

Turning, she met his eyes. "It'll give me a chance to see if I can persuade him to allow me to treat him."

He held her gaze, then quietly said, "I was going to ask you to leave—now, this afternoon."

She looked steadily back at him. "Because of the adder."

Not a question, he noted. Still, he nodded. "There's no chance that adder got down to the still room on its own. Someone placed it there while you and Alice were out in the herb garden."

Momentarily, her gaze grew distant, then she refocused on his face. "The herb garden is exposed—anyone from the house or elsewhere could have seen us there, and the doors are never locked here, are they?"

Jaw firming, he shook his head. "The house of a laird is always open to the clan. Which brings me back to my request. Is it possible for you to leave now? Perhaps return tomorrow to continue instructing Alice?"

She stared at him for long enough that his hopes started to rise—then she grimaced. "No. Not really. I don't want to leave Alice until she's confident she can manage on her own—in our calling, confidence is a foundation stone. Without it, without being certain and sure, it's hard to take the decision to prescribe and treat people. But quite aside from that, the truth is that I'm more concerned by what I see in Manachan."

She laid a hand on his arm; he felt her light touch through coat and shirt, and had to shackle his instantaneous response. They turned and started back along the terrace, and she took back her hand, clasping her fingers before her.

He lowered his arm, glad to be free of her distracting touch, yet, perversely, wanting the contact back. He clasped his hands behind his back the better to ensure he didn't reach for her.

She glanced at him. "Manachan should not be as he is—I'm convinced of that. There really is no reason he should be so. I can accept that some illness dragged him down, but he should have recovered much better than he has." She met his eyes and her chin firmed. "I *know* I can, if not completely cure him, at least make him very much better. But to do that, we have to persuade him to accept my help—and the best chance we'll have of doing that will be over dinner tonight.

"He'll be dragged down again, but *wanting* to be strong enough to come down to dinner, to interact and play the host. That's the perfect time to dangle the prospect of greatly improved health before him. He'll be feeling his weakness and be frustrated by it—we can use that frustration to tip the scales our way."

The prospect she was dangling in front of *him*—of having Manachan largely restored—was too tempting, too desirable, to dismiss. "If he agrees…you can return to the Vale after dinner, and send whatever tonic you prescribe over tomorrow—"

He stopped speaking, stopped walking, because she'd halted and was shaking her head. Vehemently. Her lips had set in a mulish line.

"No." The eyes that met his were crystalline hard. "That won't work. If he agrees—and you'll allow that if he does, we'll need to strike then and there, and not let the moment lapse?"

Knowing Manachan, he had to nod.

"Well, then," she continued. "If he agrees, what I propose is that I'll examine him, which is a relatively simple thing, and then make up a boosting tonic immediately—something he can take tonight that will make him feel very much better in the morning. If he agrees, I need to take advantage and convince him that, yes, medicine really can make him feel better. Then, in the morning, once I gauge how well he's responded to the boosting tonic, I'll make up a restorative that he can take every mealtime to keep rebuilding his energies."

Lucilla caught Thomas's gaze and firmly stated, "So I'll stay for dinner, and if Manachan agrees to let me treat him, I'll stay for at least one more night." And, if she could, she would push that to two nights. At least. What with everything that had gone on, she hadn't had a chance to advance her cause—the Lady's cause—with him. And if she meekly returned to the Vale, she couldn't see how that would help, not with him remaining here and, it seemed likely, all too soon retreating to Glasgow.

She'd waited for years for him to come to her. Now that he had, she wasn't about to let him ride away.

Let him set her back in her usual place and leave.

Her gaze locked with the gold-flecked amber of his, she could feel his resistance as an all-but-tangible force. It was alive in his eyes, in the set of his lips, in the squared masculine beauty of his jaw.

That resistance didn't waver, but then another insight bloomed. Without shifting her gaze from his, she arched her brows. "If I understood you correctly, in order to help your clansmen with the strange problems that have cropped up on the estate, you need Manachan hale and strong once more. Strong enough to, if not retake the reins of the estate, at least exert influence over how they are managed. I want to help your uncle because that's what I do—it's a part of my duty just as much as helping your clan is to you. He might not be one of my people, but he is, indubitably, living under the Lady's protection. To walk away without making every effort to help him...that's not something I will readily do."

She infused enough determination into that last phrase to leave him in no doubt that she would refuse to leave if he attempted to pressure her. It only remained for her to point out, "As I see it, our goals are aligned. Both of us want the same thing—Manachan well again."

He didn't argue; he couldn't.

But when his capitulation came, it was no real capitulation at all. "Very well." The words were quiet and clipped. "But the instant you've dealt with Manachan and Alice is able to manage on her own, I will escort you back to the Vale."

There was little she could say to that, either. She inclined her head regally and turned to continue their perambulation back to the front door. Ultimately, him returning her to the Vale wasn't of itself any real threat. It wasn't the same as him leaving.

Nine

The gathering about the dinner table was similar to that of the evening before. The same people sat in the same places. The only real change was that Manachan was, as Lucilla and Thomas had expected, even more worn down.

That, and the clear impression Lucilla received that Nigel and Nolan had decided to blame her and her presence for their father's stubbornness in insisting on exerting himself and coming down to dinner.

The brothers were the last to arrive. On walking into the dining room and discovering Manachan already seated at the table's head, Nigel frowned. "I'm sure, Papa, that Miss Cynster won't be offended if you remain abed. This is too much for you."

Manachan slowly turned his head, and, from beneath his heavy brows, studied Nigel. Although his voice had yet to regain its strength after his slow journey down the stairs, there was no mistaking the temper in his tone when he stated, "It's not she who would be offended by the slight, but the clan, and while I have breath and strength enough left in this aging body, I won't shy from what I know should be."

Nigel clamped his lips shut. With a sour look at Lucilla, he took the seat to Manachan's left.

Nolan followed, taking the chair beside Nigel's and likewise directing a look of distinct antipathy at her.

She ignored them but seized the opening they'd given her. Under cover of the soup course being served, she leaned closer to Manachan and said, "Shortness of breath and general weakness often linger after an illness, but are usually quite easy to treat."

Manachan's blue eyes fixed on her face. After a moment, he murmured, "Is that so?"

She sat back to allow Ferguson to ladle game soup into her plate. When the butler moved on, she met Manachan's eyes, which had remained on her face. "Indeed. There are several tonics that are effective in reversing the debilitation caused by an illness."

Manachan arched his brows. "What about the debilitation that comes with age, heh? Do you have a tonic that can turn back the clock?"

Nigel was listening, of course; he snorted in disparaging agreement.

Serenely, she replied, "The effects of age cannot be reversed, but are you so very sure that age alone is the cause of your current state?"

Manachan paused in sipping his soup, his spoon suspended.

She didn't give him time to respond but rolled on, "The truth is that you cannot be sure, any more than anyone else can be certain. But, therefore, what harm can there be in trying a tonic or two to see if there's any improvement?"

Lightly shrugging, she returned her attention to her soup. Lifting a mouthful to her lips, she paused and softly—for Manachan's ears only—added, "I know the clan would rejoice to see you up and about again."

She fixed her gaze on her plate and ate her soup. Although she felt Manachan's gaze—and Nigel's and Nolan's, too   on her face, she didn't react, didn't meet their gazes, but left them to consider the seeds she'd sown.

Thomas asked Niniver about the gardens on the far side of the house. Although Lucilla pretended an interest, she kept most of her attention on Manachan, waiting and hoping that he would, of his own accord, return to the subject of his health.

They were most of the way through the main course before she was rewarded with a rumbling humph and the question, "Do you really think this godforsaken weakness isn't just old age?"

Shifting to face him, she met his eyes. "I've never known you that well, but from what I remember, bolstered"—she glanced briefly at Edgar, standing as usual within reach of his master—"by what those closer to you report, I would say that there's a very real chance that much of the tiredness that's holding you back has nothing to do with old age but, instead, is a lingering aftereffect of some illness." She paused, then added, "One thing age does affect is the body's ability to recover after an illness. It could simply be that you had some illness and have never thrown off the effects. And that sort of lingering weakness can become entrenched."

Manachan's gaze bored into her eyes. She met it without flinching and just waited.

After several long moments, he sat back in his chair, his gaze still locked on her face. "*If* I decided that it was time to put myself in a healer's hands—given, as you say, that there's surely no harm in trying a potion or two—

and if *you* were the healer I challenged to put me right again, what treatment would you recommend?"

He was a wily old fox. A challenge? As if he were merely amusing himself, merely accommodating a guest...but she could see how to use that, too. Letting a smile infuse her features, she leaned toward him and replied, "If I were given the opportunity to test my skills on you, I would need to briefly examine you—to check your eyes and your skin, and see what you can tell me about how you feel, and whether you can recall what illness precipitated your weakness. And then I would work up a boosting tonic for tonight." She held his gaze. "You would know by morning if it had had any effect, and if it had, I would make up a restorative you can continue to take, which will help you to improve further."

Manachan studied her for several long moments. No one else about the table said a word.

Then he pulled a face. "Why not?"

Ferguson hovered, waiting to remove Manachan's plate. Manachan noticed and waved; Ferguson replaced the plate with one for the poached pears in syrup that a footman had placed on the table.

Once the fuss of changing the courses had ended and they were all engaged with eating the dessert, Manachan returned to the topic now exercising the minds of all those about the table. "As you said, no harm in trying, and indeed, one might even say that it's my duty to the clan, heh?"

She inclined her head, although she suspected the words were more for the benefit of everyone but her. Nigel, for instance, looked plainly shocked at the notion of his father allowing her to treat him. Nolan looked blank, Niniver hopeful, and even Norris had blinked and taken notice. As for Thomas seated beside her, she hadn't turned sufficiently to see his face, but she could feel his relief that she'd succeeded where he had doubted she would, together with his hope that she could, as she'd claimed, set Manachan back on the road to health.

The instant they completed the meal, Manachan laid down his napkin and beckoned to Edgar. "I've had enough for today—I'm going up." He focused on Lucilla as she rose, along with Niniver. "You go off and have your tea—I'll send for you after I've had my nightcap."

Lucilla met his gaze, smiled confidently, and nodded. "I'll be waiting."

Manachan humphed as, leaning heavily on Edgar's arm, he turned away. "And then we'll see if you and your Lady are up to the challenge of healing an old reprobate like me."

Everyone heard his soft cackling as he stumped out of the room.

Eyes wide with hope as well as surprise, Niniver joined Lucilla. They followed Manachan and Edgar out, and headed for the drawing room.

* * *

Thomas remained at the dinner table with Nigel, Nolan, and Norris. Ferguson and the footmen quickly removed the platters and plates, then set the usual three decanters on the table before Nigel, along with a selection of cut-crystal glasses.

Nigel reached for the whisky decanter, poured a healthy dose into a tumbler, then passed the decanter to Nolan, on his right. Nolan did the same, then passed the decanter to Norris, who somewhat absentmindedly poured himself a dash.

Thomas seized the moment to study Norris; as always, Manachan's youngest son's mind seemed to be far away—on a different plane, or at least in some different place. He was increasingly getting the feeling that Norris had cut himself off from everything around him. Thomas wondered how Norris spent his days, and made a mental note to inquire…probably of Niniver.

Norris pushed the decanter Thomas's way. He reached out, snagged the neck, and proceeded to pour himself a restrained single finger of the rich malt Manachan favored. Setting the stopper back in the decanter, he considered the relief, and the strange pride, he'd felt over Lucilla inveigling Manachan to agree to her treating him. Sitting back, he felt his lips curve and raised the glass to conceal his smile; she had, in fact, gone one better, and allowed Manachan to couch his agreement in terms of obliging a guest with a challenge.

But Manachan's health was no game.

Thomas sipped and, pretending to have no particular interest in anything beyond the taste of the whisky, waited to gauge his cousins' reactions.

Abruptly, Nigel drained his glass and reached for the decanter again. After sloshing another three fingers into his glass, he slumped back in his chair and looked at Nolan, who was sipping in rather more moderate fashion alongside him. "I don't know that this is wise—allowing her to raise his hopes like this."

His gaze on his glass, on the light refracting through the amber liquid as he turned the crystal between his hands, Nolan shrugged. "We all know it's just age that's made him so. She'll try her tonic, it won't work, and that'll be the end of it."

Thomas noticed that even Norris nodded in agreement. Thomas was puzzled. "How can you know? Has a doctor examined him?"

Nigel snorted. "I suggested it, but you know what he's like. He wouldn't have it—insisted he was just poorly and would come about, but that was last September." Nigel glanced at the glass dangling from his fingers. "I'm just surprised he agreed to letting her, of all people, treat him."

Nolan sipped and mumbled, "It's all nonsense, this healer rubbish. But when it doesn't work…" He shrugged. "Underneath it all, he knows that it's because he's old and his time is coming. I think he agreed because she's a guest, after all, and he's old-fashioned about such courtesies."

Thomas kept his lips shut; it would be easier all around if Nigel as well as Nolan believed that. It would keep them out of Lucilla's, his, and Manachan's hair while Lucilla tested her tonics. And while he was a touch surprised that both Nigel and Nolan, and even Norris if his occasional nods were any guide, had such a poor regard for the healer's arts, it was perfectly possible that, other than with long-ago childhood ailments, they, personally, had never seen the difference a good healer could make in people's lives.

Quite aside from her reputation, he'd seen Lucilla act, not once but twice. There was a young girl, Lucy, who lived with her parents, Jeb and Lottie Fields, in one of the more distant shepherd's cabins, who would not be alive if it hadn't been for a much younger Lucilla. Likewise, the Bradshaws. He would never have thought of the well as the source of their illness. She had—it had been she who saved them.

"Mind you," Nigel said. "I'm rather impressed by her fortitude in remaining after stumbling on that adder. I would have thought she would have run screaming from the house and all the way back to the Vale."

Nolan glanced across the table and caught Thomas's eye. "A bite from an adult adder at this time of year..." Nolan smirked, then hid the expression behind his glass. "I'm surprised, cuz, that you didn't insist on taking her home yourself. After all, you were the one who brought her onto Carrick lands."

Nigel snorted. "Just think what will happen if any harm befalls her while here." Nigel shuddered melodramatically, then drained his glass again—and, again, reached for the decanter.

Cradling his own glass, Nolan nodded. "And—worse—think of what the situation will be if she treats Papa, but instead of getting better, he gets worse. How will the clan react to that news, I wonder?"

There was a malicious glint in Nolan's eyes when they touched Thomas's.

Thomas didn't respond, didn't outwardly react at all, but it took effort to keep his body relaxed, his fingers gently wrapped about his glass. Because regardless of Nigel and Nolan's motives in sending those barbs his way, their comments held more than a passing acquaintance with the truth.

Yet regardless, Lucilla remaining at the manor and treating Manachan was the right path—the one he had to follow for the good of the clan. Moreover, Lucilla, in her capacity as the Lady's local representative, had insisted, and despite the impulses riding him, he had no right to gainsay her.

Rationally, logically, he knew all that, yet his cousins' comments still pricked and prodded that part of him that, when it came to her, was neither rational nor logical. The part that wanted her safe at any cost, and at present, he was fairly certain that meant back in the Vale and away from here.

The Bradshaws. Joy Burns. Faith Burns. And now the adder in the still room. Coincidence could only stretch so far, and his belief in it had died long ago.

Norris drained his glass, set it down, and rose. "I'm going up." He directed a general nod around the table. "Good night."

Thomas murmured a good night in response. Nigel and Nolan just watched Norris leave.

Thomas drained his own glass. He felt no inclination to sit with Nigel and Nolan; if he did, he might be tempted to raise issues that, at present, would be better left unbroached—at least until he saw if Manachan regained his strength as Lucilla hoped he would.

Setting down his empty glass, he pushed back from the table.

Nigel and Nolan did the same.

Thomas strolled to the open doorway, went through, then paused and glanced back at his cousins. "I'm going to the drawing room. Will you be joining the company?"

Nolan exchanged a glance with Nigel, then Nigel met Thomas's gaze. "My apologies to Miss Cynster, but Nolan and I have important business to attend to."

Thomas kept his brows from rising in cynical disbelief; instead, he inclined his head and continued on his way.

But at the far end of the corridor, before he turned into the front hall, he paused and glanced back—and in the dimness at the end of the long corridor, saw Nolan follow Nigel through the billiard room door.

Lips twisting cynically, Thomas walked on.

* * *

Nolan leaned over the billiard table and lined up his shot.

Nigel stood at the end of the table, chalking the tip of his cue.

Nolan potted a ball into the side pocket and circled the table to line up another shot.

Nigel stared at the tip of his cue. "Do you think Lucilla's tonic will improve Papa's health?"

Nolan waited until he'd taken his shot, then straightened. His gaze remaining on the table, he shrugged. "Who can say?"

"But she is supposed to be an excellent healer—I've heard people say she's even better than her mother."

"She might be able to make him feel a touch better for a little while, but you know as well as I do that he's simply old. Not even Lucilla has access to the Fountain of Youth. He'll be better for a day or so, and then exhaust himself and slide back again—you know he will. Just like he's done again and again over the last few months." Nolan bent over the table again.

Nigel glanced at him, waited until he took his shot, then softly said, "But what if he *does* get better?" When, straightening, Nolan met his eyes, Nigel went on, "What if he actually recovers enough to see and learn, and understand what I've done? He won't approve—not of any of it. And you know as well as I do that he'll take back the reins, and then we'll be back where we used to be—with no hope of living the sort of life we've only just started to enjoy."

His eyes flaring, Nigel stepped closer to Nolan. "What if he doesn't just overturn the changes, but does something to make sure we can't change things even after he's gone?" Panic had his tone rising. "What if he disinherits us and makes Thomas the laird instead?"

Nolan appeared to consider the prospect, then shook his head. "No—he won't do that. Regardless of all else, he'll never admit you're anything other than the best candidate for the lairdship once he's gone." Nolan drew a slow breath. "And as for the rest, you're making a mountain out of a molehill. Lucilla's no miracle worker. Papa might improve, but only temporarily. She'll leave, and in a day or two he'll slide back again." Nolan turned to the table and bent over it once more. "See if I'm not right."

"But even temporarily might be long enough for him to get wind of what I've done."

Nolan shook his head. "It'll take more than a day or two of improvement before he's back in the library and leafing through the ledgers. And even then, things won't seem to be that different."

Nigel brightened. "I forgot you keep two sets of accounts."

Nolan dropped another ball and straightened. "I told you we might need them, and if we do, everything's there, already in place. Papa can look to his heart's content, and all he'll see is that you running the estate is no great change at all—that all you've been doing is keeping things ticking over, much as he would have done."

Nigel chuckled.

Nolan circled the table to line up the last ball. "But I doubt we'll need our fake ledgers—he's not going to get that far. Trust me—once Lucilla goes home, Papa will lapse again."

Nigel watched the last ball roll into a corner pocket. "The way he's been going, he can't be all that much longer for this world."

Nolan straightened and met Nigel's gaze. "Very likely not."

* * *

Thomas was waiting with Lucilla in the drawing room when Ferguson came to tell her that Manachan was ready to receive her.

Niniver had, again, excused herself and retired as soon as they had finished their tea. Once she had, Lucilla had asked for a more detailed account of what Thomas had discovered when he'd ridden out that afternoon; he'd obliged, and once again, her insightful questions had demonstrated her comprehension of how the local people thought. She understood what others from outside the area would not.

Carrying a lamp to light their way, he walked by her side up the stairs and around the gallery to the door to Manachan's room. He paused and met her eyes. "Ready?"

She blinked. "Of course." Before he could, she reached out and rapped on the panel.

Several seconds later, Edgar opened the door, then stepped back and held it wide. The normally dour man almost smiled. "Thank you for coming, miss." The words were barely a whisper. Edgar waved her into the sitting room to one side. "The laird is waiting for you through there."

"Thank you, Edgar." Lucilla led the way into the room, but just over the threshold, she halted and looked back at Edgar. "I would appreciate it if you were present, too. Your past observations will be helpful."

Edgar inclined his head.

Lucilla turned and swept into the room. She had no idea if Manachan was already regretting agreeing to let her treat him; he could turn crotchety and difficult, but she was determined to keep control of the examination and extract from him—and Edgar, too, if necessary—all she needed to know.

She was somewhat reassured to see that Manachan had changed into his nightshirt; swathed in a multihued velvet dressing robe, he sat waiting in a large, ornately carved straight-backed chair.

Fixing her most professionally reassuring smile on her lips, she inclined her head to him. "Excellent. This will do nicely."

He glowered at her. "I warn you—I haven't let a doctor near me for decades, so if you think to poke and prod me, you'll have to wait until I'm a great deal iller."

She managed not to smile too broadly. "I've no need to poke and prod. I just need to check your eyes, your hands and your feet, and then I'll need you to answer my questions truthfully."

He snorted, but he allowed her to examine his eyes. She noted the paleness of his skin, but it was simply pale, not sickly; the areas around his eyes looked as healthy as they should, with no bruising or indication of current illness. She had Edgar hold a lamp just over her shoulder and studied the faded blue of Manachan's irises at some length.

"What can you see?" he mumbled.

"Your age, for one," she tartly replied. After a moment, she admitted, "I can also see that you had some serious illness, something to do with your digestion and blood, some months ago." The striations were quite clear and sharp; whatever it had been, the attack had been intense.

"Aye," Edgar murmured. "That'd be right."

"Hush, you." Manachan directed a sharp glance at

Edgar as Lucilla stepped back. "Let's see what she comes up with on her own."

She arched a brow at him, but after checking his pulse at both throat and wrist, she moved on to examining his hands and, lastly, his feet and ankles. There was no unnatural swelling, and the color of his nails and cuticles was, for a man of his age, quite good. But his pulse was weaker than she would have liked, and his skin tone, and the resilience of the flesh beneath, could definitely be improved.

How much of his symptoms were due to the length of time he'd been weak and run down, rather than to any irreversible damage, she wasn't yet sure.

Rising, she sat in the second of the pair of straight-backed chairs. Thomas stood at her shoulder, while Edgar took up a similar position behind Manachan's chair. She fixed her gaze on Manachan's face. "Right, then—now I need some answers. First, it appears that you suffered a major gastric attack of some sorts, I would say not quite a year ago. Is that correct?"

Manachan grimaced. "Aye." He nodded. "You're right. That's when this"—he waved at himself, indicating his weakened state—"all started."

"Near to midsummer, it was," Edgar offered.

She nodded. "Very well. Let's start from then." She proceeded to interrogate Manachan as to his symptoms at the time of the attack. Some of her questions made him squirm, but under the combined weight of Thomas's and Edgar's gazes, he grumbled and mumbled his way through the answers. As she had hoped, if Manachan attempted to slide past anything, or not mention something, Edgar was close enough, and assured enough of his position and his place in Manachan's life, to fill in the gap.

By the time her interrogation had advanced to the present day, she had a fairly firm notion of what was ailing the old tyrant.

When he finally rapped out a "Well, what is it? What have I got?" she smiled and rose.

"I'm pleased to say you haven't anything at the moment. You did catch something fairly serious last year, but after this time I can't even begin to guess what it was. You appear to have had a relapse or two in the following months, but you're not ill now, and although you might feel weak and lacking in strength, the only reason for that is that you were, indeed, so dragged down by that recurrent illness that your body simply hasn't bounced back." She held his gaze. "You need a tonic to push your body back onto the road to health again, and then keep it moving forward. Rebuilding your strength won't happen overnight, and I can't promise that you will ever regain the strength you once had, but in time, if you continue to take the medicine I prescribe, you will be much stronger and more able than you are now."

Manachan looked at her, and in his eyes, she could see the hope he tried to hide. "If I can manage to walk up the stairs under my own steam again, I'll be happy."

She tipped her head. "I think that's quite possible."

Manachan grunted. "All right—what do I have to do? No eye of newt, mind."

She laughed. "I can assure you that nothing I give you comes from anything but plants."

He waved at her to get on with her prescription.

"I'll make up what I call a boosting tonic for tonight. You can take it and go to sleep. Tomorrow, when you wake, I expect you will be feeling considerably better."

She looked at Edgar. "Don't wake him but let him sleep until he wakes of his own accord."

"And then?" Manachan demanded.

She looked back at him. "Then I'll examine you again, and depending on how well you've responded to the boosting tonic, I'll make up a restorative to leave with you. That's a syrup that will last much longer—at least several weeks. You'll take doses every mealtime, and it should keep you moving forward into improving health, improving strength."

Manachan studied her for several moments, then he inclined his head. "Thank you."

She held his gaze. "And you promise to take the restorative as prescribed?"

He humphed. "If you had any idea of how much I want and need my strength back, you wouldn't even ask."

Satisfied, she glanced at Thomas; he'd remained all but silent throughout. "I need to get into the still room, but I just realized that Alice has the key."

Thomas nodded to Manachan and waved her to the door. "Ferguson will fetch it for us."

Us, because he wasn't leaving her in the still room alone.

Lucilla looked at Manachan. "I'll wish you a good night. I'll bring the boosting tonic—Edgar can help you take it. Then I'll see you in the morning when you wake. I won't need to see you immediately. Have Ferguson fetch me once you're up and ready for the day."

Manachan nodded. "I will—and if I don't feel much better, be prepared to hear a lot of complaints."

Both Thomas and Lucilla were grinning when they left. But once he drew Manachan's door closed behind them, Thomas sobered. He met Lucilla's green gaze. "Will he be much better?"

She looked into his eyes, then, lips curving, she shook her head. "Oh, ye of little faith." She started for the stairs. "I can tell you that he will definitely be better. How much better, just overnight? That's in the lap of the Lady."

* * *

Thomas sat on a stool in the still room and watched Lucilla work. The soft lamplight laid a gilt sheen over her flame-colored hair and warmed her alabaster skin, leaving her lips a lush rose.

She was totally focused on what she was doing; he might not have been there at all.

And it was intriguing to realize that she allowed him to see her thus—as she was, without any chance of screen or veil, uncaring of—or was it unbothered by?—what he might see as she concentrated on mixing her tonic.

She measured and weighed, and muttered as she did. "Two drops of the hawthorn oil should be enough. Just a hint of betony. And a dash of poppy juice to balance it all out."

He sat and listened to her voice, to its cadence and tone. Regardless of the actual words, her monologue fell on his ears like a soothing litany.

And he realized how comfortable he was, there in what was essentially her domain. He'd never really been inside the still room before; as a child, he'd been sent to the door to ask for an ointment for this or that, but he hadn't dared set foot inside.

Now he sat and breathed deeply, and let the peace of the place—and a strange sense of security and belonging—seep into his bones.

Eventually, Lucilla gave the greeny-yellow concoction she'd mixed in a beaker a final stir, then poured the liquid into a waiting bottle and stoppered it. Setting the bottle aside, she quickly cleared away the various elixirs she'd used, then she glanced around to make sure all was tidy, turned down the still-room lamps, picked up the bottle, and turned to him.

He rose from the stool and lifted the lamp he'd brought with them from the counter. His gaze fixing on the bottle, he murmured, "Let's pray he takes it." So much rode on Manachan's strength returning.

"He will." Lucilla led the way into the corridor. She waited while he closed the door and locked it, then handed her the key. Accepting it, she smiled. "Your curmudgeon of an uncle will never back away from a challenge, and although it's me he challenged, not obeying my instructions will mean he backed away, so he won't do that." As they walked toward the steps to the ground floor, she added, "Besides, he *wants* to get better—everything I saw and heard screams that."

Starting up the steps beside her, Thomas nodded. "He's still the laird, and now that he knows his people need him, he'll do everything he can not to let them down."

They walked into the front hall and made for the main stairs. They climbed, the light from the lamp swinging from his hand creating shifting shadows on the dark paneling.

As they reached the landing, Lucilla murmured, "I've heard Manachan called many unflattering names over the years, but I've never heard anyone ever suggest that he hasn't, always, acted in the best interests of your clan."

Thomas inclined his head. They reached Manachan's door and he tapped on the panel.

Edgar appeared and Lucilla handed over the stoppered bottle. "He has to drink the entire dose, every last drop, and then he can sleep. Send for me when he's ready to see me in the morning."

Edgar had been examining the bottle. He looked at Lucilla and bowed. "Thank you, miss. I'll make sure he drinks it all."

With a nod to Thomas, Edgar shut the door.

Lucilla turned and, with Thomas pacing beside her and the lamp in his hand lighting their way, walked around the gallery toward the visitors' wing and their respective rooms. A sense of anticipation, of pending satisfaction, coursed through her; she was keen to see how much of an improvement her tonic wrought in Manachan by the morning. She had every expectation that the improvement would be significant, and that would rank as a true accomplishment, one she had every intention of building on with the subsequent restorative. On that front, she was eminently pleased with her progress.

But as for progress on the Thomas front, while she hadn't lost ground, neither had she gained enough to feel secure. She had a long way yet to go before she convinced him that his path was entwined with hers—that his future was already defined, and that it lay in the Vale with her.

They walked under the ornately carved archway and into the corridor that ran down the center of the visitors' wing. Despite having stood for several centuries, Carrick Manor was a much younger structure than her home in the Vale. Casphairn Manor was built around the keep of a very old castle, and over the centuries had grown and spread out on all sides; the resulting shape was roughly circular, with the old Great Hall still very much the center of the place, its structural and emotional lynchpin.

Here, there were two separate wings attached to opposite sides of the main wing, which was essentially the original block-shaped manor. Instead of the stone walls of her home, here the walls were plastered and paneled with dark-stained wood. Ceilings were coffered with the same wood, and relatively low compared to those she was accustomed to.

This house had a very different feel. Despite the predominance of pale gray stone, her home was filled with light and warmth, with energy and laughter and the heartbeats and footsteps of many people; it was very much alive. In contrast, Carrick Manor, although inhabited, struck her as sleeping, as somehow dormant, in a form of stasis.

The knowledge swept over her and she suppressed a shiver. Whether it had started with Manachan's illness, or perhaps long before when his wife had died, she didn't know, but the house had drawn back, drawn in, shut down, and was now waiting…although for what, she couldn't say. But unless something happened to breathe life into it again, this house would ultimately die.

Pulling her mind from the thought—she might not know what would bring this house alive again, but she did know it wasn't anything to do with Thomas or herself—she refocused on the long corridor down which they were walking. She still hadn't decided how to advance her cause with Thomas, what her next step should be, yet the doors to the rooms they'd been given lay just ahead, opposite each other toward the end of the wing. That fact alone spoke volumes regarding the lack of proper direction in the household. Unmarried male and female visitors should have been accommodated in separate areas of the house, and despite the disused wing being disused, it was there...

Halting outside the door to her room, she looked at Thomas. "I just remembered—I found Faith Burns's candle. It was what caused me to trip in that corridor." Briefly, she described what she'd found, and where the candle and candleholder had lain.

Even in the poor light, she saw the change in Thomas's expression. Knew that he, too, was struggling to make sense of Faith somehow tripping down the stairs, but the candle landing that far back along the corridor.

She sighed and met his eyes. "I know coincidence is being stretched thin, but...there's one reasonable possibility that might account for the Burns sisters' deaths." He frowned, and she went on, "What if Faith and Joy ate something while they were together and chatting in the kitchen— something poisonous? If Faith ate more of it than Joy, it would have started affecting her first. She could well have become disoriented, taken the wrong turning in the gallery and ended in the disused wing, dropped the candle, then lurched along the corridor, and stumbled and fallen down the stairs. Joy didn't eat as much, so she reached the Bradshaws' farm, spoke with the Forresters, and started work there—but then the poison took hold, and she died, too."

He studied her eyes, thinking, assessing. "Wouldn't you have known if Faith had died from poison, too?"

She considered, then shook her head. "I doubt it, because Faith died of a broken neck, not the poison, and her body lay for so long, by the time I saw it, there was no visible trace of poison. But I doubt there would have been any to find, not unless her body had been discovered immediately and someone had known what to look for."

He stared at her for a long moment, then softly said, "That still leaves us with the question of whether it was poison by intent, or by accident."

"Given we have no evidence of any kind that anyone wanted the sisters murdered, it's hard to argue intent. And as I understand it, anyone in the clan has access to this house, day and night, so even if we harbor suspicions that the deaths weren't accidental, proving who the murderer was will be well-nigh impossible."

He held her gaze. "You've been thinking of this as much as I have."

She raised her chin. "I live in the area. I'm presently sharing the running of the Vale with Marcus. I'm equally responsible, and part of that responsibility is bringing any potential crime to the attention of the magistrate." She paused, then went on, "I have to weigh everything and decide what path is the correct one for the people here. While you and I might speculate and imagine how murder was done, we can prove nothing, not even that it *was* murder, and we have absolutely no notion of who might be responsible for such a crime."

After a moment, his lips tightened, and he inclined his head. "You're right. As much as we might suspect, we have no proof that Joy's and Faith's deaths were anything but terrible accidents."

She waited, watching him—knowing that he was trying to convince himself, to make himself accept that, as matters stood, the correct thing to do for the Carrick clan was to let their suspicions lie, and allow Joy's and Faith's deaths to remain as accidents.

Coincidental accidents. Possibly connected accidents.

She liked the situation no better than he. "If we had any proof," she murmured, "it would be a different story, but we don't, as yet, have any evidence, and even if Joy's canteen shows traces of poison, we have no idea as to who any putative murderer might be. Sir Godfrey Riddle— he's currently the magistrate—won't thank us for need-lessly stirring up a hornet's nest."

Thomas grimaced. "No, indeed." He glanced at her door. He tensed as if to step back, toward the door to his room just a few feet further down the corridor.

Lucilla's pulse spiked. Was she going to allow him to retreat without getting even one step further?

But he paused and his gaze returned to her face. "Thank you—from me, from the clan—for what you're doing for Manachan."

The words were simple, heartfelt.

She didn't stop to think. Instead of inclining her head in acceptance—as he plainly assumed she would—she stepped boldly across the corridor, stretched up, and pressed her lips to his.

And, this time, his response was both immediate and unfettered, unrestrained. He didn't make the slightest attempt to hold back, but immediately engaged, his lips firming against hers, then his free hand rose, and he cupped her head and held her steady as he took control.

Took over the kiss and scripted it to his liking—to his need, his desire. He plunged them both into the mael-strom of their whirling senses and anchored them there, his tongue plundering evocatively, stroking hers, drawing forth and compelling a response that reached deeper, one even more primally visceral than she'd felt before.

She curled her fingers around his lapels and clung as her wits waltzed and her senses spun.

Thomas could have avoided the engagement; he'd read her intent in the glorious green of her eyes in the instant before she'd moved. He could have stepped away, but he hadn't.

Because something in him wanted her.

After walking into the house and hearing her scream, after feeling her shaking in his arms, and now having to accept that he simply didn't know, couldn't be sure, whether a murderer lurked close or not...

Because of all that, he needed this—this contact, this moment.

It was that simple, and that devastating. To know beyond question that—as he'd always suspected—she spoke to that inner him, the primal male who lived inside him, and when she called, that side of him ruled.

She was all fire and promise in his arms, a temptation he couldn't resist, regardless of the fact that he'd made the decision, absolute and irrevocable, that she would never be his. That she wasn't his to take—or, more accurately, that accepting what she was so blatantly offering wasn't what he wanted to do.

Accepting would mean staying—with her, under her spell.

He'd spent a lifetime crafting his own life, ensuring it remained, in all respects, his to determine and define.

He wouldn't—couldn't—give that up, not even for her.

Not even for the paradise he knew he would find in her arms.

Her lure clashed with his self-will, and he was determined that his self-will would be the stronger.

But he could take this much, indulge in one last heated kiss, without risk.

So he took, and gave, and reveled in the heat. In the slick softness of her mouth, in the pliancy of her lips, in the warmth of the curves she pressed against him.

She was a quick study, yet there was much more he could teach her; figuratively taking her hand, he angled his head, pressed deeper, and led her on.

Into a wild exchange weighted with the heady lure of forbidden pleasures, with the dark, pulsing heat of passionate need. Through the kiss, in his mind he could almost see her, a passionate nymph whose flame-colored tresses rippled down her back as she tipped up her head and laughed delightedly, glorying in the sweet rush of arousal, then she plunged into the rushing stream of desire, bathing herself in its heat.

In his heat, his passion.

She opened her heart, her mind, her body, and drew him in. On...

He pulled back, drew back—a primal reaction to the primitive warning of standing on an invisible brink, of being about to take one step too far.

Retreat took more effort, more strength than he'd expected—until that moment, he hadn't comprehended just how definitely he would have to wrestle with himself as well as her.

But this was one battle he wasn't about to lose. He was still holding the lamp in one hand, an added disadvantage. Blindly reaching, he set the lamp down beside him. Finally, *finally*, he lifted his head and forced his hands to do what they had to and set her back, apart from him. Then he dragged in a huge breath.

And looked down, into her emerald gaze.

She blinked up at him, swirling passion still sparking in the jewel depths of her eyes. Her gaze roamed his face, then returned to his eyes. She moistened her lips and simply asked, "Why?"

When he didn't immediately respond, she elaborated, "Why are you resisting this?" She waved between them. "What's between us."

A direct question, one he didn't want to answer, but as he looked into her face and saw both her stubbornness and her honesty clearly writ in her fine features, it occurred to him that answering in the same vein, holding to the same standard of personal clarity, might, in this instance, be the fastest route to ending this. More, to bringing an end to this in the right way, with understanding and honor.

She didn't press him but waited, a tactic only those with supreme self-confidence tended to use.

But he knew his own self-worth, had his own self-confidence. "I have a very clear idea of what my future life will be. I've planned it for years—ever since my parents died and I spent a year here. From that time on, I've been planning my path."

He had her complete attention; with her gaze fixed on his face, she nodded for him to go on.

Drawing breath, he eased back to rest his shoulders against the wall. Briefly, but clearly, he described his life in Glasgow, how he was the principal of Carrick Enterprises, what that entailed and the sort of work he did, all of which flowed into and informed his decisions about the sort of life, and the style of wife, he wanted.

He employed no obfuscation but continued to speak directly, as if to a close friend rather than a would-be lover.

And to his surprise, she listened without any strong reaction that he could see. She heard and drank in everything he said; her attention was of the same quality he'd seen her giving to mixing Manachan's tonic—complete and absolute. And because of that, he didn't need to specifically point out that she—wedded to the Vale as she was, and in several other ways so very much *not* what he was looking for in a wife—didn't fit his bill. Rather than stating that she was far too strong a character, with the potential to be far too demanding, to require too much of him, of his attention, of his time, all he had to do was describe his wife—the lady he needed by his side. A lady with the right social connections in Glasgow, who would keep his house, bear his children, manage his household, and appear on his arm whenever he required her presence.

Lucilla listened to his considered, rational, and no doubt carefully constructed vision, and was mildly surprised to discover that, far from feeling as if her heart was being rent in two, far from experiencing his words as nails crucifying her soul, all she felt was a burgeoning impatience that he was still so far from seeing the truth.

Her confidence in that truth—in the Lady's view— had never wavered, and despite his words, it didn't waver now. And that wasn't simply due to her lifelong belief in the Lady, nor yet her own stubbornness and a general unwillingness to let his direction trump hers.

Her certainty came from something even deeper. From an absolute conviction that, for him and her, there was no alternative, no matter what he thought or said.

He could argue until the cows came home, resist until he turned blue in the face, but he couldn't and wouldn't change the simple fact that he was hers and she was his.

She'd known for years that them being husband and wife was the Lady's wish, Her plan, but until now, until this minute when she sensed that deep, abiding certainty in the bedrock of her soul, she hadn't truly understood the simple fundamental truth.

This wasn't simply a matter of the Lady's decree. This was much more a matter of who they were—he and she.

They were lock and key.

Neither would ever be who they could be, not without the other by their side.

He reached the end of his recitation. His amber gaze sober, steady on her eyes, he softly concluded, "So I hope you now see why..." He paused, then mimicked her earlier gesture, waving between them. "Why this, what's between us, can never come to be."

She understood why he believed so, but she wasn't sure where to go from there. She waited, but no obvious answer came; slowly, still holding his gaze, she inclined her head. "I understand and accept that that's your decision."

At this moment. At this time.

Her lungs felt tight, but even now, she didn't feel cast down. Instead, she understood and accepted that the obstacle blocking their correct way forward was rather larger, and more deeply entrenched in his mind than she'd realized.

She could see in his eyes that her stance—her lack of the sort of fiery response he'd expected from her— was puzzling him. Confusion was already dawning in his eyes.

If he asked, she couldn't explain her position—not now, not yet. She raised her head; pressing her palms together before her, she nodded more definitely. "Thank you for telling me." She tipped her head, her eyes on his. "And now I believe I should bid you good night."

She infused just enough wryness into her expression and tone to ease his mind—to avoid his confusion turning into suspicion, as it would if left unaddressed, undistracted. Subtle relief eased through his body and he pushed upright, away from the wall.

A gentle, reassuring expression on her face, she reached for the doorknob, opened the door, then with a last dip of her head, slipped into her room.

She closed the door and leaned back against it.

Several moments passed before, beyond the panels, she heard him shift, then she heard the soft click as he opened the door to his room, followed by another click when he closed it.

He'd stood staring at her closed door for those moments; no matter he hadn't asked, he was wondering what she was thinking.

As to that, she wasn't sure herself.

Moving into the room, she reached for the pins anchoring her hair. A maid had lit the lamp on the dressing table. In the low light, she got ready for bed, going through the motions absentmindedly, her mind absorbed with the critical question: So, what now?

Now she knew of his direction, what should she do? Was the next move hers, or his?

By the time she turned down the lamp and climbed between the sheets, she'd achieved some degree of clarity on that point.

Because everything hinged on "claiming"—on reciprocal, mutual claiming.

She'd always known that, between them, "claiming" was the operative word. That in order to have the life they were supposed to live, he had to claim her and she had to claim him.

But claiming was an active decision—no one could be made to claim something they didn't wish to. Claiming was the same as a declaration, open and clear and unequivocal. A deliberate decision, one everyone could see.

She couldn't force him to that decision. Not even the Lady could. The decision to accept what she was offering, the decision to claim the position by her side, had to be made of his own free will.

The most she could do was persuade, and in the circumstances, given his view of his future, it seemed clear that whatever opportunity presented, she would be wise to seize it and use it to that end.

She couldn't afford to simply sit back and let him barrel ahead. He was stubborn, even more stubborn than she. She was going to have to use every wile, every weapon she possessed and that fate sent to her hand, to open his eyes and show him the truth.

Whether she would succeed or not, she didn't know—couldn't tell—but she had no choice.

Turning on her side, she tugged the covers up over her shoulder. "At least we've both acknowledged the existence of 'what's between us.'"

Closing her eyes, she followed that point further.

And smiled. She'd never had the chance to play the siren before.

While she considered the prospect, sleep drew her down.

* * *

She woke in the dead of night with no notion of what had disturbed her.

She'd left the window beside the head of the bed uncurtained. Faint moonlight streamed in, casting everything in grays and shadow.

Then she heard a stealthy sound, the quiet placing of a shoe on carpet.

She pushed back the covers, raised her head, and looked.

And saw a man in a cowled cloak, a cushion held between his hands, mere steps away.

Creeping closer.

She screamed and flung up her hands, ready to keep the cushion from her face.

To keep him from smothering her.

That was clearly his intention.

His head lifted. For a split second, he paused, then he cursed, flung the cushion aside, and charged for the open door.

He swung into the corridor. She heard his thudding steps pounding down the corridor runner, fading away.

A door crashed against a wall, and Thomas appeared in her open doorway. He'd thrown a loose robe over his nightclothes, although he didn't appear to be wearing a shirt. Gripping the doorframe, he stared across the room at her, then he looked in the direction the man had fled.

He cursed, too.

She'd come up on her elbows as the man had raced off. Now, suddenly struggling to breathe, she clapped a hand to her chest, over her racing heart, and fell back on the pillows.

Thomas hesitated, then stepped into the room and

shut the door. Her scream had been enough to summon him, but the visitors' wing was long and their rooms were near its end; he couldn't hear anyone else stirring, much less racing to her rescue. "What happened? All I glimpsed was a shadowy figure disappearing into the gallery—they were too far away for me to see clearly."

She'd closed her eyes; she raised her lids a fraction, studied him for several long seconds, then said, "Some man."

Her voice was thready. Coming up on her elbows, she looked about; her gaze came to rest on the pitcher of water and glass on the bureau.

Thomas found himself standing before the bureau, pouring a glass of water, before he'd even thought.

Indeed, at that moment, he wasn't thinking well at all; his entire brain seemed overloaded with impulses, furious anger, and rising need. He would have preferred to somehow levitate the glass over to her but... He walked to the bed and handed it to her.

"Thank you." The underlying tremor in her voice raked across his senses.

Taking the glass, she sipped, then sipped again, then she closed her eyes and sighed. "Before you ask, no, I have no idea who he was." Her voice quavered, and she waved to the other side of the bed. "I woke up, and he was there." Opening her eyes, she clutched the glass in both hands, then said, "He had a cushion in his hands and was coming closer."

The vision chilled him to the marrow. Rounding the bed, he saw the cushion, lifted from the armchair closer to the door and now flung against the legs of the dressing-table stool. He bent and picked up the cushion. It was nice and plump. Perfect for holding over a woman's face...

He very nearly snarled and flung the cushion away. Reining in the impulse, he carefully placed the cushion on the stool, then turned to her.

And noticed the moonlight shafting through the window. He looked at her. "You didn't see his face?"

She shook her head. "No. He had a cowl up over his head. He'd pulled it forward. It completely shaded his features. I didn't even catch a glimpse of his chin."

His face felt like granite; he couldn't manage even a grimace. "So it could be anyone—anyone at the manor, anyone in the clan."

She didn't answer, just closed her eyes again. Her chest rose and fell as she breathed deeply. Reaching for calm.

"Are you all right?" The question fought its way out of his chest and emerged in a tone one step from a growl.

She didn't open her eyes, but her head shifted as if she was considering... "I took no harm, but I'm not sure, at this moment, that that equates with being 'all right.'"

He glanced at the closed door, then at the armchair. "I'll remain for a while." In case her attacker returned; he truly hoped the bastard would. He started for the armchair.

"Wait."

The command brought him up short. He glanced back and watched her open her eyes and sit up, reaching, stretching, trying to place the glass on the small table beside the bed.

He stalked back to the bed, took the glass from her, and set it on the table.

Her fingers locked in the silk of his robe.

He wasn't wearing a nightshirt; the brush of her thumb against his skin sent desire lancing through him.

He looked down at her hand, at the knuckles white beneath her fine skin. As declarations went, it was fairly clear. "Lucilla..."

He couldn't look at her face, not while standing at the side of her bed, with her en déshabillé a mere foot away, with her skin warm and her hair sleep-tousled—the whole made even more compelling by the inevitable consequence of shock and fear he knew he would see in her wide green eyes.

He knew he shouldn't look, not if he wished to save himself, and her, from what raged inside him.

From the primal, primitive urges that her scream and the need swimming in her eyes had sent rocketing through him.

Possession had never felt so desperately *needful*.

Desire had never ripped at him so powerfully, with such sharp claws.

"Stay."

The single word had him meeting her eyes. They captured his soul.

"Stay." Her lips moved again, a siren whispering in the night. "Stay and be my protector until dawn."

He swallowed, fighting, battling his own urges as well as her. "The armchair," he croaked. He felt amazed he'd managed even that much.

Without easing her grip, she shifted and swung around, then smoothly rose onto her knees. Fisting her free hand in the other side of his robe, she held him. Anchored him.

She held him even more tightly with her eyes.

The green was deeply shadowed, but he could still feel her power, the heated caress of that passionate fire that was such an intrinsic part of her.

"Here," she said. "With me. In this bed."

He opened his mouth, but no words came out.

Her lips curved; intent and more burned in her eyes. "That isn't a request." She tugged with both hands, hauling him to her. "You're mine, and I need you."

She pulled him the last inch and pressed her lips to his.

Ten

He was hers—he *could* be hers—for tonight. For just one night.

He told himself that even while he closed one hand over hers, clamped it against his chest and fought her for control—of the kiss, of the engagement that was already spiraling out of control, either hers or his.

Dangerous. *Beyond* dangerous.

But oh, so very needed.

So necessary.

For them both.

Some part of him recognized that. The rest didn't care—not about anything but having her in his arms.

Her lips holding his captive, hands clenched in his robe, she tipped backward. He started to topple, realized, and sank one knee onto the edge of the mattress, held back, held fast, and caught her against him.

Not a wise move, yet the alternative would have been much worse. He could feel passion's fire licking over his skin, heat flaring everywhere her lithe body pressed to his. Then, leaning back against his hold, she hauled his robe wide, released the sides, and her hands were on him.

On his skin, palms like hot silk sweeping across his chest—burning him.

Branding him.

Alarmed, some part of him tried to pull back; the rest rejoiced and gloried.

Dipping his head, he wrenched control of the kiss fully from her. Pressing her lips wide, he ravaged her mouth. For one finite instant, he caught her full attention and held it—seized her senses and trapped them in the hot melding of their lips. Focused them both on the heated communion, on the evocative plundering—and her hands, those greedy hands, stilled.

He almost caught his mental breath, but temptation whispered. Locking one arm about her waist, he raised his hand, cupped and held her face, angled her head, and took the kiss one step deeper—into the realm of more primitive possession. He held her trapped, his to take from as he wished, and he took—claimed—more.

And wondered if she would take fright and retreat.

Vain hope? Or unwelcome fear?

Regardless, he should have known better. She barely paused to find her feet in the sensual maelstrom he'd unleased before she met him, boldly matched his aggression with her own fire, her tongue dueling wantonly with his.

She plunged them both into a battle for supremacy, one it seemed neither could win. Despite his expertise, whatever move he made, she was there, countering, enticing—forever tempting, challenging, and luring him on.

Deeper into the madness.

He knew he should resist, that he ought to call a halt and draw back.

He didn't.

Couldn't...wouldn't...

The brutal truth was he couldn't make himself step

away from what she offered. Not tonight. Not when her scream still echoed in his ears and all it had called forth still raged through his blood.

Demanding.

Her.

She—here, now, in this way—was exactly the reassurance everything that was male within him hungered for.

And if, even after her entreaty, he harbored any doubts of her desire, she was hell-bent on eradicating them. She remembered her hands and reached again, fingers splaying, gripping, fingertips sinking evocatively—demandingly—into the muscles of his upper chest, kneading like some imperious cat. Splintering his concentration, snagging and fixing his attention on the heat of her touch, the blatant desire burning behind it.

Then she pushed her palms flat to his skin again, ran them up, over his shoulders, now bared, and up to the column of his neck.

His breath caught; his chest tightened.

Cupping his nape, she slid the fingers of her other hand into his hair, slowly, seductively ruffled the dark locks, then she gripped.

She tipped back and succeeded in toppling them onto the bed.

Lucilla landed on her back. He landed half over her, half beside her. She would have grinned triumphantly if she hadn't been so deeply immersed in their kiss that even breathing no longer seemed worthy of attention. Nothing could possibly compete with this—with the clear and present sense of physical connection. Of unscreened, unrestricted physical communion.

She'd always imagined that a kiss—a true kiss between lovers—would be like this—open, direct, and heated.

With no screens, veils, or polite modesties to mute the power of their burgeoning need, to shield them from the conflagration.

They—he and she—didn't need shielding.

Even as the thought slid through her mind, they were already reaching, seeking more.

Opportunity had come knocking, as she'd hoped, albeit not in any way she'd imagined. And yes, she'd seized the moment, but she hadn't been driven by anything so logical or deliberate as tactics or strategy. She'd reached for him and pulled him into her arms because—as she'd admitted—she *needed* him.

Needed to hold him, to feel his hard body against hers, and feel *alive*. Feel as truly, gloriously alive as only he could make her.

She needed this—him, here, now. Them, together, wrestling amid the rumpled covers of her bed, lips locked, mouths melded, body against body, hands on heating flesh as their senses rioted and their hearts surged, and they filled their minds with each other.

With their passion and its inherent power.

She finally succeeded in tugging and pushing his robe far enough down his arms that he softly cursed through the kiss, then drew his hands from her, from where they had held her, as if debating whether to attempt to hold her back, and with swift, jerky movements, he stripped his arms of the sleeves.

Instantly, she whisked the material away, blindly flung the garment off the bed, and immediately returned her hands to him. To the heavy curves of his shoulders, the broad sweep of his chest, created by some master celestial sculptor expressly to make her senses salivate.

Bracing his forearms on the pillows on either side of

her, he sank back into the kiss, his tongue stroking heavily over hers. She tipped her head back, hands grasping his sides as she urged him over her—and he obliged. Shifting so she had even greater access to the splendors of his body—his heavy chest, broad and so superbly muscled, his ridged abdomen, and the relative hollow of his stomach.

She touched, traced, caressed all she could reach. His skin burned from within, pulled taut over muscles tense and tight. A smattering of coarse hair teased her fingertips. She brushed her fingers back and forth, and felt him battle a shudder.

Sensed the hunger that rose to that simple touch.

In him, and in her.

He was leaning on his forearms, holding his weight off her. His hands framed her face, his fingers tangling in her hair.

And suddenly the kiss was not enough. Nowhere near enough to appease her rising need.

She traced the sculpted beauty of his back, ran her hands down, reached as far as she could. Slipping her fingers beneath the drawstring waist of his sleeping trousers, she ran greedy, grasping fingers over the upper curves of his buttocks.

Muscles bunched, flexed, then hardened.

Through their kiss, she felt the fracturing of his attention—could all but see, watch, as he battled to restrain the impulses she'd provoked.

Deliberately, she slid her hand around the curve of his hip, sweeping forward to capture—

He caught her wrist in a viselike grip.

Broke from the kiss enough to growl, "Not yet."

"No" she wouldn't have accepted, but "not yet" she could live with. At least for another minute.

Perhaps two.

She gave him the moment, twisted her wrist, and when, his senses alert and watchful, he eased his hold, she drew her hand from his and slowly skimmed it upward between them. Knowing that, with their lips still parted by a breath, almost brushing but not, he was following the movement of her wayward hand, she walked her fingers up the placket of her nightgown. Halting at the top button, she slid it free.

On a tortured groan, he closed his eyes and dropped his forehead to hers. "You are going to be the death of me."

She debated being offended. Instead, she tipped her head enough to trace the soft upper edge of his lower lip with the tip of her tongue. "Not true."

Her whispered words washed like fire over the flesh she'd just slicked. Thomas felt his entire body clench, as if she'd licked him elsewhere.

But she wasn't finished. "To you, I will always bring life. This—you and me like this—is as things should be. Life for us as it needs to be."

There was so much certainty in her tone; with those simple words, she pushed aside the doubts and questions his more rational, cautious side had been piling up in his brain.

This—her and him together in her bed—didn't fit with his plan for his life. He didn't know—had no idea— how it might fit with hers. But here and now, none of that mattered; as her words had confirmed, this was what needed to be.

That undeniable need—to have her beneath him, her

long, slender legs wrapped about his hips as he drove deep within her—still thrummed, an irresistibly compelling beat in his blood.

A beat that, through the last minutes, had only grown more insistent.

And with every prompt, every push from her, that need only grew. Escalated.

He opened his eyes—in time to see her slide another of the tiny buttons free. Her white nightgown, the placket edged with delicate lace, gaped enough to expose the swell of one surprisingly plump breast.

The sight transfixed him. She was so slender, he'd thought...

His mouth watered.

On a half-smothered groan, he tipped her chin up, recaptured her mouth—anchored them both for one fleeting moment, long enough to submerge their senses in the kiss. Then he brushed her hand aside and, with expert flicks of his fingers, rapidly undid button after button.

Then with the back of his hand, he brushed one side of her nightgown wide and set his hand to the taut mound of her breast.

Just that one touch, silken skin to his palm, and he knew there could be no going back.

Her heart leapt at his touch; as his fingers closed about the tight peak, he felt her senses soar.

His did the same.

Her flesh firmed beneath his hand, heated and with skin unimaginably delicate and fine; her nipple, already puckered, ruched tight as he rolled it between his thumb and forefinger, a pearl just begging him to caress it with his lips, to taste it with his tongue. To lick.

Deserting her lips, he bent his head and did. He

licked, laved, then drew the tight bud into his mouth and suckled.

Her fingers clenched tight in his hair as she swallowed a small scream. He licked again, and she arched beneath him, her body undulating beneath his in a provocative, infinitely arousing surge...

Any lingering possibility of somehow bringing this engagement to some end other than total intimacy vaporized. The last shreds of his resistance fell, fled.

Blown apart, blown away by the tide of sheer need— his and hers combined—that erupted and raced through them both.

From that point on, there was no him and her, no separate thoughts, no individual agendas. All they knew was one driving need, an overwhelming urgency that flooded them both.

He couldn't rein it back; he couldn't contain it. The best he could do was to steer it, and even that much control was tenuous and shaky.

Driven, at the mercy of that urgent need, he stripped her of her nightgown and she urged him from his trousers.

Then she wrapped her fingers about his straining erection, and he thought—for several excruciatingly tense seconds—that he'd died.

Or that he would spend before he got inside her.

His jaw felt as if it might have cracked, but he found the strength to open his eyes and *not* focus on the delight in her face as she explored and traced.

He managed to force his limbs to his bidding. He caught her hands, drew them from him, then, raising her arms, he bore her back down, anchoring her hands in the froth of the pillows on either side of her fiery head.

Their bodies met, naked skin to skin.

He'd forgotten just how potent that first jolt of sensation could be—how momentarily disorienting.

Lucilla's senses seized. Her eyes remained open, but she couldn't see. The feel of him, of his skin so hot, of his muscled strength surrounding her, pinning her—covering her in this most primitive of ways—stole her breath.

Stole her senses and claimed her mind.

His hands held hers trapped, the weight of his arms anchoring hers to the bed, the broad sweep of his chest pressing against her breasts, declaring his dominance. His hips lay heavy over hers, immobilizing her; the columns of his thighs felt like steel between hers.

She should have felt fear, or at least wariness. With any other man, she would have.

But with him...gripping his hands, she opened her senses wide—wider—the better to drink in every last scintilla of tactile sensation.

Of the raw intimacy of his naked body lying atop hers, of his skin, hot and rough, firing hers, abrading hers—feeding her passion.

With effort, she drew in a tight—so tight—breath.

As he did the same.

Her breasts rose as his chest expanded; the swollen mounds flattened against his hard planes, her tightly furled nipples pressing into his skin.

She blinked, refocused. For one instant, in the soft shadows of the bed, their eyes met—hers felt impossibly wide. Their gazes locked. Time stood still for just that instant, then he dipped his head.

He found her lips with his. She parted them, welcomed him in, then drew him deeper. The kiss was all liquid heat, desire made manifest, the thrust of his tongue a presaging of the joining and sharing to come.

He angled his head and plunged deeper yet, and their passions rose and whirled again, higher, then higher.

She let go and followed, surrendering again to the compelling beat fashioned of need, of desire and yearning.

When he drew back from the kiss, she let him go without complaint. The kiss had been intense enough to leave her senses reeling. Feeling him draw away, his hands releasing hers as he eased down the bed, she lay with every nerve on high alert, tense and flickering, and waited, expectant, to see what came next.

Slow down, slow down, slow down. Thomas repeated that mantra as he slid down her body. His didn't want to comply, but it was obvious a little finesse was required. He was large, distinctly so, and she...wasn't.

No matter how experienced she might be—and of that he really had no idea—given he didn't want to, couldn't bear to, hurt her, he needed to find the strength to slow them down...

The only way he could think of to do so was to spread her legs, wedge his shoulders between, and dip his tongue in her nectar.

Predictably, she shrieked, but as she'd earlier proved, no one would hear her. Only him—and, he discovered, he liked hearing her scream with pleasure. So very different from her screaming with fear.

Those delectable screams grew increasingly breathy; she grew increasingly breathless as he ministered to her senses and his. Her tartness was ambrosia on his tongue; the restless, needy, almost mewling sounds he eventually drew from her were exactly what he'd hoped to achieve.

With calculated expertise, he drew the nubbin of her pleasure between his lips and flicked it with the tip of his tongue.

And sent her flying.

She shattered on a broken scream.

After one last long lick, he rose, shifting over her. His body aching with need, he settled his hips between her widespread thighs.

Her slickness coated the head of his erection in scalding welcome; even before he'd thought, he'd flexed his spine and pushed past her tight entrance.

He caught his breath.

Letting his head hang, he closed his eyes against the sight of her lying wantonly naked and spread beneath him. He forced himself to pause and breathe in. Deeply. His muscles bunched and shifted as he fought down the urge to thrust in to the hilt. She was tight and hot and open to him—his to take, to claim.

He didn't need to be brutal about it.

When he was sure he had enough control to last the distance, he eased his reins and pushed further. Deeper.

Even though she was all but boneless, he felt her tense; he halted, but almost immediately her tension eased, faded. In the next heartbeat, she raised her arms and wrapped them about his chest. Reaching, holding. Her hands flattened on his back and pressed; wordlessly, she urged him on.

Dragging in another tortured breath, he held it and obliged, forging deeper into her slick sheath, aware of the tightness as he stretched her… He paused and eased back a fraction, then he flexed his hips and thrust in.

She tipped her hips at the same moment.

He ended fully embedded in her body. She gave a soft,

smothered squeak, and his mind seized as she clamped, hard, all along his length.

The membrane that had marked her virgin had been barely there. She was twenty-eight, had ridden all her life, yet even though, from her flagrant encouragement, he'd assumed that she'd long ago indulged in the act, he'd had just enough mind left to register the slight resistance, the sudden give—and know.

Opening his eyes, he stared down at her in shock and confused disbelief, but she didn't open her eyes and look back. All he saw was the faintest hint of awareness crossing her features—leading him to imagine what she was so suddenly aware of—and then she moved. Smoothly shifting beneath him, relentlessly and inescapably she urged him into the age-old dance.

His mind shut down. His senses whirled.

He closed his eyes and answered her call, responded to the primal rhythm she set, and joined with her and rode on. He was unable to do anything else, even to pause long enough to ask…a question she clearly didn't wish to answer, at least, not then.

Not with the fires of passion, finally released and free, raging through them.

Not with need sinking its spurs deep, then deeper, driving them, raking them, forcing them on.

The flames they'd spent the last half hour stoking rose up and engulfed them.

And they rode. She might have been a novice, but she knew the ways of this riding. Knew when to cling and hold him in her body, when to release and let him pull back.

So he could drive into her again, and drive them both on.

Into the landscape of their melded desires, created

from the interlocking complementary aspects of their passionate souls.

That they were well matched—in passion, in desire, and, tonight, in need—could not have been clearer.

They moved as one, increasingly confidently, increasingly forcefully, driving and urging each other on.

They gasped, clung, panted; breaths mingling, skins slick, she writhed, he plundered, and they strove for yet more.

To you, I will always bring life.

With crystal-like clarity, he remembered the last time she'd done exactly that, when he'd been running through the forests as Herne, god of the hunt. She'd seen him, known him, and had saved him from a hunter's bullet.

It seemed, now, that he was running as Herne again— the same ancient, thudding, repetitive beat filled his heart and pounded through his veins—and she was there again, with him again, his goddess come to claim him.

Naked and willingly spread beneath him, she offered herself to him, his to claim in return.

With her passion and her power, she held him to her and urged him on, and he plunged deeper into her fire, deeper into the slick heat of her body, and wild and free, together they raced on.

Together through the heat, the raging flames, through the tumult of their combined desires.

Beneath the skin, she was as wild as he, as unfettered. As unrestrained in her pleasure, as open in her ardor.

Angling his head, he found her lips, supped, then sank deeper, another element of this untamed mating.

And suddenly they were there, teetering on the cusp of paradise.

He hung back for one second, and she sank her nails into his back—in desperation, scored his skin.

He thrust deep and she shattered.

And took him with her.

Straight over the edge into the blinding heat of ecstasy.

And on, on. The cataclysm wracked them, wrung from them the last drops of their passion, then left them limp, clinging to each other as glory bloomed, spread, and dragged their senses down.

* * *

Sprawled on his back with Lucilla slumped across his chest, her long hair in glorious disarray, the tendrils warm where they caressed his body, he slowly returned to the land of the living, his mind swimming up from the depths of satiation.

A satiation deeper than any he'd previously known.

He frowned as his mind fully re-engaged. Eyes still shut, he considered, compared.

He'd never experienced anything remotely similar in his not-uneventful, considerably varied, and extensive sexual life.

He didn't understand why that should be so; they hadn't done anything he hadn't done countless times before, yet…

The notion that the quite startling result might be because it was *Lucilla* he'd finally indulged in the act with wasn't one he wished to examine too closely.

The truth hit him like a brick. He'd finally succumbed and had surrendered to the attraction between them, and to her, and let both lead him here, to this. They'd shared their bodies; he was sharing her bed. Very definitely the last thing he'd wanted to do and the last place he'd wanted to find himself.

Yet despite that…he didn't regret it. Couldn't even pretend enough to conjure the emotion. Even so…

Opening his eyes, he glanced at her, but her head was tucked down, her cheek resting on his chest; he couldn't see her face. "That was your first time." He didn't make it a question.

"Yes." The admission sounded…dreamy. She was clearly still awash with pleasure.

He tried not to feel smug, but failed.

Slowly, languorously, she rolled over in his arms until her breasts were pressed once more to his chest. Her still naked breasts; he wasn't about to complain.

Finally lifting her head, she looked into his face, into his eyes. He couldn't guess what she saw there, but after several moments, her lips slowly curved, then she patted his chest, turned again, and settled as she had been, her head over his heart.

"My decision," she softly said. "Not yours."

He wasn't sure he liked that; wasn't sure he liked the implication. He'd been very much an equal participant.

That said, despite the extreme provocation of the situation they'd been plunged into earlier that night, with her so shaken and him so ridden by a protective possessiveness he even now didn't fully comprehend, he would have done the gentlemanly thing and walked away—if she had let him. His resistance would have held if she hadn't demolished it with her insistence.

Only hours prior to that, he'd done the right thing and told her, clearly and unequivocally, why he and she could never develop a formal relationship. Why they could never marry. There had been several strands in his reasoning, all contributing to that conclusion, and she'd understood them all. More, she'd said so.

She'd known he and she would never wed, yet she had—as she'd just confirmed—made her own decision to take him to her bed.

To demand he share it with her.

She—and the situation—had made it well-nigh impossible for him to refuse.

He wondered what that meant in terms of where they were now.

She'd relaxed in his arms, but she wasn't asleep. Briefly, he hugged her tighter to get her attention. "So this is what? Your first fling?"

She didn't immediately answer. Then she shrugged the shoulder not pressed to his chest. "It is what it is." She paused, then more quietly added, "And I'm content with that."

He couldn't think of anything to say in response— nothing that he wanted, at that point, to say.

And while there were several other pertinent questions he wanted to ask—such as whether she would consider indulging again later—he didn't feel now was the moment for such inquiries.

He thought, then murmured, "I'll stay until dawn."

"Yes. Please." She settled deeper into his embrace. "Until then...at least."

Another statement he saw no reason to challenge. Closing his eyes, he let his senses sink back into the satiation that still had a firm grip on his body, and was waiting, still, to snare his mind.

* * *

Lucilla left her room and headed for the dining room, eager to discover what effect the events of the night would have on more mundane interactions between Thomas and her.

She'd spent a lifetime following her instincts, even when they'd urged her to acts that, on the face of it, had at first led to what seemed like disasters. In the clearer light of hindsight, said disasters had always proved to be turning points leading to the correct path—not just for her but for all those involved.

Last night, she'd followed her instincts. They'd spoken loud and clear, and she'd surrendered herself to their guidance. She'd followed their insistent compulsion without question, without hesitation.

And had reaped a glorious reward. A reward that had been a great deal *more* than she'd expected.

She had thought she'd known, that she'd understood, but the clinical explanations and whispered confidences hadn't prepared her for the sheer, glorious physicality of the act. At moments—such as when he'd first joined with her—her senses had nearly overloaded; she hadn't had any notion of how it would *feel*—what it would feel like to have him inside her like that, stretching and filling her *like that*, with such strength and weight, such raw male power.

And the sensations associated with that fabulous muscled power had rolled on through the ensuing intimate engagement.

Lips curving, she paused at the head of the stairs as the memories rolled through her, leaving remembered warmth beneath her skin. Thus far, her instincts had proved correct, and a lifetime of experience reassured her that, in this instance, too, her instincts' directives had started her and Thomas down the road they needed to take.

She didn't know the details of how matters would work out, only that they would.

Serenely assured, and in exceedingly fine fettle, she swept down the stairs and on toward the dining room. She and Thomas had slept until dawn, then they'd woken and indulged in another bout of lovemaking, one much slower and gentler, yet regardless, the moments had left her feeling as if sensation had been lavishly burnished over every inch of her skin.

When she'd woken again, not long ago, he'd been gone. While she'd been washing, she'd heard his door open and close. His footsteps had paused outside her door, but then he'd walked on.

Now, seated at his usual place at the table, he'd heard her footsteps; he was looking at the doorway when she walked through. His gaze locked on her face, searched her features.

She smiled—for one instant, let all the effervescent joy and delight bubbling inside her show—and saw his gaze—indeed, all of him—still, then he blinked. Then, eyes widening a fraction in warning, he glanced at Niniver and Norris, who were seated at the table with their backs to the door.

By the time Niniver turned and smiled a shy welcome, Lucilla had muted her smile to one of mere contentedness.

"Good morning," Niniver said. "Did you sleep well?"

Lucilla turned to the sideboard to mask her grin. "Excellently well, thank you." She laid two pieces of toast on a plate. "And you?" Turning, she glanced at Niniver—then raised her eyes and met Thomas's gaze.

Niniver shrugged. "I always sleep well, but it is my own bed. I thought you might have been more unsettled." Niniver moved the teapot to within reach of Lucilla's chosen place as, circling the table, she took the chair Thomas rose and held for her—the one beside his.

She settled her skirts, intrigued to discover that her awareness of him, of his nearness as he resumed his seat, although still strong, seemed to have a softer edge, a more gentle impact.

Niniver stirred her tea. "I wanted to ask…have you seen Papa yet? Was he improved by your tonic?"

"I haven't yet seen him." Lucilla glanced at Norris, but other than a vague nod in her direction as she'd sat, he seemed thoroughly absorbed with the food before him. If he had any interest in his father's health, she could see no sign of it. Transferring her gaze to Niniver, who was much more transparently concerned, she went on, "The Burns sisters' funeral is to be held this morning— I expect I'll examine him before we leave for that. I'm sure he'll want to attend, and indeed, I hope my tonic will have done enough overnight to make the occasion easier for him."

Thomas relaxed beside Lucilla and listened with one ear as she and Niniver discussed the details of the joint funeral. Niniver knew the clan's habits as well as all those involved…Thomas knew, too. He didn't really need to refresh his memory. That left him free to continue puzzling over all that had happened since he'd retired to his bed the night before.

So much had changed between then, and when, this morning, he'd returned to his room, albeit not to his bed. Lucilla and he…he still couldn't quite understand why he'd acquiesced to her necessity, acceded to her demands and stepped so far from the path he'd been so determined to tread.

What he understood even less was why, even now, even recognizing what had happened, he still did not feel the least perturbed.

What he felt was…a curious hiatus. As if he were living in a different world, on a different plane, in some other, alternate reality to that of his life in Glasgow.

As if this life with her and that one did not connect, did not touch, did not impinge on each other.

Stay and be my protector until dawn.

Here. With me. In this bed.

That isn't a request.

This—you and me like this—is as things should be. Life for us as it needs to be.

It is what it is, and I'm content with that.

All words she'd said, and every one had held the ring of truth. For all her inexperience, she seemed to see this—whatever it was that had grown and then flared so powerfully between them—more clearly than he did.

Given that, given the unwavering self-assurance he could feel radiating from her with respect to him, her, and them together, he was fast coming to the conclusion that, for however long their liaison lasted, his best way forward might well be to follow her lead.

The thought brought him up short, made him mentally blink.

For the last twenty years, ever since his parents had been taken from him, he hadn't followed anyone else's lead, had allowed no one to arrange his life for him. He'd followed his guardians' advice not because they were his guardians but because that advice had furthered his own self-determined ambitions.

Yet now, even though he stood at a pivotal point in his

wider life, he was contemplating—more, advocating—following Lucilla's lead.

He turned his head and looked at her. Studied her face as she spoke to Niniver, and wondered what spell she'd worked on him.

Sensing his gaze, she glanced at him. She searched his eyes, then faintly arched a brow.

Suppressing a frown—he could detect no sign that she was intent on bending him to her will, nor could he see any reason why she should be—he shook his head slightly.

"So…" Niniver was frowning down at her hands and had missed their exchange. "When will you start the next stage of Papa's treatment?"

Looking across the table, Lucilla replied, "Assuming I examine him before we leave for the church, then when we return after the funeral, Alice and I will make up a restorative—something he can continue to take that will build on the improvement I hope he'll have experienced overnight."

She placed her napkin beside her plate and glanced at Thomas as she pushed back from the table. "Which reminds me that I should check with Alice in the still room."

Thomas rose and drew back her chair. She met his eyes and smiled—a private smile between them.

He held her gaze. He hesitated, but then nodded. "Have them fetch me when Manachan calls for you. I'm sure he will before getting ready for the funeral." His lips twisted wryly. "Either he will, or Edgar will remind him."

She smiled and inclined her head. "Indeed."

Entirely satisfied with how matters were progressing on all counts, with a nod to Niniver, she left the room.

* * *

Thomas quit the dining room shortly after Lucilla. He resisted the urge to reassure himself that she was safe in the still room; at his suggestion, Ferguson had stationed a footman in the lower passageway within sight of the still room door, with orders to go in and sit inside once Lucilla arrived.

While she remained on Carrick lands, until they solved the mystery of whatever was going on, and until he understood who had come to her room last night and why, she would be watched over.

Going out of the front door, he circled the house to the side terrace, where he could be assured of privacy while he paced.

Lucilla seemed to have shrugged off last night's attack—if it had been an attack. He'd got the impression that, as in the end nothing had happened—and indeed, the incident had given her the opportunity to indulge in an activity she'd clearly wished to embrace—in her view all was… How had she put it? *It is what it is, and I'm content with that.* Although she'd been speaking of what lay between them, the same words seemed an accurate reflection of her attitude to the man who had crept up on her while she'd slept, a cushion clutched in his hands.

Thomas felt his face harden. It had to be comforting to have such faith and belief in fate, for want of a better term, but he was much less sanguine. He remained deeply unsettled by the incident. And, even more, by how it might connect with all the other odd things that had been, and apparently still were, going on.

Yet as he'd told her, the man could have been any

clansman; everyone knew the manor doors were never locked, and most knew the layout of the house well enough to look for her in that particular wing.

But had the man actually intended to harm her—or had he come hoping to speak with her, perhaps to warn her, but he hadn't wanted her to wake and scream?

That notion might seem far-fetched, yet Thomas knew of several men in the clan who were...unsophisticated enough to have thought that way.

Halting, he sighed. Turning, he looked out unseeing over the stretch of coarse lawn. The incidents were accumulating. While they yet lacked the evidence necessary to prove it, all the previous incidents up to last night had clearly been acts of malicious intent. The odds favored last night being another.

Which, in turn, suggested his inner conviction that Lucilla herself was in danger, that she, specifically, might now be in the perpetrator's—a murderer's—sights, could very well be true.

He remained staring, unseeing, out over the lawn as the minutes ticked by, then, his face feeling more like stone than flesh, he turned, walked back to the front door, and re-entered the house.

Eleven

Lucilla returned from the Burns sisters' funeral, which had been held at the small local church in the village of Carsphairn, in a carriage with Thomas, Niniver, and Norris.

She spent the short journey finalizing the composition of the restorative she planned to make for Manachan. He'd summoned her to his room a bare half hour before they'd been due to leave the house, but five minutes had more than sufficed to convince them all that his vigor had been almost magically improved, courtesy of her boosting tonic.

He was a long way from full strength yet, but he'd been able to come down the stairs merely leaning on Edgar's arm. He'd been slow, but he hadn't needed any real help in moving his large frame. His legs were still weak, and his balance wasn't certain, but he'd been able to stand by the graveside alongside the vicar with nothing more than a cane to prop him up.

His color, too, had returned, his face more ruddy than pale, and his grip had firmed, too. But for her, his eyes had shown the greatest improvement—that, and the alertness and incisiveness of the mind behind them.

All in all, she was thrilled and deeply satisfied with what she'd achieved—a true reward for a healer.

And if the gratitude directed her way from virtually everyone at the funeral was any guide, the clan as a whole was delighted to see their laird on the road to recovery.

It had been important for them to see Manachan there. He'd sat in the front pew through what had been a short but moving service, and he himself had risen to go to the lectern to deliver the eulogy, a tribute that had brought tears to everyone's eyes.

Subsequently, Lucilla had risen and gone to the lectern; she'd spoken words she'd said before, at other similar ceremonies, binding those who had lived, worked, and died on these lands with the spirit of the land itself— "dust to dust" meant something quite explicit in the Lady's domains.

As one of the few non-clan present, she'd stood a little removed from the grave and had watched the members of the clan as they interacted with each other; sharing grief brought families—in this case, clan families—together. And so it had seemed, with one notable exception. Nigel did not appear to command the confidence, much less liking, of his clansmen. All had been polite and, to some degree, even respectful, but she had to wonder how much of that had been in deference to Manachan's presence. The coolness directed Nigel's way—the standoffishness of the men, let alone the women—had been, to her eyes, marked.

In contrast, Niniver had been embraced, and even Norris had been treated as "one of them." Nolan had hovered, as ever, in Nigel's shadow; Lucilla had got no clear indication of how the clan saw him.

The carriage slowed as it neared the house. She rapidly reviewed her planned composition and mentally nodded; her decisions and selections were sound.

She was, truth to tell, still somewhat puzzled over what, months ago, had brought Manachan low in the first place, but whatever it had been, she'd found the right counter to it. She would reinforce and build on that.

Thomas alighted first and turned to hand her down.

She placed her hand in his and felt the warmth of his clasp through the fine leather of her glove. The sensation was comforting, rather than discombobulating. Taking that as a sign that their relationship had, indeed, turned a corner, courtesy of their endeavors through the night— and feeling distinctly satisfied on that front, too—she walked beside him into the front hall.

Norris, followed by Niniver, made straight for the stairs.

Lucilla paused before the corridor leading to the steps down to the still room and swung to face Thomas. "I'm going to make up Manachan's restorative."

Hearing footsteps in the corridor, she turned to see Alice, who had come back from the church in one of the carts, hurrying up. Alice paused by the head of the steps.

Lucilla smiled and waved her on. "Open up—I'll join you in a minute."

Facing Thomas, she added, "I'll teach Alice to make the composition, so she'll be able to keep Manachan supplied after I've returned to the Vale."

Thomas nodded; since before they'd left for the funeral, his expression had been severe, and it hadn't yet lightened. He met her gaze. "Come and fetch me when you have it ready—I'll go up with you."

Assuming he wanted to ensure Manachan gave some

undertaking to continue with the treatment, she nodded and turned for the steps. "I'll ask Ferguson if I can't find you."

Making the restorative took less than twenty minutes, even repeating the process several times to ensure Alice had the order of additions—in this case, quite critical— correctly memorized.

With the tonic in a stoppered dark blue bottle in one hand, Lucilla climbed the steps to the ground floor, then walked into the front hall, intending to find Ferguson. Instead, she found Thomas sitting in a chair against one wall, long legs stretched before him and crossed at his ankles, his chin on his cravat as he stared broodingly at his booted toes; he looked up at the sound of her footsteps.

Seeing her, he uncrossed his legs and rose. His gaze locked on the bottle in her hand. "Ready?"

"Indeed."

He fell in beside her, and they walked to the main stairs and started up.

She waited until they reached the landing before saying, "Choosing the right ingredients for a restorative is tricky. I've selected those herbs and tinctures I believe will work best, but I will need to check on him later, to ensure I have the balance correct."

Thomas glanced at her face, but she was looking down, holding up her skirts with her free hand as she climbed. Beyond his brief wonderings at breakfast, he'd been so engrossed in thoughts of Joy's and Faith's deaths, of what was going on at the manor, and of Manachan and his illness, that he hadn't, yet, reached any real conclusion regarding her and him. Until last night, he hadn't known there would ever be a "them"—that there would ever be anything more substantial than unfulfilled desires connecting her and him—yet now there clearly was... Was that connection an ongoing one, or had it ended when he'd left her room that morning?

He didn't know.

Even more disconcerting, now he'd finally thought of it, was that he didn't know what he actually wanted— if he would be happy to let their liaison end after just one night, or...

But there wasn't any future in it, so perhaps he should simply let matters flow as they would—as she seemed so adept at doing.

As they stepped into the gallery, he glanced at her as, letting her skirts fall, she raised her head. Calm certainty, that serene self-assurance of hers, infused her features. Given his own less-than-certain state, he could almost resent that inner certitude.

He prowled by her side, wondering why he felt so oddly off-balance with her, even though interacting and dealing with her, and generally being in her company, had grown easier in the wake of the events of the past night.

They were nearing Manachan's door when it opened, and Nolan, followed by Nigel, stepped out.

Seeing Thomas and Lucilla approaching, the pair halted and watched them. Nigel pulled the door closed behind him.

Lucilla stopped a few yards away.

Thomas halted beside her.

Nigel's and Nolan's gazes had gone to the bottle in Lucilla's hand. After a second of staring, Nigel asked, "Is that it? The medicine that will keep Papa improving?"

"It is," Lucilla replied. "How is your father?"

Nigel's gaze rose to her face. "Better." The admission was grudging. "Even after the funeral."

"Amazingly better." Nolan's tone was matter-of-fact. "I just hope it lasts."

Lucilla's chin rose; her smile had sharp edges. "I know of no reason his strength and vigor shouldn't continue to improve." She raised the bottle. "This will help." She paused for a split second, then imperiously said, "If you'll excuse me, gentlemen?"

No real question, of course. With reluctance, Nigel and Nolan moved aside.

Lucilla tapped on the door. When Edgar opened it, she held up her bottle and smiled. "I'm here to see my patient." With that, she walked in.

Thomas inclined his head to his cousins, still loitering, and followed her, letting Edgar close the door behind him.

Lucilla was already with Manachan in his private sitting room. She was checking his pulse when Thomas walked in.

He stood to one side of the fireplace and listened as she questioned his uncle, queries that were clearly designed to assess his relative strength compared to how he'd been earlier, before the funeral.

When she ended her inquisition, Manachan fixed her with a sharp glance. "Satisfied?" He tipped his head at the bottle she'd placed on the mantelpiece. "Going to give me the rest now?"

She studied him for a moment, then smiled and reached for the bottle. "This won't have as dramatic an effect as what I gave you last night, but if you consistently take a spoonful every morning when you wake, and again with your luncheon, and at night before you settle for sleep, then over the next week, and week by week after that, you should see further improvement." After showing the bottle to Manachan, she handed it to Edgar. Her gaze returning to Manachan, she continued, "You can't make yourself ill by taking too much. However, taking more than I've prescribed won't get you better any faster. It's designed to work steadily over time, as your appetite improves."

Manachan humphed and glanced at Thomas. "I can't say I'll be sorry to get my appetite back. The only thing worse that eating pap is wanting to eat pap because all else is too much bother."

Thomas managed a grin.

"I've already instructed Alice in how to make more," Lucilla said.

"Aye, and how are you finding her, heh?" Manachan slanted a glance at Lucilla. "I have high standards in healers, these days—will she do, do you think?"

Thomas listened as Lucilla responded, and Manachan confirmed for himself that despite having buried Joy that morning, the clan would nevertheless be adequately served.

"And if she runs into any problem she doesn't know how to treat," Lucilla concluded, "she now knows me, and I've already told her to feel free to send to the Vale for any assistance we can provide."

Manachan accepted that as the final word; knowing his uncle, Thomas suspected it had been the final declaration he'd been angling to hear. Manachan inclined his head to Lucilla in as much of a bow as he could manage. "Thank you, my dear. I'm honestly not sure what me and mine would have done without your assistance."

While Lucilla repeated that the Vale would always

answer any call for help from the Carricks, Manachan's gaze rose to Thomas's face and, lips lightly curving, Manachan fractionally inclined his head—a gesture that brought to mind the words: *Well played.*

Unsure what his uncle had meant—on what aspect of Lucilla's presence Manachan had been commenting— Thomas followed her out of Manachan's suite and into the gallery.

She swept to the head of the stairs, then turned and looked back at Manachan's closed door. There was calculation in her expression, then she looked at Thomas as he halted beside her. "The one thing I still cannot understand is why he never asked Joy to, at the very least, take a look at him. She might not have been as skilled as I or my mother, but she would still have brought him some degree of betterment."

That was one of the many issues he'd spent the morning pondering. He held her gaze for a moment, then glanced around before waving her down the stairs. "Let's go for a stroll."

She immediately took his meaning and nodded. "An excellent idea."

Side by side, they walked down the stairs, out of the front door, circled the house, and started along the side terrace.

As they settled to an easy pace, she simply asked, "Why?"

Looking down, he considered his words. "Because," he eventually said, "someone in the clan has to be behind what's going on. At least one member, and it might be more."

After a moment, he went on, "As to your point, I originally thought, as I believe you did, too, that Manachan's refusal to see a healer stemmed from his pride, in one aspect or another. Yet as we've seen, he was ready enough to allow you to treat him. But according to Edgar and Ferguson—and Mrs. Kennedy, too—Manachan's been more or less in the state we found him for months." He paused, then continued, "I've asked, and no one knows of any reason Manachan might have taken against Joy, yet he steadfastly refused to listen to Edgar's suggestions that he consult her. Yet you heard him today, at the funeral—he told us what he thought of Joy. Manachan might be many things, but he isn't good at prevarication, at putting on a polite show."

She snorted. "According to my parents, that's never been his style."

"Exactly. So what he said about Joy, he meant. Which means there was no reason he didn't ask her to help him *except*—and this is what I now believe purely because I've seen no evidence of anything else—someone convinced him, whether intentionally or otherwise, that everything he was suffering from was simply due to old age."

She walked on for several seconds; like him, her gaze was fixed on the flagstones ahead of them. "We have heard that explanation put forward several times since we've been here."

Her tone was exceedingly even; he had to give her points for remaining, apparently at least, detached. "Indeed." His own temper wasn't so accommodating; the word had been clipped. Then again, Manachan was his uncle, not hers. "But setting aside the question of why he didn't seek help before now, I wanted to ask—your tonic and restorative. How do they work?"

Glancing at her, he saw a slight frown claim her face.

"Do you mean what aspects of a person's vitality the two potions are designed to affect?"

He hesitated, then admitted, "I think that's what I mean. I was wondering if knowing what you're building up might tell us anything of what brought him low."

"Ah, I see." She raised her head. "Unfortunately, the answer is no. The treatment is specifically to boost his strength—muscle tone, but even more his energy levels. That's circulation, breathing, and digestion. But lack of vitality—vigor, strength, whatever one calls it—is a general symptom. If I had seen him soon after he'd first been taken ill, I probably could have said what caused it, but after such a long period of debilitation, it's not possible to define what sent him into that state to begin with."

He grimaced. "What sort of things might it have been?"

"It might have been something relatively ordinary— like a lung infection." They reached the end of the terrace and turned to walk back. She shook her head. "It's not really possible to guess after all this time."

He took two paces before saying, "Would it be true to say that, regardless of what initially brought him low, the critical issue that's kept him ill for so long was that he didn't seek help?"

She nodded decisively. "Definitely. That can be stated without any equivocation."

After a moment, she turned her head and studied him, then said, "And yes, if you'd visited more often, you would have ensured he got treatment earlier and he wouldn't have been so drawn down for so long, but no one told you, so you weren't to know. But now you've come, and I've seen him and treated him, and that's all that can be done."

Jaw setting, he halted and waited until she did the same. Locking his eyes on hers, he simply said, "Indeed. So will you leave now?" When she blinked, he added, "Please."

She frowned. "What brought this on?"

"An adder inexplicably appearing in the still room. A man creeping into your room in the dead of night, apparently intent on smothering you while you slept. Those two incidents, for a start." Along with his growing conviction that whoever was behind whatever was going on had already committed murder twice. He kept his lips clamped, holding back those words.

Much good did the restraint do him.

Her frown grew black. "No. I will not simply waltz off home, not until I'm sure Manachan—who is now officially my patient—is firmly on the road to recovery." With a swish of her skirts, she started walking again. "And before you ask, I imagine that will take at least two more days."

He gritted his teeth and followed. "Do you have any idea what"—exasperated, he waved—"*interfamily ructions* will ensue if anything happens to you while under this roof?" He threw out a hand. "More, with your standing in the area, something happening to you while you're here will very likely break up the clan."

After finally getting him into her bed, Lucilla wasn't going to meekly pack up and go home. She halted and swung to face him. "That's—"

The warning struck her like a mental slap.

She stopped speaking and looked straight up.

A grinding scrape drew her gaze to the roof—to a stone gargoyle as it tipped, then tumbled and fell.

She screamed and grabbed Thomas, flinging them both to the side.

He'd followed her gaze. Seizing her in return, he added his much greater strength to throwing them both along the terrace.

They landed on the flagstones—or rather he did; she landed more or less cushioned in his arms.

She heard a dull crack—then a horrendous *crash* drowned out everything else.

Stone shattered and flew, shards lancing into their clothes, a thousand tiny pinpricks. She ducked and covered her head. Wrapped around her, Thomas jerked and grunted. A rock rolled against her shoe and halted.

Then fine dust spread, a cloud enveloping them, and silence fell.

She choked, coughed, then struggled up, pushing back Thomas's shielding arm.

His arm slid away. He didn't move.

She looked at his face.

And felt the blood drain from her own. "Oh, God."

He was unconscious. He was injured somewhere.

For a second, panic clutched at her throat, then her healer's training rose through her. She hauled in a deeper breath and dragged herself up to a sitting position. Then she gently touched his face. Slowly easing her hands and fingers around his skull, she closed her eyes and felt...

No break. No blood. Just one sizeable, already thickening lump above his left ear.

"God!"

"Miss!"

"Are you hurt?"

"Mr. Thomas!"

The exclamations came from multiple throats. The stablemen came rushing up, and other staff streamed from the front of the house.

She didn't look up but continued her careful visual examination, scanning down Thomas's body—to his left calf.

A large shard of splintered rock had embedded itself in the thick muscle.

"Miss?"

She glanced up as Sean crouched beside her.

He looked into her eyes. "Are you all right?"

She nodded and drew in another breath.

Mitch and Fred, hunkering beside Thomas, reached to turn him onto his back.

"No! Don't move him. Not yet." The sharpness of her tone had the desired effect; they all froze and looked at her. She nodded again, this time more determinedly, and reached for her usual brisk manner. "There's a fragment of rock in his calf. See?" She pointed it out; it had been screened from Mitch's and Fred's view. "We need to take it out first. Moving him with it still in there risks jiggling it and doing more damage."

From the fragment's position, it might well have cut a major blood vessel; she wasn't going to take any chances.

She'd worn a black silk scarf to the funeral. It still hung about her throat and shoulders—the perfect material from which to fashion a tourniquet. Drawing it off and starting to twist the long length between her hands, she explained to Sean, Mitch, and Fred—and Ferguson and several maids and footmen who came to join them— what they were going to do and why.

Mitch, Fred, and two of the footmen set to work clearing the shattered stone and the remains of the gargoyle, giving her, Sean, and Ferguson a clearer area in which to work.

While Ferguson and Sean cut away Thomas's trouser

leg and applied and tensioned the tourniquet under her direction, she confiscated the maids' aprons, folded the material into a thick pad, then pressed the pad around the wound—and nodded to Sean to pull out the offending shard. He did and blood gushed, but she immediately pressed down and, using her weight, leaned on the wound. Thomas grunted and stirred, but then fell unconscious once more.

"Just as well," she muttered. She looked at Sean and Ferguson. "Now we can move him—to his room and his bed."

Despite her words, she didn't like the fact that Thomas was still unconscious. But she hadn't succeeded in finally taking him as her lover only to lose him—that wasn't going to happen.

* * *

Thomas swam back to consciousness while they were laying him on his bed. Which seemed more than passingly strange. They were all there—Sean, Mitch, Fred, and Ferguson, and other members of the staff...

He tried to remember what had happened, why they were placing him fully clothed on his bed, but his head felt as if it were being used by someone as a drum while also being stuffed full of wool... Ordered thought eluded him.

They laid him down, so very carefully, on his back. His head sank into the pillows, and blinding pain erupted above his left ear. He sucked in a breath even as he registered that one lower leg of his trousers had vanished and there was something tied over his exposed calf— then Lucilla was there, leaning over him, offering him a glass, urging him to drink.

He was parched.

Sean helped raise him, and he drank long and deep.

As they eased him back onto the pillows, his eyes drifted closed, and he fell into a dreamless sleep.

* * *

When next he awoke, he'd regained full command of his wits. The pain in his head was still there, but had receded to a dull throbbing ache. Unfortunately, it had been joined by a more definite, more focused pain in his left calf. Eyes still closed, he sent his awareness searching; he decided that what he could feel in his leg was the pull of stitches. As for his head, he must have hit it on the terrace flags...

Memory flooded back.

He opened his eyes—and saw Manachan sitting in a chair beside the bed. Thomas scanned the room; no one else was there. He returned his gaze to his uncle's face. "Lucilla?"

Manachan nodded, as if approving the question. "She escaped unharmed—oh, a few scratches and a bruise or two, maybe, not that she's admitted to even that much."

Thomas frowned. "Where is she?" She'd been there earlier, when they'd laid him on the bed; he remembered that much. And his leg had been stitched—her handiwork, no doubt. A glance at the windows beyond Manachan showed the fading light of late afternoon. It had been late morning when he and Lucilla had gone out on the terrace... He met Manachan's eyes. "What happened?"

"You and Lucilla were walking on the terrace when someone pushed one of the gargoyles off the roof with the clear intention of killing you. You, her, or both of you—clearly they didn't care which." Manachan made the statement with no inflection, simply stating facts.

"Ferguson and Edgar went up and checked—there's no other explanation. A statute that heavy doesn't shift a foot or more to fall on its own."

When he simply lay there, staring unseeing past his uncle while taking all that in, and said nothing, Manachan added, "I heard about the adder, too."

Thomas refocused on Manachan's face, then sighed. "A man turned up in Lucilla's room last night. She woke and saw him creeping toward the bed, a cushion in his hands. She screamed, and he fled. I saw his back at the end of the corridor, but I couldn't tell who he was. He was wearing a cowled cloak, so she didn't see his face, either."

Manachan grunted and scowled. "That's even worse."

"I was trying to persuade her to leave—and not getting anywhere—when that damned statue fell." Thomas gritted his teeth and pulled himself up to sit with the pillows at his back. Grimly, he stated, "After this, I'll make sure she goes." After a moment, still frowning, he glanced at Manachan. "In fact, I'm surprised you haven't already sent her packing."

Manachan studied him for a long moment—then, to Thomas's disquiet, his uncle grinned. "You've come along nicely. I always knew you would. You've learned to think with your head, which is all well and good, and especially necessary for running a business or any other enterprise. But, my boy, you haven't finished evolving yet." Manachan wagged a stubby finger in gentle admonishment. "You need to learn to think with your heart as well as your head. That's what connects us to others, to those we need to be closest to as well as to our communities, such as clan. Such as family. If you don't learn to think with your heart, you might amass all the wealth in the world, but you won't have anyone to share it with. You won't have anyone to share your life with, and then what use will it be?"

Thomas was momentarily at sea, unsure how his uncle's sudden lurch into philosophy connected with any of the topics they needed to discuss.

Yet with no more than a pause for breath, Manachan rolled on, "I want you to take Lucilla back to the Vale, and then I want you to turn north and head on back to Glasgow."

Thomas blinked.

Before he could argue, Manachan continued, "You need to recuperate, and you can't do that here." Manachan's blue eyes met Thomas's, and there was no give in Manachan's steely gaze. "You can't remain on the estate because, for whatever reason—and clearly there is some very pertinent reason—someone here, someone in the clan, doesn't want you—or Lucilla—around, and their antipathy toward the pair of you extends to the point of murder."

Manachan paused. "I can't have that." His jaw firmed. "As Laird of the Carricks, I can't *allow* that."

And suddenly Thomas was very aware that he was, indeed, facing *The* Carrick. His uncle's strength had returned in no small measure. Even while he rejoiced in that improvement and delighted in his own satisfaction that Lucilla had been able to restore Manachan to such a degree, he also recognized that dealing with a restored Manachan would be very much more difficult than dealing with a run-down Manachan had been.

As if reading his mind, Manachan continued, "As leader of the clan, I'm ultimately responsible for yours and Lucilla's health while you're on clan lands. More, you're my dead brother's son, and as dear to me as he was." Manachan stirred in the chair. "And as you can see, I'm not dead yet, and thanks to Lucilla's tonics, I'm now well enough and able enough to do what needs to be done."

He caught and held Thomas's gaze. "Yes, something is going on here—something that can't be tolerated. Not by the clan, not by me. You haven't yet told me the whole of it, but you will—before you leave. Because I won't be able to get to the bottom of it, whatever it is, while you're here. That's a simple fact—one of the heart—that I understand, and that you must accept."

Manachan paused, his gaze shifting, turning inward as if he were consulting some map, some plan. "The lairdship was never to be yours, and to your credit, and to your father's before that, neither of you ever challenged that truth. More, you've both honored it, which is something all the clan knows, approves of, and appreciates. Not necessarily in their heads, but definitely in their hearts. You are a laird by birth, by nature, by stature, but you were never to be theirs—that's one of those unsaid things that everyone knows and, again, one that I know you've always accepted. You will never be The Carrick, and it's precisely because of that that you must leave."

Meeting Thomas's gaze again, Manachan stated, "Nigel will never be as strong as you—and he resents it. That's understandable, but not helpful. Regardless of his shortcomings, he's able enough, and he can and will, in time, carry the mantle of the laird well enough, but I cannot make him concentrate and focus as he must while most of his attention is fixed on you."

Plain speaking, and there was nothing in that that Thomas could argue.

Then Manachan's lips lifted in a puckish grin. "And

there's also the little problem that Lucilla won't leave while you remain. So I need you to leave and take her from here, away from any danger. Her remaining is simply untenable."

Thomas grimaced. "You'll get no argument from me on that score, but..." He frowned. "I can't understand why you haven't pulled rank and sent her home already. It's not like you to allow another's will to override yours, especially when clan standing and security are involved."

Manachan snorted. "You're still not thinking straight. Would that I could send her packing, but not only am I her host, for goodness' sake, but she's also the daughter of a powerful neighbor, one I have no wish to alienate. And on top of that, her rank is akin to high-priestess-in-waiting of the local deity—and quite aside from how *I* feel about the Lady, which is complicated, I admit, I'm not about to disendear myself to those of the clan who do believe by insulting the Lady's representative." He huffed. "I can't send her packing, and she knows it, damn it."

Thomas studied his uncle, Manachan's words rolling through his mind. "I didn't think you gave any credence to the old ways."

"Aye, well." Manachan shrugged. "My mother, your grandmother, was a cousin of that old witch, Algaria. She, my mother, believed, and a lot of the clan still do, and I'm too old and wise to discount something just because I don't understand it." He sighed and met Thomas's eyes. "The long and the short of it is that I can't ask Lucilla to leave, yet if anything happens to her while she's here, Cynster will flay me alive—and I'd have to let him."

Thomas heaved a sigh, too. Lying back on his pillows, he stared at the ceiling, juggling Manachan's demands—

the commands of his laird—with his own and Lucilla's wishes.

He'd come to Carrick Manor to learn what was going on and to ensure that things were put right. Instead, he'd uncovered a far more widespread and malignant malaise. He hadn't succeed in learning who was behind it, or even how far it had spread—but he had, along the way, brought Lucilla to the manor, to Manachan, and that had resulted in him and the clan getting their laird back. Even without looking at his uncle, he could sense Manachan's greater strength, and there'd been a clarity and incisiveness behind his words and thoughts that simply hadn't been there days before.

Did he believe Manachan was now in a position, health-wise and understanding-wise, to get to the bottom of what was going on and resolve the issues troubling the clan?

And if the answer to that question lay on the positive side of the ledger, as it did, did he then have reason, or the right, to refuse a direct request from his laird? Especially a request he understood—even if, in some respects, that request ran counter to his own inclinations and rubbed against his pride?

Two minutes passed, then he pressed his lips together and lowered his gaze to Manachan's face. "All right." Even he heard the resignation in his tone as he said, "I'll leave—and I'll take Lucilla with me."

Manachan formally inclined his head. "Thank you. And now, if you please, you can tell me all the rest that you haven't yet mentioned, but that I need to know."

Thomas settled back and obliged, relating all he and Lucilla had discovered, linking the facts and laying out their suspicions, detailing the samples they'd sent for analysis—the evidence for which they were still waiting. They still had no clue as to who was responsible, but if anyone could learn the truth, it was Manachan. A Manachan returned to vigorous strength and the full use of his faculties—and thanks to Lucilla, that was what they now had.

* * *

Apparently, Lucilla had been kept from Thomas's room and his side only by a strongly worded decree from Manachan. After Manachan had left him, Thomas had Edgar carry a message to her that he needed to speak with her and would meet her in the drawing room before dinner.

After dressing for the evening with Edgar's help, Thomas slowly made his way down the stairs, gripping the bannister and leaning heavily on a cane Ferguson had found for him. His head was still hurting, but the pain was dull, a throbbing ache he could ignore if he had to. The sharp slicing pain from the wound in his leg was another matter. Every time he put his weight on that foot, he was forcibly reminded that he shouldn't be walking.

He gimped through the open drawing room doors and found Lucilla already there. Her emerald gaze fixed on his leg, as if she could see the injury and feel his pain.

From the way her eyes narrowed and her lips pinched, he suspected she was holding back a string of acid observations he really didn't need to hear.

He reached the armchair opposite hers, and she opened her lips. "Don't." He caught her gaze when it flicked up to his face; holding it, he slowly sat. "I wouldn't be here if there was any other way."

She frowned. "You should have stayed abed. I could have come to your room."

No, she couldn't have; he was perfectly sure he wasn't that strong. Leaving her comment unanswered, he went on, "I had a long talk with Manachan this afternoon, as an upshot of which there are several matters we need to discuss."

He'd spent the time since his uncle had left him rehearsing his points; he laid them out in concise and logical order.

She heard him out in silence. When he reached the end and Manachan's request that he leave and take her back to the Vale before continuing on to Glasgow, a definite frown formed in her eyes, but she didn't, even then, respond.

Not knowing from which direction she was intending to attack his and Manachan's decision was, he decided, worse than arguing with her. When silence stretched, and she continued to stare, frowningly, apparently unseeing, at him, as if her thoughts were far away, he sighed—a touch exasperatedly. When she refocused on his face, he arched a brow. "Well? Will you agree to leave with me and go back to the Vale?"

She studied him for a second, then turned her head and looked at the open door.

She rose, walked across the room, and quietly shut the door, then she turned and, rather more forcefully, stalked back. She didn't resume her seat but started pacing before the hearth, back and forth between the two armchairs. He hadn't seen her pace before, but he didn't think it was a good sign.

Lucilla laced her fingers before her waist, paced, and tried to see some way—tried to weigh the best way—to secure what she wanted and needed from the shifting situation.

She'd got Thomas into her bed—now she needed to keep him there. At least long enough that he would agree to remain there, by her side, of his own volition. Clearly he hadn't yet reached that state; she hadn't expected him to, not after just one night.

She needed more of his nights, and his days, too.

Flinging a glance his way, she asked, "Are you satisfied that Manachan can carry on on his own, without your support? That he can find who's behind all these odd happenings and bring them to justice?"

He didn't immediately agree, but he considered…then nodded. He met her eyes. "He's a great deal better—far better than I imagined he might be after so short a time of your treatments."

So because her treatments had been so perfectly gauged, she was to have her time with Thomas cut short? No—that wasn't going to happen.

She could understand why Manachan wanted Thomas to leave Carrick lands, and she agreed with both Manachan's assessment and his directive. Indeed, she, too, had already concluded that she ought to leave, if only to ensure there were no further attacks on her person; such attacks would only escalate tensions within the household and the clan, which were already high enough. So she understood and agreed, but she didn't have to tell Thomas that.

Folding her arms, she halted and faced him. "I believe I should remain here and make sure Manachan continues to improve. That he continues to be able to deal with whatever the problem affecting the clan is. As my duty encompasses doing what's best for the people here, then clearly that's what I ought to do."

Thomas looked up at her, then he sighed and pointed

to the chair she'd vacated. "Would you please sit down so that we can discuss this more easily?"

Seeing the tension around his lips, she humphed and sank onto the cushions. "And that's another thing—you can't yet travel back to Glasgow. I stitched the gash in your leg, but it was deep, and serious, and not something to leave to mend without appropriate care. You won't be able to ride at present, not given the position of the wound, and traveling in a carriage for even an hour will be more than you'll want to do."

That he didn't argue spoke volumes.

He studied her, his gaze steady on her face, reading the resolution that she made no effort to hide.

His lips thinned; his amber eyes narrowed. He drummed his fingers on the head of his cane, then simply asked, "What do I have to do to get you to agree to return to Casphairn Manor?"

She felt her eyes widen; that was a great deal more direct than she'd expected, but she was entirely willing to engage on that plane. She held up a hand to indicate that she was thinking—and did so rapidly—before saying, "You are now, in effect, my patient, until your leg heals well enough for you to ride. I will concede that Manachan should continue to improve without being under my day-to-day care, so I can accept that I do not need to remain here, in this house, on his account. I can also understand that Manachan's way forward will be easier without you in residence, so I would not argue against his request for you to leave the estate. *However*, while I will agree to travel with you back to the Vale, I must insist that you remain there, at Casphairn Manor."

Thomas blinked. He rapidly compared what she was suggesting with what he—and Manachan—needed to achieve. He hadn't thought to remain in the Vale, but if he did, at least for the next few days, he would be close enough to respond quickly if Manachan needed his support again. Regardless of his uncle's returning strength, given they had no idea who was behind the recent incidents, being close enough to step in and assist might be a very real boon.

He looked at Lucilla, opened his mouth to agree, but she halted him with an upraised hand.

"I have one more stipulation." Her eyes captured his; her emerald gaze held him captive. "While at Casphairn Manor, you will share my bed."

A shaft of pure desire lanced through him. He stared at her.

He should have been shocked; instead, he was intrigued.

He let himself remain within the green fire of her eyes—didn't bother fighting free. Not yet.

He hadn't realized—not with his conscious mind—how much of his awareness, of his less-conscious self, had been absorbed with her, with the question of whether one night was all she wished for or if, somehow, their liaison might continue…for at least the few days that she was now insisting on.

One night hadn't been enough for him—indeed, had only whetted his appetite; apparently, one night hadn't sated her, either.

Which was…good, wasn't it? To his advantage? Somewhat oddly, he wasn't so sure of that.

He blinked free of her hold and refocused on her face, her figure—all of her and not just her mesmerizing eyes. "What about your reputation? Your household? What about your brother?"

She waved dismissively. "I'm twenty-eight, and as my mother's successor in the Vale, everyone knows and accepts that I have my own eccentric road to follow. No one will question—will feel they have the right to question—whatever route I take. Our staff have always supported me, and always will. As for Marcus, he knows me too well to stand in my way."

He could well believe that—all of that—yet...he felt as if he were being lured down a path that a wiser—less attracted—man would avoid.

But he wasn't that man; he was as he was, and what she was offering, stipulation and all, was precisely what he wanted on all fronts, personal as well as clan. In this, it seemed his clan and personal needs ran parallel.

For one instant more, he hesitated, but then surrendered to the overwhelming pressure of his instincts and inclined his head. "Done. And we'll leave immediately after dinner."

Her brows rose in consideration, then she nodded. "Very well." She met his gaze. "With that decided, the situation we're leaving Manachan to pursue... He mentioned that someone had been on the roof and the falling statue had been pushed off."

He nodded. Guessing—knowing—what tack her mind would take, he concisely recounted the essential findings, much as he had with Manachan a few hours before.

She listened gravely. When he reached the end, she thought, then said, "Assuming that the results of the analyses confirm our suspicions, showing that the Bradshaws and Joy were deliberately poisoned, and although we can't prove it, we're also fairly sure someone pushed Faith down the stairs and killed her—and, of course, someone put the adder in the still room, crept into my room with fell intent last night, and then pushed that statue off the roof… Yet in spite of knowing all of that, we can't point the finger at anyone, because virtually anyone on the estate could have done all those things."

He nodded. In the hall beyond the door, the dinner gong rang, summoning them to the table.

Shifting forward, he leaned on his cane. Even more swiftly, she rose, came to his side, and offered her hand.

He hesitated, but then put aside his pride, gripped her hand, and allowed her to help him stand. On his feet, he released her, drew breath, then met her eyes. "Not only can't we point a finger at anyone, we can't even tell whether all those incidents are connected—whether whoever did for Joy and Faith was also the person who poisoned the Bradshaws' well, or pushed the statue from the roof today, or…"

She grimaced and turned to the door. "So, in reality, we really do have to leave this to Manachan, because, when it comes to it, you and I can do no more."

She walked slowly so he could keep up. He followed her from the room, her words repeating in his mind.

And indeed, she was right. In the matter of discovering what was behind the strange happenings on the Carrick estate, there was nothing more he and she could do.

Twelve

They left Carrick Manor in Manachan's carriage shortly after dinner. Lucilla had insisted on re-examining Manachan before she left, and on overseeing his evening dose of the restorative.

Manachan had been surprisingly acquiescent, even jovial, throughout; Thomas suspected that, as his uncle was getting precisely what he wanted, he saw no reason not to be magnanimous in victory.

As they rattled slowly down the long drive that led to the main road, he spared a thought for Phantom, following the carriage on a lead rein. The gelding wouldn't be happy. Then again, like his master, Phantom had a rare female to distract him, in the form of Lucilla's black mare.

Thomas felt much the same way he imagined his horse must be feeling. Unhappy over the manner of his leaving, yet distracted by the company.

As the miles fell behind, he remembered all the little things he'd forgotten through having to deal with more serious events.

He shifted; Lucilla had been right in predicting that he wouldn't be able to sit in a jostling carriage for long. "I never did learn what was behind Nigel's changes to the seed supply. Or his other changes on the estate. Or, I suspect, the true story about those horses and carriages in the old barn." Stretching out his injured leg, frowning, he massaged his thigh.

Seated beside him, Lucilla shrugged lightly. "You told Manachan about them. I can't imagine he won't inquire and set things right."

The carriage slowed, then ponderously turned out onto the main road, heading south, toward the entrance to the Vale. As the wheels picked up speed, rolling more evenly along the better surface, Thomas looked out of the window to the right, into the darkness toward Carrick Manor. "I wish I hadn't had to leave—to leave him to handle things on his own."

"But you had to. There was no other way." She paused, then, as if understanding the frustration he felt in having to accede to Manachan's wishes, she added, "Sometimes one has to accept that someone else's right to direct their destiny takes precedence over one's own desires."

The comment drew his attention back to her. The carriage running lamps were lit; every now and then the flickering light from outside illuminated the dimness within, enough for him to make out her expression, to catch glints from her fire-red hair.

After several seconds of considering his words, he remarked, "I find it curious that, given your temperament, you seem to so easily accept what you term your Lady's decrees."

She turned her head, met his eyes through the shadows, then raised one shoulder and faced forward again. "I've heard Her—received Her guidance—from my earliest years. Not all of us do. But experience, especially from a very young age, is an excellent teacher. Despite directives that at the time I thought exceedingly strange, She has never steered me wrongly."

No doubt that accounted for her unwavering certainty, something he sensed so strongly in her. Leaning his aching head back against the squabs, he closed his eyes and found himself pondering that clear difference between them. They were both strong-willed, independent characters, yet even though she recognized what she was doing, she was able to bow to the directives of fate. He, conversely, instinctively opposed any decree that came from any source other than himself.

They passed the rest of the journey in silence, for which he was grateful. He knew of no other lady, young or otherwise, who would have left him in peace, yet not only did she apparently feel no need to converse but that sense of deep calm that was so peculiarly hers spread out and enfolded him—and soothed and calmed him, too.

Yet when the carriage drew up in the forecourt of Casphairn Manor, on the gravel before the steps leading up to the front door, he discovered he was still very far from recovered. His head ached, pain thudded in his temples, and his leg throbbed. He had to allow Lucilla to descend from the carriage first so that she could help him down.

Sean, who had driven the coach, came to help. Once Thomas was steady on his feet, Lucilla sent Sean to ring the doorbell. She remained by Thomas's side, supporting him as, leaning heavily on the cane, he slowly made his way up the thankfully shallow steps.

He'd just reached the porch and had paused to raise his head and draw in a deeper breath when the door swung open.

It wasn't the butler who looked out but Marcus Cynster. Midnight-blue eyes pinned Thomas, but then rapidly skated down his length before, his expression impassive and growing ever more so, Cynster looked at his twin sister. Their gazes met, then Marcus arched a brow.

Imperious as ever, Lucilla waved him forward. "Come and help Thomas   he has a wound in his left calf, so be careful."

Before Thomas could blink, Marcus was there, coming up on his good side. As tall as Thomas, Marcus gave him his arm; Thomas leaned on it. Marcus's presence was like that of an oak, solid and unbreakable, beside him.

Somewhat to his surprise, he detected no animosity from the man he'd left unconscious outside Lucilla's sacred grove. What he did sense was a very shrewd mind paying very close attention to everything, and even though they exchanged no words, Thomas got the clear impression that Marcus and Lucilla were swapping comments back and forth across him.

As they passed through the arched front door, Lucilla announced, "Mr. Carrick will be staying for at least a few days, until his wound is healed well enough to ride."

With his gaze on the floor before his feet, Thomas thought she was speaking to Marcus, but then the three of them paused and he raised his head—and a veritable sea of friendly faces, all beaming, bringing with them a tangible tide of warmth and concern, engulfed him.

The housekeeper, a Mrs. Broome, patted his arm and told him she'd get a room ready for him immediately. Maids grinned and bobbed curtsies, then whisked off in the bustling housekeeper's wake. The butler, Polby, was there, consulting with Lucilla while footmen had already gone out to help Sean with his bag, and several grooms had followed, presumably to tend to the horses.

If Thomas had thought about what his welcome at the manor would be like, it wouldn't have been this; he found it a touch disorienting. For several moments, he stood in the center of that welcoming wave—then scrabbling sounds heralded the arrival of dogs.

Hounds—deerhounds, a small pack of them—came pouring out of one archway. The foyer was large and irregular, with stairs and lots of corridors and archways leading from it; the hounds came out of the largest and most impressive archway. The dogs were young or in their prime; sniffing and snuffling, ears flapping, jaws open, and tongues lolling, they surrounded Thomas, Marcus, Lucilla, and Polby—all of whom absentmindedly greeted them, patting huge heads and scratching ears and shaggy chins.

And at the rear of the pack came two animals Thomas hadn't seen in ten years; although they'd been much smaller then, something in him recognized them instantly. His cane balanced against his leg and with both his hands absorbed with stroking and petting, Thomas glanced at Marcus. "You bred from them?" With his head, he indicated the pair ambling toward them.

Marcus, likewise absorbed with the dogs, nodded. "We got others from other breeders." Briefly, he met Thomas's eyes. "You're responsible, in a way—you gave us Artemis and Apollo, and everything started from there."

The two older dogs had finally reached them. The younger beasts instinctively gave way, falling back. Both Artemis and Apollo halted in front of Thomas, looked up and, with their amber eyes, searched his face, then both sat and raised their paws.

Thomas was disarmed. He laughed and took each

paw, squeezed lightly, then he released the dogs and rubbed their shaggy heads. "They're in excellent condition." He might not have bred them any longer, but he still knew everything there was to know about deerhounds.

Marcus shrugged. "They were good stock to begin with."

The front door had been shut, and the press of people had thinned; Thomas had distantly registered the sound of Manachan's carriage being driven away, and he'd glimpsed a footman disappearing up the main stairs with his bag.

Lucilla turned to him. "Would you like to join Marcus and me in the drawing room for a nightcap, or would you rather retire? Mrs. Broome has your room ready."

She'd insisted that he would share her bed but, given they'd only just arrived, perhaps he would get a reprieve for tonight—which, considering how woozy he felt, was probably just as well. "I'm...not thinking as clearly as I would like." The simple truth. "I suspect I had better retire." While he still had some hope of negotiating the stairs upright.

A burly footman stepped forward. "If you'd like to lean on me, sir, we'll get you up to your room."

Marcus stepped back. He caught Thomas's eyes and gave a curt nod. "I'll catch up with you tomorrow."

There was a promise in the words Thomas would have had to have been dead to miss, yet there was no aggression in Marcus's expression or stance.

Which, as he allowed Lucilla to take his arm, and between her and the footman, he made for the stairs, Thomas had to wonder at.

The effort of ascending the stairs wiped all thoughts

beyond lasting long enough to fall into the wonderfully plumped bed from his mind. Luckily, the room they'd prepared for him was on the first floor, at the base of one of the turrets.

He dismissed the footman, but he lacked the strength to dismiss Lucilla. He tried, but she just sent him a "don't be ridiculous" look and set about helping him undress.

Finally semi-decently clad in his sleeping trousers, he had to stop and catch his breath. Sitting on a chair, arms braced on his thighs, his head hanging forward, he murmured, "Even though I dislike the notion of taking any of your potions, if you have something that will ease the pain, I'll gladly swallow it."

She regarded him for an instant—he could feel her gaze—then she touched the top of his head. "Wait there."

He had no idea how long she was away, but it seemed no more than a moment before she was back and pressing a small beaker into his hand. It contained a reddish-pink potion, not the usual green her potions seemed to be. He glanced at it, then downed the dose in one gulp.

She took the empty beaker, set it aside, then urged him up and into the bed.

He literally fell into it. She'd pulled down the covers, and as he rolled to his side, she drew them over him.

A soothing sense of peace enveloped him.

Warmth ran beneath it, the lingering threads of the welcome in the foyer.

How very different from the welcome he'd received from his cousins.

Acceptance, and the gentle contentment that came from that, closed around him and dragged his senses down.

Lucilla watched him slide into slumber.

While his pain and his present lack of strength didn't please her, she hadn't been surprised by either, and she was immeasurably reassured that he'd asked for and accepted her aid.

He was there, in the Vale, under the manor's roof, and only one floor down from where he ultimately should be—in her room, in her bed.

With the Lady's help and by Her grace, she'd accomplished that much. As for the rest…she had to have faith that the following days would play out as they should, and the rest—Thomas's realization that he was hers and she was his—would come in time.

One step at a time.

His breathing had evened out, slow and steady; his features had eased, showing no signs of tension, of continuing pain.

Satisfied with the outcome of the day, she picked up the lamp, went out, and shut the door. She paused on the landing, debating, then accepted the inevitable and started down the stairs. Marcus, she knew, was waiting.

* * *

Lucilla walked into the drawing room and closed the door behind her. Although it could be used for formal gatherings, it was the room the family used on a daily basis to gather in before and after dinner. Her mother had accordingly decorated the room with comfortable rather than fashionable furniture, the sort of well-stuffed chintz-covered sofas and armchairs that invited ladies to relax and sink into, and gentlemen to sprawl at their ease in.

Occupying one of the armchairs near the hearth, Marcus was engaged in the latter. A glass of whisky cradled in his long fingers, he sipped and watched her as she crossed to the armchair opposite his.

When she sat, he lowered the glass and met her gaze directly. "First question—do you know what you're doing?"

She held his gaze and let him see her certainty, her commitment. "Yes." That was all she needed to say.

He read her eyes, then inclined his head in acceptance. "All right." He took another brief sip, then asked, "So what's been going on at Carrick Manor?"

She told him from beginning to end, leaving out nothing bar her interactions with Thomas—those, her twin definitely didn't need to hear described, although she suspected he would still guess that such interludes had occurred.

Regardless, he took her report in his stride and focused, as she'd hoped, on the conundrums.

When she reached the end—Manachan's request for them both to leave, and them acquiescing and doing so— Marcus grimaced. He rose and crossed to the tantalus, and tipped a little more whisky into his glass.

He arched a brow at her, but she shook her head.

He returned to the armchair and all but fell into it. Frowning, he sipped, then broodingly said, "Manachan made the right decision. If the culprit lies within the clan, as it seems certain he does, then, as Manachan's now able to manage again, he—and only he—is the right person to deal with the situation. No one from outside can, and although Thomas is clan, with Nigel resenting him and all the others preferring him, Thomas being there will only make things worse." Marcus drank, then added, "Especially as worse might stretch to murder."

"Indeed." She paused, then said, "I couldn't see any

way around it—around leaving Manachan to deal with it on his own. Aside from all else, over all these years he's earned everyone's respect—he's always been uncannily shrewd over anything to do with his clan."

"Exactly." Marcus nodded. "Although I don't in the least approve of having a murderer or murderers—including one who had and may yet have you in his sights—wandering around still free, now that Manachan's back to reasonable strength, we all, Thomas included, need to give him the time and the space to sort it out—within clan, if at all possible."

She could only nod in agreement. That, in a nutshell, was what had brought her home.

Marcus's dark gaze rested on her; she couldn't read his expression, but she could sense his approval. "Presumably"—he paused to drain his glass—"rescuing the Bradshaws and then restoring Manachan to viable strength were the reasons Thomas was summoned back from Glasgow."

She knew her twin wasn't referring to Bradshaw, and then Forrester, writing to Thomas, but to the hand of fate—the fate both she and Marcus accepted ruled them and the lands they watched over.

"And"—Marcus tipped the empty tumbler, watching the light spark in the cut crystal—"why he had to fetch you, and by extension, why I was left nursing a very sore head."

She humphed and rose. "I checked you over before I left you—it wasn't that bad. And"—she arched her brows at him—"as we all know, you have a very hard head."

Marcus's smile was slow and rather intent. "You and I know that, but I have no intention of letting Carrick off the hook."

She snorted and, unsuccessfully battling a smile, turned and walked to the door. Opening it, she left her twin plotting, secure in the knowledge that Marcus understood who Thomas was to her, and that tease him though Marcus undoubtedly would, he would nevertheless protect Thomas in the same way he did her—with his life if need be.

* * *

Lucilla climbed the stairs to the first floor, then headed for the southeast turret in which her room was located; one level up, her chamber was circular with views over the green of the summer pastures to the distant horizon where dawn first arrived.

She was grateful that Marcus had refrained from asking more questions about her and Thomas, because, as yet, she didn't know the answers herself.

Reaching the guest chamber at the base of her turret, the room in which Thomas was sleeping, she quietly opened the door, went in, and equally quietly eased the latch closed.

Not that she needed to have worried—he remained deeply asleep.

She walked to the end of the bed and stood looking down at him.

Letting her eyes trace his features, the fall of one thick lock of dark hair across his brow, the elegant length of his palms and fingers relaxed on the covers, she let the essence of all he was, and all she needed him to be—lover, consort, husband—impinge and sink in to her mind, to her soul.

She'd secured the first; they were lovers, and he hadn't tried to pull back from or deny that connection. As for being her consort, he'd been protective of her from the first; with regard to her, that was a part of his nature he hadn't attempted to suppress, nor, she suspected, would he be able to. It was the last title that would be the hardest for him to embrace; it would, in effect, be a public declaration that he was hers and would remain by her side for the rest of his days.

Him agreeing to be her husband would be the true and final commitment—the only one that, for her and him, really mattered.

She knew beyond doubt that he would never be at peace, would never find any true and lasting satisfaction in life if he wasn't there, living beside her, where he was supposed to be.

Filling the role he was supposed to fill, destined to fill, despite his resistance fueled by his belief that his life lay elsewhere.

But there was nothing she could do to advance their cause—hers, his, and the Lady's—tonight.

Although he'd insisted on his sleeping pants, he apparently slept without a nightshirt; the muscled strength of his arms, the power inherent in the heavy width of his shoulders, lay exposed, displayed against the ivory sheets.

The potion she'd given him had contained enough poppy juice to take the edge from his pain and tip him into a healing sleep; he wouldn't be stirring any time soon.

She stood silently considering his sleeping form for a moment more. She'd insisted that, here in the Vale, he had to share her bed, but in gaining what she needed, she was willing to be flexible.

* * *

Thomas woke to find the gray light of predawn filtering through the uncurtained windows—and Lucilla, a warm armful, tucked against his side.

He was lying on his back, his head cushioned on thick pillows. Without shifting his head, he studied the segment of room he could see. Although his memories were hazy, he was fairly certain this was the room, the bed, in which he'd fallen asleep last night.

So she'd adjusted her strategy; not her room, not her bed, but she was still sharing it with him.

His lips curved. He let his lids fall again, thinking that would improve his ability to think clearly. Instead, with his eyes shut, his other senses expanded, and awareness of her presence swamped him.

There was an earthy reality in the moment. An adult man, an adult woman, sharing a bed. Simple. Uncomplicated.

They lay warm beneath the sheets, their muscles relaxed, heavy in slumber. The door was closed, and beyond it, no one was stirring.

Slowly, his nerves, his skin, came alive.

She'd donned a nightgown, the fine cotton an insubstantial barrier separating naked skin from skin. The ripe swell of her bottom was snuggled against the side of his waist, the elegant curve of her spine pressed along his side.

The ache in his head had eased to almost nothing; he could still feel the wound in his calf, but the pain had dulled and was easy to ignore.

Not so the intensifying ache in his loins.

He drew in a deep breath, filling his lungs—with the alluring scent of her. A mixture of herbs and flowers, a complex medley of scents that reminded him of spring edging into summer, of bright freshness transforming via a luscious ripening into something beyond desirable—into something to be coveted.

That promise was there in her, carried to his senses in so many ways, on multiple planes.

He reached for her, for that promise—compelled, unable to resist.

Having no need to resist, not here, in this quiet, private world.

He opened his eyes and turned to her, careful not to jostle her.

She was curled on her side, facing away from him, her head ducked, her face half buried in the pillow, the covers drawn over her shoulder. Her hair lay in wild disarray over the pillows; several tresses lay beneath his cheek, the silk strands catching in his stubble.

The soft fabric of her nightgown caressed his chest. He was already hard and ready for her, his erection tenting the front of his sleeping trousers. But relief was pending and so very near to hand; the tug of desire was so real, so palpable, he gave up trying to think, surrendered all thought of attempting to plot and control the engagement and, instead, simply sank into the moment and let it lead him where it would.

However it would.

Reaching around her, he pressed his hand beneath her arm, then gently closed palm and fingers about her breast. The mound filled his hand; he squeezed and felt her flesh firm. She stirred, the small movement languorous. He continued caressing until her nipple was a tight pearl beneath his palm, then he shifted his attention to her other breast.

She murmured, no real words, just a sound born of pleasure. Then she stretched, her spine arching like a cat, the movement pressing her breast more firmly into his hand and rubbing her derriere against his erection. She stilled for a heartbeat—then, more deliberately, shifted her hips against him, wantonly caressing him. A wordless invitation.

One he had every intention of accepting, but in his own time—or, to be more accurate, according to the rhythm that had laid hold of his senses.

He shifted closer, using the weight of his hips, his legs, his chest to pin her, not immobilizing her but leaving her little leeway to filch the reins.

Lucilla came sufficiently awake to register the sensation of him pressed to her back, of being surrounded by him, held trapped. The veils of sleep still lingered, hazy clouds of comfort, of reassurance that all was well and that no active thought was necessary, yet the feel of him so close, so warm, so strong, sparked her nerves to alertness and brought her senses alive.

Intrigued, dazedly wondering, she caught her breath on a soft sob of pleasure as his hands continued to massage her breasts with a touch that, while firm, was almost languid.

One of his legs lay heavy over hers; he lay half over her. She debated turning to him, into his arms, but…all her intentions fell away as, having opened the front of her nightgown, he slid one large hand beneath the gaping side and wrapped his hard palm—slowly, gently, yet inexorably—about her swollen breast.

Her senses focused solely on his touch, on the simple claiming.

Her breath hitched, and what conscious thought she'd managed to marshal unraveled and slipped away.

Eyes closed, she tipped her head back and let her senses take her, let them and him overwhelm her.

His shoulders against the backs of hers, he raised his

head and dipped his lips to the curve of her throat. He traced the taut line with his lips, all the way up to the hollow beneath her ear. Then he opened his mouth and placed hot, wet kisses down along the same line.

All the while, his hand continued to play, continued to knead and claim her breasts.

Until they grew unbearably heavy, the peaks excruciatingly tight.

Until she could barely breathe through the pulsing weight of the heat rising inside her.

With one hand, she reached blindly back, found his face, and with her fingers lightly traced one lean cheek. "Thomas..."

She hadn't known she had so much need in her, yet it thrummed in that word—that plea.

He murmured something, but she couldn't make it out; hearing wasn't a priority, not then, there, in their sensual cocoon.

He drew his right hand from her breasts, but only to curl that arm around her and lift her enough to slide his left arm beneath her. He settled her on that arm, tucking her even more securely against him. To her body's relief, his left hand replaced his right, sliding through the opening of her nightgown to caress her breasts, his touch just as hot, as heavy, as expertly knowing.

Just as expertly stoking the steadily rising tide of desire he'd set welling within her.

Then his right hand trailed down, over her cotton-clad thigh. Her nerves sparked, then tightened. Reaching past her knee, he found her nightgown's hem. He slid his hand beneath, cupped his palm to her skin, and ran his hand upward. He paused to caress the hollow behind her knee, then set the back of his crooked fingers to her skin and ran them slowly up the back of her thigh.

She felt the touch to her marrow, tensed, but when he reached the top of her thigh, he drew his fingers away.

The back of her nightgown had risen, caught on his wrist and forearm. He grasped the folds and lifted them higher, pressing them up over her waist, baring her bottom. Prickling awareness flashed over her skin. She felt the brush of his sleeping trousers against her naked curves. Felt the jut of his arousal screened by that last layer of fabric. Releasing her nightgown, he eased his hips back—just enough to set his hand to the globes of her bottom.

And freely trace, stroke, and caress.

Languidly.

Heat built, inexorable and strong—edging toward fierce—yet there was no urgency, either in his touch or in the solid beat of passion she sensed rising within them both.

It thrummed beneath their skins, holding them captive to the slow, steady, swelling beat.

Her skin dewed. A restless empty ache of wanting expanded and filled her.

Then his fingers skated down, dipped to the hollow between her thighs, and delved.

Scalding wetness met Thomas's senses. Lids heavy, eyes closed, he breathed deep, and pressed two fingers further, finding her entrance and spreading the welcoming slickness over her pouting lips.

Around them, the room lay silent. The only sounds that reached them were of their own tight breaths and the thudding of their hearts.

There was barely light enough to see, and the covers hid all, and they had their eyes closed.

Yet their senses had never been so full, so alive, so overwhelmed. With his awareness reduced to touch and nothing more, her skin had never felt so silken and smooth, so fine and perfect, her curves had never seemed so lush, so delectably formed. So alluring.

And the same sensual restrictions that limited him also limited her. He could only imagine what, in this heightened state, she was feeling…just thinking of that laid a visceral edge to his escalating need.

Their heated, heavy, commanding need.

He pressed his fingers deep, then deeper, stroked, and she shifted her hips, seeking, needing—brazenly wanting.

He drew his hand from her and pushed down the front of his sleeping trousers. His erection sprang free and he pressed closer. Adjusting her upper thigh and the angle of his hips behind hers, he slid the rigid shaft into the hollow between her thighs; he gripped her hip and held her immobile as he aligned the head with her entrance, then he sank home.

In. Deeper.

His weight propped on one elbow, one hand filled with her breast, the other clamped over the curve of her hip, he held her still and steadily forged into her body, until he came to rest engulfed to the hilt in her searing softness.

Her body clamped about his in a welcoming embrace that had him shuddering—with need, with desire, and so much more.

But even as he let his weight settle on her, shifting into the best position in which to ride her, the control that the moment had imposed on him, that had held and set the pace to that point, continued to restrain him.

He withdrew from her clinging heat, almost to the point of losing it, then—slowly, heavily, and deliberately—he surged back, filling her anew, his groin pressing against the lush curves of her bottom.

She murmured and pushed back, taking him deeper yet, but even as he continued the measured dance of thrust and retreat, she, too, seemed to accept the compelling beat.

As if it thudded through both their hearts, down both their veins, not just his.

Beneath the covers in the gray light of early dawn, they continued dancing to the strict beat, so slow, so steady, so heated—so achingly intense. So overflowing with reined desire that it almost choked them. Every nerve he possessed was excruciatingly alive, seared alive by a passion so demanding, so relentlessly commanding.

They could have gone faster at any time, but neither made any move to break the spell. Instead, they clung, each to the other, and let it play out—let it unravel them both.

Sinking her fingertips into his thigh, she held him to her as the tension ratcheted one last notch—then, arching wildly, she came apart on a sobbing cry.

The sound filled his ears, and blindly he followed, holding her immobile and thrusting deep into her rippling sheath.

Release slammed through him. Scoured and emptied him.

He pumped into her surrendered body, felt his seed jet into the dark warmth of her womb—and all tension left him. Abruptly released, he collapsed over her; gasping, his heart thundering, barely aware, he tightened his arms and held her close.

And felt her sink back into him, accepting, holding him to her in her own way.

Ecstasy rolled over him—over them. It stole away the last shreds of control, of any ability to think. In a wave as long and as steady as the undeniable beat that had commanded them throughout, the glory rolled on and through them, and only very slowly receded, finally leaving them wrung out, exhausted, and steeped in pleasure. Shared pleasure, where awareness of hers heightened his, where a thrum of connection remained, resonating within him, even when the fading tide had fully ebbed away.

That connection fascinated, but he couldn't focus. The dark warmth of satiation beckoned; slumping under the covers with her locked against him, he let go and allowed his senses to slide into that soothing embrace.

* * *

Perhaps it had simply been that they were there, in the Vale, in a place of peace and assured safety, and no longer surrounded by the uncertainty, the questions, and suspicions that now haunted Carrick Manor. Lying in the bed with his arms crossed behind his head, Thomas wondered if that was reason enough to account for the contentment, the abiding sense of rightness and peace that had swamped him after the act and, even now, lay heavy and oddly reassuring within him.

He'd woken five minutes ago to discover morning sunshine streaming in through the window and Lucilla no longer beside him—indeed, no longer in the room. But the sheets at his side still held her warmth; she could only just have left. He was sorry he'd missed that—both the sight and the chance of gauging what she'd thought of their earlier endeavors. Then again, there was no reason to imagine the interlude had affected her in the odd way it seemed to have affected him.

In his eyes, some new element had crept into the moments, something unexpected that he didn't understand, and as such, it intrigued him and tugged at his awareness.

By anyone's standards, he was an experienced man. To discover something new in an act he'd indulged in times out of number was a situation guaranteed to command his attention. Admittedly, the first time he'd had Lucilla beneath him had been exceptionally intense, yet now... It wasn't so much her, herself, as her and him together—possibly in this place—that seemed to be opening new avenues to explore.

Which, for a man of his appetites, was a very real temptation...

Luckily, he had at least a few more nights of compulsorily sharing Lucilla's bed.

He let a slow grin curve his lips, then he threw back the covers. He swung up to sit on the edge of the bed and paused to assess his injuries. His head no longer throbbed at all; he reached up and traced the lump above his left ear, and was pleased to find it reduced in size and only slightly painful when prodded.

As for his leg, there was definite pain there, but a quick examination showed the redness about the gash and stitches was already fading. Whatever ointment Lucilla had smeared over the wound seemed to be doing the trick; the gash was dry, and even he could see that there was no infection.

Carefully, he stood. He'd left the cane leaning against the bedside table; he grasped the head and tried walking.

His stride was less hampered than it had been the day before, but Lucilla's estimate of several more days before he could risk riding seemed likely to prove accurate.

On reaching the washstand, he set the cane aside, picked up the pitcher, and poured water into the bowl.

He'd agreed to stay in the Vale under duress. Now, however, he was willing to admit—to himself if no one else—that coming there and staying had been the right thing to do. He'd been intending to marry for the last several years, but had dragged his heels over choosing a wife. Although he'd pretended to be seriously looking over the field, in reality he hadn't yet made the final commitment, not in his heart.

What had Manachan said about him having to learn to think with his heart as well as his head? As usual, his uncle had been correct.

He needed a wife, and when he returned to Glasgow, he would have to act—would have to choose a suitable young lady, propose, and front the altar. And in pursuit of that goal, his liaison with Lucilla would serve to burn away the lingering shreds of his longtime attraction to her. He was well aware that that was passion's way— resisted and suppressed, it never died, but if allowed to ignite and burn, it would inevitably reduce to cold ashes.

Reducing his deep-seated attraction to Lucilla, if not to cold indifference, then at least to the sort of temperate feeling he could readily leave behind… That he hadn't done so earlier was doubtless why his memories of her had so consistently and insistently interfered with his attempts to focus on suitable young ladies. She and her inherent passion had never lost their claim on his mind, because he and she had never allowed their suppressed passions to ignite.

Now they had, and the outcome was, indeed, as enthralling as it had always promised to be, but it was only passion. A few more days—a few more nights in her bed—and he'd be able to ride away and finally, properly, get on with his life.

He picked up a washcloth and dipped it in the water. It was bracingly cold, but as he scrubbed, he thought of what the day might bring, including his first real meeting with Marcus, and how that and the rest of the day might unfold.

Thirteen

Thomas followed the sounds of voices down a winding stair and stepped out onto what proved to be a dais at one end of a huge vaulted chamber.

Lucilla sat at the long table that took up most of the dais; she was facing the rest of the room, which was filled with tables and benches at which various groups of people sat. Some were clearly manor staff, but others appeared to be stablemen and outdoor workers.

Curious, Thomas looked around. People glanced his way and smiled; some nodded.

Not entirely sure of his standing, he dipped his head politely in reply and shifted his gaze to Lucilla.

She'd noted the glances from the body of the hall. Looking his way, she smiled and waved him to the chair and the place set beside her.

He limped forward, noting that Marcus sat on Lucilla's other side, although not quite as close as the place to which he'd been summoned. Grasping the chair, he drew it out.

Marcus looked up, briefly met his gaze and nodded.

He nodded back and sat. There'd been no antagonism in Marcus's dark gaze—no great welcome either, but more a guarded watchfulness. As if Lucilla's twin was reserving judgment. Deciding he could live with that, Thomas began lifting the lids from the various covered platters arranged on the board before the three of them.

No one else sat at what he gathered was a high table of sorts.

After sampling the excellent porridge laced with the most delectable honey he'd ever tasted, he murmured, "You have other brothers and... Is it just one sister?" He glanced at Lucilla. "Are they here at the manor?"

She shook her head. "No—not at present." Busy slathering marmalade on a slice of toast, she explained, "Annabelle—she's twenty-four—is presently in town staying with our uncle and aunt, the duke and duchess. She's of similar age to their daughter, Louisa, and also to two of our other girl cousins, so the four of them are keeping themselves amused through the Season."

A grunt from Marcus suggested just how four young ladies of that age might be "keeping themselves amused" through the London Season.

"And Calvin—he's the next in age at twenty-one—is also in town, staying with one of Papa's cousins and his family. Calvin and their son, Martin, and two others of the family have recently come down from university, so they're enjoying their first Season on the town."

Marcus pushed aside his empty porridge bowl and reached for the covered platter containing the kedgeree. "I'm sure they'll be getting up to all sorts of hijinks, but Papa's brother and cousins are there to pull them into line." He paused, then dipped his head toward his twin. "Not to mention our aunt, the cousins' wives, and our grandmother and her cronies, too."

Lucilla chuckled. "Indeed. And that leaves Carter, our

budding artist—he's just twenty and has gone traveling with Mama and Papa on the Continent."

"But," Marcus said, "while they'll be seeing the sights, Carter will be haunting every museum and gallery he can find."

"Well," Lucilla said, "that's why he went—to see the old masters' paintings and all the other famous works that he could."

Thomas paused, then ventured, "By my reckoning, that leaves the pair of you holding the fort."

Beyond Lucilla, Marcus nodded. "Indeed." Then he shrugged and looked down at his plate. "But that's our role, after all—watching over all those here."

Thomas had listened carefully, but he'd caught no hint of resentment, not even of mild reluctance, in Marcus's deep voice. Reminded by their comments about their siblings that these two, even more than the others, could command places at any fashionable table in London, he had to wonder why neither had gone south; most in their places would have—and with alacrity. They might have been born in the Vale, their mother might be Scottish, but their father was English, a scion of an English dukedom. Over Lucilla's head, he glanced at Marcus. "You don't mind?"

Although he directed the question at Marcus, he was asking Lucilla, too. He lowered his gaze to her face. "You could have gone to London and been the toast of the ballrooms, yet you've remained here."

She met his eyes, held his gaze for an instant, then simply said, "Here is where we're supposed to be." She paused, then looked out at the hall before them. "We wouldn't be happy anywhere else, so"—she shrugged lightly and reached for her teacup—"neither of us bothers to go down and pretend."

Marcus chuckled rather darkly. "Much to the consternation of our aunt and her peers. Our parents, however, are more understanding."

Thomas ate for several minutes. He'd noted Lucilla's unwavering certainty about her direction in life; it seemed her twin shared the same conviction—the same assurance that this was where his future lay. Where he needed to be for that future to evolve as it should.

It must be…comforting, and anchoring, to have such absolute knowledge.

Finally pushing his plate away, he reached for the coffeepot and poured himself a mug. Both Lucilla and Marcus had finished their meals; like him, they were enjoying a last cup—tea for Lucilla, coffee for Marcus.

He would only be there for a few days, but he was accustomed to business, to being actively engaged with something through the days…and he was curious. Most of those in the body of the hall had departed, although a few last stragglers were still being served by the maids. He gestured at the hall. "I take it this is a communal place?"

Lucilla nodded. "It's the Great Hall—the original Great Hall of the manor—and still functions as such. Everyone who works on the manor lands, including all those on our farms, come here for their meals."

"That isn't as odd as it sounds," Marcus said, "because all our farms radiate outward from the manor. If you wander around the perimeter fence, you'll see some of the farmhouses, and all are within sight of the manor's turrets. So the manor is at the center of the Vale in a literal as well as figurative sense."

"And as we are also—like the Carricks—snowed in for part of the year," Lucilla said, "it was decided very early in our history that it made best sense for everyone on the estate to come into the manor during those times." She met Thomas's eyes. "It's safer that way."

He nodded. "I remember that Christmas Eve when we were all stuck in the Fieldses' cottage. Bad enough when the blizzards rage now, but a century or more ago, it would have been hellish getting stuck for weeks in those flimsy shacks." He idly tapped the table, then admitted, "I could wish the Carricks had a similar system, but sadly, now the various families are too...shall we say independently minded? If the first Carrick had instituted a system similar to yours, perhaps it might have worked, but now the farms are too far-flung and each family, or group of families, tends to struggle through on their own, only asking for aid when they're in desperate straits."

Marcus inclined his head. "Pride. It's a fine edge one needs to tread when balancing independence and community."

The housekeeper came bustling up. Smiling, she halted before the table, bestowed brief nods on Thomas and Marcus, then fixed her gaze on Lucilla. "If you would, m'lady, I'd like to get the menus sorted so I can send the boys off to Ayr. We put off the usual trip to market while you were away."

"Yes, of course." Lucilla pushed back her chair.

Despite his injury, Thomas was on his feet before Marcus could rise; he drew the heavy chair back for her.

She smiled—distinctly warmly—at him. "Thank you. Feel free to wander wherever you like. Your wound will let you know if you overdo things, but it won't help you to sit all day, either. If you have any questions, ask anyone. All here will be pleased to assist you."

He inclined his head. "I'll endeavor to keep myself amused."

She laughed and left, stepping to the side and down two shallow steps to join the housekeeper. Heads together, they walked away across the huge hall.

Thomas hadn't quite finished his coffee; he slipped back into his chair and lifted the mug.

Having drained his mug, Marcus glanced at Thomas. "She meant that literally." Something like amusement lurked in Marcus's dark blue eyes. "You may be perfectly certain no one here will let you get lost, and everyone will be happy to answer whatever you wish to ask."

Thomas wasn't quite sure what to make of that—neither the words nor the amusement behind them. He'd expected to get off to a much more fraught start with Marcus, but apparently Lucilla had been correct, and Marcus would, indeed, take his lead from her.

"I have to ride out and look over the state of the crops with our farmers." Marcus set down his mug and met Thomas's eyes. "Last night, Lucilla told me about the strange happenings on the Carrick estate. She mentioned there was some question about the supply of seed. I'll be seeing the local seed merchant today—he's due to join us out in the fields. He's the same merchant the Carricks use. If you like, I can ask if there have been any problems. The man knows me and values his business with us—if I ask, he'll tell me what he knows."

Thomas gazed at the table for several seconds, turning over the offer in his mind. If it had been Manachan who had been dealing with the merchant, he wouldn't have contemplated checking up, as it were, but...if it had been Manachan dealing with the seed merchant, he suspected there wouldn't have been a problem at all. Looking up, he met Marcus's steady gaze and nodded. "Thank you. I have no idea what's going on, but hearing from the other side of the deal might be the fastest way to find out."

Marcus nodded and rose. "I'll let you know what I learn." He pointed to the archway to the rear right of the hall. "The library's through there. Feel free to investigate, and if you need to write letters, you can use the desk there. The news sheets from London, Edinburgh, and Glasgow arrive about lunchtime, and will be put in there, too."

Thomas didn't fancy sitting inside all day—he did that too often in Glasgow. He eased his chair back. "Which way are the stables?" He should check on Phantom.

Marcus grinned and pointed to the largest archway. "The front foyer is through there—you want the corridor to the left. Head down it and through the door at the end, then turn left down the path. It's actually not the shortest way distance-wise, but I suspect it'll be your fastest way."

Thomas dipped his head, then, using his cane, pushed to his feet. "Thank you. I rather think, in this instance, that fastest will be best."

Marcus chuckled and left him, striding off down the hall.

Thomas paused, wondering how he felt over being left to his own devices—to do as he wished, with no restraint or direction... It had been a long time since he'd had such an opportunity.

Shaking himself to action and deeming it best to get out of the hall and let the serving maids clear the table, he gimped down the steps to the hall floor and headed for the main archway to which Marcus had directed him.

And realized, as he passed under the broad arch, just how he felt.

It had been a long time since he'd felt so free.

* * *

Thomas limped into the stables and asked for the head stableman.

A grizzled man came forward; when he saw who waited for him, the man's face creased in a smile. "Ah—Mr. Carrick, sir! I'm Jenks." Jenks bobbed his head respectfully. "I suspect you've come to take a look at your horse. Lovely animal."

Jenks waved Thomas toward the stalls further down the long stable. "Yon Sean said as how the beast's name is Phantom. Nice conformation, if you don't mind me saying."

"Not at all." Thomas glanced at the older man, who had slowed to keep pace with his own halting gait. "I'm rather partial to his points, myself."

Jenks laughed. From that promising beginning, it was an easy step to discussing the finer points of horseflesh. Phantom looked quite pleased with his new digs; after admiring the big gray and trading tales of horses they had known, Jenks invited Thomas to look at some of the other horses under his care.

"Right lucky, we are, with Mr. Cynster's cousin being a trainer of Thoroughbreds and all. He—Mr. Demon Cynster, that is—picks all the family's horses, so we get some gems. Like this little beauty." Jenks stopped and leaned on a stall door. Thomas joined him in looking at Lucilla's black mare.

Jenks sighed. "So elegant, she is."

Just like her mistress. Rather than saying anything so revealing out aloud, Thomas said, "I recall when last I saw Miss Cynster riding—years ago, now—she had a black mare then, too. Does she always ride blacks?"

Jenks pursed his lips, thought, then admitted, "Now you mention it, all her horses have been blacks, but I'm not sure as that's been deliberate." He arched his brows. "Must remember to ask her, when I next see her, if she really is partial to blacks, or if that's just been an accident."

They chatted about the riding in the area, Thomas drawing on his memories, and from there the talk veered into hunting and the other horses in the stable. Eventually, Thomas perched on a bench to ease the pressure on his leg and happily watched as various grooms, all of whom Jenks had introduced, paraded some of the most superb horseflesh Thomas had ever laid eyes on.

"Aye—when it comes to hunters, it's Miss Prudence—Mr. Demon's daughter—who has the best eye. Even better than her father, she is, although he'll never admit that!"

Thomas grinned. With his cane, he pointed to a heavy dappled gray. "Whose is he?"

"That's Mr. Marcus's favorite, Edward—better known as Ned."

"Ned?"

Jenks shrugged. "He was named after the king, Edward the Third, but he's so fractious, Mr. Marcus said he was more obstreperous Ned than kingly Edward."

That, Thomas thought, sounded like Marcus.

The talk meandered this way and that, over horses and the various eccentricities of the Cynsters, both those of the local branch and the more far-flung members, who, Thomas gathered, frequently visited.

"They'll likely be back once the Season in London is over with and the master and mistress come on home. The duke and duchess and the other couples—always together, that lot, and they keep an eye on each other's broods as needed, too."

That was said with approval, and Thomas didn't disagree.

An hour and more flew past, then Jenks excused himself to see to some ponies in the farther fields, and Thomas made his halting way back to the house, taking the same roundabout route he'd come out by. The path ran around the side of the manor above a set of terraced gardens stepping down to a burbling burn. It was a lovely sight, with a profusion of plants and flowers brought to vigorous life by the warmth reflected off the manor's high stone walls; nothing else could account for such lush and vibrant growth.

The beds were edged with stone, the nearer walls at the perfect height to sit and look down over the colorful carpet to the rippling, rushing waters. Thomas grasped the opportunity to rest his leg—and rest his soul in the peace and tranquility that rose with the perfume of the flowers and, like their scent, wreathed through his mind.

The view was simply lovely—and made lovelier still when, between the bobbing flower heads, he saw Lucilla further down the slope. She was working in the garden; he realized it must be the source of all her herbs. Two other young women of much the same age worked alongside her, presumably her apprentices.

He sat and watched and let the peace claim him. For today, at least for this morning, there was nothing more he needed to do—he could rest and enjoy this strange sense of freedom. The time and space to commune with others on subjects he enjoyed, and the opportunity to let his eyes feast on the cynosure of his desire.

* * *

After luncheon, once again taken in the Great Hall with the cheery bustle of the household all around, Thomas told himself that he couldn't waste all day on country pleasures. He needed to remind himself of who he truly was—Carrick of Carrick Enterprises.

He repaired to the library. After chatting with him over a tasty soup, followed by a cold collation, Lucilla had excused herself to return to the gardens; she was, she had told him, harvesting the first flush of herbs.

Marcus hadn't appeared at luncheon; from what he'd said at breakfast, Thomas had assumed he would be out for most of the day.

The library proved to be another enormous room, this one longer than it was wide. The windows weren't large—the winters were too cold—but in this room they were frequent enough that, with the long velvet curtains drawn back as they presently were, the room was filled with light.

As was the case elsewhere in the manor, the focus was on comfort rather than on fashion; deeply cushioned armchairs, well-stuffed leather chairs and sofas, and side tables with lamps abounded. The parquet floor was covered with a series of large, oriental rugs, their deep jewel tones adding a luxurious richness to the ambiance. The wide hearth hosted a cheery little fire, just enough to keep the natural chill of the stone walls at bay. Thomas limped down the room, his gaze roving the many bookcases lining the walls. All were packed with tomes, most leather-bound and showing signs of use. It was clear that this was no formal reception room but a room a large family actively used.

The desk Marcus had mentioned sat across one corner, facing down the room and toward the windows. On reaching it, Thomas balanced his cane against the nearby bookshelves, then carefully eased down into the admiral's chair behind the desk.

His first order of business was to write a letter to Quentin, advising his uncle that it was likely to be several more days before he returned to Glasgow. Despite his intention, it took him a good few minutes to push his mind back to his office there, to recall what matters had been on his desk when he'd left, which issues were still pending. Dipping the nib he'd found and sharpened into the inkwell, he set down his thoughts and suggestions for how those matters might be best addressed, and stated his confidence that Quentin and Humphrey would be able to deal with said matters in his absence.

As for that absence, after due deliberation, he wrote that he had inadvertently sustained a minor injury that would keep him from traveling for a few days, and that while Manachan had been poorly, he was now much improved. However, subsequent tensions on the Carrick estate had made it advisable for him, Thomas, to recuperate at the neighboring property of Casphairn Manor. He needed to tell Quentin and his office where to find him in case of need, but he didn't want to unnecessarily alarm them.

He concluded with a statement of his intention to be back in Glasgow within a handful of days. He paused, rereading the words, knowing he should be more definite and wondering why he wasn't setting down a specific date for his return, but in the end, without amending the message, he signed, blotted, and then sealed the missive and scrawled the address across the front.

A silver salver sat on one of the sideboards, several letters already reposing on it. Grasping his cane, he levered himself to his feet, limped across, and laid his letter on the pile. Some footman or groom would no doubt be dispatched to take the letters to the post office in the village later in the afternoon. Thomas knew coaches passed up the main road every evening; his letter would reach Glasgow tomorrow morning.

He had earlier noticed a pile of news sheets stacked on a low table before the longest leather sofa. Limping over, he let himself down into the embrace of fine leather, set his cane aside, and reached for the pile.

Glasgow, Edinburgh, and London. He went through the news sheets for the last three days—the days since he'd left Glasgow—in that order, reading all the business news, glancing briefly at the political and general news, and the editorials, and even more idly scanning the society columns, but found nothing of real interest. Nothing to excite him and engage his mind.

He'd just tossed the last of the news sheets back on the pile when the door opened and Marcus walked in.

Thomas looked at the clock ticking on the mantelpiece and realized that more than three hours had passed. A glance at the window showed the golden rays of a westering sun slanting over the fields.

Marcus dropped into one of the armchairs facing the sofa. His expression was impassive and gave nothing away, but his eyes rested on Thomas as if weighing him, or something relating to him.

Leaning back, Thomas arched his brows.

Marcus grimaced. "I asked the seed merchant about

the supply of seed stock to the Carricks. According to him, they—by which I gather he means your cousin Nigel, who is now managing the estate?" When Thomas nodded in confirmation, Marcus continued, "Apparently, Nigel arranged to have the Carricks supplied from what the merchants call the 'dregs.' That's the bulk of seed left over after all principal orders have been filled. Because the seed will deteriorate with time, the merchants don't want to keep it, so they offer what's left at significantly reduced prices."

Thomas frowned. "But by the time something that's 'left' has been delivered…how much time has elapsed?"

Lips tightening, Marcus nodded. "That's the reason so few estates around here, or south of here, buy from the dregs. By the time that seed stock is delivered, we're too late to get it into the ground—at least not to allow two full crops. But buying from the dregs is a common enough practice for estates further north, where they can only hope to get one decent crop a year. Those estates can afford to wait for the cheaper prices—and, of course, it saves money. But for us"—Marcus met Thomas's eyes— "and also for the Carricks, starting the season with seed bought from the dregs means we start too late to get our usual two crops harvested."

Marcus sat forward. "The reason the farmers and I— and later the merchant—were out in the fields today was to assess the strike rate of the seed he'd supplied. Our first crop is already out of the ground, and we met to confirm our order for later in the year. That order is already set aside from the original stock. And that's the other major drawback of ordering from the dregs—you are effectively wagering that there will be sufficient seed left over to supply you in the first place, and your estate also goes to the bottom of the list for fulfillment of orders later in the year."

Thomas digested that. "When Manachan asked about the seed supply, Nigel said that there was a new system in place, and that the seed had just been delayed. Strictly speaking, he told the truth." Thomas raised his gaze to Marcus's face. "Do you know what the current situation with the Carrick farmers is?"

"Their seed order was delivered yesterday." Marcus grimaced. "Even getting the seed into the ground immediately, the only way they'll get a full second crop is if we have a very late summer and a mild autumn. Most likely they'll end with one decent crop, and a second that's immature and only useful for stock feed." Marcus pushed upright. "Drink?"

It was early, but...Thomas nodded. "Thank you." He watched as Marcus crossed to an elegant tantalus against one wall. "Whisky, if you have it."

Marcus humphed as if to say that was an idiotic question.

After returning and handing Thomas a cut-crystal tumbler containing two fingers of deep amber liquid, Marcus raised his own glass, sipped, then sank back into the armchair.

Thomas considered him, then asked the question circling in his brain. "What reason would an estate manager have for ordering from the dregs?"

Marcus met his eyes. "Money." He considered, then shrugged. "I can't think of anything else."

The whisky was excellent; it burned a trail of fire down Thomas's throat. Tapping one finger against the tumbler, he frowned. "If I understood your explanation correctly, although one might save money initially by buying from the dregs, an estate such as the Carrick estate, where two crops can be brought in, risks losing much more by having a failed second crop." Catching Marcus's gaze, Thomas arched his brows. "Is that a reasonable summation?"

Marcus inclined his head. "Entirely reasonable." He sipped, then more harshly added, "Also almost certain." He paused, then said, "What I can't understand is why Nigel would do such a thing. If you need money, you increase production, not restrict it. As a move driven by prudence, it makes no sense."

"No, indeed." Thomas sipped, then sighed. "Unfortunately, I have no idea what straits the estate might be in—perhaps there was a problem with available cash— but without knowing the full circumstances, looking in from outside, we can't properly judge." He shifted, easing his injured leg. "We'll have to leave it to Manachan to sort out—he'll find out the same details as soon as he asks." He paused, thinking of all the other questions about the Carrick estate that were as yet unanswered, but there was nothing he could do about them, either; as he'd agreed, he would have to leave it all to Manachan. He grimaced. "I'll write to Bradshaw and Forrester— the farmers whose summons brought me down here. At least I can explain what's been done—not that that will appease them or the other farmers growing crops."

His expression severe, Marcus shook his head. "The point I find hardest to comprehend is that Nigel took such a decision without consulting his farmers—those most crucially affected and also most aware of the variables."

"Do you do that here?" Thomas asked.

Marcus nodded. "All the time." He sipped, then said, "Admittedly, the Vale doesn't run on quite the same principles as the Carrick estate—we're not clan-bound, but rather bound by historical allegiance and practice. Our ways are those we've found over the centuries work best for us—and if anything stops working, we find a new best way, one that works for all of us."

If Thomas had an enterprise like an estate to run, he would run it in the same fashion; his years at the helm of Carrick Enterprises had taught him that the best returns came when all those involved felt their voices were heard.

He and Marcus sipped and a companionable silence fell. Marcus nodded at the pile of news sheets and asked if anything truly important had occurred; Thomas's reply—that while according to the pundits, the skies were close to falling, as they always were in the pundits' eyes, nothing had changed that might even remotely impact the lives of those in their small corner of the world—made Marcus grin.

In the ease that ensued, Thomas stared into the last of the really quite remarkable whisky in his glass. Slowly swirling it, he said, "At the breakfast table this morning, you and Lucilla..." He frowned, searching for the right words, for his true meaning. "Both of you are strong people, the sort who reach out and wrest from life what they want. The type of characters who demand and establish their own place, their own life, as they wish it to be. That's in your characters and in your ancestry. Yet"—he gestured, encompassing the room and more—"here you both are, fulfilling roles prescribed for you—expected of you. Designed by others for you." Thomas raised his gaze and met Marcus's steady blue eyes. "That seems a very contrary thing for characters such as you, that both of you seem to have so easily accepted that your futures lie here, in the Vale."

He paused, but could read nothing in Marcus's eyes or his expression. "I'm curious—and a trifle confounded, truth be told." And he wanted to know how such an apparent contradiction could be.

Marcus didn't immediately respond, but after several pensive moments had ticked by, he sipped again, then, lowering his glass, replied, "I think a large part of"— his lips curved lightly, a touch self-deprecatingly—"our apparently easy acceptance of our roles here stems from having known of them for all of our lives." His gaze resting on his glass, he went on, "There never was a time when either of us didn't know—simply know with absolute certainty—that our true path, our way to our most satisfying and fulfilling future, lies here. That the roles we're destined to fill—our true destinies—lie here." He seemed to catch himself, then tipped his head and qualified, "Or, at least, that living here, doing as we're doing, is the right path to our true and final roles."

Thomas said nothing but, his gaze on Marcus's face, tried to follow the nuances running beneath his words.

Marcus sipped, then his lips twisted, again with that hint of self-deprecation. "All that said, I can assure you that knowing, even with absolute certainty, that a particular path is the right one to take doesn't necessarily make it any easier to bow to a power that, to all intents and purposes, is greater than your own will." Raising his glass, he saluted Thomas. "You had that right—it isn't in our characters."

"Yet you've both done it—bowed to that greater power."

Marcus nodded. "Yes, but not, I contend, *easily*. How-

ever, as I said, we—Lucilla and I—have had the experience of being…for want of a better term, chosen for our
destinies since childhood. We learned from an early age
that fighting against your own destiny is, to put it mildly,
a complete waste of time." Marcus paused, his dark gaze
resting on Thomas. "If you're chosen, you can't escape.
You can try, but you'll end by ruining your life and living in misery—and you still won't escape." After a moment, he added more quietly, "That's a lesson Lucilla
and I learned long ago. And neither of us are the sort to
fight battles simply for the sake of fighting."

After a moment, Thomas dipped his head. "Thank
you."

They let silence fall again. Marcus picked up the news
sheet on the top of the pile, one from London, and started
to read.

Leaving Thomas sorting through his thoughts, through
Marcus's words, and the understanding he'd gained. Marcus's talk of personal destinies—of being unable to escape regardless of what one might do—rippled through
his awareness, reminding him of the unsettling sensation he'd had of being herded—steered, prodded, and
ultimately *guided* down a particular path. One that had
led him from Glasgow to where he now was—sitting in
the library at Casphairn Manor.

In his case, *people* had been behind the herding—
Bradshaw, Forrester, Lucilla, Manachan, and Lucilla
again.

A whisper—that perhaps those people were merely
the pawns of some greater power—slid through the
depths of his mind and sent a sensation suspiciously
like a shiver down his spine.

Deliberately, he focused on Marcus and asked the

other question he had. "You"—he paused until Marcus looked up and met his eyes—"and everyone else here have accepted my arrival in Lucilla's train without so much as a blink." He had no intention of alluding to, much less underscoring, the nature of his relationship with Lucilla, so he simply asked, "Why?"

Any doubt he'd harbored that Marcus didn't comprehend the true nature of his relationship with Lucilla was slain by the hardness that infused Marcus's eyes...but, after several seconds, Marcus dropped his almost-challenging gaze and shrugged. "No one has any reason to take exception to your presence here. You arrived quite clearly under Lucilla's aegis, and whomever she brings to this house will always be welcomed with open arms."

Marcus raised his gaze and met Thomas's eyes—and this time Thomas got the impression that Marcus was studying him, trying to see past his mask and into his mind. But then, his lips easing into what might have been a gently commiserating smile, Marcus said, "There really is nothing more to it than that. As we've already discussed, she is who she is, and all of us here accept that."

There was a finality in Marcus's tone that Thomas, in turn, had to accept. He tilted his head in wordless acknowledgment and let the subject drop.

* * *

Thomas had wondered if Lucilla would rethink her insistence that he share her bed, but no.

That evening, after another meal in the Great Hall shared with the entire manor household, during which the company had been entertained by a group of children practicing madrigals, he, Lucilla, and Marcus had retreated to the drawing room, where he'd learned that

Lucilla played the harp like an angel. They'd chatted about music; he hadn't felt the passing of time, but then the tea trolley had arrived, and after duly partaking, he'd claimed tiredness—and hadn't been entirely surprised when she declared that she would retire, too.

They left Marcus engrossed in a book in the drawing room; as they climbed the main stairs, she linked her arm with his. They reached the first floor and walked to the door of his room, but instead of releasing him, she tightened her hold and drew him on—to the narrow stairs that spiraled upward a few yards further on.

She had to release his arm, but caught his hand and, raising her skirts, led the way. Curious, he allowed her to tow him, haltingly, up the curving flight and into the turret room above the chamber he'd been assigned.

That the turret room was her private domain was, to his eyes and all his senses, instantly apparent. The room wasn't a girl's, but a woman's, powerfully yet elegantly decorated in myriad shades of green—from the softest spring-green of the sheets, to the vibrant leaf-green of the silk comforter, to the lush velvet draperies that cloaked the windows and the corners of the four-poster bed in the deep dark green of the forests.

She drew him further in, then released his hand and turned back. Behind him, he heard the door shut with a quiet, solid *thunk* of fated finality.

Soft lamplight glowed from sconces on either side of her mahogany dressing table; another lamp sat on the small table beside the bed, shedding light over the wide expanse, laying a shimmering golden sheen over the green silk.

He was vaguely aware of two dressers and two armoires set against the walls and, beyond the bed, a comfortable setting of two armchairs with footstools angled before a fireplace. A fire burned in the hearth, and the tang of pine underlay the perfume infusing the very air. Tempted, he breathed deep, filling his lungs—and recognized the pervasive scent. That curious blend of herbs, flowers, and spring sunshine he associated with her.

He would recognize that scent were he blind; that hook had already sunk deep.

He started to turn toward her, but she came up beside him, took his hand again, briefly met his eyes, then faced forward and drew him on.

The bed was her ultimate goal.

He understood that and was willing enough to follow.

She halted by the bed's side, released his hand, and with a swish of her silken skirts, turned to him—stepped to him, framed his face with her hands, pulled him down as she stretched up and kissed him.

Her passion hit him full force. No warning, no gentle rise of desire, but with the sudden impact of a raging storm.

She parted her lips under his, but the instant he responded, she changed tack and boldly slid her tongue past his lips, found his tongue, and heavily stroked.

Incited.

With each successive, deliberate caress, she demanded and taunted.

For long seconds, he reeled, rocked back on his mental heels by the sheer force of her desire, the heat, the raging beat, the power—the sheer need she poured into him.

He drank it down—suddenly couldn't get enough. His own need roared to life, answering hers.

Rising to her call.

His hands had instinctively closed about her waist, holding her… His fingers curled, his palms seized.

His cane cracked on the floor as he moved into her and closed the last inch, then he hauled her against him, into a crushing embrace as he forced her head back, took control of the kiss, and pressed his passion on her.

She didn't give ground. Didn't back away an inch.

She speared her fingers into his hair, clutched, and came up on her toes the better to press yet another scorching kiss on his mouth, on his slavering senses.

Curiosity flared; she'd dispensed with all shields, all care, all caution.

How far would she truly go?

The primitive male in him wondered.

Yet he wasn't prepared to cede to her in this, not in this arena. His fingers tensed, then eased, his senses registering the feminine vitality between his hands, the supple, resilient skin beneath the layers of clothes; once he got his hands on her, on the silken curves of her body, she would yield and the reins would be his once more.

Yet she wasn't ready to end the passionate plundering of their mouths—and neither was he.

Awareness fracturing, he wrenched enough of his wits free of the kiss, enough to send his hands searching. Tonight, her lacy bodice closed down the back. Starting at the high collar at her nape, he swiftly slid the tiny buttons free, driven by a rising desperation to feel the silk-satin of her skin again, to taste the succulent peaks of her breasts and hear her moan.

Her kiss pulled his mind one way, his desperation pulled in another; he almost felt giddy.

The bodice was loosening, gaping at the back, almost undone… What wits he'd reclaimed from the heated, hungry savoring of their mouths were focused on that. Then his neckcloth whisked away, and the witch in his arms hauled apart the sides of his shirt that she'd already freed—and set her greedy hands to his chest.

To his body; from the way she swept her palms, here, there, and over every inch of bared skin she could reach, it was transparently clear that she wanted it all—wanted to, intended to, seize and lay claim.

The *need* infused in each sweeping caress had him closing his eyes—made him shudder.

This was passion of a different stripe—of a power and force he hadn't before encountered.

Life. I will always bring you life. Life, indeed, at an elevated level.

A temptation he couldn't resist.

He had to step up, had to match her; some innate part of him recognized and accepted that he had no other choice.

He pushed the last button free and hauled open the back of her bodice, then by main force, unrelentingly pulled the garment forward and down—trapping her arms and inexorably forcing her to draw her hands from his already burning skin.

Lucilla had no intention of stepping back, slowing down, or allowing him to dictate this engagement. She— her instincts—saw tonight as hers—her time to convince him of all they could have, of all they could be. The cuffs of her sleeves weren't tight; in virtually one movement, she lowered her arms, with two swift tugs freed her hands, drew her arms from the confining sleeves— and reached and grabbed handfuls of his shirt, waistcoat, and coat level with his collarbone, then lifted and pushed the garments up and over his shoulders, trapping his arms in return.

She broke from the kiss as, with one last, downward shove, she pushed his bunched clothes to his elbows. Then she seized a second for the battle to catch her racing breath.

Her bodice fell away; she heard the *clink* of the buttons as he let it fall from the fingers of one hand to the floor.

His hands, large and strong, were splayed on her back, his touch burning through the fine silk of her chemise.

She'd broken the kiss, but their faces remained only inches apart. They were both breathing rapidly, heated breaths mingling. Their gazes met and locked—his glinted, gold in amber, from beneath the thick lashes of his lowered lids. She flicked the tip of her tongue over her lips. "How's your leg?" The one restriction still hovering in her mind.

Thomas blinked. For an instant, he didn't know what she meant…then he remembered and inwardly checked, but it wasn't his leg that was aching. "It's not hurting." The words came out in a low growl.

"Good." She shifted closer and, with calculated deliberation, pressed herself to him like a cat, rubbing her barely clad breasts against his lower chest, the warm, curvaceous mounds impressing his skin, his senses.

His jaw locked as he battled vainly to ignore the provocation—in the movement, in her intensely green eyes.

With his arms trapped, he was at her mercy, but to free himself, he would have to take his hands from her—lose the last vestige of control over her.

Her eyes on his, she swayed, the tight peaks of her breasts dragging across his skin; the sensation made the muscles of his abdomen quiver, then lock even harder than before.

He muttered a curse and drew his hands from her. Lowering his arms, he pulled and shook the constricting garments down and free of his hands.

But she was on him the instant he moved. Small hands bracing, fingers spread, on the heavy muscles on either side of his chest, she placed a hot, wet, open-mouthed kiss in the small hollow in the center of his chest—and branded him.

Scalded him; the heat from that claiming touch raced through him and spread, igniting a need he had to assuage.

He reached for the laces anchoring her skirt.

Lucilla pressed her lips once more to the beckoning hollow, then she licked, laved. Closing her eyes, she gave her senses over to tasting him as he had her—to savoring the slightly salty tang of him and drawing the arousing scent of pure male deep, to her bones.

He filled her senses to overflowing, and she welcomed and embraced the knowing. Then she set about tasting him some more. She found the flat discs of his nipples hidden beneath the fine mat of curly dark hair. She fingered them—learning them by touch, by feel—then she closed her lips about them and tasted, closed her teeth and lightly scraped, then with her lips tugged.

She read his response in the flickering of his skin, in the tensing of iron-hard muscles, in his increasingly harried breathing.

Her own breaths were shallow; if she thought of it, she'd feel giddy, but in that moment, she was focused on only one thing.

Him.

On claiming him.

She felt the frantic tugs at her waist and knew she was on the right road. Recognizing the opportunity, she used the moment to let her hands slide down, fingers lightly gripping, tracing over the tensed ridges of his abdomen to his waist.

To the buttons securing the waistband of his trousers.

Two flicks and she had the buttons undone.

He cursed and yanked her skirt down, pushing it down in a profusion of silk folds, then he set about unraveling the laces of her petticoats.

It fascinated her that he could unknot the laces without seeing, yet he seemed quite adept; she left him to it.

Left him worrying at that while she peeled back the front placket of his trousers, sought and found the slit in his linen underpants, and slid her hand within.

She palmed his erection and his breath hitched, then halted. She closed her fingers about the rock-hard length, heavy as marble, corded with thick veins, the skin unbelievably delicate and fine. And sensitive. His breath stuttered and shook when she brushed her fingertips over the smoothness of the broad head. Her fingers dallied on the moistness of the slit—and he came at her again.

He yanked the laces loose, shoved her petticoats down to join her skirt.

Before he could seize her and lift her—and break her hold on him—she stepped out of her skirts and kicked them aside. Closing her hand more firmly about his erection, she reached with the other for his nape. She caught him and hauled him into another kiss.

This time, he dove into the exchange—as determined as she, as ravenous for control, but even more for the outcome. No reluctance, no resistance. Just need and raw desire.

She moved into him, and he hauled her closer. For a protracted moment, they caught each other, seized each other's senses and held them immersed in the scorching duel of their tongues, the blatantly sexual mating of their mouths.

She was no longer thinking—she didn't need to; she reacted and stroked the hard hot length in her palm, then sent her other hand skating down from his nape, tracing down the side of his chest to slide around to his back and splay over the center, holding him to her as with her other hand she played.

He groaned through the kiss. The guttural sound was music to her ears.

Then his hands, until then spread on her back, slid down, blatantly sculpting her body, her skin screened from the heat of his hard palms only by the flimsiest of silks. Those large hands swept lower, over the indentation of her waist and down, to close, possessive and greedy, over the globes of her bottom.

Her own breath shook as he gripped, then provocatively kneaded.

Although their lips were still supping, neither was any longer trapped in the kiss—they were trapped by their own desires and the sensations battering them. She could barely breathe, but by her judgment, it was her turn.

She slid her hand from his back to his side and gripped the loose waistband of his trousers; simultaneously, she eased her hold on his erection just enough to score upward with her nails, all the way to the tip.

His focus fractured. The grip of his hands on her bottom eased.

Just enough for her to wiggle and slide out of his hold and sink to her knees.

With her free hand, she held the front of his trousers open, while with the other she angled his erection to her lips.

Thomas froze. Emotions lashed him—a vivid medley of leaping passion, straining desire, disbelief, and surging expectation. Anticipation triumphed, sank its claws deep—and held him immobile. Every muscle he possessed locked; he was unable to move, barely able to breathe—all he could do was watch as, kneeling amid the pile of her discarded skirts, she closed both hands about his straining length, and gently, delicately, kissed the weeping head.

His senses teetered; she was going to kill him—slay him—if she didn't do more. Did she know how?

The answer came in the next second. She parted her lips and took him into her mouth, and his senses rioted.

Her hair was still more or less up in the knot she'd worn it in that evening, exposing the delicate curve of her neck as she bent her head at his groin. He stared, then she suckled and ripped a groan from him.

If he watched any longer, he'd be lost. Closing his eyes, he rode out the exquisite slide of her hot wet flesh closing about him. He reached for her head, needing that anchor—needing that pretense that he had some control, when in reality he had none. She'd razed his defenses.

She proceeded to reduce every last barrier he had to ash.

Every lick set him quaking, clinging desperately to fast unraveling sanity; every time she sucked, he teetered on the brink of losing all control and simply ravishing her.

If she realized that, sensed that, she didn't stop.

Her hairpins pinged and scattered on the floor as, his head tipping back, he desperately clung to some semblance of sophistication while she, with her hot mouth and her wandering hands, hands that ultimately came to close about and lightly knead his heavy balls, tried to cinder even that.

Bit by bit, suck by lick, she succeeded.

Life. I will always bring you life.

But some part of him was dying. Under her committed, direct, and determined ministrations, that part of him that was not truly him was withering and falling away.

And all that was left was the true him—nothing like the Thomas Carrick the ladies of Glasgow knew, but a man of even stronger passions, of needs that went so much deeper than any of them had ever known, ever touched, much less satisfied.

Under her hands, under the touch of her lips and the wet heat of her mouth, the true him burned.

Then she shifted her head and took him deeper yet.

And he knew beyond question that he wouldn't last.

"Enough." He forced the word out, could barely make it out himself, but she heard and paused—he seized the moment to slip his thumb between her lips, to spread his fingers and grip her head and, as he drew free of her mouth, haul her up.

Against him. He held her head clamped between his palms and pressed a searing kiss on her swollen lips.

Tasted a trace of himself in her mouth and plunged deeper, forcing her lips wide, sweeping his tongue over hers, claiming every inch of her softness anew. Then he released her head and caught her instead, crushed her to him and, angling his head over hers, holding her trapped in the kiss, proceeded to conquer the rest of her.

Lucilla wasn't about to be conquered—at least not so easily. Especially not now that he'd finally dropped his shields and was interacting with her as just him. She hadn't realized what a difference there was between this inner man and the other, the one she'd known until now. This man was harder, more demanding—even more inclined to command.

She didn't care—*he* was the one she coveted. Her true lover, her true husband, her true mate.

His hands shaped her body, ruthlessly pressing fire beneath her skin.

She returned the act with interest, then pushed things even further, touching, tracing—teasing and taunting. Passion thudded in her veins; desire surged through her even as delight coursed down every nerve.

She was burning, almost as hot as he; his skin was like a brand wherever she touched, sinking into her senses. She could feel urgency building in them both, in the tension in their muscles, in the desperation driving each caress and in their fractured breaths, yet still they battled, waging a sensual war of sorts, neither willing to surrender even though both were reaching the limit of what they could withstand... They were racing flat out toward that threshold beyond which passion wouldn't allow them to hold back.

He reached that breaking point first.

A guttural sound escaped him, then he swung around and backed her against the bed. The high mattress met her thighs.

His arms eased from around her, but instead of gripping her waist and lifting her—either to the bed or against him—he closed both hands in the open collar of her chemise. The eyes that met hers were burning gold. Then he ripped.

In one violent move, he stripped the fine garment from her.

Cool air washed over her flushed skin, and she rejoiced.

Dragging in a shallow breath, she reached for his trousers, still hanging open from his hips.

Her fingertips had barely touched the material when he caught her shoulders and spun her to face the bed.

She caught only a glimpse of his face, of his eyes, as she turned, but what burned there was so powerful, so passionately alive, she lost what little breath she'd managed to catch.

Then his hand pressed heavily between her shoulder blades, and she had no choice but to bend over the bed.

Turning her head to one side, she tried to peek through the fall of her hair, tried to reach back, but he caught her hands, anchored them in one of his in the small of her back, and leaned enough of his weight on that hand to keep her in place.

Then with his feet, he pushed hers apart, and touched her.

He caressed the bare globes of her bottom, then he dipped his long fingers into the hollow beneath.

He found the slick wetness between her thighs, spread it over her sensitive lips, tracing and caressing. He found her entrance and circled it with one broad fingertip, then he pressed his fist between her thighs and thrust that finger into her, as deeply as he could.

She squirmed, but he held her down.

He stroked, and she panted.

Then he added a second finger to the first; she moaned as he slid both fingers deep.

She could feel his hand flexing between her thighs as he worked his fingers in and out of her sheath. Gasping, burning, she rolled her hips, riding the repetitive penetrations.

Her lids fell. She caught her lower lip between her teeth in an attempt to hold back the scream she knew would come...

The nameless peak of passion had risen before her and she was almost at its lip—teetering on the brink of ecstasy—when he abruptly drew his fingers from her.

Before her raging senses did more than register that fact, he'd released her hands and taken her hips in an unforgiving grip, then with one long thrust, he drove into her to the hilt.

Her scream was forced from her lungs and half muffled by the comforter. Passion sizzled down her veins, and she clamped tightly about him.

As he rode her. Through the moment of unraveling control—through that first surrender.

And straight on into the next.

She hadn't thought the peak could get any higher, but it could—it did. He made it so. Made her nerves unravel further yet, made her senses unaware of anything beyond the earthy evidence of their joining—the slap of his belly against her bottom, the brush of his balls between her thighs, the hard grip of his fingers anchoring her before him, the repetitive push as he filled her and the slide of her cheek against the silk of her comforter, the scent of her arousal and his, the weak, panting breaths that fell from her lips, and the unrelenting heat that had her writhing on the bed.

She didn't think she could reach the pinnacle, not a second time—not so soon. But he drove her up and over, thrusting deep and rolling his hips, then pushing deeper yet, and she screamed again as blinding ecstasy took her and frazzled every last nerve.

She was boneless, utterly boneless, but as he withdrew from her, she realized that he hadn't yet sought his release.

Quite deliberately, she assumed, and wondered. Waited.

She heard him dispense with his shoes and remaining clothes. Then he scooped her up, lifted her against his chest, and crawled onto the bed.

He laid her down with the huge mound of pillows at her back; that left her half sitting, but that seemed to be his intention as he followed her down. Settling his hips between her thighs, he planted an elbow beside her shoulder, angling his chest so he could look at her—at her body lying supine beneath his.

Her wits long gone, operating on instinct alone, she studied his face. There was a hardness, an angularity that hadn't been there before, as if the moment had stripped away all superficial softness and left only the true bedrock behind.

That sight—what she could see revealed—fascinated her. Raising one hand, she lightly trailed her fingertips down one chiseled cheek.

He'd been surveying her body; he turned his head and met her eyes.

His were gold in amber, and they burned with a passionate, possessive flame.

His lids lowered. He turned his head a fraction more and kissed her fingertips. Then he caught her hand and pressed a searing kiss to her palm.

Raising his eyes to hers again, he held her gaze—and set his other hand to her breast.

And plunged them back into the fire—theirs, born of their desires, of their passionate natures, and fueled by a need neither could deny.

He moved one thigh up and wide. Holding her open, he pushed deeply into her. Anchoring her as he wished, sinking deep between her thighs, he filled her.

Closing his eyes, he gave himself up to the moment, to her.

She raised her arms, wrapped them about him, and drew him closer yet. Until his body was truly riding hers; the friction of his hair-dusted limbs and chest against her skin was beyond exquisite.

She surrendered and claimed, opened her arms and embraced him—this, all.

Thomas bowed his head and, in the final desperation, found her lips, covered them with his, sank into her mouth, and let the pounding need of their combined passions have its way as he raced them up and on—and then over the final, impossibly high and jagged peak.

She was burning beneath him, as ferocious in her passion as he as they soared into that critical moment of heightened need—of shattering oneness.

Of true intimacy.

Glory beckoned and she fell. She came apart, and he drank deep, drank in her cry, let his greedy senses draw her passion and total surrender deep into his soul—then his thoughts disintegrated. He was dimly aware of plunging into her body, of the clinging rippling clutch of her sheath, of his own body finding an elementally shattering release—but as ecstasy painted a sunburst on the inside of his lids, what he was most deeply conscious of was the incredible peace.

The sense of rightness and belonging that filled his soul.

He was too wracked by passion to fear it, too deeply exposed to do anything other than recognize just how precious such a feeling was.

He accepted it, let it stretch.

With her pinned beneath him, he let himself slump into her arms, and let her hold him as they and their senses tumbled over the edge into satiation, into the pleasured oblivion of their sensual sea.

Fourteen

In his chamber below Lucilla's room, Thomas washed and got ready to face another day of ambling about Casphairn Manor.

Until Lucilla had got him into her bedroom, the previous evening had been a *subtle* seduction; in many ways, the day had been, too. Once she'd shut her bedroom door behind them, the seduction had turned blatant, yet... while on one level he wasn't entirely at ease with how far into uncharted territory they'd ventured, most of him was still reveling in the aftermath—a curious sense of freedom.

She was the only bed partner—the only female of any sort—with whom he'd openly been simply himself. He'd adopted the façade of a gentleman of society so long ago, he'd forgotten what it was like to set it aside and simply be him.

He'd forgotten a lot about being simply him. About what he truly liked, about what appealed to the real him.

So many of the previous day's interludes had reminded him of what he had, in his early years, liked about living in the country; those moments had reawoken a forgotten appreciation for the minor mundane occurrences that made up the heartbeat of country life. In this sort of country.

He'd been born not far away. He'd spent some of the most formative of his months and years close by, in these lands.

He hadn't realized the connection still lived, buried beneath the layers of his Glasgow personality, the sophisticated façade he'd fallen into the habit of using as a perpetual mask while living there...where, if he was honest, he'd grown increasingly bored over the last several years. Not with the business, the running of it, but with all the other aspects of living there.

He'd missed coming back to these lands, missed connecting with his roots. Roots he hadn't realized had remained so strong, so immutable.

But for today and those following, until his leg was sufficiently healed to ride Phantom back to Glasgow, he could indulge his inner self; he was, indeed, looking forward to discovering what the day might bring.

He heard Lucilla's footsteps coming down the stone stairs; an instant later, she tapped on his door. Shrugging on his coat, he walked to the door, opened it, and found her waiting outside.

She met his eyes, read them, then smiled—one of her direct, open-hearted smiles that felt like warm sunlight to him.

He smiled easily back with just a hint of smugness, which she saw, but there was no reason to employ any façade with her. Her nose tipped up slightly, her challenge still there in the set of her head, her posture.

She stepped away. "I don't know about you, but I'm ravenous."

He picked up his cane, drew the door closed behind

him, and followed. "A night of interrupted sleep can have that effect."

She smothered a laugh.

They found Marcus already at the high table. Thomas sat Lucilla in her usual chair, then settled beside her in what had already become his accustomed place. He and she helped themselves from the array of platters and settled to eat.

A comfortable silence enfolded them, which, it appeared, none of them felt compelled to break. He continued to be curious about the relationship between Lucilla and Marcus; both seemed to know what the other was thinking, and possibly what they intended to do. They exchanged few questions along the lines of "What are your plans?"—presumably because they knew the answers.

It was curious to feel included, not as if he were a part of them but rather that he'd been accepted as a denizen of their small world and didn't need to be entertained with polite but meaningless chatter.

They'd pushed their plates away and were sitting back, savoring their coffee or tea, when, as had happened the day before, Lucilla was summoned to deal with some household matter. She immediately excused herself, rose, and walked off, leaving him and Marcus still at the table.

Eventually, Marcus set his mug down and arched a brow at him. "I'm going to spend a few hours with the dogs, if you'd like to join me. I'm training the younger ones, and if you have any advice, I'd be pleased to hear it."

"Where are the kennels?"

Marcus tipped his head to the southwest. "At the far corner of the rear yard. It's not that far, and we have a training field behind the kennels, so you won't have to walk any further."

Although his wound still pricked and itched, and the muscle tensed uncomfortably when he walked, the pain had largely gone; unless he stood or walked for too long, the wound wouldn't hobble him. He nodded and set down his mug. "Thank you. I'd like that. It's been quite a while since I last worked with hounds."

As they rose, Marcus glanced at him. "You didn't keep your hand in with the Carrick pack?"

Gripping his cane, he followed Marcus off the dais. "When I realized how little time I'd be spending down here, I gave it up. Not fair on the dogs, and it's not possible to keep even a pair in Glasgow." Not in the fashionable area in which he lived. "Deerhounds would go insane from the lack of space in which to run."

Marcus grunted. He headed for the archway Thomas had assumed led to the kitchens. Reaching it, Marcus paused to glance at him. "So who keeps the Carrick pack now? I know some are still there, even if Nigel sold off more than half—which, incidentally, seemed another very strange thing to do. I bought several of the bitches and a good-looking sire, too."

Thomas shrugged. "Nigel was never that interested in the hounds—well, other than for hunting. He never saw the point in breeding them." He hesitated—then, accepting that Marcus was unlikely to act in any way that might harm the hounds, he added, "I understand that several of the clan disagreed with his culling, and they spirited the most valuable breeders to one of the outlying farms. I'm not sure who is running the breeding now, but Nigel knows nothing of it."

"Ah. I see." Marcus led the way into the wide corridor.

"Speaking of breeding hounds," Thomas said, limping behind him, "where are Artemis and Apollo? They were here when I arrived—or did I dream that?"

"No dream." Marcus walked through another archway into the bustling kitchen. He moved to one side, out of the way of the maids, and halted; Thomas joined him. "That evening, I had the dogs in to show the children. I do that every now and then, so the dogs learn children aren't prey to chase, and the children get used to them. Normally Artemis and Apollo are the only dogs allowed in the house, but they have the run of the place. They used to stick to me and Lucilla like glue, but now they're so old, they spend most of their days moving from fireplace to fireplace on this level." Marcus tipped his head to a pair of shaggy heaps stretched before the main kitchen hearth. "At this time of day, they're invariably here, waiting for leftover sausage and bacon."

Thomas grinned; he watched the two dogs for several minutes. "They look like they're dreaming."

Marcus smiled. "Let's leave them to it. We can go out this way."

Thomas followed his host into another corridor that led to a rear door. They stepped out into a cobbled courtyard and walked slowly toward the southwest corner of a very large rear yard.

As they walked, he looked around. The ancillary buildings made Casphairn Manor feel more like a village; he noted a blacksmith's forge, and what appeared to be a tannery, and an active buttery with butts of ale neatly stacked along one wall.

Marcus had noticed him looking. Thomas arched a brow. "You have a strange and different mix of trades—not just the ones for farming."

Marcus nodded. "From the first, we've always had all the trades needed to survive. Historically, given how much of the year we're snow-bound, that made sense, but even now, we don't need to rely on the outside world for anything vital. Every necessary trade is here somewhere, either at the manor itself or on the farms—which, as I mentioned, are relatively close."

Thomas had looked out of Lucilla's window that morning and had seen several of the farmhouses. Although not so visible at ground level, they weren't far from the manor at all.

The kennels proved to be a relatively new structure, at least as far as buildings at Casphairn Manor went.

"We built it when I—and Lucilla, but mostly me—decided to seriously breed the hounds." Marcus led him down the central aisle toward a large open area at the far end. Along the way, he unlatched the doors of the large pens to either side, and dogs of all sizes and a good blend of colors rushed out, eager to hunt, eager to please—and hoping to run like the wind.

Thomas laughed as the dogs brushed and jostled him, and younger pups scampered around and about, but after circling and scenting him and deciding he posed no danger, the older dogs led the milling pack on down the aisle, to gather, curious and eager, in the clear area at the end.

The next two hours went in a pleasure he hadn't so much forgotten as set aside. How to deal with the large, strong, and ever-curious deerhounds instantly returned to him; he joined Marcus in putting the older dogs through their paces, then, once those dogs were satisfied and ready to slump, tongues lolling, and rest, he and Marcus ran through a succession of training exercises with the year-old youngsters. The puppies were too young to train, but the yearlings needed to start learning the signals, whistles, clicks, and waves by which a hunter controlled his dogs.

At the end of the session, assisted by the two kennel keepers, they steered the dogs back to their pens. Thomas paused to rub the shaggy head of one brindle-coated yearling.

Marcus leaned on the gate of a nearby pen. "That's one of Apollo's descendants."

"Really?" Thomas pushed back to study the dog's lines. "Yes—I can believe that."

Marcus straightened. "Perhaps we should close the circle, as it were." When Thomas looked his way, Marcus pointed to the dog. "I could give you a pair of hounds—one from Apollo, one from Artemis."

The notion tugged at something inside him, but Thomas shook his head and stepped back, allowing one of the kennel keepers to pen the dog. "That's the one thing I truly dislike about Glasgow—it's no place for hounds."

Marcus stared at him for several seconds, his expression—never easy to read—especially inscrutable, but when Thomas arched his brows in question, Marcus merely dipped his head and said, "There is that."

With a wave, Marcus started them walking out of the kennels.

Thomas had crouched more than a few times; his injured calf was now reminding him that he still carried a wound.

Although he said nothing, and he was damned if he showed anything, Marcus seemed to sense his discomfort and kept to a slow, ambling pace.

They were still some way from the kitchen door when a voice called, "Mr. Carrick, sir!"

He and Marcus both looked and saw a farmer—one from the Vale who Thomas had seen in the Great Hall, but could not put a name to—standing on the other side of the yard fence, leaning on the top rail.

"I was wondering, sir, if you'd mind if I picked your brains over the sheep—the longhairs the Carricks run. I oversee the herd here, which is all white-faced natives, but I wondered if you had any pointers you could share."

Marcus glanced at Thomas, a query in his eyes. In reply, Thomas changed direction and limped across to lean against the fence. Marcus followed and introduced the farmer as Mr. Gatehouse. Thomas exchanged nods. "They're Lincoln Longhairs, as I recall."

"Aye, that'd be them." Gatehouse nodded solemnly. "We've been wondering"—he included Marcus with a tip of his head—"whether there'd be any sense us getting a few in, just to see."

"That," Thomas said, settling more comfortably against the rail fence, "depends on what you want to achieve." To his surprise, details of the breed several of the more isolated crofters ran to supplement their income from logging were still clear in his memories. "The Carrick crofters chose the Lincolns because they could get a decent return even with just a few animals, principally because of the weight of the fleece."

The three of them stood leaning against the fence, swapping observations and weighing the benefits of the longhairs versus the local white-faced breed, which was highly prized for its silken fleece as well as its succulent meat.

At one point, remembering his earlier exchange with Marcus, Thomas asked, "What do your weavers think?"

And that opened up another field for extensive discussion.

It was nearly an hour later when they parted from Gatehouse and continued their ambling progress toward the manor's back door.

Halfway across the open section of the yard, Thomas halted. Leaning on his cane to ease the pressure on his leg, he lifted his gaze to the surrounding hills, scanning their forested lower slopes and the higher, bald peaks.

Realizing he'd stopped, Marcus halted a few paces ahead and turned to look back at him.

His gaze resting on the hills to the north, on the ridge that separated Carrick lands from the Vale, Thomas murmured, "It's been so long since I was here, on the land and with my feet on the ground, so to speak. I hadn't expected my memories to be so clear—so sharp and precise."

Marcus considered him for a long moment; Thomas felt his steady gaze, but before he turned to meet it, Marcus, too, looked up at the hills, at the northern ridge. "Once this country claims you, it sinks talons into your soul, and as far as I've seen, as far as I know, it never lets you go."

That sounded like some old saying. Given all he knew of Marcus's situation—his unquestioning acceptance of his future in the Vale—Thomas wasn't sure how to respond, so he merely tipped his head and resumed his journey toward the house.

Marcus watched Thomas for several moments, then sighed and followed him.

* * *

Late that night, when the manor had fallen silent and all were abed, Thomas lay sprawled on his back between Lucilla's pale green sheets, with his head on her pillows and with her stretched half over him, sated and asleep.

He was sinking toward slumber, too, equally sated and so deeply satisfied—so very deeply relaxed on the mental plane as well as the physical—that his mind seemed to be floating, hovering, observing.

Able to see and recognize aspects of himself that normally lay concealed.

Such as the reason he was so very at ease, at peace on a level he couldn't remember ever having attained.

Despite the limitations imposed by his injury, his day—this day—had…suited him. Had unexpectedly fulfilled him. From the first, it had been pleasant—pleasing, engaging, and satisfying in an unprecedented way—and, courtesy of what flared so hotly between him and Lucilla, had ended in soul-wrenching pleasure.

His mind dwelled on the revelation—on the answer to the question of what he needed in order to feel this way. A question he hadn't previously asked for the simple reason that, until now, he hadn't realized it was possible to feel so content. So sunk in contentment.

Now he knew, but he also knew it couldn't last. His wound would heal and he'd leave for Glasgow—and by then this…madness, whatever it was, with Lucilla would have run its course. If their mutual fire hadn't reduced to ashes by then, the flames would at least have started to subside. To lose their potency, their power.

They hadn't yet, but they would. Such was the way of life.

To you, I will always bring life.

Perhaps, but all things died with time. Like the screen he'd originally deployed between him and her that their passion had reduced to cinders.

He had to admit that being himself—simply himself— as he was with her was a special boon, yet no matter how much he wished to cling to it, he couldn't. Being with her would end when he left the Vale and returned to Glasgow and his other—controlled, safe, and forever—life.

She stirred. Tightening his arms around her, he shifted onto his side and rested his jaw on the top of her head. All tension leached from her limbs, and she sank into his embrace. As the delectable perfume that spoke to him of her weaved through his mind, sending tendrils into his dreams, he felt again the swell of that golden emotion— amorphous, but powerful and very real—that she and this place seemed to evoke in him, and mentally smiled.

It might be slated to end, but there was no reason not to enjoy it—even to wallow in it—until then.

The arms of Morpheus closed about him and dragged him down.

Lucilla felt him slip over the threshold into sleep. She reached with her senses, checking again, and once again felt reassurance wash through her.

She could feel his contentment like a tangible thing. While she wasn't a mind reader and couldn't even guess his thoughts with any certainty, she was increasingly able to read his emotions, especially now that he'd dropped the last barrier he'd used to screen his true persona and engaged with her directly, man to woman, heart to heart.

The breaching of that barrier had been her first real sign of success. The deep contentment that now held him was another.

Earlier in the evening, Marcus had stopped her in the corridor. Her twin had met her gaze and simply asked, "Are you *sure* you know what you're doing?"

He hadn't needed to specify what he was asking about. She'd inwardly frowned but had answered truthfully, "Yes."

He'd grimaced but had left it at that, and they'd gone down to the drawing room.

Bothered that it had been Marcus who had—again—doubted her, she'd watched Thomas closely, paying attention to his tone, his gestures, to everything she could read in him—and, of course, she had consulted her own feelings and her sense of the Lady's directives again, but nothing there had changed.

And now the advances she'd hoped for were falling into place.

So she was on the right track, following the right path—the one she was supposed to lead Thomas down. She'd been convinced she needed to bring him to the Vale and keep him there until he understood what he was to her; what she hadn't fully appreciated was that a part of what he had to see and learn was what she and the Vale were to him. He'd needed to comprehend that his position as her consort was not simply a matter of standing by her side, but that he had a real and active role to fill in the community and the people were ready to accept him.

This—including the bliss of this night in her bed—was how things were meant to be.

All was well and progressing as it should.

Reassured, satisfied, and as deeply content as he, she let herself slide into dreams.

* * *

Thomas enjoyed two more days of bucolic bliss before the pleasant cocoon of life in the Vale fractured and shattered around him.

He'd known this strange time would end, yet he hadn't expected that end to come in quite such a dramatic fashion.

Not that the final act had yet been played out; that was still to come. Once he'd realized... The right place and the right time to ask his questions was patently after he and Lucilla retired to her room, so with steely resolve, he'd waited through dinner and now sat in the drawing room with her and Marcus.

As they had over the previous evenings, he and Marcus idly discussed this or that—or, as they were presently doing, flicked through the gentlemen's periodicals with which the manor seemed well supplied, while Lucilla entertained them and herself by strumming airs on her harp.

Those previous evenings had struck him as immensely comfortable; tonight, he was impatient for the tea trolley to arrive. But he was adept at hiding his emotions, a necessity in business negotiations; Marcus, at least, seemed to have no inkling of any storm brewing, of any tension in the air.

Lucilla was more sensitive. She'd been watching him from the instant she'd first seen him after he'd strung the pieces together and had finally seen her design, but he'd made sure she couldn't see past his façade. That the façade was back in place was, of course, what had alerted her to the change in him.

There was nothing he could do about that; she would

just have to wait until they could speak privately and he could drop that screening façade and let her see just how much anger was roiling behind it.

Looking back, the clues had been there all along, on open display from the instant he'd crossed the manor's threshold, but he hadn't been aware of what was really going on, and so he hadn't noted them. But that morning after breakfast, when Lucilla had departed about her daily chores and Marcus had been summoned to deal with a broken fence, leaving him sitting sipping his coffee alone at the high table, a man had approached, introduced himself as the head herdsman, and asked for his opinion on the manor's herd of Highland cattle.

He'd explained he had little knowledge of the beasts, but the man had seemed set on showing him the manor's breeding stock, which were accommodated in the nearer pastures; with nothing else on his plate, he'd mentally shrugged and gone. He'd wanted to walk anyway, to check how far he could go without the cane. Although the stitches were still there, and would remain for some days yet, he'd discovered the injury no longer troubled him. So he'd walked the fields, observed the beasts he'd been shown, absorbed quite a lot from the knowledgeable herdsman, and had discovered that, as with the sheep, he hadn't forgotten snippets he'd picked up long ago and that he did, therefore, have something to say. Something to contribute.

He and the herdsman had parted on good terms.

Immediately after luncheon, the head forester of the estate, a grizzled older man named Gibbins, had stopped him on his way out of the Great Hall and asked for his views on logging. As it happened, he knew considerably more about that subject than about cattle, or even sheep. Gibbins had been excited to hear of his experiences with the export and import of timbers; several others—the other farmers who were involved in logging on the estate—had gathered around, and they'd spent a comfortable hour discussing the current state of the local forests and the demand for various timbers.

Eventually parting from the men, he'd been left with a strange feeling—something about the way the men had looked at him at the end, as if they'd expected something more from him, some directive, but that wasn't his place.

He'd been ambling toward the library, musing on what might have been behind that air of expectation, when Cook had come hurrying after him.

"Mr. Carrick, sir." Halting before him, the ruddy-faced woman had bobbed a curtsy. Wiping her hands on her apron, she'd said, "I've been meaning to ask, sir, if you could let me have a list of your favorite dishes." Bright-eyed, she'd rattled on, "What with you joining the household and all, we in the kitchen like to make sure we provide favorite dishes for the family every now and then…"

She'd gone on, but he'd stopped listening, his mind seizing on the words "joining the household" and "for the family."

That had been the first crack in his pleasant world.

In a daze, he'd agreed to make a list—not that, even then, he'd had any intention of doing so—but saying anything else would have revealed too much, risked exposing too much of the turmoil erupting inside him.

Cook had beamed, dropped another curtsy, and hurried back to her kitchen.

He'd walked on to the library, gone in, and shut the

door. He'd been relieved to discover that Marcus wasn't there.

Over the next two hours, he'd paced before the hearth while his mind had ranged over every incident of the last days—replaying every conversation, reassessing from the perspective of what he now suspected.

Most especially, he'd reviewed every single word he'd exchanged with Lucilla.

And now he waited to have it out with her.

Finally, the tea trolley arrived. She stopped playing, and he and Marcus set down the magazines they'd been perusing.

She poured and handed around the cups, and they all drank. In between sips, they made idle conversation, which, thanks to his years in Glasgow and his reinstituted façade, he managed well enough.

But his impatience was rising, and she, at least, sensed it.

When he set down his empty cup and declared he would retire, she rose with him.

Leaving Marcus picking up a magazine, he and she quit the library and walked to the foyer. They climbed the stairs and, as they had for the past several nights, ignored the door to his room and continued up the turret stairs to her chamber.

She led the way inside; he followed and shut the door.

He turned—to find she'd halted and swung to face him; she was watching him, and for the very first time in all the years he'd known her, her emerald gaze was unsure.

"What's wrong?" Her voice was steady. He sensed she truly had no idea.

He locked his gaze with hers; despite a wish to remain impassive, he felt his jaw clench. "What have you told the people here—the household and all those in the Vale—about me? About why I'm here?"

She frowned in open puzzlement. "I haven't told them anything." She shook her head. "I haven't discussed you at all."

"Ah." He'd left his cane in his room; he wished he had it—something to grip, to have in his hands. He remained where he was, his back to the door, and kept his gaze locked with hers. "So the desire of so many to hear my opinions—on the crops, on the cattle and sheep herds, on the blacksmith's new forge, on logging, and on so many other matters—is merely them being friendly?" He saw realization flicker in her eyes. "And what about Cook's request for a list of my favorite foods? Because every now and then, the kitchen likes to provide favorite dishes for the family."

The flicker steadied and strengthened; realization flooded her features. "Oh." She blinked, then grimaced. After a second, she refocused on his eyes. "As I said, I haven't told them anything, but of course, that doesn't mean they haven't guessed, doesn't mean they don't know."

"Know *what*?" He rapped out the question and felt his façade of sophistication fracture and fall. "What do *they* know that *I don't*?"

She studied him for an instant, as if realizing he was dealing with her directly again—without that façade of manners between them—then she drew breath and lifted her head. "That according to the Lady, you are my consort."

He blinked, sensed a ripple in the atmosphere, and put it down to pure shock. He drew in a breath, then breathed deeper still, forcing himself to take an extended moment to grapple with his surprisingly diverse reactions, to muzzle and suppress them without examining them and allowing them to distract him. That accomplished, he fixed his gaze once more on her eyes and, with carefully reined aggression, asked, "What, exactly, does that mean?"

He needed to hear the whole story, and he needed to hear it directly from her rose-red lips.

They parted, and she said, "My consort is the man fated to be my one true lover, my protector, my husband, the father of my children."

Again, he felt that odd ripple in his awareness—stronger this time, a schism opening within him as if reality had ruptured. It wasn't hard to pinpoint the cause; her words had evoked, provoked, a torrent of turbulent emotions, half of which he didn't recognize—he shoved them down, locked them away. He couldn't *want* to be her consort—couldn't want any part of the position, the life, she was defining.

That, apparently, she and everyone else in the Vale had been anticipating he would accept.

As if to confirm that, she added, "He will rule here by my side."

He frowned. "What about Marcus?"

She shook her head. "His path lies elsewhere. He can't rule in the Vale—only the Lady of the Vale, the one chosen by the Lady in each generation, can. She and her consort together."

Me and you together. She didn't say the words, but he heard them.

It didn't really matter. This wasn't the life he wanted—

the life he'd chosen, the life he'd spent years crafting for himself. The life he was determined to have.

That life lay in Glasgow, not here.

But anger and resentment simmered—that she'd brought him to this, to feeling the tug he was determined to deny. To *feeling* the connection with her, with this place—to experiencing again the comfort of his roots, the very real pleasures he'd so steadfastly blocked from his mind.

All that he'd turned his back on long ago. All he'd consistently refused over the years.

Including her.

Yet *she* had pulled him back—back to where emotions he didn't want to acknowledge, much less feel, seethed in a restless reckless sea inside him.

And she'd done it deliberately, even after he'd explained it wasn't what he wanted.

That life here, with her, wasn't something he would accept.

"How long have you believed that your fated one was me?" Some part of him was curious; he wanted to know.

She hesitated, but then she raised her chin and, her gaze still meshed with his, replied, "Since that Christmas Eve we spent in the Fieldses' cottage. I had suspicions before, but after that, I knew."

"And you never thought to mention it?" It took effort not to pace, to prowl; he forced himself to remain where he was and return her steady gaze. "We've met often enough since, yet not even over the last week and more we've spent together did you feel it appropriate to say a single word?"

Her chin firmed. Her eyes narrowed; the green started to sharpen and spark. "When, exactly, could I have told you? You didn't believe—you *still* don't believe. And without some degree of acceptance of the Lady's power, of her influence, telling you that you were one of Her chosen—chosen to be my consort—would have achieved precisely what?"

Her voice had grown stronger, her accent more clipped. Before he could answer, she went on, "It was patently obvious that the only way you would ever come to accept the position that is rightly yours was if you spent time here—with me, in the Vale—long enough to see and understand for yourself." She crossed her arms and stared him in the eye. "That was all I could influence—all I could accomplish. All I could do was bring you here and trust that you would open your eyes and see."

Her plan had worked, but he wasn't, even now, going to concede. "That's all very well, but the life of your consort is not the life I want."

He made the statement coldly, clearly—deliberately brutally. Although she didn't move a muscle, didn't flinch, he felt her reaction—he might as well have slapped her.

But then a furious flame erupted in her eyes; she seemed to grow taller as she lowered her arms and raised her chin. Her eyes seared his. "So. You've decided on a particular path, and no matter what evidence is laid before you—nor how compelling that evidence is—you will not turn aside." Her voice resonated, thick with power—the power of her personality, of all she was. Ruthlessly, with a harshness all her own, she stated, "The path you've chosen is the *wrong* path, but because it's the one you've decided on, you refuse to turn from it. Pigheaded doesn't begin to describe you, for in this you are deliberately harming yourself."

He managed a sneer. "Some men prefer not to live under a cat's paw."

"And some men are blind beyond reason."

There was hurt as well as fury in her voice.

He shackled the emotions that tried to erupt—to respond, but in what way he wasn't sure, and he wasn't about to trust what he felt. Not about her.

It was she who flung away and started to pace. "You've been shown the right path, and you *have* seen it—you've recognized it." She tossed a raking glance at him. "Don't bother to deny it. I can see. I can tell."

Lucilla stalked back, trying desperately to harness her temper, her fury—and her fear. The words that fell from her lips came from she knew not where, yet still they came, tumbling free. She had no idea if they were what she should say—if they were the wisest response she might make. So much hung on this, yet she couldn't seem to think; she'd so rarely felt uncertainty, much less real fear.

She'd done *everything* she could to make him see, given him all she could—everything, every last piece of her that she had to give—and she'd succeeded in doing what she was supposed to do, yet still…he was refusing. Her, the position of her consort. All.

Her lungs had locked; she could barely draw breath. Her mind seemed on the brink of true turmoil. Yet she had to speak—had to try to reach him and make him rethink.

Make him change his mind.

"If I have it right"—she kept her eyes on the floor, heard her rioting emotions still straining her voice— "despite understanding—as inside you truly do—that remaining here, by my side, is the right path for you, because that isn't a path you have fashioned for yourself but one offered you by another—by me, by Fate, by the Lady—you refuse to take it."

Swinging to face him, she met his amber eyes; they were agate hard and unyielding. "Do I have that correct? That it's your *pride* that rules you in this—*even* in this?"

His face hardened; his expression closed. She saw a muscle in his jaw tighten.

An instant passed, then he stated, "You can analyze all you like. I am not going to change my mind. Allow me to repeat—being your consort is not a position I wish to fill."

Something inside her fractured; emotion geysered. Inside, she trembled with the force of it, yet she stood rock-steady. She breathed in, deeply, then raised her head and, still holding his gaze, replied, "You can fight Fate all you want, but it will not end well." She'd let all the considerable power at her command infuse those words. She continued with the same deadly calm. "Allow me to make something perfectly clear. There *isn't* anyone else for me *or for you*—and there never will be. If you turn your back on me, on us, on all we might be, there will be no other chance—not with anyone else, not in any other place."

His features impassive, he held her gaze for a long moment, then, with apparently dismissive nonchalance, quirked a brow. "Is that a curse?"

Her control very nearly ruptured; curling her fingers into fists at her sides, she fought to hold her fury back. Eventually, in a voice every bit as cold as his, she replied, "By asking that, you show how limited your understanding, how little you've thought this through. Fate is not something anyone can run from—no matter your desires, no matter how immutable your determination, you will not escape."

She paused, then remembering that, regardless of his pigheadedness, he *was* still her consort, made one last bid to sway him. "I cannot stop you—your life is yours to live. Yet it's one thing to condemn yourself to lifelong misery, but in this, you condemn me, too."

His gaze had been stony, but at her last words, the amber of his eyes fractionally softened. She saw, dared to hope—but then he looked past her, at the bed. When he returned his gaze to her eyes, everything about him was granite again; although he hadn't moved, she could see he'd stepped even further back—putting even more distance between them.

He was leaving her.

Panic clutched her chest. What else could she say? He was locked against her—against her and everyone else and everything else in the Vale; she could all but feel him holding her and them back, pushing them all away. Rejecting and refusing to hear. To believe—to even consider.

She had no idea where such a ruthless, almost violent, and comprehensively adamant rejection sprang from. She had no notion of what might be behind it, what gave it such power—yet the force of it had hardened his heart as well as his face, and had set an impenetrable shield behind his eyes.

There was nothing more she could do.

The realization closed like an icy vise about her heart.

In brutal reality, free will trumped even Fate.

It trumped even the Lady.

The bottom fell out of her world.

When he spoke, his tone was distant, as if he was already viewing their association as something in his past. "Our time together hasn't been what I thought it was. I was honest about how I saw my future—you knew what I thought—yet against my wishes, you sought to change my path. You and your Lady failed, and you will have to live with that." He tipped his head a fraction—a travesty of a bow. "And now, I'll bid you goodbye. I'll be leaving at first light."

She said nothing; there was nothing she could say.

She watched the only man for her turn away, open the door, and leave her room.

He pulled the door closed behind him.

She stared at the panels. She had to let him go. Even through the turmoil raging inside her, she knew that. Understood that.

Even accepted that.

Regardless, she still felt as if her heart had been ripped from her chest, sliced, and stamped on.

And that, she was quite sure, she would never forget.

Fifteen

She stood at the window of her room and watched him ride away. Dawn was still streaking the sky when he set out, riding his gray into the future. His self-determined future, the one that didn't include her.

She had no tears left to shed—either of fury or of pain—not even in anticipation of the misery she knew now hovered on her horizon. If this was how it was meant to be, then it was; ranting and railing wouldn't change anything. As he'd said, she'd failed to convince him to turn aside and take the right path with her.

In the way he looked at things, that was her loss and his gain.

She watched him go until he rounded the curve in the drive and she could see him no more.

Only then did she draw a deeper breath. Folding her arms across her chest, she stared out unseeing and, finally, allowed herself to look inside.

Desolation lay heavy on her soul. A barren wasteland littered with powerful yet powerless feelings stretched, unending, inside her.

She breathed in, out. Waited.

Nothing in life was set in stone, not if it involved people. Every single soul possessed free will; every person, no matter how weak, was entitled to choose their own destiny.

He had chosen his self-determined path with deliberation and intent, and in repudiating so adamantly the alternate destiny she and the Lady had laid before him, he had, at least in part, rescripted her future.

Irreversibly.

So where did that leave her? What about *her* right to define the life she wanted—to claim the life she'd grown to adulthood expecting would be hers?

What now for her?

For long moments, she stared out at the land she had accepted as her birthright, to which she remained committed to protect and to nurture. Eventually, she exhaled and, closing her eyes, reached…and to her surprise, found the usual calm waiting. Waiting to enfold her and draw her in, to center her, to anchor her…

She'd expected to feel far less sure, far less stable.

Life, apparently, went on—and she was strong enough to endure. She breathed in again and felt steely resolve infuse her. She came from a long line of women who had found their way through turbulent times—through emotional storms and defeats as well as physical ones; no more than they would she give up, would she eschew her duty.

She would endure.

She'd been born to this—however it played out—and she would go forward.

More assured, she allowed herself to examine her emotions, recognizing and acknowledging them before setting them aside. Yes, there was hurt, layers of it, and beneath that a level of devastation—a disbelief that he truly had gone without even making any real attempt to understand—and beneath even that, beneath all, lay a yearning. A hollow core of emptiness; that was something she had expected to feel, along with the nagging, useless thoughts of whether she could have—should have—done this or that, something else, something other, to hold him and bind him to her.

From the first, she had understood that this decision had to be his. Entirely his, without undue influence from her.

Without the full impact, the full pressure, of her love.

Did he love her? She doubted he did, not as he might have—not as he would have if he'd claimed the position by her side. Acknowledging a possibility gave that possibility the potential to become a reality, but he'd turned away without giving love a chance, without even considering doing so.

Did she love him?

Her mind balked, unwilling to delve deeper.

She opened her eyes, stared outside, and forced herself to acknowledge even that. "Yes."

The truth resonated inside her, inviolable, immutable.

She had loved him for years; a quietly patient, undemanding kernel of unconditional love had been planted in her soul so long ago that she'd fallen into the habit of taking it for granted. But her love was no longer that gentle bud. Although she'd been aware of gradual changes through the years, until that moment she hadn't truly appreciated how much had altered over the last days, how their constant adult interactions had nurtured that long-buried seed to rampant, full-flowering life.

Love wasn't something one commanded. It came on its own terms, was governed by its own rules, and needed no permission to grow into a force that compelled, and held, and never, ever, let go.

Such was her love for him now, and all she could do was feel it, acknowledge it—honor it and herself and hold true to it, and wait to see if he ever rode back to claim it and her.

Time would tell.

So she was back to waiting again, to relegating her heart and her private life to the back of her mental shelf again.

She dragged in a breath—forced air deeper into her lungs. Then, exhaling, she lowered her arms and turned to the door, to her day.

Life went on.

She accepted that she'd had to let him leave, that she had to wait for him to reach understanding and acceptance on his own…but for the first time in her life, she no longer had faith that through following the Lady's dictates all would eventually be well—not in this case. Not for her and him.

He'd taken that faith from her when he'd ridden away, and she didn't think she would ever get it back.

* * *

Thomas hadn't even reached Ayr before the feeling that he'd made a horrendous mistake engulfed him. He felt it like a weight crushing his chest, making it harder and harder to breathe with every mile that fell behind him.

He refused to acknowledge the nonsensical feeling, gritted his teeth against the sensation, and rode doggedly on.

* * *

In the cool of the evening four days later, he pulled the door of his lodgings shut behind him, settled his hat on his head, gripped the head of his cane—once again more fashionable accessory than required support—and set off to walk the short distance to his uncle and aunt's house in Stirling Street. His aunt was holding a soirée and had, as usual, insisted he attend; she'd dropped in at the office to make sure he'd received her invitation, and with patient reasonableness had pointed out that he couldn't hope to marry well if he didn't properly pay attention to the available young ladies.

He couldn't argue that. Indeed, he now saw the sense in making up his mind sooner rather than later. The sooner he chose the young lady he would make his wife, the sooner Lucilla and her enduring temptation—that relentless tug on his soul—would fade.

Pausing at the corner to let a carriage pass, he flexed his left leg. He'd called on his doctor the day before and had had the stitches removed; Henderson had spent most of the session waxing lyrical over Lucilla's exquisite stitchery and the apparently marvelous efficacy of the salve she'd used. He'd shut his ears; he'd just wanted the stitches out and gone, the last physical reminder of Lucilla and his time in the country eradicated.

Would that he could wipe his mental slate clean as easily.

With night slowly falling and deepening the dusk, the residential streets lay largely quiet. The rattle of carriage wheels came from here and there as ladies traveled to their engagements, the strengthening glow of the gaslights setting the brass and silver on harnesses and carriage bodies gleaming. A brisk shower earlier had washed the air clean and slicked the pavements and streets, making them appear darker than they were, yet glistening where the light played in the tiny puddles between the stones. Like him, a few gentlemen had grasped the opportunity afforded by a nearby social event to stretch their legs, but otherwise, this section of the city was sliding into its customary evening repose.

A repose that invited introspection; although the last thing he wished to dwell on was his recent past, as he turned up Candlerigg Street and continued strolling, he couldn't—simply couldn't—stop his mind from reviewing and reliving the past few days.

After riding—fleeing—from Lucilla and the Vale, he'd reached Glasgow by late morning. He'd blamed the continuing heaviness in his chest on the sulfur-laden atmosphere of the city—the wind had been absent, and the smog had been hanging heavily, after all.

So very different from the crystal-clear air of the Vale.

He'd thrust the comparison aside and had ridden Phantom to the stables where the gray was quartered, then had limped to his lodgings carrying his bag and trying to ignore the renewed throbbing in his calf. He'd *had* to leave the Vale—had had to leave immediately without risking seeing Lucilla again—and at least he'd reached there and was safe in Glasgow, once again focused on following his own path.

With that justification firmly fixed in his mind, he'd walked into his lodgings only to realize it was Sunday. So he hadn't been able to immediately lose himself in work. He had a key to the office; he could have gone in, but the offices would have been cold and empty—no distraction. He'd debated calling on his uncle and aunt to let them know he'd returned, but given the hour, that would have meant sitting down to luncheon and having to describe his time at Carrick Manor and the Vale... He hadn't been up to that—not even up to evading the questions.

He'd gone to a nearby tavern for a pint and some food,

then had settled to spend the rest of the day and evening in his lodgings. His rooms were by any standards well-appointed and comfortable, bordering on luxurious, yet the walls had suddenly seemed too close, the rooms too dark, and an unexpected coldness had sunk to his marrow.

Writing to Manachan that he was now back in Glasgow had been his only occupation, and even that, involving as it did an acknowledgment that he hadn't succeeded in resolving whatever it was that was afflicting his clan, had scraped at several raw places inside.

He'd told himself that all would be well as soon as he settled back into his position as principal partner of Carrick Enterprises and immersed himself in his usual routine.

Despite the tiredness brought on by the long ride, he'd slept poorly.

He'd risen early and, with his goal of reclaiming his true life in the forefront of his mind, had gone into the offices. He'd needed to re-establish his norm, find his previous anchor, and feel his world steady beneath his feet.

He'd walked through the door with its gilded logo. Mrs. Manning and Dobson had already been at their morning tasks; both had greeted him warmly, and he'd responded as usual and waited for a sense of coming home to embrace him.

But it hadn't.

Suppressing his disquiet, he'd walked down the corridor to his office. He'd gone in, shut the door, walked to his desk, and sat behind it. He'd looked at the files and documents waiting there and had felt...nothing.

Just a horrible gaping emptiness where he'd expected eagerness and some semblance of relief.

Shaken, he'd stared at the files and letters, unable to

accept that he couldn't summon any degree of enthusiasm for what previously had so effortlessly commanded his attention. For what previously had been the cynosure of his existence, the focal point of his life.

Reliving the moment, he drew in a tight breath and, head rising, cane swinging, paced slowly on. He wished he could haul his mind from its newfound obsession—from reliving the recent days and all the shortcomings that he was determined to excuse and put behind him—yet his recollections rolled relentlessly on, refusing to let him bury them as he so desperately wanted to do.

That first morning back, he'd been forced to face a realization he still refused to accept as anything like a final truth—a momentary truth, a passing state perhaps, but no more than that. He wouldn't *let* it be more than that. He'd spent a decade and more crafting a life for himself there, in his office as the principal partner of Carrick Enterprises, and now he was supposed to believe that it no longer meant anything? That he might, all along, have been misguided in pursuing that path?

That it didn't hold his attention because it didn't hold his heart?

You need to learn to think with your heart as well as your head.

That morning, sitting behind his desk, shaken and shocked, he'd heard Manachan's voice in his head. Manachan was as wily and as cunning as they came, but how could his uncle have known about this? About the situation he now faced?

He'd closed his eyes—then, jaw setting, he'd shaken his head, opened his eyes, and got down to business.

He'd told himself that the distraction caused by his time in the country would fade.

Quentin and Humphrey had arrived, and for the first time in his life he'd had to deploy, strengthen, and rely on his façade to greet them, to talk and exchange news with them, all the while hiding the deadening numbness inside him.

It had quickly become apparent that the business had run smoothly without him there. Quentin knew the guiding framework Thomas and he had set in place as well as Thomas did, and Humphrey had stepped up and filled Thomas's shoes in terms of his day-to-day role, and had done very well.

Why Thomas had done it, he didn't know, but he'd used his injury as an excuse not to take back all that Humphrey was now handling.

More than any of his reactions, that one had rocked him to his foundations.

What am I doing?

He'd asked himself that through the rest of that day and into an evening spent with a bottle of whisky.

At some point during that night, he'd found himself staring at the prospect that, deep down, he didn't really want his old position back.

Carrick Enterprises didn't need him—indeed, could function perfectly well without him. He didn't need to be there, in the office, for it to flourish.

And if that were so, then his position there couldn't give him what he needed, couldn't ground him, anchor him, ultimately wouldn't satisfy him. It wouldn't—couldn't—fulfill his deeply rooted need for *his* place—the right place for him, with the right passion and with people who needed him in a position he and only he could fill.

Despite his long-held belief, his position as principal

partner of Carrick Enterprises hadn't sunk its talons into his soul and refused to let go.

Yet something—someone else and another place—had.

He'd drained his glass and had refused, outright, to believe that. Any of that. Not wanting his established position back equated with him not wanting his carefully constructed life back, and that couldn't be—*wasn't*—true.

He'd decided it had been the whisky talking. He'd stoppered the bottle and had gone to bed.

Not that he'd slept, not even after the whisky.

Since then, he'd steadfastly lived as he had before, done all the things he'd done before, exactly as he had before, and had waited for the effect of his sojourn in the country to fade—for the talons to loosen and slip free.

They hadn't.

Yet.

He remained adamant that, with time, they would. That with time he would reclaim his passion for this life, and be able to go forward as he'd always intended, following his carefully defined, self-determined path into the future.

Attending his aunt's soirée that evening was to be his first new step along that path since he'd returned.

He hadn't wanted to arrive too early and have to stand in any receiving line, chatting with matrons and their hopeful daughters while waiting to greet his uncle and aunt, so he'd taken a roundabout route from his lodgings in Bell Street; he'd headed north along Candlerigg Street, then had crossed the road to amble about the gardens surrounding St. David's Church. Stepping out along Canon Street, he walked east, intending shortly to veer south to Stirling Square, and so on to Stirling Street and the Hemmingses' house.

Unfortunately, the diversion also gave his mind the perfect opportunity to remind him of all he was striving to forget.

Like the need he'd sensed—had been so openly shown—by Lucilla, and also by so many in the Vale.

He hadn't immediately understood what it was that had so called to him; in her, he'd seen it as simply another emotion in her mesmerizing emerald eyes, another element of her fire, another aspect of the fierceness of her loving.

Only now, with his mind so insistently revolving about his own need—a need to be truly needed by others—did he finally recognize that emotion in her eyes for what it was—for what it had been.

She had shown him, had exposed and put on display, her deepest vulnerability, and had trusted him to see it, to recognize and honor it.

He had seen, but he hadn't...allowed himself to know, to consciously recognize the reality for what it was. Because that reality—being needed by her—was a large part of what powered the talons that were still sunk so very deeply in his soul.

His mind had refused to accept, but his heart, it seemed, had known. Not allowing himself to register the truth hadn't saved him from it—from its effect, from its power.

And it wasn't only from her that he'd sensed the tug; the lure of being needed—of being wanted—had been so pervasive, coming from so many people and directions in the Vale, that he'd been drunk on its seduction.

Lips thinning, he flexed his shoulders as if he could thus dislodge the memories.

Regardless of all temptation, regardless of all the potential benefits, he couldn't give in. His jaw clenched; despite the clear assumptions of Lucilla, Marcus, and all in the Vale that, having seen and appreciated the role they believed he was fated to fill, he would surrender and stay, he couldn't. He couldn't, in effect, bend to their Lady's will.

He'd made up his mind long ago that nothing else in his life mattered—could ever matter—more than that he remain in control of it, that *he* defined and directed his path without interference from any other source.

When he'd finally understood what had been happening in the Vale—the trap that had been set for him, however well-meaning—he'd felt…in essence, betrayed. He hadn't seen until his eyes had been opened—and it had almost been too late to wrench back. He'd almost been unwittingly press-ganged into a life quite different from—and far more dangerous than—the one he'd set his mind on.

His *mind* on—not his heart on.

The words whispered through his consciousness as he reached the railings of Stirling Square; he didn't remember turning south, but his feet had carried him along by rote. As he paced along the wrought-iron fence, he reminded himself why following one's heart wasn't a wise thing to do. Wasn't a safe thing to do. Why following the directions laid down by a cool and calculating mind was far better.

As he turned into Stirling Street, he squared his shoulders in preparation for the ordeal ahead.

Ordeal by young lady and matchmaking matron; he really would rather be somewhere else.

A fleeting image of that somewhere else, with Lucilla, flared in his mind. In hindsight, his anger—all the righteous anger he'd felt when he'd realized just what she'd done and why—had been misdirected. And overwrought. A concurrence of Fate and some villain's machinations had delivered him into Lucilla's hands, and although she'd manipulated the situation, she had done so purely to show him the possibilities, the prospect that lay before him and her, giving herself and all in the Vale a chance to lay the full gamut of their temptation before him. Yet, at the last, she hadn't tried to hold him against his will. She'd let him go—she hadn't wanted to, but she had, as if she'd understood that she could never bind him, not against his will and not counter to his commitment to self-determination, to his own way forward.

He had to give her that, had to credit her—and her Lady—with that much understanding and integrity.

You need to learn to think with your heart as well as your head.

Manachan, again.

Reaching Quentin and Winifred's open front gate, Thomas shook off the yoke of his memories and climbed the steps to the front door. It was opened by their butler, who smiled in welcome, took his hat and cane, then showed him into the drawing room.

The cacophony of dozens of voices, all striving to be heard through the babel, washed over him. Winifred, standing a few steps from the doorway, saw him; she beamed with genuine delight as he bowed over her hand. Straightening, he leaned in to kiss the cheek she tipped his way. "A very good crowd, dear Aunt. Are you pleased?"

"I'm more pleased to see you here, dear boy." Winifred waited while he exchanged a nod with Quentin, who was having his ear bent by one of the local politicians. "Now!" Winifred tapped his sleeve with the furled ivory fan she was carrying. "There are several young ladies you should meet."

He inwardly sighed but didn't try to resist; when it came to his aunt's matchmaking aspirations, he'd learned that it was better to surrender gracefully. Now that Humphrey was settled with his Andrea, Winifred had turned the full focus of her attention on settling him respectably—and as her goal was, in this case, aligned with his, he did his best to be grateful.

Winifred introduced him to a Miss Mack, who had recently arrived from Perth to visit with her sister. As soon as he'd exchanged a few words with her, Winifred drew him on to make his bow to Lady Janet Crawley, whom he'd met previously, but who, this evening, had a cousin, Miss Vilbray, in her train.

After several such introductions, he felt a deep ennui descending over him; the faces of the ladies seemed to blur—they were soft, charming, sweet, shy, or coy, yet none seemed able to hold his attention for longer than the few minutes he spent conversing with them before Winifred whisked him on.

This was, in reality, no different to other soirées he'd attended, but for some reason, it felt more oppressive.

More senseless.

Winifred finally released him to his own devices, and he was standing for a second in the middle of the room, with streams of conversations swirling around him, yet, for all that, he was essentially alone...when the truth struck him.

And that sense of having made a cataclysmic mistake rose up and nearly choked him.

To you, I will always bring life.

Every young lady he'd met that evening had lacked precisely that—*life*. True vibrancy, the sort that welled from the soul and set fire flaring behind clear eyes and added a tangible glow to their presences.

Lucilla embodied the quality, at least to him. And with her life, she brought *him* alive. Fully alive in a way that nothing and no one else ever had.

And with his eyes now fully opened to what might be, to what he might have—to what waited for him in the Vale—he *could* no longer pretend that any other, here or anywhere else, would ever hold a candle to her.

She *had* brought him life, exactly as she'd promised, a deeper, truer appreciation of what life might be—what his life *could be*.

His eyes *had* opened, and he wouldn't ever be able to close them again.

He was no longer able to pretend that any lady there would suit him.

In his heart, he knew only one ever would.

The epiphany—its depth, breadth, and completeness—left him reeling.

This was the trap—the real trap—one fashioned by his own self-will, his own...cowardice.

His head spinning, he managed to maintain a mask of languid bonhomie while he made his way out of the crush to the side of the room. He found a small space on the edge of the crowd where he could expand his lungs and drag in a tight breath.

*There isn't anyone else for me or for you—and there
never will be. If you turn your back on me, on us, on all
we might be, there will be no other chance—not with
anyone else, not in any other place.*

She had warned him, but he'd thought she'd over-
stated her case.

Now he knew she hadn't.

It was impossible to even think of spending more
than a few minutes with any other woman; the thought
of being intimate with any of them simply left him cold.

Chilled and alone.

She'd warned him that misery would dog his steps;
he'd thought she'd been indulging in hyperbole.

And, indeed, it wasn't so much misery as emptiness—
a widening, deepening pit of lonely yearning that nothing, it seemed, could ease, much less fill.

He'd left his heart and soul behind when he'd ridden out of the Vale. Standing in the middle of Glaswe-
gian society, he had to face the fact that *that* was what
it felt like—that that was how leaving the Vale had affected him.

This wasn't his place; there was nothing for him here.
His true place, the role he needed to fill—for his own
sake, let alone anyone else's—was not here.

That role, his rightful role, the only one that would
satisfy him, lay south, in the Vale. By her side.

Along with his soul that the land had claimed and the
heart he now realized he'd left behind.

Did he love Lucilla?

He honestly didn't know.

Did he crave her unrelentingly?

Yes.

She'd been a potent lure hooked under his skin and

deep in his psyche for over a decade, and as they'd matured, her attractiveness and his awareness of it had only grown.

Could he, in all honesty, envision a life—a future—that did not include her?

The answer to that, a resounding negative, resonated through him.

He refocused on the crowd before him; regardless of how sophisticated, elegant, beautiful, charming, and powerful they might be, every minute he spent in their company only served to emphasize the truth. To him, they and their community were without substance; they didn't matter to him. And more, here in their company, *he* was a mere shadow of who he could be.

If he wanted the chance to live a fulfilling and meaningful life, if he wanted to reclaim his heart and his soul, he would have to go back, face Lucilla, and do whatever he had to do to reclaim the position she'd offered him and that he'd so arrogantly and misguidedly spurned.

He had to change his course.

Now, tonight.

He dragged in a huge breath.

From the time he'd left the Vale, no matter what he'd tried, the power behind that urge to return had been growing, minute by minute, hour by hour, until now, *nothing* but that urgent need to return seemed important.

He couldn't stand against it any longer. He no longer had the strength to deny that power, that compelling force.

Something inside him broke. Gave way.

And the man he could be, the man he had tried so hard to corral, to deny and never risk being, broke free of all restraint and took charge.

He searched the room and spotted Winifred and Quentin. Cloaking his near-desperation to be gone, he tacked though the crowd to their side.

Quentin looked inquiringly at him.

Winifred smiled. "Any possibilities?"

His mind was already racing ahead. Despite his inner grimness—how could he have been such a fool?—he tried for a smile, but from Winifred's fading delight, it wasn't much of one. He turned the expression into a grimace. "My leg's playing up. I took the long way here, and I think I overdid it."

"Oh." Winifred's concern was immediate; he felt small. "But," she said, patting his arm, "at least you came, and you did meet some new ladies. Next time, you'll have more time to talk."

He couldn't force a nod. Instead, he held out his hand to his uncle. "Sir."

"Take care, my boy." Quentin's grip was strong. "And don't come in if your leg needs more rest."

He nodded, then he gave in to impulse and bent and kissed his aunt's cheek. She'd been as much of a mother to him as he'd allowed, yet he doubted he would share much of their lives from now on.

Winifred blinked up at him, trying to read his face and failing. Again, she patted his arm, but this time in benediction. "Yes, Thomas—do take care."

With a half bow, he left them, left the room, collected his hat and cane, and quit the house.

On the pavement, he glanced back, then looked around at the quiet streets. He might visit, but this would never be—could never be—his home.

He set off to walk back to his lodgings by the shorter, more direct route.

About him, the heart of Glasgow thrummed, but this wasn't where his heart was, nor his soul.

His heart was someone else's and his soul had found its true home.

He would be leaving in the morning, and he wouldn't be coming back.

* * *

He had a lot to arrange—an entire life to restructure. He sat at the small desk in his lodgings, and with the lamps turned high, worked steadily through each aspect.

Carrick Enterprises was surprisingly straightforward, up to a point. That point being how much involvement he wished to retain in the years ahead. He wasn't sure; when he looked inside and examined the new prospect, the new landscape of his life taking shape, he could see a place for the firm, see a value in retaining his interest and keeping a connection in the importing and exporting trade. The Vale was largely an agricultural concern, and some of its produce could easily be exported.

He was somewhat surprised by how readily the decision about the firm came; now he'd faced his reality and, guided by said reality's harsh light, had revised his direction, he felt little lingering attachment to the firm, much less than he'd expected. Carrick Enterprises had been his father's dream; Thomas had assumed it was also his, but it wasn't. It never had been, because his heart had never been involved. The people, he would miss, but the firm itself?

All of which underscored that he'd made the right decision and was, finally, marching down the correct road.

His goodbyes would initially have to be made by letter. The compulsion to return to Lucilla and the Vale was now full-blown; he wasn't prepared to dally in Glasgow a moment longer than absolutely necessary. He—perhaps with Lucilla by his side—would return at some point, to visit and explain in person, but for now, the written word would have to suffice.

Nib scratching, he penned letters to Quentin, Winifred, and Humphrey, and short notes to several others in the firm, and still briefer notes to Mrs. Manning and Dobson, wishing them well until next he saw them.

His landlady, his banker, his solicitor—to them, he wrote that he was heading into the country and expected the change to be permanent, but that he wished his current arrangements to stand, at least for the time being.

Then he threw himself into cataloguing the many and various deals and potential contracts and contacts he hadn't yet passed on to Humphrey. It was like emptying his mind, clearing out the past and creating space for his true future.

With the act came clarity and a burgeoning peace—a simple confidence he hadn't known since childhood. A clarity of vision, a sureness of purpose, and a certainty that his feet were following the right path.

It was past two o'clock when he tidied the desk and turned down the lamps. Outside the windows, Glasgow slumbered.

Half an hour later, he was packed; when it came to it, he had little by way of meaningful possessions. He set the trunk by the door with a note for his landlady, asking her to send it on.

He was burning bridges, eradicating his past. Eliminating the man he'd spent the last decade striving to be.

With a self-deprecatory grimace, he fell into bed. Was he cutting off all chance of retreat so that no matter what happened with Lucilla in the Vale, he wouldn't be able to take the easy way out and come running back?

He had to wonder.

He expected exhaustion to claim him—not the exhaustion of physical exertion but that of emotional turmoil. He felt scoured inside, as if, when he'd reached the point of being unable to suppress the fundamental truth any longer, it had erupted and he'd accepted it, embraced it, and just let go...let everything else go.

He'd let the truth in and let it own him.

Let it clear everything else out and become his new reality.

He closed his eyes. His body relaxed and sank into the mattress.

Exhaustion claimed his limbs, then crept higher to claim his mind.

In the last instant of rational thought, in the cavern of clarity his mind had become, he saw where he had been, and where he now was—and where she had been, where she still stood.

At her core, she possessed one attribute he didn't have. Faith. Which led to commitment. Faith in the fact of simply knowing, and commitment to the path that that knowing led her down.

She'd followed the flame of her faith all her life. He... he could at least follow her.

Whether he had it in him to fully embrace his own knowing—the impulses he felt—he didn't know. Presumably he would find out, because, as things stood, in setting out along his new road, those instincts, those impulses, were all he had to guide him.

There isn't anyone else for me or for you—and there never will be.

In going forward, he was counting on that. He couldn't deceive himself over how much he had hurt her in turning his back and simply walking away.

At the time, he'd been so angry—and, underneath that, so frightened and shaken—that he hadn't truly appreciated what she'd been offering—*all* she'd been offering—but now...?

He didn't know if she loved him—if she could or would, if that was a part of their fated interaction. He didn't know if he loved her, or if he could or would, either. What was love? What, between them, did love mean? That was one aspect he and she would have to learn.

But that he couldn't live without her—*that*, he knew. That to be the man he needed to be, he had to return to her and claim the position by her side—that he now accepted without reservation.

The mists of sleep rolled in. One last thought drifted through his consciousness.

He might not know what love was—not enough to define it and, with honesty, own to it—but she'd won his heart long ago. His battle to win hers was just beginning.

* * *

He set out from Glasgow just after dawn, riding south into his true future.

Going home.

If home, and she, would have him.

That was the only question remaining in his mind; all the rest had been answered, or had proved to be unimportant.

Jaw set, the wind whipping through his hair, he rode Phantom down the road spooling south before them.

He was finally on his true and correct path. His mind was clear, his thoughts focused, and he was determined.

He might not yet have faith, but he was committed.

One way or another, no matter what was demanded of him, he would find his way back to her side.

Sixteen

The first hurdle Thomas hadn't expected manifested when, in response to his jangling of the doorbell, Polby opened the front door of Casphairn Manor.

The butler beamed at him. "Mr. Carrick, sir! Welcome back. The master will be so pleased to see you."

Thomas blinked. Master? Stepping over the threshold, he asked, "Marcus?"

"Oh, no, sir. I meant Lord Richard. He and the mistress returned two days ago." Polby looked out at Phantom, standing placidly in the forecourt. "I'll get one of the lads to take care of your horse and have your bags taken up to your room." Polby shut the door and faced Thomas; his smile knew no bounds. "The mistress said you would return shortly. One learns that she's rarely mistaken."

Mistress… If "master" meant Richard Cynster, then by "mistress," Polby meant Catriona, the current Lady of the Vale.

Thomas was already wishing he'd never been so foolish as to leave in the first place.

Hands clasped at his waist, Polby was regarding him with a mildly hopeful air. "I expect you wish to see Lord Richard, sir."

Thomas debated that. If he had to face any of Lucilla's male relatives, he would prefer to face Marcus, but…he supposed he should start as he meant to go on. He assented with a dip of his head.

And delighted Polby all over again. "If you'll come this way, sir. The master is in the library."

Thomas followed Polby along the wide corridor and waited outside the library door while Polby announced his arrival and his request for an audience, and inquired whether his lordship was willing to see him.

His lordship was; the deep growl of Richard's voice carried a menacing quality.

Polby opened the library door wider and waved Thomas through.

He walked into the room feeling very much as if he was stepping into a cage with a potentially dangerous beast. The sound of the door quietly clicking shut only added to the atmosphere.

Richard was standing by a small table covered with fishing flies and the apparatus to create them; he'd clearly just risen from the chair at the table's end.

He was middle-aged, now, with silver streaks at his temples, the strands very white against his black hair. Other than that, age had treated him kindly; his carriage remained military-upright, his long legs and arms well-muscled, and his shoulders still filled the width of his coat. He cut a fashionable figure in buckskin breeches and top boots, with a hacking jacket over a plain waistcoat and a simply tied cravat.

His face still resembled chiseled granite, and his expression couldn't have been less forgiving. The dark blue gaze that rested on Thomas as he walked forward was razor sharp.

When Thomas halted, Richard growled, "Carrick."

There was absolutely no welcome in the word.

Thomas inclined his head. "My lord." He held Richard's gaze. "I wish to ask for your permission to pay my addresses to your daughter Lucilla."

Richard's expression remained impassive. After a long moment, he arched his black brows. "Is that so?"

Maintaining his own blandly uninformative mien, Thomas merely responded, "It is."

"I heard you were here. Staying here."

In the room below Lucilla's. Thomas had not a doubt Richard knew that—and understood rather more. But he wasn't going to cross swords with Lucilla's father, not if he could help it. Remaining silent seemed his wisest course.

"I should perhaps mention," Richard went on, the aggression in his tone unmasked, "that although I don't know the details of what passed between you and Lucilla, I have seen the effects." Richard's gaze, fixed on Thomas's face, darkened. "I would really like to do some physical damage, and I've no doubt Marcus would, too. However, while such actions might allow us to vent some of our aggravated feelings, those actions would, sadly, be frowned upon by the ladies in our lives, so that won't improve our situation."

Thomas said nothing, just steadily returned Richard's hard gaze.

After several long moments of studying him, Richard humphed. "At least you came back—I suppose that's a start." His stance eased fractionally, and he turned away, but then he glanced back to ask, "You do realize that, regardless of what I say, permission granted or not, it's what she says that will count?"

"Of course." Thomas hadn't imagined anything else.

"Well, at least you've got that much clear." With that muttered comment, Richard abandoned his prickly, disapproving father pose and headed toward the large desk. Waving Thomas to the chair before it, Richard rounded the desk and sat. Hands flat on the desk's surface, he arched a brow at Thomas. "So—reassure me." Leaning back in the chair, Richard gestured. "We both know her assets. If you succeed in gaining her consent, what will you bring to this marriage?"

Thomas had anticipated the question and had rehearsed his reply while riding down. Somewhat to his surprise, Richard had a keen grasp of business and asked several shrewd questions, but in the end, his putative father-in-law seemed satisfied, pleased—or, at the very least, appeased—by his answers.

In turn, he asked how Richard saw the Vale being run, and was relieved to detect no hint of reservation in Richard's assertion that he, Richard, would teach him all he would need to know. He resisted asking about Marcus; Lucilla had mentioned that her twin's place lay elsewhere.

When the questions and answers from both sides had been exhausted, Richard studied him again. Then he briskly nodded. "All right. Permission granted, for whatever good that will do you."

They both rose. Coming back around the desk, Richard grasped the chair at the smaller table; he waved at the table's contents as he sat. "Do you fly-fish?"

Thomas nodded. He picked up one of the intricately tied flies. "But I haven't assembled a fly in years."

Richard grunted. "It's a family interest—at least among us males. You'll have to get back into it."

Thomas set down the fly. Richard appeared to have focused his concentration fully on the fly he'd been tying, yet Thomas sensed he hadn't yet been dismissed.

Sure enough, an instant later, his gaze fixed on his fingertips and the feather he was binding into place, Richard said, "Before you go to seek your fortune, I feel compelled to offer you a word of advice."

Thomas said nothing. Simply waited.

"You left." After a moment, Richard shrugged. "I left, too. Like you, I came back."

Thomas hadn't known that; he listened even more intently as Richard continued, his gaze still on the fly, "I had to make amends, and you will have to do the same. But I had a fire to deal with and a life-threatening rescue to effect, which illustrated my revised direction and made further declaration unnecessary. In your case, however, given that Marcus and I are both here, you won't have any dragons of that nature to slay to demonstrate your change of heart, so you're going to have to find some other way."

Thomas had already foreseen the necessity of making amends and, while learning that Richard had undergone a similar battle and, like Thomas, had surrendered, was comforting, it offered little material help. He was about to ask if Richard had any suggestions regarding "some other way" when Lucilla's father grunted and said, "Sacrifice usually works."

He frowned. "Sacrifice?"

Richard glanced up at him, his dark gaze faintly irritated. "What's the one thing you have that you haven't yet laid at her feet?"

Thomas blinked and tried to think.

Richard snorted and looked back at his work. "It's simple, man—and if you have to, crawl."

* * *

Leaving Richard once more immersed in his hobby—or at least pretending to be—Thomas walked back out to the foyer, hoping to find Polby and ask where Lucilla was.

Instead, he came face to face with Marcus.

Lucilla's twin had clearly just come in from the stables; he was carrying his crop and his top boots were dusty.

Marcus's expression was contained. He nodded to Thomas. "I saw your horse."

Thomas met Marcus's eyes, very similar to his father's dark and rather impenetrable midnight blue. Somewhat curiously, Thomas could detect very little emotion emanating from Marcus—neither aggression nor sympathy, not anger or support. Carefully, he said, "I'm here to see Lucilla. Do you know where she is?"

Marcus tipped his head back along the corridor he'd stepped out of, the one that led to the side door. "She's in the garden harvesting herbs. Beware of her shears—they're sharp."

Thomas blinked.

Marcus snorted. "You did notice she has red hair?"

"Ah." So she was angry with him—angry enough to attack him?

Marcus hesitated, then said, "Just so you know, it was Mama who insisted that you would come back. Lucilla said nothing."

Thomas considered the implication of that, especially given who it was who was telling him.

"Mama also said that you would be worth it in the end." Marcus met Thomas's eyes, and if it wasn't quite a threat, at the very least it was a challenge that Thomas saw in the hard blue of Marcus's gaze.

"If I were you," Marcus said, "for all our sakes, I'd make sure you prove Mama correct."

With that, Marcus turned and walked on and up the stairs.

Thomas watched him go, turning over the warnings in his mind.

Apparently, someone had faith in the outcome here, had faith in him, although whether that someone was the Lady or simply Catriona—and whether her words were merely a hope or something more certain—he had no way of knowing.

He turned and walked down the corridor toward the side door. The critical moment was nearly upon him; he needed to marshal his thoughts and stick to the script he'd rehearsed.

He was mentally scrolling through his speech when the side door opened and Catriona walked in.

Immediately, her gaze lifted to his face; he got the distinct impression she'd known he was there, in the corridor—that she'd come in expecting to meet him.

Catriona smiled, and her smile conveyed a wealth of understanding and acceptance. "Thomas." She shut the door and came forward, her gliding walk a ladylike attribute she shared with her eldest daughter.

Halting, he half bowed. "Lady Cynster."

She laughed softly. "Just Catriona, please." She halted before him and looked into his face. "I'm glad to see you, Thomas. I knew you would come."

"So Marcus mentioned." He remained where he was—felt held where he was—while Catriona openly searched his eyes. He had no idea what she read there, but, apparently, whatever it was, she found it satisfactory.

With a gentle, encouraging smile, she tipped her head toward the door. "Lucilla's in the garden, but you might not see her at first—she's further down by the burn." She stepped out of his path and continued past him. "I don't know if she knows you're here, but she might."

With that, Catriona walked on.

Turning, Thomas watched her go. After she reached the front foyer and disappeared from his sight, he thought through her words, then shook his head and continued to the door.

Reaching it, he paused to draw in a last, too-restricted-for-comfort breath.

Then he grasped the latch, opened the door, and went out to face his fate.

* * *

Lucilla lifted her gaze to Thomas the instant he stepped into view on the lip of the upper terrace of the gardens.

Emotions—the immediate leap and roil of so many powerful feelings—stole her breath.

For several heartbeats, she felt giddy, but then the emotional storm coalesced, the tumultuous emotions aligning to form a single, cohesive force.

He had left—and now, as her mother had assured her he would, he'd returned.

Apparently, leaving and returning was something strong men had a habit of doing when grappling with the reality of being a consort in the Vale; until her mother had mentioned it, she hadn't known her father had done the same thing, but that snippet had gone some small way toward allowing her to view Thomas's flight in a more equable light.

Still…he'd left. And she was very far from forgiving him for the nature of his leaving.

Some men prefer not to live under a cat's paw.

Of all the words they'd exchanged, those were the ones she remembered most clearly. True, she hadn't been open about her motives, but, given his stubborn blindness, what else could she have done?

Straightening from the verbena bush she'd been trimming, she glanced at the two apprentices working alongside her harvesting the wormwood and rue. "Agnes, Matilda—if you would, please take what we've cut up to the still room. There's enough to start with—you know how to hang the bunches to best catch the drafts."

"Yes, my lady," the pair chorused. They gathered the various trugs, including one Lucilla had filled with verbena, then started the long trudge up the garden.

The pair hadn't seen Thomas, but he'd seen them. Rather than pass them, he came down the terraces by a different route.

She was standing in the lowest of the walks. The bed hosting the verbena she continued to snip was raised, the wide coping of the stone wall level with her thighs. At her back, the other side of the walk was bordered by another wide bed at ground level—the last of the terraced beds above the path that wended along the edge of the burn.

Today, the burn was running freely, burbling and tinkling as it tumbled over rocks and rippled over stones. The air close to the banks was always a touch cooler, a touch damper than elsewhere. Refreshing.

Her mind was registering those mundane observations when she heard the soft thud as Thomas's boot met the sod of the walk.

Her senses locked on him.

He prowled closer, his stride one she recognized like someone plucking a fiber of her soul. Her senses expanded, stirring, restless and distracted. Reaching...

He halted by her shoulder.

She didn't turn to meet his eyes.

She could feel his gaze on her, felt the intensity increase as he tipped his head and studied her face.

"Lucilla."

One word, but it was greeting, question, supplication, and much more.

She forced air into her suddenly tight lungs, then glanced briefly at him—too briefly to get caught in his amber gaze. "Why are you here?"

Refixing her gaze on the verbena and carefully clipping another long shoot, she waited—for the answer to the only question that mattered.

He sighed softly, so softly she wasn't sure she was supposed to hear. Then he shifted to face the burn; after a moment, he sat on the stone wall alongside her, his hands gripping the coping on either side of him.

Not so close that he was in her way, but within easy arm's reach.

She glanced at the leg closest to her. "How's your wound?"

That was the healer in her speaking; she hadn't meant to show any interest, at least not yet, but that other part of her had raised her head and claimed her tongue.

"A lot better. I had a doctor in Glasgow take out the stitches." He paused, then added, "He was amazed by your work—both the stitches and the effect of your salve."

She humphed.

And waited.

More than a minute ticked by before he said, his voice low, but without any real inflection, "You asked why I'm here—why I've come back. The answer is because…I was a coward."

That hadn't been any part of Thomas's rehearsed speech, but sitting there in the quiet of the garden, with the one woman who meant so much to him, he'd finally understood what Richard had meant when he'd said: *What's the one thing you have that you haven't yet laid at her feet?*

He hadn't given her the truth—the simple unadorned truth—because he hadn't wanted to lay aside his pride.

He looked down at the toes of his boots. From the corner of his eye, he could see her face—see her arrested expression, see her hands paused, hovering, no longer smoothly working.

She was as surprised by that confession as he.

So he had an opening—a moment when her guard was down.

Drawing breath, he seized the chance and plowed on, "You asked, and I explained why I resisted the attraction between us—because it wasn't a part of my plan, the definite plan I had for my life." He fixed his gaze on the tumbling waters of the burn. "I told you of my plan—but I didn't tell you *why* I had a plan. Why adhering to that plan was so important to me."

At the edge of his vision, he saw her blink, saw her expression grow distant as she remembered that night and what he'd told her in the corridor—before some blackguard had invaded her room and made it all irrelevant.

Head tilting slightly, she murmured, "I didn't think to ask, either."

"You were caught up in absorbing what I said." He remembered her concentration, her focus; even then, before they'd been intimate, the connection between them had run deep.

After a moment, she flicked him a glance, this time allowing their eyes to meet. "So," she said, "why did you have a plan—one that you've clung to for so long, and so doggedly?" She looked back at the straggly bush and rather viciously snipped another long shoot. "That same plan was behind you returning to Glasgow, wasn't it?"

He nodded, then realized she couldn't see and said, "Yes." Shifting his gaze back to the burn, he drew in a breath. Held it for a moment as he ordered his thoughts. "I can remember when I first started working on my plan. I was ten years old. It was a month or so after my parents died." He nodded beyond the burn, to the north, toward the Carrick estate. "I was at Carrick Manor at the time—after my parents died, Manachan brought me back to the clan, and I spent that next year there."

He fell silent.

Lucilla glanced at him but didn't prompt. She wanted, so much, to understand, and she only would if he told her in his own words, in his own time.

After a moment, he went on, his voice deeper, his normally smooth tones rough, "I was an only child—my parents and I were close. Very close. We were holidaying in the Highlands, but I had a tutor and still had lessons. My parents left me with my books and went out for an afternoon drive in my father's curricle." He looked down. "Only their broken, lifeless bodies came back."

She resisted the urge to reach out and touch his arm. It was an old wound, one that needed no more healing.

After a moment, he raised his head and drew in a

breath. "When I finally...woke up again—that's what it felt like when I came fully back to myself and re-engaged with normal life—I was at Carrick Manor with the clan. And I decided that what had happened...that I was never going to let that happen to me again. So I started to plan exactly how my life would be—I thought that if I controlled all the important aspects, if I determined my own life and always kept control, then I could make sure that whatever happened, I would never be hurt like that again. But even as a ten-year-old, I knew that the most important aspect of avoiding being hurt like that again was ensuring that I never *cared* for anyone like that again—not in the way I had cared for my parents."

He looked down at the ground before him. "I was a boy, a male—I didn't use the word 'love.' But that's what I meant—I needed to remain in control of my life so that I could ensure I never again loved anyone to that extent. To the point where it opened up a vulnerability inside me—to where, if anything happened to that person, my heart would again be ripped in two."

He exhaled, then raised his head. "That was the real reason behind my plan—it was my way of ensuring that I was never hurt again—and that's why I clung to it so tenaciously." His voice lowered. "And that's why, above all other reasons, my carefully planned life could never include you."

She looked at him.

He turned his head and met her gaze, and there was no screen in his amber-gold eyes, just an open heart and honesty. "You couldn't be a part of my life because I knew I would care for you. In exactly the way I didn't want to care for anyone. You were my Achilles' heel, and

I've known that for a very long time. I've felt the connection between us, the attraction, for as long as you have."

She saw in his eyes that that was the truth, and her heart started to lift, to lighten.

His focus turned inward. "Over the last years, when you didn't marry and it became clear that that attraction wasn't fading, I deliberately avoided meeting you. But then the Bradshaws and everything else happened, and... you stepped past every barrier I erected, and I wasn't strong enough to hold you back—or to hold myself back from you." He paused, then with a tip of his head, admitted, "And, for a while, I fooled myself that a liaison would work. I wanted you and you wanted me, and as long as I never forgot my plan and the reasons behind it...I told myself that I would be safe."

He looked down at his feet, and she got the impression that it was getting harder, not easier, for him to speak—to expose himself as he was.

He drew a short breath, and the planes of his face hardened. "But then, here, when I finally realized that I was teetering on the brink of giving up my plan, that... *coerced* by what I felt for you, blinkered and overwhelmed by yours and your Lady's seductions combined, I was bordering on doing exactly what I had always held so strongly against...when I realized that, I panicked and fled."

Thomas rolled straight on, giving himself no time to rein back the words, to censor them. "And in that, I was a coward, because I knew all along exactly what I was fleeing from, and why. I've always known the reason behind my plan—it was a conscious decision, not an unthinking, instinctive one. I knew I was running from..." He glanced briefly at her. "If not love, then the prospect of it. So I ran because, even after all these years, I was still too much of a coward to risk the pain of loving and losing again."

Dragging in a tight breath, he shifted on the cold stone. "So I rejected you and hurt you. I turned my back on all that I might have had here and ran back to my tightly controlled, forever-to-be-safe life in Glasgow."

Gazing, unseeing, at the rippling burn, he felt faintly lightheaded from the effort of forcing the words out, yet, at the same time, he felt curiously lighter, lightened—not precisely absolved, but as if, in cataloguing his actions aloud, he'd at least acknowledged his failings and had regained a measure of honor through that.

"And?"

Uttered in a quietly encouraging rather than imperious tone, her question slid across his mind.

The answer was there, obvious and true. "My carefully organized, eminently safe life didn't fit me anymore." Raising his gaze, he looked north and east, toward Glasgow. He filled his lungs, then shrugged. "Something happened while I was here—when I reached the city again, I wasn't the same man who'd ridden south. I'd...tasted ambrosia, if you like. I'd sampled a different sort of life, one that suited me so much better than my carefully constructed life in the city. Living here, in the Vale by your side, satisfied me in ways that I hadn't known were possible. Just those few days here opened up parts of my soul that I hadn't known were there and filled them up."

He turned his head and met her eyes. "You asked me why I'm here. I came because I've changed my mind. I want to claim all you offered me—the position by your side. To be your lover, your defender and protector, your consort—your husband."

He'd hoped to see…forgiveness, compassion, perhaps even sympathy in the emerald green. Instead, all he saw was a shield—an impenetrable screen he'd never seen before. She'd never screened herself from him before. The realization rocked him, but almost immediately his instincts steadied him; he'd known she wouldn't make this easy.

He hadn't known she could cut him off so completely—hold him so much at a distance.

Instead of directly replying to his statement, still holding his gaze, she slowly—imperiously and a touch arrogantly, too—arched her fine brows. "So you ran from love? Does that mean you love me?"

He'd hoped against hope that she wouldn't ask, yet he'd known she would. He thought of simply saying yes, but…after what he'd done, lying to her seemed a very bad idea. He searched her eyes yet saw nothing; it was as if she held a reflective screen between him and all hint of her feelings. He felt his jaw clench but forced himself to say, "The only honest answer I can give is that I don't truly know. I've avoided love—steadfastly and concertedly—for twenty years, all my adult life. I don't know what love looks like, feels like. I don't know that love for you doesn't already live inside me—I only know that, if I remain here, with you, it might and most likely will."

Truth. Absolute truth. And no matter what it cost him; that was what he'd vowed during the ride there to give her. He owed her that, at least. And so he went on, "You ask whether I love you. While I can't answer that, I can say that I know, beyond a shadow of a doubt, that I cannot exist—not as I wish to exist—without you." He dragged in a breath and forced the rest of his declaration—the only one he could, with complete honesty, give—from his chest to his lips. "I now know that, after this, after returning here, if you refuse me and my suit and send me away, that I won't go far."

A short, rather hollow laugh slipped past his guard and expanded on the words "I'm so in thrall to you that I seriously doubt I would ever be content with letting you out of my sight, my reach, my keeping. Even if you didn't want me close, I would still be here, compelled to be here to keep watch over you."

"I did tell you that you couldn't escape." Calmly, she turned from him. Returning her gaze to her hands, she snipped a leafy branch. "Precisely because you *are*, in truth, my consort, my protector and defender, you will always feel that way. I warned you that it's not possible to avoid the effects of what links us."

So she was going to be difficult; he supposed he deserved that. All but gritting his teeth, he pointed out the convoluted logic behind her statement. "Being your consort, your protector and defender, isn't what links us."

She gave a little nod, as if he'd passed some test. "No, it's not. Those qualities are consequences, not the cause."

When she said nothing more, he narrowed his eyes on her face and quietly asked, "So what does link us?"

She had the answer ready. "A power greater than any other—and one even less likely to let you go."

He sighed and pinched the bridge of his nose. "So what am I supposed to take from that? That because I feel so strongly about protecting you, I must be in love with you?"

When she didn't answer, he spread his arms in appeal.

"What do you want me to *say*, Lucilla? I can't claim to love you if I don't know that I do."

She didn't respond, just cut another bloody branch; his temper was starting to fray. Then he remembered. "Manachan said something on that last afternoon we were there, when he was convincing me to bring you back to the Vale. He told me that I needed to learn to think with my heart as well as my head. I didn't understand then, but now perhaps I do. I tried—with everything in me, I tried—to keep my heart closed against you. And I failed. This connection between us, whatever it might be, isn't something my heart will allow me to walk away from." He tried to bite back the next words, but they tumbled out. "It certainly wasn't my head that brought me back to your side."

He saw a faltering in her shield—a brief primming of her lips as if she struggled to hold back a smile.

But still, she said nothing.

He watched her openly and saw no sign of encouragement, yet neither did he feel any sense of being pushed away. Not even of being truly locked out. She just hadn't let him in again, hadn't yet accepted him back.

He sighed. He could see that they might go around and around for hours, even days, debating the fine point of whether he loved her or not—whether he would say the words, even if he wasn't yet certain.

Looking down, he linked his fingers, stared at them for several seconds, then said, "I went to Glasgow because I didn't believe the position by your side was the right one for me—for the man I wanted to be. But in Glasgow, I learned a deeper truth: That I can't be the man I wanted to be—I can only be the man I am."

He looked at her—waited, and waited, until at last she

glanced at him. Capturing her gaze, he simply said, "The man I am is yours, Lucilla—the only life I now want is one by your side, filling the position of your husband, your consort, and all that comes with that." He drew in a deeper breath, exhaled, and said, "So if that position's still vacant, I'm here to claim it. Will you have me?"

She didn't really have a choice. Lucilla knew that, yet still she held back. Not from any wish to prolong the discussion, to extract more revelations from him, or to make the interview more difficult for him. He'd come back to her of his own accord, exactly as she'd needed him to, exactly as she'd prayed he would. Yet his going had opened a vein of uncertainty inside her, and that was something she was ill-equipped to deal with; she had no experience handling...not being sure.

So now she hesitated, wanting to simply say "yes" and have done, yet...

She continued to hold his gaze. He'd been open and honest; she had to be the same. She dragged in a breath, and let it out with the words "If I accept you as my husband, are you sure you won't, at some point in the future, come to regret it—to resent the demands the position makes of you—and leave me again?"

With those few simple words, that straightforward question, she cut Thomas to the quick. She didn't lower her shields, didn't let him see her emotions, yet those words communicated them oh, so clearly. She had never doubted her power—would never have questioned the very force they'd been discussing—before.

Before he'd turned his back on her and walked away.

He drew in a long, slow breath—then, his eyes still holding hers, he slipped from the wall to stand beside her.

She shifted to face him, her shears in her hand. He

recalled Marcus's warning but ignored it. She wasn't going to stab him with her shears; she'd already stabbed him with her words, with the proof of the vulnerability *he* was responsible for creating inside her.

He'd spoken of his own vulnerability; he knew what it felt like, recognized the effect of it in others.

Slowly, giving her plenty of time to react if she would, he raised both hands and cupped her face.

Instinctively, she shifted closer as he tipped her face to his.

He looked down into her eyes, reached as deeply as she would allow. With the force of everything inside him, he stated, "I will never—ever—leave you again. I will never quit the place by your side. I want you, but more, I *need* you—you and only you. You are the center point, the pivot, the fulcrum of my life, the anchor about which I must and always will revolve." Drowning in green, he paused to draw breath. "You are, and always will be, all and everything I want—all and everything I need."

Her free hand rose to cup the back of his.

And, at last, with that feather-light touch, through that and the thinning of her shields, he saw acceptance bloom within her, gradually strengthening in her eyes.

He lowered his head, drawn to kiss her, to claim her mouth at least.

She didn't retreat but came up on her toes to meet him.

He paused with a bare whisper separating their hungry lips. So hungry—he could feel her hunger rise to meet his. Once their lips touched, all talk would be behind them.

He spoke breath to breath. "Do you accept me as yours, forever and always?"

Her lids rose; green fire met his eyes. "Yes."

He exhaled and briefly closed his eyes. "So my lady's—your Lady's—prophecy is fulfilled."

She didn't answer, just slid her hand to his nape and drew his lips to hers.

* * *

So my lady's—your Lady's—prophecy is fulfilled.

But it wasn't. Not quite.

Thomas knew that as surely as he knew the difference between a negotiated agreement and an effective partnership. They'd managed the first; they had yet to achieve the second.

They walked up from the gardens hand in hand, with their awareness of each other, courtesy of that kiss and the several that had followed, back in full force, and acceptance, carried in the warm clasp of their palms and the gentleness they showed to each other, slowly settling upon them.

It was a curious transition, with them trying to find their way back to the path that his leaving had taken them from.

And even then, it wasn't quite the same path; they'd rejoined it several bends further along.

As they walked into the house, the luncheon gong rang. Instinctively, he steeled himself. Lucilla cast him a reassuring glance, wordlessly assuring him that all would be well; tightening her grip on his hand, she drew him on.

And she was proved correct. Catriona beamed upon him; Marcus appeared neutral, yet he nodded easily and talked about the dogs. Richard was the only one who appeared watchful, assessing, waiting to see how matters played out.

But most importantly in Thomas's eyes, Lucilla in-

teracted with him not just as she always had but with a
more personal, tentative, exploratory connection that set
him apart from everyone else.

He was perfectly willing to work with her on that—
to allow what linked them to evolve and deepen, to let it
infuse their actions and strengthen the ties that already
bound them.

Given the smiles directed their way from everyone
in the body of the hall, the existence of those ties was
obvious to all.

That was reassuring, but as, seated beside Lucilla,
he supped and ate, he realized he wanted, and needed,
more. And with his awareness of her deepening with
every breath, he knew—somewhere inside, where everything about her wants and needs now resided—that
she, too, needed more. Having lived through the drama
of his leaving and his return, they both needed to move
on more quickly. More definitely.

The meeting with Catriona and Richard in the drawing room after lunch was unavoidable, but as Thomas
had expected it and was prepared for all the inevitable questions and Lucilla was increasingly confident
of her new footing, the discussion passed off surprisingly well—and Richard stopped viewing him quite so
critically.

Richard still watched, but it was more in the way of
reassuring himself that all continued well.

Thomas was certain that the full implications of his
return had, by that time, occurred to Lucilla's nearest and
dearest; none of them was the least bit slow. Certainly,
all of them seemed increasingly amused at his expense.
As it happened, he was entirely willing to admit that his
return signaled his agreement to living under the paw

of a certain flame-haired cat; as the day wound on, he was increasingly impatient to get on with doing just that.

It hadn't escaped him that the one subject no one had broached was when their wedding was to be. That, apparently, was going to be left entirely to Lucilla and him to decree.

The point was never far from his mind through the later afternoon, when Lucilla had to go down to the still room to deal with her apprentices, and Polby, still beaming, came to ask him what to do with the trunks that his landlady had duly sent down.

By dinnertime, he had made several decisions. He bided his time through the meal—the usual combined gathering of the household in the Great Hall—and through Richard and Catriona's announcement of the pending union between Lucilla and him, a declaration that was greeted with thunderous cheers and a wave of goodwill that was all but palpable.

The smile he directed over the occupants of the hall was entirely genuine, as was the warmth in his gaze as he looked at Lucilla.

No more shields. None. Not for him, or for her.

She read enough in his eyes for color to rise in her cheeks; raising her napkin, she patted her lips, then reached for her wine goblet.

He felt his smile deepen and looked away. Content, for now.

As usual, the ladies led the way from the Great Hall. Catriona had linked her arm in Lucilla's; from the snippets of conversation drifting to his ears as he followed alongside Richard and Marcus, Lucilla and her mother were discussing fabrics for redecorating the drawing room.

Richard grunted. In a low voice, he murmured, "Just as long as they don't decide to redecorate the library."

"Don't even think it," Marcus murmured back. "You know that's enough to put ideas into their heads."

Thomas slowed as he reached the archway to the front foyer; stepping through, watching the ladies go ahead, he slowed still more, then halted.

Richard and Marcus had instinctively matched their pace to his. Both halted, too, and turned to him.

He flexed his left leg and winced. "I left Glasgow at dawn and rode hard—I might have overdone it."

Neither Cynster male looked as though they believed the lie, but neither did they challenge it.

Realizing that they—being the sort of men they were—probably understood, and might even applaud his direction, he went on, "If you would proffer my apologies to Catriona and Lucilla, I believe I'll retire."

Marcus tilted his head as if considering the strategy.

Richard slowly blinked, then nodded. "Sound idea. Best to conserve your strength rather than fritter it away in the drawing room. We'll make your excuses."

Thomas didn't wait for more; he turned and strode for the stairs.

* * *

Lucilla wasn't sure whether Thomas's leg was truly troubling him, or if his retreat signaled something else.

What else? was the question.

On learning that he'd retired, she dallied for just long enough to take tea—only waiting until then because she didn't want to appear so needy before her family—then she excused herself and made for the stairs. She was walking briskly toward Thomas's door, intending to go in and inquire about his health, when that lurking, uncertain part of her reached out and hauled on her reins.

She halted and stared at the door.

What was she doing?

He'd retreated—retired—and immediately she was running after him.

They were partners, yes, but what did that mean?

And regardless of what it might come to mean, what did it mean now? Tonight?

If his leg was troubling him, if he had exhausted himself riding down from Glasgow, she should leave him to recover; they had the rest of their lives to grow closer and spend their nights together—she shouldn't be so needy as to demand even this one.

And if this was some sort of convoluted ploy?

She didn't think it was—didn't see him playing those sorts of games—yet he had made it plain what he thought of her manipulation. Would he, perhaps, stoop to using the same, just to see if he could? If she would respond to him tugging on her heartstrings?

Whether she believed that or not, that scenario, too, suggested that the last thing she should do was go to him.

She wanted to go to him, wanted to lose herself in his arms so they could find their way back to what they'd had; until they did that—at least that—the lurking unease inside her, a lack of confidence she'd never before known, wouldn't leave her.

Life had been so much easier when she'd always been sure.

She sighed. She was *dithering.* For a second, she closed her eyes, feeling that uncertainty still wrapped about her heart, seeping into her soul, then she opened her eyes and forced her feet away from his door.

She climbed the turret stairs. Eyes cast down, absorbed with her thoughts, she opened the door to her room, went in, turned, and shut the door, then swung back and took two steps into the room.

And noticed the unusual brightness of the lamplight. Slowing, she blinked, raised her head—and saw Thomas sprawled in her bed.

He didn't appear to be wearing a stitch.

Her steps faltered; she nearly tripped over her toes before she halted.

Her eyes grew round, then rounder; her mouth dried.

He was lying against her pillows, his magnificent chest fully on display. One powerful arm was bent, that hand behind his head; his other arm lay invitingly relaxed on the sheets beside him.

Beyond her control, her gaze—which had been absorbed in tracing every last line of his powerful shoulders and upper chest—tracked down, over the hollow in the center of his chest—the one she loved to set her lips to—and down, over the muscled ridges of his abdomen to his narrow waist...the sheet was draped across his hips, but so low...as she looked, the sheet shifted.

She jerked her gaze back to his face. And registered how warm she'd grown. This was ridiculous. They'd been intimate how many times?

But she hadn't seen him like this before—this naked, this exposed.

This much hers.

She understood the declaration. He'd said he was hers, and here he was, in her bed, with not so much as his sleeping trousers to shield him from her.

And he'd taken steps to ensure that she could see; he'd moved the lamps so they surrounded the bed and flooded the interior of the four-postered expanse with soft, golden light.

She looked, saw, and her mind blanked.

He was patently, blatantly, waiting for her.

"Ah…" And, yes, she was speechless. What could she possibly say—to this?

He didn't seem to have the same problem. "I wondered how long you'd be." His eyes held hers, golden fire smoldering in the amber. Then he raised his hand and gently beckoned. "Come here."

Not an order, a suggestion.

One she followed.

Instinct took over; she could almost see the threads of what linked them glimmering in the air between him and her.

She reached the bed, raised her skirts, and set one knee on the edge of the mattress. She extended an arm, placed her hand in his, and let him grasp and pull her up. On her knees, she shuffled closer, still upright. Still gripping his hand, still lost in his eyes, held by them and the promise—the future—she saw burning brightly in their depths.

This was what she wanted, what she needed.

Him. All of him.

She let go of all restraint and let him lead her on— let the power that held them swell, coalesce, and take control.

Leaning down, curling her fingers in his and using his grip for balance, she framed his face with her free hand and kissed him.

Opened her mouth and, when he responded, drew him in.

Their fingers eased; they drew their hands apart only

to place them on each other. To relearn the curves, the hollows. To reacquaint their senses with the delight each brought the other; to taste and breathe each other in—until their hearts beat in time and the familiar urgency rose within them.

Passion shivered around them, all but tangible as—together, piece by slow piece—they shed her clothes. As, together, to an unhurried and deliberate beat, they knowingly and willingly surrendered and slid deeper into love's embrace.

Even if he wouldn't yet acknowledge the affliction, he had already admitted openly to having every symptom.

And that, she acknowledged, as she rose up and—her skin afire, her nerves thrumming with desire—sank down and took him in, sheathed him in her body, held him deep, and pleasured them both, was enough. Enough from someone who had been so very afraid of loving at all.

The lamplight played over his skin and hers, allowing neither of them any shadows in which to hide any part of what they now were, of what together they could be.

And together they reached for that, strove for that moment of elemental joining.

They touched the glory and came apart, shattering, then shuddering as ecstasy claimed them.

Gasping, barely able to breathe, they sank into each other, and with nothing any longer held back, with every last barrier breached and cindered, with their fingers locked, their hearts in rhythm, and their souls entwined, together they reached...and let incandescent love, honored and accepted, fill them, fuse them, and forge them, finally, into one.

* * *

Thomas eventually stirred. He wanted nothing more than to lie exactly where he was forever, but the lamps were still burning.

On a long, almost silent sigh, he gently eased her from him.

Immediately, her fingers clutched, sinking into his sides, and she raised her tousled head.

"*Sssh*. I'm only going to turn down the lamps."

Huge green eyes, still utterly dazed with spent passion, blinked at him, twice, then she eased her grip and let him slide from the bed, but shifting onto her back, she continued to watch him as he circled the bed, turning down the wicks.

He'd left her windows uncurtained; faint moonlight guided him back to her.

Back to the soft arms that were waiting to wrap around him once more.

He lay down and, for an instant, closed his eyes—unable to imagine how he had ever thought to walk away from this.

From this indescribable wonder.

If he'd known that this was what true surrender felt like, he wouldn't have fought it—not for an instant.

She settled half across him, her silky red head in the hollow of his shoulder, one hand splayed over his heart. Gently, he closed his arms around her, holding her there.

He debated, for a moment, if this was the right time—decided he wouldn't find a better. He shifted his head and pressed a kiss to her hair. "Our wedding." Various approaches ran through his mind. He settled for "How soon do you think we should marry?"

She huffed, her breath tickling his chest. In a questioning tone, she suggested, "Tomorrow?"

He grinned. "That would suit me, but I suspect your parents might have something to say to that." He drew in a breath. "And I have to confess that I wasn't so sure of my reception here that I stopped to get a special license. So unless you know a local bishop who might be prevailed upon to grant us one, I assume we'll still need the usual three weeks..." He squinted down at her face, what he could see of it. "Or am I presuming and there's some other form of ceremony here?"

She sighed. "I wish there was—I'm sure, if left to the Lady, the entire matter would be much simpler—but no. We need to get married in the church, just like everyone else, or it won't be legal."

He'd assumed as much. "So, when?"

"Sunday's the day after tomorrow, so four weeks after that." She snuggled deeper into his embrace. "That will please everyone—the family will have time to gather, which they will appreciate." She glanced up and through the dimness met his eyes. Her lips curved. "And you'll have time to get used to us all. We're considered a fairly *robust* clan."

He picked up the hand resting on his chest; holding her gaze, he raised it and pressed a kiss to her palm. "As long as you're there, by my side, I'll endeavor to endure and survive."

Her smile grew pensive. She slipped her fingers free of his and traced the line of his cheek. "I know you will. We're here, together, as we were always fated to be. You're mine at last, and I'm yours." She drew breath, then murmured, her voice dreamy, faraway, "And no matter the challenges, no matter the years, we will never turn from each other. Come what may, we will hold to each other, and we will never let each other go."

The words rang softly through the night.

He closed his arms around her, she settled in his embrace, and finally, for both of them, everything felt right.

Those Fate had linked, no one and nothing would ever part.

Lover, consort, protector and defender—husband.

Thomas closed his eyes as the words rolled through his mind, echoed in his heart, then rumbled through his soul. He would always be hers. He would always be here, because this was his place—this was his destiny—now, tomorrow, and forevermore.

Seventeen

Their marriage was formalized before the altar of the tiny church in Carsphairn village.

The Cynsters turned out in strength; Thomas's Glasgow relatives, several old friends, and all those on the Carrick estate helped balance things out somewhat.

The bride wore pearls and a gown of tiered lace; the bridegroom stood straight and tall, broad shoulders clad in regulation black. Everyone agreed they were quite the handsomest couple in the county.

A hush fell over the congregation, packed into every nook and cranny in the small stone church, as Thomas, then Lucilla, spoke their vows. When they shared a kiss and the organ swelled in a triumphal march, joy and happiness abounded.

After the church bells finally pealed and the bride and groom emerged to circulate and talk with the guests spread out on the lawns, every face wore a smile; Thomas's shoulders were constantly being slapped, and Lucilla's cheeks were rosy as relative followed friend in kissing her and wishing her and her handsome new husband well.

Standing at one corner of the church's open porch, Catriona looked out over the throng and smiled.

"Happy?" Richard paused beside her, also casting his gaze over the heads.

"I'm very pleased," Catriona admitted. "I confess I hadn't expected quite so many to travel all the way from London."

"Helena's eldest granddaughter weds?" Richard snorted. "I'm surprised that more aren't here, but I gather she put it about that only family were expected."

"Still, when talking of Cynsters, 'only family' is now what? Well over a hundred?"

Richard twined his arm with his wife's. "I haven't counted recently, but it must be something like that. Now come along, Mother-of-the-Bride, and let's greet our guests."

Catriona laughed softly and let him draw her down to the lawns. Pausing to greet her cousin-in-law Angelica and her handsome Highland earl, Catriona glanced at Lucilla and Thomas and found them surrounded by what the Cynster parents referred to as "the older set."

Sebastian, Marquess of Earith, was their leader; tall, with near-black hair and his father's pale green eyes, he was already a commanding figure, a quality dependent not only on his stature, but even more on his personality. His brother, Michael, stood shoulder to shoulder beside Sebastian—which, in itself, said much. Alongside Michael, Christopher Cynster was holding the group's attention by relating some story; he was a natural raconteur, yet Catriona sensed he used that art as a deflecting shield behind which dwelt a far more complex character. Marcus, of course, was one of the group, but aside from Lucilla, leaning on Thomas's arm, the only female was Prudence, she of the curly blond-brown hair, blue eyes, and passion for all things equine.

Prudence, Catriona knew, entertained few thoughts of marriage, reasoning that horses were much more accommodating beasts.

Given the males Prudence had spent her life surrounded by, Catriona had to admit that, as far as it went, Prudence's reasoning was sound. Cynster males, and those like them, were only as accommodating as a lady could persuade them to be.

Or, as usually happened, love persuaded them to be.

Catriona glanced at the Cynster by her side. They'd been married for nearly three decades, and the magic was still there, as was the love. For them, for all those like them, love was the great leveler between the sexes—the critical element required to make a marriage work.

As they moved on through the crowd, Catriona heard Lucilla laugh. She glanced across and saw her daughter look up at the man she had taken to her bed—the man that, Lady-chosen or not, Lucilla had brought to her side, and together they had bound themselves with love and passion.

They had the right foundation; Catriona had no doubt they would thrive.

Richard leaned close and whispered in her ear, "One down, four to go."

Catriona smiled. "Time enough for the others. Today is all Lucilla and Thomas's."

And yet…through the crowd, Catriona glimpsed a head of pale blond ringlets at the far side of the lawn.

Niniver Carrick. Thomas's cousin had given Thomas and Lucilla a female deerhound as a wedding gift; no one was quite sure where she had got the elegant brindle-coated animal, as most had thought the Carrick kennel sold and dispersed. Marcus, meanwhile, had given Thomas and

Lucilla a male deerhound from the line he was breeding. There hadn't been any collusion; the match was simply a happy coincidence.

In Catriona's world, happy coincidences were often signs.

Thomas and Lucilla had, for reasons not even they could explain, wanted the deerhounds at the church. Niniver had offered to hold them. As Marcus had stood as one of Thomas's groomsmen, the offer had been welcomed.

But that now left Niniver holding the young pups on leashes to one side of the lawn, out of the crush of the crowd, yet a potent magnet for every one of the many children, Cynster and local alike, who was there.

Niniver was a quiet, reclusive beauty. Catriona doubted that Niniver liked crowds, yet she was surrounded by a veritable army, all demanding and questioning...

Marcus must have realized the same thing. He arrived, and moving around to stand beside Niniver, he wisely made no move to take the leashes from her, but started to intercept the questions—and the children, both those who knew him and those who did not, responded to his presence and focused on him, allowing Niniver to breathe.

Even from a distance, Catriona could see the relief in Niniver, in the loosening of her muscles, in the lines of her face. In the grateful glance she threw Marcus, even though he didn't notice.

Catriona watched for a minute more, then—satisfied that all was well on that front, too—moved on.

"But how fast can they run?" Eleven-year-old Persephone Cynster stood at the rear of the crowd of children and directed her question not at Marcus but at the blond goddess beside him. "Faster than a horse?"

"For a time." Niniver looked down at the shaggy head she was stroking; the pups were fretting, wanting to run and leap—initially on all the nice friendly people in their Sunday best.

"They can run faster than horses for a short way." Marcus stepped in before Persephone, with the un-flinching confidence of her heritage, could further in-terrogate Niniver. "But they can't keep that pace up for long—nowhere near as long as a horse can run."

He could see that Persephone—intrigued by the fact that it was a girl who had control of the dogs—wanted to pursue Niniver, but Niniver was there, where he knew she truly didn't want to be, partly because of him, and he wouldn't have her badgered. Appealing with a look to several of the local boys, who were crouched as close as they could get to the dogs, he invited a question—and they obliged with alacrity. Most were, he noted, Car-rick clansmen.

Given the interest shining in their eyes, he had to wonder from whom Niniver had got Eir, the female she'd given Thomas and Lucilla. Marcus would have sworn the hound was a purebred from the old Carrick line, and Thomas had mentioned that breeding was still going on somewhere on the Carrick estate—*he* hadn't been sur-prised to see Niniver arrive at the door with the squirm-ing bundle under her arm.

Thomas would know, or could guess, from whom she'd got the dog; Marcus made a mental note to pick his new brother-in-law's brain.

He glanced over the crowd at his twin and her new

husband and found himself grinning. He would ask, but maybe not tonight.

"No," he replied to the next question. "Their coats are never flat and smooth."

And, speaking of smooth, he gave thanks that, thus far, the crowd and the width of Thomas's shoulders had blocked Sebastian, Michael, and Christopher from noticing where he'd gone. If any of the three sighted Niniver, they'd be over to lend a hand in a flash, but situated as they had been at the front of the church, they hadn't known she was there, at the rear holding the dogs, and she'd come out ahead of the rest of the congregation. Thus far, she was safe.

While he knew none of his cousins would intentionally do anything to hurt or harm Niniver, he was also convinced that them not noticing her would be best all around for everyone.

He wasn't sure how he would screen her from them at the wedding breakfast in the Great Hall, but he would worry about that later.

Right now, he had children to deflect, and Niniver to protect from their constant encroachment. He pointed to three little boys who'd been sidling nearer. "Back. We don't want to startle the dogs."

Or Niniver; she was jumpy enough as it was. He could all but feel her nervous tension.

He wished he could do something to ease it, but the best he could do was keep the children amused and that weight, at least, off her shoulders.

In the middle of the crowd, grasping the distraction created by Antonia Rawlings joining their group, Thomas dipped his head toward Lucilla's. "Have you seen Manachan?"

She looked around. "No. And I have been looking."

So had Thomas. After their engagement had been announced, he and Lucilla had wanted to call on Manachan, to confirm that his recovery was progressing and also to learn if he'd made any headway in identifying who had been behind the various incidents on the estate, but the day after their banns had first been read, Manachan had written, both to heartily congratulate them and to ask them to stay away.

He'd written that matters were tense within the clan, and he would appreciate it if they kept their distance at that time.

They had, of course, acceded to that request. Their lingering concerns had been somewhat allayed when Manachan had responded to the invitation to the wedding, both on behalf of the clan and of himself and his family, declaring that they would all be present.

But Manachan hadn't come forward to take the position reserved for him at the end of the front pew. Thomas and Lucilla had both noticed the empty spot, but as yet they'd seen none of the Carrick family other than Niniver, who was presently engaged.

"I can't imagine," Lucilla said, "that after what he wrote, he wouldn't have come. Perhaps he didn't feel up to being swallowed by the crowd and stayed at the back of the church."

Thomas nodded. If Manachan had stayed back, Nigel, Nolan, and Norris would have, too. Raising his head, he scanned the crowd. "Perhaps we should circulate and see if he's by the edges somewhere."

Lucilla squeezed his arm. "We should circulate anyway, but that's an added incentive."

Turning to her cousins and Antonia, she excused the pair of them, and they moved into the crowd.

A stone wall surrounded the church grounds, keeping the crowd tightly packed; the day was fine, if cool, and no one was in any great hurry to pile back into their coaches. For all those present, weddings were gatherings designed to catch up with family and friends; everyone was content to stand in the fresh air and chat.

Several chairs had been carried out from the church and set here and there. Helena, Dowager Duchess of St. Ives—old and frail but with eyes that still saw everything—sat in one, commanding a small circle of attendants; Lucilla and Thomas had already paid their respects, so they didn't pause there, but continued wending around the edges of the crowd.

They finally found Manachan; he was standing at one corner of the lawn, leaning heavily against the stone wall and gripping two canes, both planted in the lawn to either side.

His hat was pulled low over his face, and a fine woolen scarf swathed his jaw, rising nearly to his beak of a nose.

When Lucilla and Thomas reached him, Manachan dipped his head as low as he could. "Congratulations to you both." He straightened, and his piercing eyes, just visible in the shadow cast by his hat's brim, lifted to Thomas's face. "You've made me very proud, boy. Your father and mother would have been thrilled." The corners of his eyes crinkled. "I did tell you to learn to think with your heart and not just your head."

"You did, indeed." Thomas dipped his head; although his uncle was swathed top to toe, with only a small section of his face visible, it was clear the earlier improvement in Manachan's health hadn't lasted. Lowering his voice, he asked, "How are you?"

Edgar was, as ever, at Manachan's side. Thomas glanced at Edgar as he spoke—and was even more disturbed by the stony blankness in Edgar's expression. Rather than meet Thomas's gaze, Edgar stared straight ahead.

Manachan waved irritably. "I'm well enough—well enough to be here to see you wed."

Lucilla's eyes had narrowed on his face. "Which means you're not as well as you should be." She would have stepped closer and peered at Manachan's face, examined his eyes, but he shifted one of his canes into her path, forestalling her.

"Never you mind about me. As I told all of my dear family"—Manachan flicked one of his canes toward Nigel and Nolan; having spotted Thomas and Lucilla speaking with Manachan, the pair had detached from the crowd and were approaching—"I will not be the black witch at your wedding."

Nigel halted beside Thomas, his gaze on his father. "We tried to tell him you wouldn't mind if he didn't come, not given his ill health, but, of course, he wouldn't listen."

"I'm still The Carrick, boy," Manachan growled. "You mind your manners—and have you wished Thomas and Lucilla well?"

Nigel's lips tightened; turning to Thomas, he offered his hand. "Congratulations, cuz."

Nolan followed Nigel; releasing Thomas's hand, he bowed to Lucilla. "Miss—" Nolan paused, then amended, "Mrs. Carrick." His brows rose and he glanced at Thomas. "I suppose that makes you a part of the clan, too."

Lucilla smiled. "Indeed. And my new position gives me an even better right to treat the head of the Carrick clan, don't you think?" She turned her green gaze on Manachan.

He held up a hand in a fencer's gesture of surrender. "Tomorrow. You can come and see me tomorrow afternoon—both of you. But for my sake, promise me you'll enjoy this day without a care—it's your wedding day, and by the grace of God and the Lady, you'll only ever have one."

Even shadowed by his hat brim, even though he was physically weak and, it seemed, under some degree of strain, Manachan's gaze was still strong; Thomas could feel its weight as it rested on him and Lucilla, demanding and compelling acceptance, obedience.

Inwardly sighing, Thomas inclined his head. "Tomorrow afternoon, then. We'll call on you then."

Manachan went to say something, but his breath caught in his chest. He half bent, wheezed—but when Thomas and Lucilla reached for him, he fended them off. "No—off you go. You've your other guests to see to." He managed to breathe again. Straightening, he continued, "Now I've seen you and paid my respects, I'm going to head off home." He looked at Lucilla. "If you see your parents, please give them my regards and my apologies for not dallying to speak with them."

"Of course." The look Lucilla threw Thomas was questioning.

He understood what she was asking, but Manachan patently did not want any fuss made.

Pride. He understood the emotion. And given that Manachan seemed even more infirm than he had been before, leaning heavily on Edgar as he pushed away from the wall and turned toward the gate, perhaps his pride was one thing they needed to acknowledge and support.

Closing his hand about Lucilla's, he held her beside him as Manachan moved away. "Until tomorrow."

Manachan gave a small tilt of his head and continued making his way very slowly toward the gate. Beyond it, Thomas could see his uncle's carriage waiting in the lane. Two good-looking hacks were tied to the back.

His gaze on Manachan's retreating back, Nigel paused beside Thomas. "We'll follow the carriage home." Nigel turned away, and Thomas followed his gaze to Norris.

Manachan's youngest son had held back, hovering on the edge of the crowd. He dipped his head to Thomas and Lucilla and murmured his congratulations.

"You'd better fetch Niniver." Nigel's tone was hard, as was the gaze he directed at Norris. "The pair of you should go in the carriage with Papa."

Norris's expression remained impassive, but he gave a slight nod. "I'll get her." He inclined his head again to Thomas and Lucilla, then turned and made his way into the crowd.

Lucilla glanced at Thomas, clearly wanting to follow— to question Niniver, the one person who might tell them more about Manachan's condition.

Thomas agreed; he gripped her hand and, with brief nods to Nigel and Nolan, parted from them.

He and Lucilla started back through the crowd, following in Norris's wake—but there were many who had not yet had a chance to speak with them and wish them well. They progressed by fits and starts. By the time they'd traveled far enough that Thomas could look over the heads, he searched along the wall where Niniver had been, then sighed. "She's already gone."

Lucilla looked up at him. He let her see his welling concern for Manachan; she read his eyes—and he saw the same anxiety reflected in hers. But then she sighed. Leaning closer, she squeezed his arm. "I think this is one of those times we have to accept that whatever will come, will come."

He dipped his head and brushed his lips to her temple. "He did want us to enjoy our day."

"Indeed." With a brisk nod, she straightened. "So that's one thing we can do for him—we can honor his wish." Settling her arm again in his, she turned him to the next group waiting to speak with them. "And tomorrow," she murmured, "I'm going to ask Mama and Papa to come with us."

Thomas thought that an excellent idea.

Leaving dealing with tomorrow for tomorrow, he joined with his new wife in honoring his uncle's wish; thereafter, they devoted themselves to enjoying their day, on every level and in every way.

* * *

The wedding breakfast proved a riotous event. Speeches were declared the order of the day, and they were many and varied, from the sincere to the hilarious, delivered by a host of characters ranging from Helena, Dowager Duchess of St. Ives, to Christopher Cynster.

Even Quentin, Winifred, and Humphrey joined in, along with several of Thomas's old school friends.

And from noon until late in the afternoon, the feasting rolled on.

Later, after waving away all those returning to their homes, the contingent who were staying at least until the next day adjourned to the drawing room, the library, the

Great Hall, the large schoolroom, or Carter's attic studio, as their ages, genders, and inclinations disposed them.

Thomas and Lucilla ended lolling on a sofa at one end of the long library, surrounded by their Cynster peers, along with Antonia Rawlings, who had claimed a small love seat facing the sofa. Sebastian lay sprawled in an armchair, Marcus in another, while Prudence had curled on the other end of the sofa. Michael and Christopher had elected to lie on their backs on the floor, all but filling the space between sofa and armchairs.

"So," Sebastian murmured, his gaze traveling the group, "who's going to be next?"

Eyes closed, Michael replied, "Not you."

Everyone laughed, but none of them volunteered any further reply.

Antonia asked whether Thomas and Lucilla had any plans for coming south that year, and the talk, desultory as it was, moved on.

Thomas listened and learned; he'd never been a part of a family such as the Cynsters, yet in the same way he had so quickly felt at ease with Marcus, so, too, he felt surprisingly relaxed with and accepted by this group—those closest to Lucilla, her particular circle within the larger family.

And while family was very like clan, in this particular family, while the similarities were there, it still wasn't quite the same. He finally decided it was because clan was so hierarchical, with so much power vested in the head of the clan, while the Cynsters were a family of powerful individuals, linked by blood and heritage, yet each strong and capable in their own right—the combined strength of the Cynsters would outweigh that of any simple clan.

And, if anything, they worked together and looked out for each other even more than clansmen did.

In proof of that, a few hours later, Marcus, Prudence, and Antonia arranged a diversion that allowed Thomas and Lucilla to escape all further imminent teasing and retire.

Laughing, her hand gripping his, Lucilla rushed up the turret stairs. She hauled him into their room and slammed and bolted the door.

Laughing, too, he fell back with his shoulders against the door. He tipped his head at the bolt. "Is that really necessary?"

"Oh, yes." Lucilla's face was flushed, her eyes sparkling. "You don't yet know my cousins. Sebastian, Michael, and Christopher are bad enough, although I expect self-preservation will exert at least some tempering influence on them, but the younger ones?" Smiling fondly, she shook her head. "Trust me—we'll need to exercise great caution when we walk out of that door in the morning."

He studied her—the light dancing in her emerald eyes, the glow happiness had laid over her skin, the rumpled glory of her hair. Earlier, she'd changed out of her delicate bridal gown into a simple round gown—which was just as well; given the emotions rising within him, he doubted he would have been able to manage the lace without ripping it.

She was studying him, too.

Lucilla drank in the reality that was now acknowledged to be hers—her husband. His strength, as always, was blatantly on display in his shoulders and chest, the thews of his arms and thighs. Her gaze swept over him, noting the thick fall of his hair that would feel like silk as she raked her fingers through it, and the telltale tenting of his trousers.

Passion shimmered in the air, now so potent and powerful between them.

She raised her gaze to his face, took in the golden embers smoldering in the amber of his eyes.

His lids were low; he was watching her with the calculation of a lion eyeing its next meal.

A giggle bubbled up.

Another joined it, and she laughed, whirled, picked up her skirts, and raced for the bed.

He caught her before she reached it.

Thomas swept her up in his arms and tumbled them both onto the bed.

Onto her silk comforter, into the softness.

They fell on each other with hands, lips, and tongues. Clothes flew, then they fell into each other, joined and whirled each other on, into and through the heady dance of their passions.

Of their needs and desires, fueled by their yearnings and their hopes and dreams for now and the future.

All swirled about them in the confines of her bed.

And that night, they grabbed all—gave and took and seized *everything*.

Every last nuance, every last gasp of ecstasy.

"I love you."

"Never leave me."

"You're mine and I'm yours."

"I'm yours until I die."

The words fell from their lips—from her, from him—breathed at the last with knowledge and acceptance. With a reverence, a devotion, nothing could hide.

Between them, they no longer hid anything; no screen

or veil was able to hide her heart from him, much less his from her.

They were ruled by a togetherness that sank deep, abiding and binding.

This they had; it would be theirs, come what may.

Ecstasy raked them, shattered, then remade them.

Separate no more.

Sated and satisfied, certain at last and buoyed beyond belief, they slumped into each other's arms, and let their future have them.

* * *

Lucilla woke before dawn and knew what she had to do. Turning over in her bed, she rose on one elbow and leaned over Thomas. He was still asleep, held deep, his heavy body more relaxed than she'd ever seen it.

Framing his face, she kissed him, woke him.

Drew him down the long slow road that was now theirs to travel. To enjoy these sweet minutes that were solely theirs, to glory in the pleasure of their love.

She didn't need to hear him claim the emotion; it lived in his heart, in his mind, his soul, and nothing, she felt certain, would ever mute it, much less cause it to fade.

Later, eminently pleased with this way of waking up, she lay boneless over his chest and listened to his heart thud.

When the beat had slowed sufficiently, she raised her head and looked into his eyes.

At her movement, he'd raised his lids. From beneath his lashes, he searched her face. "What?"

"I should go—I need to go—to the sacred grove."

"To pray?"

When she nodded, he lightly shook his head as if

clearing the cobwebs of sleep away. "What does it say that such a manic idea actually makes sense to me now?"

She was starting to love the way he made her laugh—usually at the most unexpected times. Growing serious again, she looked into his eyes. Held his gaze. "It's tradition for the Lady of the Vale—or in my case, the Lady-in-waiting—to introduce her consort to the Lady in the grove. It's also tradition—one my father keeps to this day—for a consort to keep watch over his lady while she prays." She hoped he would want to do the same, but she wasn't sure. "Will you come?"

"Of course." He sat up, tumbling her from her position across his chest. "By keeping watch, you mean like Marcus was doing that day I came to plead with you to help the Bradshaws?"

Climbing from the bed, she nodded. "Just like that. It's not as if there is any danger—it's more symbolic."

Thomas glanced at her lithe, naked figure as she walked to the washstand. Symbolic be damned. She was very real, and so was the protectiveness he felt—had always felt—for her. He tossed back the covers and rose. "I take it we'll ride there."

* * *

They did; through the freshness of a late spring dawn just breaking, they cantered across the fields—fields he found himself studying with a proprietary eye. He'd be working alongside Richard managing the estate, the Vale, from now on.

Upon reaching the sacred grove, they dismounted, leaving their horses in the same area he'd found her black mare and Marcus's mount long ago. It seemed long ago—so much had happened since—yet in reality only six weeks had passed since he'd last walked down the winding path that led to the heart of the grove.

The experience, this time, was quite different.

He'd thought he didn't believe, but somewhere in some long-forgotten, unrecognized corner of his soul, he must, because now, through Lucilla, through the ceremonial words she used, he could feel the power.

Old, ancient, it stirred—around him, through him.

And he *had* to believe.

Closing his eyes, he swayed slightly, sensing that power washing around and over him, then sinking through his soul to anchor him.

Once the introduction was complete, Lucilla led him out to the stone at the entrance to the path. With a quiet word, she left him sitting there and retreated to complete her devotions.

He sat and stared out at the land spread before him and let his thoughts flow unfettered. Let appreciation of land, of place, of people, of family and clan rise up and claim him.

This was their future, his and hers, to protect and guide and nurture.

This was his place, here, beside her.

Finally, he'd found his true home, his true role. The life he needed to be all he could be—all he had it in him to be.

He breathed deeply; closing his eyes, he held the pristine air in his lungs and gave thanks—to Fate, to God, to the Lady—for all he had found, for all life had offered him.

For all he would hold to the end of his days.

Epilogue

After a noisy, boisterous breakfast, one blessed with a great deal of laughter, most of the remaining guests departed through the morning.

Lucilla stood on the porch and, one arm linked with Thomas's, waved them away. "I'm glad they all came, but I have to confess I'm happy enough to see them go." Meeting Thomas's eyes, she saw the questioning lift of his brows, and smiled. "I'm eager to get on establishing *our* version of married life."

He chuckled and bent to kiss her—lightly—then, twining his fingers with hers, he allowed her to tow him back into the house.

The luncheon gong boomed as they entered, so they continued on into the Great Hall. Holding Lucilla's chair, then subsiding into the one next to it—into his already accustomed place—Thomas looked out over the hall, at those filing in and gathering at the tables in response to the gong's summons. Not everyone came in for luncheon; regardless, he felt pleased that he could already put a name and occupation to most of those present.

"I've been meaning to ask"—Marcus dropped into the chair on Lucilla's other side—"from whom did Niniver get Eir? She couldn't be one of the dogs spirited away before

Nigel could sell them—she's too young. So who's over-seeing the breeding now—presumably without Nigel's knowledge?"

Thomas swallowed a mouthful of rich chicken soup. "I'm not really sure. They're keeping the pack at old Egan's place."

Marcus picked up his soup spoon but didn't start eating. He frowned. "Could it be Niniver herself? She seemed very capable with the dogs, very competent in handling the pups."

"I doubt it's just her, but undoubtedly with her help." Thomas looked down at his bowl. "Possibly under her direction. I think they have not quite half, but the better half of the original breeders. But whatever you do, don't mention that to anyone. I assume Nigel saw Eir at the church, but he might not know she was a gift from Niniver, and even if he does, I'm certain he doesn't know where she got the pup from."

Marcus was staring out at the hall, but he nodded. "The secret's safe with me." He stirred his soup, then added, "Nigel was a fool to sell off the dogs—the litters had always brought in a nice sum to the estate. No one could understand why he did it."

"I certainly don't." Thomas felt his jaw clench, then Lucilla laid a hand on his arm.

Leaning forward, she caught her mother's eye and proceeded to explain their concerns about Manachan's health and also, given the decline in his strength, that they feared the problems that had beset the estate might still be unresolved.

Thomas glanced at Richard. "As you know, Manachan hadn't wanted us to call at Carrick Manor before the wedding, and when we spoke with him yesterday, he insisted that we did nothing but enjoy the day—"

"But he agreed that we could call on him this afternoon." Lucilla looked at her mother, then transferred her gaze to her father. "We thought it might be helpful if you could accompany us." She looked back at Catriona. "Both of you."

Richard considered, then exchanged a glance with Catriona. Then he nodded. "That sounds an eminently sensible idea." He paused, then added, "There have been a lot of strange decisions taken on the Carrick estate over the last year, and while none of us—the surrounding landowners—would dream of interfering—" He broke off with a short laugh. "Not that Manachan would ever allow us to, but still, we've noticed and wondered."

"Which is to say," Catriona said, regally gracious, "that your plan is a sound one. We'll leave immediately luncheon is done."

* * *

Rather than taking a carriage, they rode, albeit via the road. Both Lucilla's and Catriona's mounts bore saddlebags stuffed with herbs and potions; Thomas had felt the bottles as he'd tied Lucilla's bag to her saddle.

Marcus had wanted to come, but they'd decided that that might make their party look too much like an invasion. Manachan had a long history of taking offense over such minor social nuances.

So the four of them trotted two abreast, Thomas and Lucilla in the lead, Catriona and Richard close behind, up the long drive to Carrick Manor.

They rounded the last curve and the front of the house, sitting beyond the gravel forecourt, came into view. A small figure huddled at the top of the steps. Riding closer, they recognized Niniver's pale blond hair. Her shoulders were slumped; she looked dejected and forlorn. She was twisting a limp handkerchief in her hands.

The face she raised to them as, alarmed, they reined in, dismounted, and rushed to her, was tear-ravaged, her blue eyes awash, puffy and red-rimmed.

"Oh, my dear." Catriona sank down beside Niniver and gathered her in. "What is it?"

Leaning against Catriona, Niniver gulped and weakly waved. "He's gone—Papa. He didn't wake this morning. Eventually, Edgar—his man—tried to rouse him and realized..." She hiccupped. "He was so set on attending the wedding—we all argued, but he wouldn't stay at home... and now he's *dead*." She caught her breath on a sob. "And Nigel's disappeared, too."

Niniver ducked her head, dabbing at her face with the sodden handkerchief.

Thomas's face had set. He exchanged a look with Richard. Catriona waved them to go in; leaving Niniver with her, Thomas and Richard climbed the steps and headed for the open front door. Lucilla debated, then followed them.

Halting in the foyer, Thomas looked around and saw no one—no footman, no Ferguson. But a rumble of voices came from the direction of the servants' hall. Thomas called, "Ferguson!"

A second passed, then heavy footsteps came hurrying along the corridor. Ferguson appeared. He looked at Thomas, Richard, and Lucilla and visibly sagged with relief. "Thank God you're here, Mr. Thomas, sir—the master's dead, Mr. Nigel's disappeared, Mr. Nolan's refusing to send for the doctor, Mr. Norris is no use to anyone, and Miss Niniver is distraught—and none of us knows what's best to do."

Others had followed Ferguson; Sean, Mitch, Fred, Mrs. Kennedy, Gwen, and several maids and footmen crowded into the hall behind the butler. All looked shocked and also incipiently angry.

Sean explained the latter. "Nigel should be here, but he's gone off, and no one knows to where. What use is that?"

Others murmured darkly in agreement.

Thomas agreed, too, but in Nigel's absence… "Where's Nolan?"

"Sitting with his da's dead body in his room," Sean said. "Edgar's there, too."

Thomas nodded. "We'll go up." To Ferguson, he said, "Lady Cynster is on the front steps with Niniver—you might see if they wish to move to the drawing room, and I'm sure a pot of tea would be welcome."

"Yes, of course, sir." Mrs. Kennedy bustled forward. "Come on." She tugged Ferguson's sleeve. "We can at least give Miss Niniver what comfort we can—only one of the lot of 'em who's crying for her dad."

Thomas exchanged a glance with Lucilla as, side by side, they made for the stairs. Richard followed close behind.

They reached Manachan's room and found the door ajar. Quietly pushing it open, Thomas led the way in. He walked into Manachan's bedroom and halted just past the threshold. His uncle lay on his back, his hands clasped over his chest. The shadows cast by the curtains screening the head of the bed largely hid his face; he might have simply been sleeping.

But Nolan sat by the side of the bed, one arm stretched out, his hand on his father's sleeve; his head was bowed, resting on his outstretched arm. Edgar stood on the other side of the bed, almost in the corner of the room. His expression was devastated, his complexion ashen. He'd been with Manachan for a very long time.

Thomas inclined his head to Edgar and moved further into the room.

At the rustle of Lucilla's gown, Nolan raised his head. He looked at them almost blearily, as if he'd been asleep, then he blinked and dragged in a huge breath. His face, always pale, looked strained, his features edging toward haggard. Slowly straightening, he waved vaguely at his father's body. "As you can see, he's gone."

Thomas felt that truth—the realization that his uncle had, indeed, passed on—close about his heart, tightening his chest almost unbearably...but then Lucilla slipped her hand into his and lightly gripped, and the pressure eased. The weight of grief remained, but not the strangling sensation. He gripped lightly back, then drew in a breath. "The doctor needs to be sent for."

Nolan snorted. "What for?" He slumped back in the chair and stared at the body. "He's dead, and nothing any quack can do is going to bring him back."

"Be that as it may," Richard said, "the law dictates that in the matter of the death of a landowner, a doctor must attend the body and issue a certificate."

Nolan's expression darkened; mulishly, he shook his head. "He wouldn't have wanted any quack poking at him." He looked at Thomas and Lucilla. "You know how he felt."

"What he might have wanted is beside the point," Richard calmly replied. "Not even for The Carrick will the law bend."

Nolan slouched in the chair. He crossed his arms and stared broodingly at Manachan's body. Raising a hand, he bit the nail of one thumb; he didn't look at Thomas, Richard, or Lucilla again.

Thomas looked at Edgar.

He stirred and glanced briefly at Nolan. "I'll get Sean to send one of the grooms for the doctor."

Thomas nodded. "Thank you."

When Edgar had left, closing the door behind him, Thomas refocused on Nolan. "Where's Nigel?"

Without looking at Thomas, Nolan shook his head. "I don't know."

Thomas felt Lucilla slip her fingers free of his; quietly, she walked around the bed, her goal clearly the small table beside its head and the bottle of tonic that stood there.

"When last did you see Nigel?" Richard asked.

Looking at the nail he'd been biting, Nolan replied, his voice all but toneless, "Yesterday. We rode away from the wedding following Papa's carriage, but we didn't stick to the road—we cut across the fields." Nolan shifted on the chair, sitting straighter. "Nigel pulled up about halfway home. He said he wanted to ride for a while. I pointed out that Papa was ill, but he brushed me off and said that if I cared, I should ride on to the manor. Then he took off. He…was in one of his wild moods. I decided I should let him go and come back here, so I did."

"He hasn't returned since then?" Richard asked.

Nolan sullenly replied, "I don't know—I haven't seen him, but someone else might have. But he wasn't at breakfast, and he isn't around now. And Sean said his horse isn't in the stable."

Thomas shifted. "How was Manachan when he reached home?"

Nolan lifted a shoulder. "As well as he's been these last few days." He paused, then grudgingly added, "He's been getting steadily weaker for about the last week." Nolan jerked his chin at the door. "Edgar and the others can tell you."

Half screened from Nolan by the fall of the bed curtain, Lucilla had been studying the bottle of restorative; it was a replacement for the one she'd left with Manachan weeks ago. She'd tested a drop of the tonic on her tongue, and it had tasted as it should; Manachan hadn't grown weak through any fault of Alice's. She set down the bottle and, frowning, turned—and looked directly at Manachan's face.

For a moment, what she was seeing, what her eyes were noting, didn't properly register.

Then it did and she froze.

She felt her eyes grow rounder. Swiftly, she drank in all she could see...then she swallowed and softly said, "We should have Mama come up—she'll know for certain. But I believe you should send for the magistrate, too." Drawing in a breath, she turned and met Thomas's gaze. "I think your uncle was poisoned."

* * *

Shock froze Thomas, Nolan, and Richard, then Thomas swore and looked for the bellpull.

Richard clapped him on the shoulder. "Don't bother— I'll get her."

Ten minutes later, Catriona and Lucilla had independently completed detailed examinations. Catriona settled the covers back over Manachan's chest, then straightened and faced the three of Manachan's children now gathered at the foot of the bed. "I regret to say that Lucilla is correct. Your father was poisoned." Her gaze rose to Thomas and Richard, standing a little further back. "My guess would be with arsenic."

Nolan frowned. "But you can't be sure, can you?"

"No, I can't." Catriona walked toward them; with her arms spread, she urged them to the door. "But the magistrate can order tests, and then we'll know for certain. I suggest we go downstairs and wait for the doctor and Sir Godfrey to arrive."

As usual, Catriona got her way. Nolan, Niniver, and Norris appeared dazed; they sat in the drawing room and stared either at their hands or vacantly into space. The rest of the household wasn't much better.

Thomas knew how they felt.

Lucilla sat on the sofa beside him, one hand in his, the other tracing comforting circles on his back. Leaning closer, she murmured, "If someone here—Nigel, for instance—was intent on poisoning Manachan, there was nothing you or I could have done to save him."

He nodded; his rational mind recognized the truth in her words, yet he still felt numb inside. Still wondered…

But as the minutes ticked by, his mind cleared enough for several questions to rise above his inner desolation. Ferguson and Mrs. Kennedy brought in the tea tray; while Catriona poured, Thomas caught Lucilla's hand, rose, and, drawing her with him, walked to the end of the room. Halting by the window, ostensibly looking out, he settled his hand about hers. "If it is arsenic, as you and your mother think, could Manachan's illness have been due to that poison? The illness he's been battling for the last months? I read somewhere that a fatal dose can be built up in a body over time."

Lucilla raised her brows. "You could be right."

Catriona came up, carrying a cup and saucer for each of them.

Lucilla reached for one cup. "Mama—I told you that Manachan had been ill for months, on and off. Could that, too, have been due to arsenic?"

After handing Thomas the second cup, Catriona quizzed him on what he'd witnessed of his uncle's symptoms, and Lucilla added what she'd observed while staying at Carrick Manor and treating Manachan. Catriona grimaced. "It's certainly possible. For a man of Manachan's previously rude health, gradual poisoning might well have caused those effects." She looked at Lucilla. "Which brings me to ask—what did you put in the boosting tonic and in the restorative you gave him?"

Lucilla rattled off a string of herbal essences; Thomas could make nothing of them.

But Catriona nodded. "I can see why your treatments worked. You had several ingredients in there that would have bound up the poison in his system and cleansed his body of it. You weren't targeting the poison intentionally, but your potion nevertheless reduced it, and so he improved."

Lucilla sighed. "I can't believe I saw no sign of poisoning while I was here—not even when I examined him."

Catriona looked grim. "Don't distress yourself on that account—that's one of the difficulties with arsenic poisoning. You can take a person right up to the brink of death, and yet all the symptoms are easily explained—in Manachan's case, by old age. Only once they die…" She shrugged. "And even then, if a doctor isn't looking closely, or isn't summoned in time, then the death will still be recorded as due to natural causes—heart seizure, congestion of the lungs, or the like. The external evidence fades quickly."

The doctor arrived soon after. He went upstairs with Catriona and returned looking exceedingly grave. By then Sir Godfrey had arrived; the doctor was relieved to be able to place the entire matter into Sir Godfrey's hands. After a low-voiced conference with the magistrate, the doctor departed.

A heavy-set, bluff, and—under normal circumstances—genial gentleman, Sir Godfrey returned to stand before the drawing-room fireplace. He, Catriona, and Richard were old friends, and Sir Godfrey had known Manachan as well as any of the surrounding landowners. With gruff courtesy, Sir Godfrey expressed his condolences to the family and the clan, then informed Manachan's children that, as it appeared their father had been murdered, he—Sir Godfrey—was obliged to investigate and report on the matter.

Richard had already apprised Sir Godfrey of Nigel's disappearance. Sir Godfrey's questions, primarily directed at Nolan, but also seeking confirmation from Niniver and Norris where possible, ran over much the same ground as Richard and Thomas had already covered.

Unsurprisingly, Sir Godfrey came to the same conclusion everyone else was entertaining. He harrumphed and stroked his chin. "Well, we don't yet have proof that it was arsenic, but with the samples the doctor has taken, no doubt such proof will come in time, and meanwhile…well, the stuff's not called inheritance powder for nothing, what?"

From under his shaggy brows, Sir Godfrey eyed the three Carricks lined up on the sofa before him. "As Nigel's gone missing, I fear I must trouble you to allow me to search his rooms."

Niniver and Norris stared at Sir Godfrey blankly, then both looked at Nolan.

Eventually realizing that it was up to him, Nolan assented with a frowning nod. "Yes. Of course." He glanced to the door, where Ferguson had stood throughout.

Without waiting for direction, Ferguson bowed to Sir Godfrey. "I can take you to Master Nigel's room, sir."

Thomas couldn't sit still; he followed Ferguson, Sir Godfrey, and Richard up the stairs. He was halfway up when he heard Lucilla's boots on the treads behind him. He halted and faced her; as she joined him, he said, "You don't have to come."

She met his gaze. "He might have been your uncle, and as irascible a curmudgeon as ever there was, but he was also my patient." She tipped up her chin. "Besides, do any of you know what arsenic powder looks like?"

He guessed. "It's white."

She humphed and pushed past him. "It can also be slate gray, and all shades in between."

As it transpired, the arsenic powder Nigel had been using to poison his father was pure white. Packaged in brown paper, but with the label on the inner packet still present and legible, it was hidden at the back of the bottom drawer of the tallboy in Nigel's room.

Sir Godfrey snorted. "Sadly, the stuff's easily enough had from any apothecary."

Richard sighed and sat on the end of the bed.

Sir Godfrey set the damning packet on the dresser. "So...I assume we're all supposing that the reason Nigel has fled is..." Sir Godfrey blinked. "Why, exactly? If you four hadn't come to visit, and Lucilla hadn't noticed what she had, in a few more hours, Manachan's death would have been ruled as due to natural causes, or so the doctor said. I wouldn't have been summoned, and Nigel would have gained all he presumably wants—the leadership of the clan and ownership of the Carrick estate."

"Nigel knew we were coming here today." Lucilla gripped her elbows, suddenly feeling chilled. "We made the arrangements yesterday, outside the church, and Nigel was there. Niniver—and the others, too—said that Manachan was set on attending our wedding, but according to Nolan, and Edgar, too, Manachan's health started to deteriorate last week."

Thomas put an arm around her shoulders and drew her against him. He looked bleakly at Sir Godfrey. "If it was Nigel, then he knew about the wedding, knew Manachan was insisting on attending, knew that Lucilla, at least, would see Manachan and know that something was wrong, and possibly Catriona might see…" He glanced down at Lucilla, met her gaze as she looked up at him. "Nigel probably gave Manachan a large dose before the wedding, thinking to finish him off—or, at the very least, to force him to remain at home, possibly to die while everyone else was at the wedding…that would have worked."

"It certainly would have," Sir Godfrey said. "But Manachan was an obstreperous old coot—he wanted to attend your wedding, so damn it all, he did. He held on until then. But if he'd remained here instead of going to the church…Nigel's plan would likely have worked and left no one the wiser."

"So," Richard said, "Nigel gave Manachan a large dose intending Manachan to first fall ill—too ill to attend the wedding—and subsequently to die, possibly while no one but Edgar was around. But despite the larger dose, Nigel failed to stop Manachan from going to the wedding, and he couldn't stop the pair of you from meeting Manachan, noting how ill he was, and arranging to call… things started looking dangerous, so he took himself off."

"To parts unknown." Lucilla shivered.

Richard narrowed his eyes. "As to that…I would think he'd go into hiding, but would keep an eye on the place to see what happened. Then if there is no talk of murder, he'll know he's got away with the deed, and as he's apparently made a habit of going off without warning, he can simply ride in again and claim his inheritance."

"Not a chance." Sir Godfrey scowled. "I'll raise a hue and cry for the blackguard as soon as I get home."

* * *

The murder of Manachan Carrick by his eldest son, Nigel, caused a county-wide sensation. Everyone in the district was thoroughly shocked; Manachan might have been a difficult, overbearing despot to everyone outside his clan, but he was widely acknowledged as having always done right by his clansmen, and for that he had always been respected and, in passing, was rightly honored.

Most of the local men, from farmhands to landowners, joined in the ensuing manhunt for Nigel Carrick, but neither sight nor sign of the miscreant was found.

After three days of fruitless riding about the countryside, the searchers returned home, weary and disappointed, to get ready for the funeral of The Carrick.

The day dawned a misty gray, and the light remained muted throughout the morning, which seemed entirely fitting for such a somber event. The well-polished dray draped in the clan's colors, with Manachan's coffin on the bed, rolled slowly through the soft morning light. Manachan's three younger children walked behind, with the rest of the clan at their backs.

All the others who had gathered to pay their respects to Manachan, and to his bereaved family and clan, were waiting outside the church. Sir Godfrey and his wife were there, along with all the other landowners and their wives, although all gave precedence to Richard and Catriona and the rest of the party from the Vale.

Everyone waited, hands clasped, heads bowed, as the

coffin was carried inside, hefted on the shoulders of eight of Manachan's clansmen, Ferguson, Sean, Mitch, and Fred among them, as well as Thomas. He'd considered Ferguson's suggestion long and hard, but at Lucilla's encouragement had accepted the position—his last duty to his uncle, to whom he owed so much.

But once the coffin had been settled on the stand before the altar, Thomas joined the Vale household in the pews on the opposite side of the church from those the Carrick clan occupied.

It was a subtlety, but an important one. He was still a member of the clan, but his first allegiance was now to the Vale.

For him, a new and deeper commitment had finally trumped clan.

Lucilla slid her hand into his as she slipped into the pew alongside him.

Thomas closed his fingers around hers and steeled himself to listen to the service.

It was a moving one, with tributes from several sources, both from within the clan—Bradshaw, Sean, and Ferguson all spoke—as well as the wider community, represented by Richard and Sir Godfrey. Somewhat to everyone's surprise, it was Niniver who delivered her father's eulogy. Although it cost her significant effort to hold her tears at bay, she spoke in a clear, quite lovely voice, painting a picture of Manachan that was both recognizable, but also deeply personal and immensely affecting and poignant. When she finally stepped away from the lectern, there was not a dry eye in the church.

Then the service was over, and the pallbearers stepped forward again and hoisted the coffin up. Pacing slowly and steadily, they followed the vicar out of the side door into the graveyard, where a freshly dug grave in the Carrick section waited to receive Manachan's earthly remains.

Many of the ladies hung back, ultimately going out to wait on the lawn in front of the church, but Lucilla stepped up to support Niniver, and Catriona followed on Richard's arm.

Marcus took station on Lucilla's other side. He noted that Nolan and Norris both seemed absorbed, deeply sunk in their own thoughts; neither exhibited any care for their sister. Inwardly disgusted with the pair's behavior, as he followed Niniver and Lucilla from the church, Marcus switched to walking on Niniver's other side. If she grew faint or was overcome—and who could blame her?—he wanted to be in a position to steady her.

With Lucilla on her other side, Marcus deemed Niniver safe; although Lucilla wasn't tall or large, Niniver was, if anything, even more finely made, more delicately ethereal.

The ceremony for interment was blessedly brief; once the first sods were cast by the family, those who'd gathered about the grave made their way around the church to join those waiting on the lawn.

Thomas had returned to Lucilla's side. When they reached the lawn, their party stepped out of the stream of mourners returning from the grave and halted. Thomas looked at Niniver; her head was still downbent. "You did well with the eulogy—he would have been pleased."

Niniver drew in a breath and raised her head. Meeting Thomas's gaze, she inclined her head. "Thank you. I know you cared for him as I did."

Thomas's features were hard, a rigid mask concealing his feelings. "His passing marks the end of an era—you were right in saying that there will never be a Carrick such as he."

Niniver nodded. Her gaze shifted to Nolan where he stood in the center of the lawn, receiving the condolences of the more far-flung gentry who had yet to speak with him. "I fear that in that, you'll be proved correct."

Marcus had noted the direction of her gaze.

Thomas had followed it, too. "What's the general feeling in the clan over Nolan becoming The Carrick?"

Marcus glanced at the others, but no one seemed to register that that was an odd question for Thomas to ask Niniver—Manachan's daughter—yet from all Marcus had seen and heard from Thomas and Lucilla, it seemed that Niniver was, indeed, the Carrick most closely connected with the clan, the one to whom the rest of the clan would speak freely.

Niniver shrugged and settled the black shawl she'd worn over her hair on the long walk to the church about her shoulders. "Despite his gruff ways, everyone in the clan liked and respected Papa. I don't know of any who liked or trusted Nigel—if he'd become The Carrick, there would have been trouble at some point. But Nolan was always in Nigel's shadow—it was Nigel who made all the decisions no one liked—so overall, everyone is withholding judgment while they wait to see how, to use Sean's words, Nolan shapes up."

Like Niniver, Thomas was studying Nolan as he interacted with other local landowners.

After a moment, Thomas stirred. He looked down and caught Niniver's gaze. "If you and the clan need help, know you have only to ask."

Lucilla added her voice in support of that offer, as did Richard and Catriona, who had joined them in time to hear it.

As did Marcus.

Niniver cast them all a small, grave smile, at the last glancing rather shyly at Marcus, then she ducked her head. "Thank you. I'll keep that in mind." Raising her head, she looked across the lawn, then drew in a deeper breath. "And now, if you will excuse me, I should join the others. No doubt they'll soon be wanting to return home."

With murmurs of farewell, they let her go. As Thomas, Lucilla, and his parents moved on to speak with others, Marcus hung back, watching Niniver as she found Norris in the crowd, linked her arm with his, and drew him to join Nolan. But Nolan she didn't touch, not even his sleeve; it seemed to Marcus that there was a schism there, between Niniver and Norris on the one hand, and Nolan on the other.

It had been agreed—in the vague way that consensus among the families of the district was usually reached—that given the nature of Manachan's death, his wake should be private, restricted to the clan. Feelings within the clan were unsettled and potentially difficult; best that the clan as a whole had a chance to get together and come to a consensus of their own, literally in the wake of Manachan's passing, when his steadying influence was still fresh. No one in the district wanted to see the Carricks riven by factional disputes.

Watching Niniver, and studying Norris, and even more Nolan, most especially how Nolan seemed to struggle to find his social feet with the others of the district—and how his expression blanked and he all but withdrew when faced with members of his own clan—Marcus had to wonder, as, from her earlier repetition of Sean's words, he suspected Niniver was wondering, too, just how Nolan would shape up.

And what would happen if he didn't.

* * *

Four weeks later, Marcus took a small pack of his dogs out hunting.

Although he carried his gun, he wasn't truly intent on bringing down any game; the excursion was merely an excuse to go walking in the peace and soothing silence of the forests.

With his twin married, things were changing in the Vale. Thomas was working diligently alongside Richard, learning all the details of how the estate was run. Although until Lucilla's marriage, Marcus had stood as his father's second in all things, from the moment of his birth, he and everyone else had known that the future management of the Vale was not a role that would ultimately fall to him.

And he didn't begrudge Thomas the role now; indeed, he was quietly amused by how single-mindedly his new brother-in-law was throwing himself into it—into learning and understanding all and everything about it.

When Richard finally passed on the reins, the Vale would be in good hands.

That change, however, had left Marcus essentially roleless—without any defined purpose to his life.

And that, he had discovered, didn't suit him—any more than such an existence would have suited his twin, Thomas, his parents, or any other of his kin.

He now recognized the driving need to have a role, a defined purpose, as a deep-seated trait that made Cynsters, and all like them, what they were.

He'd talked to his mother and he'd talked to Lucilla—not that he'd actually had to find many words for her; she'd understood why he'd come to her before he'd opened his mouth. Both she and his mother had "looked," each in their own way—Catriona by scrying, Lucilla simply by closing her eyes and consulting—but neither had been able to shed any light on his fated future beyond the facts that it lay, if not in the Vale then close by, somewhere within the Lady's lands, and that his time to claim it was not yet.

Not yet. And, courtesy of Lucilla's discoveries, they now knew that "the Lady's lands" extended far further than they'd previously thought.

So in reality, he didn't know anything beyond the fact that he did, indeed, have a fated future—some role the Lady intended him to fill, presumably needed him to fill—and that it wasn't about to find him yet.

In lieu of stepping into that role any time soon, he'd spent the last few weeks thinking, and had devised an interim plan. If he didn't have some challenge to sink his teeth into, he would go insane; when he'd explained his idea to his father, Richard had understood and had wholeheartedly agreed.

So they were in the process of buying the old Hennessy estate. It lay to the north of Carsphairn village, but on the opposite side of the main road. The estate was mostly gently rolling hills, and in the past had carried good flocks of sheep, but old man Hennessey had gradually let his flocks, and his staff, dwindle. He'd been living as a recluse for the last ten years, hiding in the old farmhouse at the center of the estate.

Richard knew the old man; he'd also known where the Hennessey children were to be found. He'd made the family as a whole a very good offer, and after much internal discussion, they'd accepted.

Soon, the old Hennessey place would be Marcus's. He would have a place to call his own, a place to *make* his own, where he could house and continue to breed his deer-hounds, and indulge in his other passion—making sheep-farming more profitable. In the latter enterprise, he already had a very useful potential partner-in-experimentation in Thomas, who through his firm, Carrick Enterprises, also had the contacts and links to better match production and supply to the most profitable demand.

They'd already drawn Thomas's cousin Humphrey, who had stepped into Thomas's previous role in Glasgow, into their discussions.

As he paced through the cool quiet of the forests cloaking the eastern slopes of the Rhinns of Kells, Marcus looked inside, and sensed that the tremors that had rippled through the bedrock of his life over the last month or so were finally subsiding.

He wasn't like his twin; he didn't have her connection to the Lady. Only when he was outside, tramping over Her land and embraced by it, did he have any sense of Her presence.

Today, he sensed that all was well, and that all would be well. His interim plan was well chosen.

The impression he received was that She approved.

Deep inside, he found that comforting. He rarely lacked for confidence; that was a trait he'd been born with in abundance, and his family and its standing had only further fostered it. But that didn't mean he didn't question, didn't ask himself those most important questions in life. Such as what was he doing there, and what did he want to achieve? What would he leave for future generations? What would his name mean to them?

The same fundamental questions he felt sure everyone asked of themselves at some point. That said, he suspected that, when facing such questions, those born with supreme confidence suffered from commensurately deeper uncertainty, simply because the doubts generated by those natural and unavoidable questions grated so very powerfully against their innate assurance, undermining something they normally took for granted.

The dogs rambled to either side of him. Halting in a deeply shadowed clearing, he closed his eyes and filled his lungs—and finally felt anchored again.

On the right path—a new path, but the right one for him, at least at this time.

Confidence fully restored, he smiled and opened his eyes.

Just as the dogs to his far right alerted.

But not in any way that signaled game. He'd brought six dogs out; all drifted to the same point, all looking, heads up, ears pricked.

Tails slowly wagging.

Then the lead dog—an experienced bitch—looked back at him, tail waving more definitely. Asking for permission to go forward.

He walked across the forest floor, his steps muted by the thick mat of fallen needles. Joining the dogs, he looked ahead but could see nothing to account for the dogs' behavior. But he couldn't see all that far; the trees grew more thickly in that direction, and the staggered boles largely blocked his view.

Murmuring to the dogs to stay close, at heel, he started forward.

The bitch kept pace with him; he took his direction from the angle of her snout.

Whatever lay ahead, it was something the dogs were interested in.

The thick band of trees ended a few yards from the edge of an escarpment. He stepped free of the shadows—

and saw another, larger pack of deerhounds scrambling to their feet. They'd been napping in the sunshine around a wide, flat-topped rock on which a lone figure sat, knees drawn up and arms wrapped around them, staring out over the Carrick estate.

The movement of her dogs brought Niniver's head around.

He'd halted, halting his dogs as soon as hers had reacted.

Meeting Niniver's eyes across the narrow strip of clear ground between the forest and the cliff's edge, he waved at his dogs, then at hers. Both packs—hers was the larger by several animals—were alert, but holding still, waiting for some indication of whether the other group was friend or foe.

He arched a brow. "All right?"

She smiled slightly and nodded. She said something to her dogs—he thought it was "friends"—and the pack stood down.

He used the same word to his dogs, then walked forward.

His dogs ranged at his sides, and then the two packs were weaving together, snuffling and snorting and getting acquainted.

Reaching the stone on which Niniver sat, he looked out at the vista. "How are things going with the Carricks?"

She returned her gaze to the view, which, as far as he could tell, took in the bulk of the Carrick lands. "Well enough, I suppose. Nolan is running things—indeed, he's so quickly picked up the reins that Norris and I suspect that, while Nigel might have been making the decisions, it was actually Nolan implementing them, handling the day-to-day management through the months since Papa gave it up." She paused, her eyes on the fields, then went on, "So Nolan is trying, but he'll never be Papa—those shoes are far too big for him to fill. That said, he's a lot less…insufferably arrogant than Nigel was. So Nolan is, one might say, easier to swallow than Nigel was, but the clan is still withholding judgment. No one is yet convinced that Nolan will be able to hold the clan together."

A formal inquest had been held into her father's death, as a result of which her brother Nigel had been charged in absentia with patricide. Yet despite all the efforts of the authorities and the clan, no trace of Nigel had yet been found. Many now believed he had fled the country, possibly taking ship for the Americas.

That left Nolan Carrick as the laird-elect.

Marcus debated asking Niniver what she thought would occur if Nolan was rejected by the clan. That could happen; the clan could elect a different laird, and the Carrick family could be forced to transfer the clan assets they controlled—namely the estate—to the new laird and his family. Marcus didn't know where that would leave Niniver and her brothers.

Not that he cared all that much about her brothers.

He shifted. "If you ever need help, remember that you can always call on us—on Thomas and Lucilla, my parents, and on me." When she turned her head and looked up at him, he caught her gaze. "If you are ever in need, please don't hesitate—just ask and we'll help."

When Thomas had said much the same thing on the day of Manachan's funeral, Niniver had replied politely, but noncommittally, *I'll keep that in mind.* Marcus could still hear her voice saying the words, but even more clearly had he heard—still could hear—the dismissal running beneath her tone; she'd had no intention of taking them up on their offer.

So he made it again, because he sensed it was important—important to her, and possibly to him.

She studied his face; her own expression was free of any guile, but she wore a faintly grave, slightly concerned air that seemed something of a hallmark.

Then, as if she, too, understood that this offer merited a different response, she dipped her head. "Thank you." She looked back out over what, in terms of her concern, she no doubt saw as her domain. "I'll remember your words. One never can tell—one day, I might hold you to them."

He tried to think of some reply, but no words came to mind, so he let the silence stretch.

Looking down at her as she gazed out over her family's lands, he was filled with an awareness of her focus and absorption—and a rising restlessness of his own.

Responding to the latter, he stirred, then whistled to his dogs. Glancing at Niniver, he caught her gaze. "I'll leave you to your cogitations."

Instead of reacting to the faint reproach in his tone, with a regal graciousness to rival Lucilla's, she inclined her head. "Thank you. Goodbye."

He echoed the farewell, then, with the dogs gamboling about him, he walked on.

He passed into the shadows beneath the trees, then paused and looked back.

Niniver sat looking out, exactly as she had been when he'd arrived—a lone figure brooding on the welfare of her clan.

He took a moment to set the sight in his mind, then he turned and strode on.

Niniver listened to his footfalls fade away. She waited until she was sure he'd passed beyond her sight before, unable to stop herself, she glanced in the direction in which he'd gone.

She wasn't Lady-touched as he, his sister, and his mother were, yet…

How much was divine inspiration, how much simple understanding?

She looked back at the pastures and the coppices spread before her. Let her gaze rove across the distant fields, now ploughed and finally planted. There was so much that was wrong, yet so much that was right—that was still good and worth fighting for.

She hadn't expected to be one of those fighting, or at least not the one leading the way, but she'd made a silent vow over her father's grave that she would do all she could—everything she could—to preserve the clan and the Carrick family's honor. And she could already see—predict—where this was heading, which road the Carricks and their clan were stumbling, all but drunkenly, and apparently irresistibly and irreversibly, down.

Shadows lengthened as she sat and pondered, as she let her mind range over every possible option.

In the end, all she could do was hope and pray, and then wait to see what happened.

And be prepared to act if there was no other way.

Finally, she rose. Her limbs chilled from the cooling stone, she shook out her skirts, called the dogs to her, then she turned and headed for the only place she had ever called home.

* * * * *

Stephanie
LAURENS

A Match For Marcus Cynster

Marcus Cynster is waiting for Fate to come
calling. He knows his destiny lies near his home
in Scotland, but what will it be? Who is his fated
bride? One fact seems certain: his future won't lie
with Niniver Carrick, a young lady who attracts
him mightily and whom he feels compelled
to protect—even from himself.

HARLEQUIN®MIRA®
www.mirabooks.co.uk

Where Cynsters gather, love is never far behind

It's December and six Cynster families come together at snow-bound Casphairn Manor to celebrate the season in true Cynster fashion.

The festive occasion brings together Daniel Crosbie, tutor to Lucifer Cynster's sons, and Claire Meadows, widow and governess to Gabriel Cynster's daughter —and the embers of an unexpected passion smoulder between them.

However, once bitten, twice shy. Claire believes a second marriage is not in her stars. Until catastrophe strikes… Will Claire learn that love—true love— is worth any risk, any price?